EXPIRATION DAY

EXPIRATION DAY

WILLIAM CAMPBELL POWELL

TOR®
TEEN

A Tom Doherty Associates Book
New York

EXPIRATION DAY

The author wishes to identify the following works and quotations as being in the public domain and to express his gratitude to the following compilers and publishers who have created online versions.

The Merchant of Venice, by William Shakespeare. All quotations taken from Grady Ward's Moby Shakespeare and are in the public domain.

"Dear Lord and Father of Mankind," by John Greenleaf Whittier (d. 1892). Hymn, taken from "The Brewing of Soma" and in the public domain.

Isaiah 61:1–3 (extract), from the World English Bible and in the public domain.

A Tor Teen Book
Published by Tom Doherty Associates, LLC
175 Fifth Avenue
New York, NY 10010

www.tor-forge.com

Tor® is a registered trademark of Tom Doherty Associates, LLC.

Library of Congress Cataloging-in-Publication Data

Powell, William Campbell.
    Expiration day / William Campbell Powell. — First edition.
        pages cm
    "A Tom Doherty Associates book."
    ISBN 978-0-7653-3828-0 (hardcover)
    ISBN 978-1-4668-3840-6 (e-book)
    1. Science fiction. 2. Robots—Fiction. 3. Coming of age—Fiction.
4. Diaries—Fiction. 5. England—Fiction. I. Title.
    PZ7.P8814Ex 2014
    [Fic]—dc23

                                              2013025453

Tor Teen books may be purchased for educational, business, or promotional use. For information on bulk purchases, please contact Macmillan Corporate and Premium Sales Department at 1-800-221-7945, extension 5442, or write specialmarkets@macmillan.com.

First Edition: April 2014

Printed in the United States of America

0 9 8 7 6 5 4 3 2 1

To Henry and Bron

EXPIRATION DAY

What a funny old day!

We got a robot today. And it was my eleventh birthday. So I thought I'd start to write a diary, because it was a weird day, and if you can't even write a decent diary when you've got something to write about, what chance have you got when the days are dry and dreary?

But I'm not going to start every entry with "Dear Diary" or anything so Victorian. That would be just so wet. Anyway, I want to decide who's going to read it. Whoever you are, my distant, unknown friend, I need to see you in my mind.

Maybe no one will read my diary, except me when I'm ninety. So just in case, "Hello, me-of-twenty-one-twenty-eight! This is me-of-twenty-forty-nine."

Maybe, though, my grandchildren are reading this. "Hello, grandkids! This is your dotty granny Tania writing, before she lost her marbles. I hope you've found me a nice home."

No, I don't hope any such thing. If I *have* to become anybody's granny, please don't let me be a *boring* granny. Instead I shall be a grand Dame, knighted for my services to the country, and I shall tell fabulous stories, mostly true, about my adventures as a spy, or a detective, or an actress. So by 2128 you'll need me, whoever you are, because there won't be many like me left.

And if you're just a boring old historian, or some kind of slimy-tentacled alien archaeologist called Zog from the Andromeda galaxy, trying to find out who on earth I am and what human beings were . . .

Do you have churches in Andromeda, Mister Zog? Weddings, christenings, and funerals? Too much detail, I think, at least for today. Anyway, my dad is a vicar. And in these times he has a lot to do. He says thirty years ago the churches were empty. Now they're full. Full of unhappy people, looking for help to make things bearable. Looking for the little rituals that make things feel normal.

The church business is good. But vicars are still poor. Mum says he's keeping half the village sane, but still we live on people's cast-offs. We have Value Beans in the larder. Our vid is someone's old 2-D model. And our "new" robot is a reconditioned '44 model, donated by a kindly parishioner.

But we *have* a robot, a real, honest-to-goodness robot. And Dad says even the bishop only has a '47 model. Ted, one of the churchwardens, dropped him off. Him? It? I'm going to keep on saying "him" for now, as his voice was rather deep, and very "Home Counties."

We called him—the robot—Soames. It seemed like the perfect name for a 1930s butler—right out of an Agatha Christie 3-Dram. Dad activated him, and I watched as the eyes lit up for the first time. I asked Dad about that, and he smiled.

"Yes, there really isn't any need for glowing eyes. They're more for show, part of a retro look, that the psychologists say makes us feel more comfortable with them around. We see all the old-fashioned twentieth-century sci-fi movies, and we laugh, because they're so quaint. This is the same thing—robots deliberately made to look clunky and antique, and act like it, too, so we feel superior, rather than feel afraid."

We had to do an imprinting, of course, to get Soames to recognize the voices of his new owners, so that he'd obey our orders.

"Michael Deeley, primary registrant. Acknowledge." That was Dad.

"Acknowledged."

"Annette Deeley, secondary registrant. Acknowledge." Mum.

"Acknowledged."

"Tania Deeley, junior registrant. Acknowledge." Me, reading from the instruction manual and sounding very formal.

"Acknowledged."

And that was it. Soames would obey Dad, then Mum, then me. In that order. There were a bunch of other commands built into his brain that we couldn't override, sometimes called the Asimov Laws, after some ancient writer who came up with the idea. Dad says Asimov's original laws were very simple, but Soames's version had been made very complicated by the lawyers. So under stress any robot just became completely useless.

Anyway, we put Soames to work doing the washing up. He didn't break anything, but I could have loaded up the dishwasher myself in half the time. Tomorrow, though, he will be faster, because he's learned what to do and where to put the plates afterward.

And then, because it was the summer holidays, there was no school, so I got him to play table tennis, because it was my birthday and Dad said I deserved a treat for that. Soames spent most of the time picking up the balls, when he didn't crush them underfoot (two destroyed) or knock them into the lamp shade (one out of reach).

Then we took him around the house, showing him where everything was. So we can tell him to tidy the house now, and everything will find its way back to where it was on my eleventh birthday. Or whenever.

Big deal.

Okay. I'm not frightened of domestic robots, honest. But can you make one that can play table tennis, please?

Hmm. If you are Zog, that probably didn't make a lot of sense, did it? I mean, you must think that Soames is the height of our technology and I haven't said who I am and where I live and all sorts of stuff. . . .

I'm Tania Deeley, though I did mention that in an offhand sort of way. Eleven years old—of course—and an only child. I live in a Green Zone village, just outside London, where my dad's the vicar and my mum's, well . . . Mum. I go to school in the village. I don't really have any proper friends at school, but there are a few I play with sometimes. . . . It's okay, I suppose.

Dad's busy right now—vicar stuff—and he's banished me upstairs, to the spare room with all his books. It's not really being banished if I'm *here*—it's my favorite place, full of treasure. Books. Proper books: books that have never been digitized. I've loved this place since I was tiny, and nobody ever told me the books were too old for me, so I just read whatever came to hand, curled up in the big reading chair, soaking up every word. For once, I'm not reading a book, but I am in the reading chair, snuggled up and re-reading yesterday's diary entry in my AllInFone.

My *new* AllInFone, Mister Zog. Not reconditioned, for once. Not some parishioner's cast-off. It was yesterday's *other* present, my actual birthday present, as really Soames wasn't *my* present. It's got this sweet diary app that can either take voice dictation, or I can type on a full-size holographic projection keyball, and it's all encrypted, so no one can snoop what I write. I won't go on about it, in case you think I'm a gadget freak, which I promise you, I'm not. But it is neat. End of gloat. Done.

Mum's upstairs, too, pottering around, doing jobs, though Dad might call her down later. She helps him a lot with the counseling. When the "parents" come round, trailing the pieces of their broken world for him to put back together.

When their Ellie or their Sammy or their Vidhesh goes back to Banbury, everything comes apart.

Today it's Mr. and Mrs. Ellis, so that means it's their Julia heading back to Oxted. Oxted, Mister Zog? The Robot People. In Banbury. And before you ask, no, Julia's not their "Soames." She's their daughter. The polite word that the grown-ups use is a "teknoid." But I've spoken to her. She's just a *Mekker*. (Dad says that's not a nice word. So don't you use it, Mister Zog.)

Listen, Mister Zog, I don't eavesdrop when Dad's doing vicar stuff, but sometimes voices do carry. And then I can't help putting two and two together. So I've got a good idea what's going on right now. Mr. Ellis is taking the lead, while Mrs. Ellis is sitting, sobbing, as they explain to Dad how Julia's too much to cope with. How it was all right when she was little, it was just like having a real daughter. But she's grown up too much. . . .

I'd asked Dad about it while we were waiting for the Ellises to arrive.

"Dad, why are they sending her back?"

"Because the illusion is broken. Because they can no longer believe Julia is their human child."

"But what's changed? I mean, she looks the same and acts the same."

"And talks the same? Yes. They wanted a daughter so very much. But they couldn't have a child of their own. So they went to Oxted and got themselves a teknoid."

"Teknoid?"

(Yes, Mister Zog. I only learned the word today, when Dad told me. So now I'm telling you. So just sit still at the back of the class and don't interrupt.)

"Sorry, Tan. Teknoid is from the Greek 'teknon,' meaning 'a child.' That's just your dad showing off his Greek from Theological College. A teknoid is an android that specifically looks like a child. So, yes, picking up from our chat yesterday, Oxted could make Soames look and speak and move exactly like a human. But it's incredibly difficult and expensive, so they don't.

"They have to do it for the teknoids, because we have to believe they're human. The thing is, Tan, if you don't do it quite right, it's really creepy. It's part of what vicars have to learn, to help them counsel people. The phenomenon is called the Uncanny Valley, after the title of the paper that first suggested the theory, back in the nineteen-seventies."

"So?"

"So something has happened to break the illusion, and Julia is now in the Uncanny Valley. The illusion is so fragile, maintained only by the initially strong desire for a child. Maybe it's an accident that's triggered it. Maybe it's just an accumulation of little oddities. I'll find out when they arrive. Either way, the illusion is ended, and the Ellises can't bear the presence of their unmasked teknoid. Love has turned to fear. And guilt. Which is what I've got to help the Ellises get through now."

At which, with perfect timing, the doorbell rang, and I scooted upstairs.

———

That made sense. Suddenly it's all over school that such-and-such is a robot, and it gets back, and the charade is over. The parents try to tough it out for a few weeks, but they know everyone else knows, and they buckle. Sometimes they move away, try to make a new start. More often they just make the phone call to Oxted. So I guess they're organizing the "memorial" service with Dad now. "Our daughter, sadly taken away before her time . . ."

And then you see every kind of silliness that grown-ups can do. Blaming each other, fights—that's just the start. Divorce, suicide, even murder—though that last was in St. Mark's parish.

Just because nobody can have kids. Well, almost nobody. And nobody knows why. It's just something that's happened. Some said that it was all the radio waves and microwaves messing up our DNA. Others said it was the gigahertz radiation from all the computers doing it. Global warming and pollution got blamed, of course. And there were some really weird theories, too. There was one scientist who claimed that every generation lost a certain amount of information from the gene pool, so we'd just reached the point where we no longer had enough information left in our genes to build a fully working human.

Wow! So I'm a real rarity. An eleven-year-old girl. Just so you know, Mister Zog. If you have a waist, you really ought to bow. Otherwise you could wave your tentacles reverently.

So there's me (and a few like me). All the other kids in the world are just robots. Realistic robots—not clunkers like Soames— but like Julia Ellis, a near-perfect copy of a human child. Good enough to fool the maternal instinct. Good enough to stop the riots.

Even good enough to play with sometimes.

Sunday, July 25, 2049

Sunday. Family service, and Julia's Memorial Service. Pretty much as I expected. Photographs of her growing up projected in 3-D. A baby, sleeping peacefully. *Flick*. A chocolate-mouthed toddler, running in the garden. *Flick*. First day at school, angelic in her school uniform. *Flick*. Prize day—Julia collecting third prize for spelling. *Flick*. *Flick*. *Flick*.

Dad stands at the front, delivering the eulogy. A beautiful little girl, with a marvelous future. A life cut short, tragically short, by an unspecified illness. God has called Julia home. May He bring comfort to the parents.

Ted's yawning. He's heard it all before. The young mums and dads, with their own kids, look smug or terrified.

There's no body and no coffin, of course. That would be silly. Oxted has already collected Julia and taken her back to Banbury.

Dad was late back after the memorial, and he was in a foul mood because of it. He hates memorials; he knows they're necessary, but he hates the lies. "It's not why I became a minister," he says, every time.

Dad believes in God. But the Bible doesn't say anything about robots, and I guess that's confusing for a minister.

And when he's said that, he sighs and adds, "I wonder how they'll cope."

As far as I can tell, they never do. I said robots were "good enough to stop the riots." Well, they were and they weren't. We still have our riots, though robots have taken them off the streets. Dad says it's just that now we have them one couple at a time, in the privacy of our own homes.

Saturday, August 21, 2049

We're on our holidays.

We're going to a theme park, of course, because that's what everybody does. It's escapism, and the parks make no bones about it. "Let us take you back," they say, and they give you a week living in the past. Pick your era, there's a park to match. Any time—except the last thirty years, because that's a little too painful for most people. So, where do you think we're going, Mister Zog? With the whole of human history to choose from, we could go back to, oh, the time of the British Empire, or the Roman Empire. Oh, yes, there are such parks. Unfortunately we can't afford them, not on a vicar's salary. So we're going back to . . . the 1970s!

It's so embarrassing.

I have to admit I was curious about the 1970s. When Dad said that was where we were going, I nearly threw a wobbly myself.

Oh, Mister Zog, where do I start about the 1970s? I knew a bit from history—the Energy Crisis, the Winter of Discontent, the IRA, the birth of Thatcherism. And Mum's got some redigitized old photos—really faded because back then they couldn't make color dyes to last—which she says are of her granny and grand-dad at Blackbushe in '78 for a Dylan gig. She sounds so awed whenever she says the word "Dylan," like he was some amazing being from another planet, come to visit us. We've been listening to some of his music in the car to get us into the feel of the decade. It's all right, I guess, but I hope we don't have to suffer a Dylan tribute band. It's not the music, you understand, Mister Zog. I just think Mum and Dad will be too embarrassing.

But as for Great-Gran and Great-Grampy, I don't honestly know which is which. The hairstyles and clothing in the photo give nothing away—all perms and frilly shirts, and shades that make them look like weird half insects. Am I going to have to dress like that? It *might* be fun, but I think it's going to be just creepy.

We're in our hotel room now, and we've come in through the modern entrance. Once we've changed, we have to put our modern clothes into sealed storage, and stay in theme for the rest of the week. There's no vid (*again*. Why do we always go on holiday where there's no vid?) and no TeraNet access. They had computers in the 1970s, but they were huge things, with whirring tapes (yes, really) and disk drives the size of a car wheel. You could afford a computer if you were a big university or a hospital—they were called mainframes—and there were minicomputers and . . .

Sorry, Mister Zog. Too much detail.

Anyway. My point is that once again we're stuck in a techno-desert, and my folks have *chosen* to come here. When I finish writing this, I'm going to have to put my AllInFone into storage with the clothes and any other contemporary gadgets, and go down to the *other* lobby in the hotel—the 1970s lobby. I'm going to try and keep notes, but the rules say only pen and paper.

They caught Dad trying to sneak his AllInFone out of the room. There's a detector at the other door, which picks up the keep-alives that all AllInFones have to transmit by law, and a very polite porter informed him, "You can't take that with you, sir."

"Oh, I didn't realize . . ."

Which was a complete lie. Daddy, you'll have to confess that to the bishop—I was watching in the mirror, and I saw you look round most furtively as you sneaked it into your pocket.

We went down to the lobby.

It was fascinating. I've done a project on the '60s and '70s, with all the fast-changing styles, and this place captured them all. Everyone was glammed up for the disco, our opening event. Everyone was covered in glitter and makeup—Dad had done a mini-strop in the room, when he realized that everyone meant *everyone*—and the clothing was equally over the top.

Platform shoes.

Huge shades.

Flares.

Hot pants.

Yep. I was wearing hot pants. Lilac hot pants. They're like shorts, but mine had a bib front and it went over a plain white blouse that was all frills and cuffs. Short little white gym socks—cute (*not*)—and the unevolved distant ancestors of a pair of trainers. I'd nearly had my own strop, but Dad beat me to it, and you don't show up your dad by out-stropping him. . . .

It was truly awful. Not least, because I still have preteen legs—like sticks, they are. There's a word for legs like mine. Gangly. I count my knees, sometimes, and I know I have just two, one on each leg. But dressed like that, I felt like it was more—a lot more, with different numbers on each leg. And hot pants are designed to go over a proper bottom and hips, and I don't have either yet.

Mum and Dad, of course, were now throwing themselves into

character; they were loving it. Dad was wearing near-luminous green flares and a sleeveless knitted jumper over a magenta shirt with a huge collar. I love my dad to bits, of course, but nothing could have been better designed to show off his pot belly. Mum . . . well, Mum had ended up in a pale lime party frock with orange polka dots. And she'd chosen to wear platform shoes, so she was . . . wobbling. Now, Mum has a nice trim figure—she exercises regularly, plays squash and tennis with some of the other young mums of the parish. So she shouldn't have been *able* to wobble. Yet, wearing *those* shoes, she quivered. . . . It was just *gross*, and I really wanted to hide. If you ever manage to break the encryption on my AllInFone, Mum, and you're reading this, I'm sorry, but that's the honest truth, written for Mister Zog.

But there wasn't anywhere to hide. I looked around me and the scene was repeated twenty-, no, forty-fold, with minor variations. The worst excesses of 1970s dress, rolled up into a lobby full of garishly attired holidaymakers, making their way toward the temple of tastelessness that is a grown-ups' disco.

It wasn't just adults, of course. This was a family holiday, and I wasn't too surprised to see myself in duplicate. Not literally, of course, but dotted around were a dozen or so embarrassed kids from maybe ages seven to thirteen, trying hard not to look at their parents, trying not to be seen by anyone at all.

We drifted over to the dance floor and found a family table. There was another family at the next table, with a young lad, who looked about my age, plus or minus. He smiled at us, a big, freckly smile beaming out from under a ginger mop. I nodded back, and his mum caught the motion, and she smiled, too. It wasn't long before we'd pulled the tables together, and the adults were chattering away. And then my dad and his dad were wandering off to the bar to get drinks.

"What's your name?"

I didn't catch on at first. Ginger Mop was talking, but I didn't register the words. I'd been looking at Mum kind of sideways.

Actually, now she'd sat down she'd stabilized, and was back to Trim Mum again.

"What's your name?"

"We're the Deeleys."

He looked annoyed.

"I know that. What's *your* name?"

"I'm Tania."

I really didn't want to say any more than that. The disco was playing early Bowie—"The Jean Genie," I think—and I was worried Ginger Mop was going to ask me to dance. Then he'd count my knees, and it would be some large odd number, and he'd laugh, and I'd have to kill him, and they'd throw me in jail—end of holiday.

"John."

"What?" I really wasn't with it.

"John. My name's John. You can use it, you know, if you want to attract my attention."

"I'd tagged you as Ginger Mop."

I didn't want company, at least, not some robot kid, so frankly, I was trying to be rude. Just a little bit, but it was water off a duck's back to him. He just grinned and pushed his fingers through his hair.

"Yeah, it is pretty scruffy. I could get a job as a mop, too. So if you're going to call me Ginger Mop, what do I call you? Raven?"

"I suppose so."

Well, my hair is pretty black, and I didn't mind him noticing. He was so determinedly friendly and cheerful, too, and he wasn't at all put off by my get-lost tactics.

"Well, then, Miss Tania Raven Deeley, how about a smile and a hello for John Ginger Mop Czern?"

I smiled briefly and nodded hello. Without much thinking, I raised my hand and carefully brushed back a stray black hair. He grinned back at me, and futilely pushed his own wild locks back, only for one to drop straight back in front of his bright blue eyes.

I couldn't help myself, and gave him a broad grin in return. For a robot, he was an all right human.

"Okay, John. I give up. I'm friendly."

"That's better."

It turned out Mr. and Mrs. Czern were from London. They owned a little corner shop, selling groceries, magazines, what-have-you. If you needed something and you couldn't be bothered to get the car out for a trip to the supermarket, the Czerns would sell it to you. John helped out in the shop, when he wasn't at school or doing his homework.

"I help out quite a lot. They treat me a bit like a servant. You know: do this, do that . . ."

"Don't you have a domestic robot to help?" But I knew what the answer would be.

"No. We don't make much money in the shop. Enough for a decent holiday. A robot, though, that would be a luxury."

Two robots, I thought. *Two* robots would be a luxury. The *first* robot is a necessity. And I thought of that gift of clunky old Soames. If my parents hadn't had good genes, there was no way they could have afforded even that necessity.

"I know. Dad's a vicar, so we don't have much money, either. We were given our robot, secondhand."

Our conversation was getting rapidly depressing. Any longer, and we'd be crying into our drinks. Which reminded me, where were the dads with the drinks?

Right on cue, they appeared out of the faceless crowd, Dad leading the way and Mr. Czern carrying the drinks on a tray. Mr. Czern served everyone from the tray. He was a round, jovial man, quite short, and he chuckled and flourished as he doled out the glasses.

"Babycham for the ladies. Watneys Red Barrel for the men. And a cola for the kids. Pretty authentic, huh?"

I wondered how he could be so sure. As Dad drank his Red Barrel he grimaced, and I asked myself, if a beer were that awful, why would anybody have kept the recipe for more than eighty years?

I caught John's eye, and I think he must have been thinking something similar, because he mimicked Dad's grimace, and then pantomimed tipping the beer away. He winked, and I winked back, and took a sip of my own drink.

Yeuch! It was foul! Cloying and sweet. Another recipe that should have been left in the vault . . .

I don't think I'll dwell on the awfulness of that disco. Or indeed the rest of that week. The '70s music was perhaps the best bit, but what did Dickens say? "It was the best of times, it was the worst of times, it was the age of wisdom, it was the age of foolishness. . . ." Perhaps it was true of the '70s, too, except I didn't see any wisdom on show at the theme park.

All in all, the '70s was a dreadful decade. One night they gave us all candles to take to our rooms, and then they staged a power cut. One moment we were all watching a grainy Panorama documentary on the TV (yes, a TV) about the energy crisis, and the next moment, the lights went off, and the picture shrank to a glowing point. There was a faint glow from the TV screen— just enough to find the candles. I think they cheated a bit, with hidden lighting in the walls, so nobody tripped over anything and broke a leg. In five minutes, everybody was stepping out of their rooms holding lit candles, and making their way, yes, down to the bar. Strangely, nobody complained that there was power for the beer pumps. . . .

The high point was a trip to a coal mine. It was a reconstruction, of course, and we used a simulator to take us "underground." I'd got sort of used to us being with the Czerns, and I liked John's sense of humor. So when we were all dressed up in orange overalls and hard hats, it seemed pretty natural to let him take my hand and lead me through the ill-lit tunnels.

They didn't go anywhere, of course—no more than ten or

twenty meters in total, with a couple of twists and short side passages to make it vaguely interesting. And everywhere there were the *oohs* and *aahs* of the tourists, and the drone of the guide talking about "the last decade in which Britain could truly be said to have a mining industry" or the "naked grasping after power of the unions." It didn't make a lot of sense, but it sounded very grand.

And so it came to the last day. There was a gala party in the bar, with a Slade tribute band. It was glittery and loud, and they stomped about on giant platform shoes, singing "Gudbuy T' Jane" and "Cum On Feel the Noize."

In between songs John had asked me for my PTI—my public TeraNet ID—and I was in a turmoil. Should I give it to him? I mean, he was nice, but he was only a robot. With a wild ginger mop that wouldn't obey orders, plus very cute freckles.

What am I saying?

Oh, dear, Zog. I think I've got my first crush on a boy. Because I gave him my PTI, and we danced—me in my ridiculous hot pants and all my knees showing—and I gave him a little peck on the cheek when I thought Mum and Dad were looking the other way. And then the band played "Far Far Away" and we danced close and I whispered to him, "Are you real?" And my heart leaped as he replied, "Yes, I am real."

INTERVAL 1

A remarkable find. Truly remarkable. I cross the galaxy to find the first records of the Dawn Civilization and I find this. Encrypted and forgotten, but surviving through uncounted millennia, for me to find.

So I am your Zog, and I will learn about you, Tania Deeley, coy and precocious as I perceive you to be. I have time to listen to you, Tania Deeley, we don't have to rush. There's no wormhole about to close. Sadly, there are no wormholes anywhere to speed us across the universe.

No, Tania, I came the long way, through normal space, though it has taken millennia.

My kind has time.

It was back to school today. The holidays are over, and it's a new school for me. The Lady Maud High School for Girls, and I have to take a bus from the village—past my old school—to get there.

Such a panic from Mum this morning. Have we been practicing the route to school for weeks, or have we been practicing the route for weeks? As I leave the house, staggering under the weight of PE, hockey, and swimming kit, plus sandwiches, ruler, pens and pencils, two sharpeners and two erasers—"just in case you lose one, dear"—calculator (why? if I have an AllInFone), padlock for locker, with five—count them—five parental consent forms, she was still calling, "Have you got your bus pass?"

And Dad was walking with me "as I have to go past the bus stop anyway," but he wasn't carrying anything for me "as you have to get used to it." He wasn't panicking—not like Mum—just being overprotective of his "little girl."

Girls of all ages and sizes waited at the bus stop, the older ones chattering already about where they'd been over the summer holidays. I'd already decided if I met anyone I knew, I'd stayed home all summer. I had not, repeat, not been anywhere near a theme park. If tortured, I'd admit to a visit to feudal England—that'd kill the conversation—but a trip to the 1970s? Uh-oh.

Dad's back disappeared round a bend in the road—I was pretty sure he'd just go round the block and return home—and I was on my own. I suddenly felt a chill—some of those other girls looked awfully tall and mean. I had to take a deep breath and remind myself that they were most likely robots, and couldn't hurt a human.

"Hi, Tania!"

The friendly voice came from right next to me, and I jumped in surprise. It was Siân, a girl I knew from the village school. I'd not seen her over the holiday—she'd been away—and I was surprised to see how much she'd grown in the few short weeks. Taller, of course, but all *her* elbows and angles had suddenly become curves—she looked awesome—and I felt totally awkward and out of place beside her.

And then I twigged. Siân had had a revision over the summer. Robots couldn't grow like humans, but to preserve the illusion of humanity, they had to appear to get older. So every year or two each robot child would go back to Oxted Corporation for a week or so and emerge with a new look—the word was "revised." The same personality, but a new body, suitably older. A standard revision was fairly basic, but was included in the contract. It didn't look like Siân had gone for the standard revision, though. . . . No, it certainly wasn't the cheap option, but Siân's parents didn't have to worry about such trifles, and had used the holidays to revise Siân into her early teens.

Of course, it was bad form to mention it, so I closed my mouth, nodded hello, and then asked casually, "How was your summer, Siân? Go anywhere interesting?"

"So-so. We went to Egypt. Daddy had to go there on business, so he took Mummy and me, too. We did the sights, took a Nile cruise. Spent a *for*-tune in the markets. Nothing special, just a lot of trash really, but Mummy says their economy desperately needs tourism . . ."

Siân was a snob, but she was okay, so long as you let her talk about herself. At least I could be sure she wasn't going to ask me what I'd done over the holidays.

". . . and then we had to go to Bangkok in a hurry—Daddy's

business again—and then before you could blink we were off again to Sydney. There was a marvelous production of *Tannhäuser* at the Opera . . ."

I didn't have to do much, just nod or grunt at the pauses. Her holiday was turning into a real world tour, but at least I didn't have to make up any lies about being a Saxon serf.

The bus came, we got on and sat together, and her chatter continued.

". . . and in San Francisco we met up with some old college friends of Mummy's—the Coulsons—he's in cybernetics and she's a neurotronic psychiatrist . . ."

So, Siân's folks were well connected to get the best for their daughter.

". . . and I must have picked up a bug somewhere on my travels, and I had to spend a couple of days in hospital . . ."

There it was, that was the revision.

". . . but I got a simply lovely private recovery suite, Tania, and the travel insurance paid for it."

No—Mummy and Daddy have deep pockets, Siân, dear, but it would be *so* crass to mention it. Oops, I just did, didn't I, Mister Zog? Will you forgive Tania a little envy?

"Oh, and Tania, I *did* think of you while I was there. It got so lonely, but then I'd think of you stuck in this ghastly hole of a village and I didn't mind so much. And when I got out, Mummy took me shopping in Haight-Ashbury and I bought you this genuine Grateful Dead 'Wake of the Flood' tour button—really rare, they said, but I know you're into the 1970s. I hope you like it."

I was really touched. Well, sort of. Siân had thought of another person, however briefly, and she had even paused in her monologue to let me acknowledge it.

"Thank you, Siân, that's so kind of you. And it's lovely."

Well, it was. Just totally inappropriate, given my own summer, but she wasn't to know that. And I'd sworn to tell nobody about the theme park. So I smiled. Noblesse oblige, and all that. I mean, she's just a robot doing her best, so how could I knock her down?

———

Senior school, I soon learned, is pretty awful. It's not like first school, where the parents are just around the corner and close enough to take a real interest in their child's progress. By the time we get to big school, a lot of parents are getting weary of the whole charade, and they let the school do what they want. In the case of the Lady Maud High School for Girls, they do still care somewhat, but most of the inner-city schools are pretty bad, I hear.

Lady Maud was a wealthy Victorian widow, we learned, who had used much of her late husband's copper fortune to endow a modest school "for young ladies of whatever social class that do display an aptitude for learning . . . so that all God's gifts in them shall be nurtured to the fullest degree." Successive governments had recognized the worthiness of that Good Lady's earnest intentions, and had invested taxpayers' money to create a school that had hovered just outside the very top academic bracket for a little over a century.

But educating robots was not a government priority, and didn't the teachers know it. The school was falling into ruin. Some of the buildings were boarded up, and I could see holes in the roof of one block. When we gathered for assembly in Main Hall, we rattled around in a cavernous space built to hold twice our number.

The Head Mistress—Mrs. Golightly—welcomed us to Lady Maud's. She—Mrs. Golightly—spoke briefly about the Great Traditions of the School, about our Oxbridge Achievements and the Daughters of the School who had achieved High Office or other Greatness. She spoke like that, too. I mean, you could hear the capital letters. Once or twice I swear I could almost see them.

"She said the same thing last year," whispered a voice from behind me.

"Word for word," agreed her neighbor.

"The rest should be pretty short, then."

It was. Mrs. Golightly trotted perfunctorily through her set speech and then abandoned us in some haste. Our Form Mistress gathered us up and led us to our classroom. Miss Gerrard introduced herself to us.

"I'm Miss Gerrard, but you must call me—and any other teacher—ma'am. Or sir, in the case of Mr. Cuthbert, our chemistry master here at Lady Maud's. Lady Maud's is a great school, with a fine academic tradition, and though times may change, we expect our girls"—she paused slightly at the word—"to perform to their highest while they are in our care. Others may fall by the wayside"—and what did that mean?—"but our *girls* are our only priority. . . ."

There was more, but the message was there, hidden just beneath the surface. Lady Maud's might promise much for her human charges, but the robots were of no interest.

And so we began. English, geography, music, divinity, French. Latin, craft, and maths. That was Monday. I turned it into a little rhyme, to help me remember where I had to go.

English, Geog
Mus, Div, Frog
Lat'n, Craft'n' Maths

Perhaps not very complimentary to the French, but it had a cadence and I found I couldn't get it out of my head.

English. Mrs. Philpott, short and dumpy, and we quickly discovered, excessively short-sighted. But she loved her Shakespeare, and in our first lesson we found ourselves reading *The Merchant of Venice*.

Geography. Mrs. Hanson. Wispy and ethereal. She started to teach us about Africa. Mud huts and grass roofs. Dark-skinned babies, emaciated and dying. I put my hand up.

"But, ma'am, surely it's not like that now?"

She coughed, embarrassed.

"No, quite right. Not since the Troubles. There are a few coastal enclaves left as I've described. But Africa has gone wild, and nobody really knows anymore what it's like in the interior. Oxted's invention solved the problem in the West, but there weren't enough robots for Africa, and perhaps they wouldn't have wanted them. Many tribes, many peoples, so proud. . . . So often stronger than the developed world. They face death better than we do. . . ."

Her voice tailed off. Her knuckles were white where she gripped the back of a chair, and her eyes glistened. I wondered what she saw. The silence lengthened and we fidgeted, looking at one another and all around. There were photographs at the back of the class, I noticed, of a young woman, who could have been a much younger Mrs. Hanson, in sun hat, tropical shorts, and blouse. Many showed her with children, brightly dressed and with beautiful smiles. In a few, she was visiting wards of a hospital, and the children looked unwell. In just one, set apart from the others, she was standing next to a tall, close-shaven black man. He was naked, except for a loincloth, but in his left hand he carried a short spear and an oval shield faced with hide, in the Zulu style. Very handsome, I thought. Mrs. Hanson clearly thought the same, for she was nestled under his right arm, and her left arm was about his waist. Husband and wife? I risked a glance at Mrs. Hanson, still staring far beyond the classroom.

The moment passed, and Mrs. Hanson continued.

"That's enough. Back to life in the Kimberley Corridor, which is what we're studying today. . . ."

Music. Miss Carr. Divinity. Mrs. Reese. French. Madame Lebrun.

They're all old, I discover. They must have been teaching all their lives . . . and don't know how to stop, even though there are hardly any real children left to teach. I realize it was like that at the village school, too, but I never thought about it. Are there no *young* teachers?

Boy, oh, boy, Mister Zog. What else have I never noticed?

Saturday already, a whole week at Lady M's. Suddenly this is my new normality—how does that happen? Siân Fuller's practically my best friend. I mean, if she were human, she'd be a total airhead. But for a robot, she's all right. I remember only last Wednesday I helped her do her homework on the bus. I smiled at the ridiculousness of it—when she wasn't looking—for what's the point of a robot learning French verbs? But I don't follow that thought often, because it leads to the future, and the future is a very scary place, with too many unanswerable questions:

What happens to robots when they grow up?

Why does Mrs. Hanson have a photograph of a handsome Zulu warrior—her husband?—in the classroom?

Why aren't there any young teachers?

What lies in the heart of Africa, beyond the Kimberley Corridor?

Why hasn't John called me?

Yes, why hasn't he called?

I dreamed about him last night. That single, daring peck on the cheek. The memory makes me feel all hot inside. I'm embarrassed, I suppose.

He hasn't called me. Not in nearly two weeks since the holiday ended. Has he forgotten me so quickly? Has he lost my PTI?

———

English. We're reading Shakespeare. Sorry, I think I already said that. Yes, I did. *The Merchant of Venice.* Mrs. Philpott. We played tricks on her. Moved things when she wasn't looking, so she couldn't find them. Her sight is *very* bad.

But she knew her Shakespeare by heart, and she never needed the books we hid. After a while we gave up our tricks—it was no fun.

Mostly we just read our lines in a bored monotone, and she'd say things like "No, no, no, imagine this is happening to *you*. How would *you* feel, dear?" And then her victim would briefly display anguish or ecstasy, with all the range and the depth and the sincerity that an eleven-year-old can muster, which is not a lot, Mister Zog. And then she'd say, "That's *so* much better," while rolling her eyes up to heaven.

And then, of course, it was suddenly my turn to read Portia, Mrs. Philpott's exhortation still fresh—"How would *you* feel, dear?"

How all the other passions fleet to air:
As doubtful thoughts, and rash-embrac'd despair,
And shudd'ring fear, and green-eyed jealousy!
O love, be moderate, allay thy ecstasy,
In measure rain thy joy, scant this excess!
I feel too much thy blessing: make it less
For fear I surfeit

Is this the trickery of Shakespeare that suddenly from nowhere an image lodges in your brain? A ginger-haired boy dressed in '70s clothing, dancing to a Slade tribute band?

Mrs. Philpott said nothing, but I felt her eyes on me long after I stopped and Bassanio spoke. At the end of the lesson, she kept me back for a moment.

"You felt something."

It wasn't a question, and I felt I could trust Mrs. Philpott.

"I did. There's someone . . ."

"Yes, I thought there might be. That's how it often begins. Our experience brings life to the words. The words enrich our experience."

"How it begins, Mrs. Philpott?"

"Our love affair with language, Miss Deeley. How dull to be an animal, knowing only emotions, or a drab mechanical, knowing only words. To be human is to *feel*, which is to give expression and texture to our emotions through language."

"Is that all?"

"It's everything, Miss Deeley. Does flesh and blood define humanity? I disbelieve it. Many born of woman do not feel— look at history and ask yourself, could this man or that have acted that way, if he could truly *feel?*"

"You mean, like Hitler?"

"An extreme example, but yes. A man born of woman, I grant, but human?"

"I . . ."

"A rhetorical question. Don't answer. In act three, scene one, there's a famous speech by Shylock, claiming his own humanity— 'I am a Jew. Hath not a Jew eyes?'—and thereafter going on to define his humanity in purely physiological terms. Then read his actions. Does he use language to leave the prison of his own head, and understand the feelings of another human? Does he, therefore, love another human more than himself? Or do his actions and his language show that he is alone, locked within his own mind?"

I think she would have gone on more, but I was fidgeting, nervous that I'd be late for my next class. She told me to run along.

I was going to take the play home and read it, but I forgot to put it in my homework bag. But later I remembered, and I cheated. I went and found an old mpeg on the TeraNet and watched Anthony Sher as Shylock. Is Shylock human? By Mrs. Philpott's definition, probably not.

But I'm going to watch that mpeg again. And again. And I promise I'll *read* it, too.

I've decided I *do* love language.

I'm glad I'm human.

I heard from John.

He's fine, he says. Enjoying school. How am I?

"I'm fine, too." *Why didn't you call me?* "It's nice to hear from you."

"Uh, yeah."

You can do better than that. Typical boy! "You must have been very busy."

"Uh, not really."

I hope you didn't call me just to grunt. I remember you used to talk. Back in the 1970s. "Well, I'm glad you didn't lose my PTI. I was beginning to think you were just going to be a holiday memory."

"No, I wanted to call you." *It constructs a whole sentence!* "But I felt awkward. Afraid you might . . ."

"What?"

"Not like me anymore."

"That's silly, John. I like you a lot."

"And I like you a lot too, Tania." *Go on, go on!* "I . . . I . . . yeah, I like you a lot."

Gosh, you're really communicating today, John. I'm going to have to do some serious work to get anywhere. "I thought a lot about our holiday, you know, John. Making friends like that hasn't happened to me before. All the people I know are, like, the kids of my parents' friends, my dad's parishioners' kids, and the kids in my class. I've never really had a choice in my friends. They're just there, and I accept it. You're different."

"Uh, thanks." *Don't grunt! And try constructing complete sentences.* "It's the same at my school, I suppose. I watch the others run around playing soccer, and there's a part of me thinking that they're just programmed to do that. It's not *fun* they're having, it's just the way they're made. So I don't want to join in. I don't have any friends. Not really."

"You mean, because they're all robots."

"Yeah." *I forgive you for grunting, this time. My own fault for asking a boy a yes-or-no question. And the rest wasn't bad for a boy, either. Lots of sentences. We'll try for a few adjectives, next time.*

"So you do understand. I never felt the same as the others at school. There's always the knowledge that they're different. I never wondered how I'd ever recognize a human kid if I met one. I knew they'd stand out. I just worried that it might take a long time to happen."

"And now?"

"Now it has happened. I'm very, very happy. So talk to me some more, and don't spoil it. . . ."

––––––––

Anyway, Mister Zog, that's enough. I think there are one or two things I still want to keep secret from you, at least for the time being.

Tuesday, October 26, 2049

My foot.

My foot.

I'm staring at my foot, like it doesn't belong to me.

My traitorous foot.

I've been sitting in my room now, for an hour or two. Longer, maybe. Mum and Dad have been up, telling me once more that they still love me, but I'm not talking to them, and they've gone away again. If I concentrate, I can hear them downstairs, whispering, crying, pacing up and down. I try not to listen, though. It doesn't help. I just sit here, staring at my traitorous foot, while my thoughts whirl in mad circles.

If only . . .

––––––––

The first If Only:

If only I hadn't let Siân talk me into a trip to London at half term.

"It'll be lovely," she said. "Mummy and Daddy will take us both in the Mercedes—there's lots of room—and we'll visit the Tower of London, and the London Eye and HMS *Belfast* and Madame Tussauds, and we'll stay in a hotel and . . ."

That was Siân all over. She couldn't stop talking. Ever.

But it sounded like fun, so I said yes.

––––––––

The second If Only:

If only I hadn't decided to show off.

We'd been round HMS *Belfast*, with its bow guns still trained on Barnet. Why Barnet? You'd think it would be more use to aim at a Yellow or Red Zone. Well, Siân had chased me round the decks, and I'd hidden from her, and jumped out and surprised her. And then we'd turned about while I'd chased her.

Harmless stuff.

And then we'd crossed Tower Bridge and watched the boats ply up and down the Thames, and ended up at the Tower of London. It had been restored a few years ago, to mark the 500th anniversary of Anne Boleyn's execution. The moat had been re-excavated, and turned into a boating environment for tourists, complete with a picnic park. They were running 3-Dram pictures of the pageant, with robot actors playing Boleyn and her executioner, Jean Rombaud, and stills of old King William officially opening the Gate and then being rowed out to the river. But mostly what Siân and I were interested in was more chasing games, hide-and-seek.

We ran out of places to hide.

At least, if we stayed in the public areas.

So we didn't. While Siân's back was turned, I raced off toward Traitor's Gate. They run boat trips nowadays, with theme parties where people dress up as condemned nobles on their way to the Tower, but only in summer. So it was all off-limits now, and the tour boats bobbed gently, chained up at the base of the steps.

I climbed over the low gate and pattered down the steps to the waterline, but now I was here, there really wasn't anywhere to hide. Except down with the boats, and I could hear Siân running closer, so I scrabbled in, and slid under a tarpaulin. The skiff rocked rather wildly as I did so, but I just stayed low and it steadied.

There were a few bumps, and I risked a peek out from under the tarpaulin.

The first thing I saw was Siân looking right at me, and as she saw my face emerge, her own expression became surprise, then horror, and she pointed at me and shrieked.

And then I looked about me, to see what the fuss was about, and there was muddy water in every direction. The little skiff was drifting away from the steps, caught by the eddies, and heading out toward the river.

Oops!

No oars, I quickly discovered, and the first gate was past, too far to reach. Siân had summoned help—a Beefeater—and he was casting off a second skiff. But it wasn't going to be in time; my own skiff was moving faster, toward the open river. Beyond the arch of the river gate, the Thames was racing past, and there were some iron railings partway across. The skiff would miss them, but not by much, so perhaps I could jump across . . .

Behind me, the Beefeater was rowing, calling something as he rowed . . .

"Don't jump!"

. . . but the railings were close, and I knew I could make it. . . .

I jumped . . .

The third If Only:

If only my foot hadn't caught in something as I jumped.

I felt something wrap round my ankle, just as I also realized you shouldn't jump from an unladen skiff. As I pushed off, the boat simply spun out from under me and I went down into the water.

And that something wrapped *tight* around my ankle pulled me down, held me down. I reached down with my hand, and felt a tangled mass of rope, and chain, tight and pulling me ever deeper.

I opened my eyes, but the murky water showed nothing clearly. There was a pressure in my ears, so I knew I must be going deep. And I could feel a terrible burning in my chest—I was going to have to take a breath and then it would all be up with me. I'm not sure if I managed a clear thought then, but perhaps I might have thought, "Good-bye" or "Sorry" or "I love you, Mum and Dad." Maybe a bit of each . . .

The fourth If Only:

If only I'd drowned.

I couldn't stop myself from taking that breath. I knew it would kill me, but I did it anyway. . . .

There was a curious sensation as the water rushed into my lungs. Only that. Just curious. There was no choking feeling. Nothing, except maybe a slight resistance as I breathed.

I *was* breathing. Breathing water. I could feel the motion of my chest as I breathed out again, and in. I wasn't dying.

Then through the murk came a figure, swimming. The Beefeater, I supposed. And he had a knife, because I felt a sawing around my foot, hacking, hacking, cutting through the rope that held me.

It was enough. My foot came free and I struck for the surface, feeling the strong arms of the Beefeater bearing me up.

I'm not sure exactly what happened then, but I remember flashes:

My head breaking water, and I coughed out a little water . . .

Hands, hauling me out of the water . . .

Siân, bending over me as I lay, her eyes flicking down, not quite meeting my own . . .

More hands, lifting me onto a stretcher . . .

A brief glance at my feet, still hurting . . .

My right foot, bloody where the knife had slashed . . .

And something else: silver-gray threads, shimmery and bright . . .

Silver-gray threads . . .

Silver-gray threads . . .

———

My next clear thought was some time later, when I realized the white blur in front of my eyes was a ceiling, and I was lying on my back, in a bed.

A hospital bed. Obviously.

I sat up, half-expecting resistance from bandages and drips and I don't know what else. But no, the covers fell away from me easily, and I flicked the sheet off the bottom of my bed, to see . . .

My foot—both feet—sticking out of the end of a pair of green-striped hospital pajamas.

Perfect.

Not a mark. Not a scratch. Not a blemish.

I leaned forward to inspect them more closely. If either of them had been hacked bloody with a knife, I couldn't prove it. I touched each foot, carefully.

Healed, I thought.

No. Not healed.

Repaired.

A memory rose, unbidden, of a name.

Martin.

Perhaps I said it aloud, perhaps I only thought the words.

I am a robot.

Martin.

We went on holiday with one of Dad's friends a couple of years back, and it was awful. You could tell he didn't like children, but his wife was besotted with their little kid. The kid's name was Martin, and he was a ghastly brat. A boy, but his father made no secret that it was a robot—at best just a little too much stress on the second syllable of the name, but occasionally cruel little remarks about "Tin Boy"—and every time she overheard him, his wife looked ready to kill him.

Boy, do you meet some weirdos . . .

That was a holiday in Wales, which is a funny place, all mountains and terraced houses made out of real concrete— really traditional. So passé. Of course, New Cardiff is properly modern, built out of proper repolymerised PET. But we weren't staying there. We were in some ghastly hole called Aber-something—all double-l's and double-d's and y's—which was at the bottom of a valley so deep the gigahertz broadcasts couldn't get in. A whole week with no vid. Well, there was sort of, and Dad said that the brochure hadn't completely lied, but the signal was so weak—Dad put on a tech-sales voice and called it at-ten-u-a-ted—that you could only get color or 3-D, not both.

Anyway, my point was that Aber-double-l's barely had electricity, let alone TeraNet. It was primitive and dangerous. So when Martin the ghastly brat went for a walk along the beach, it should have been no surprise to anybody when he tumbled off a rock and landed in a pool of seawater.

The first I knew something was wrong, was when I heard this eerie screaming sound, not loud, but insistent, and it set my teeth on edge. I'd not seen him fall, but I had a pretty good idea where the sound was coming from, and I knew immediately that Martin was in trouble.

I scrambled over the rocks, yelling for the adults to come

and help, even before I saw Martin. When I did, I thought I was going to faint. I'd expected to see blood—robots are designed to bleed—but he'd fallen onto a spur of rock, and it had gouged a hole in his side.

What showed was nothing so crude as gears and rods, but tightly packed micro-servos, pseudo-organic tensors, and weaving throughout were the silver-gray threads of Oxted's marvellous creation, the neurotronic web.

Martin wasn't moving, and the scream that had summoned me was now just a low moan. I looked back, but the adults were still sitting calmly around their picnic, unaware that anything had happened. So I yelled—quite a bit—until they got the idea that something serious had occurred, and I turned back to Martin.

The web was still bright, which was a good sign; if the web lost its silver shimmer and turned gray, then it would be all over for Martin. But what to do? How do you help an injured robot? They don't teach that in my village school. I decided to lift him out of the water a little—the saltiness couldn't be good for him.

It was hard work, but I'm fairly tough for my age, and I managed to haul him up far enough that the water could drain out of the wound. There was quite a bit of gray now, I couldn't help noticing, but still a few sparkles.

Then the adults arrived, all puffing and out of breath. Don and Suzie were completely useless; Suzie just sat down like she'd been sandbagged and went into shock, and Don tried to comfort her. So Mum and Dad had to carry Martin back along the beach to the car. Behind me I heard Suzie moan and mutter, and before you could say "Oxted's web" there was a blazing row with Suzie blaming Don for not protecting their son, and Don saying it could be mended.

We tried the doctor in Aber-double-l's. He was an old man, near retirement, I suppose, and though he'd converted to dual-practice (of course), you could see that he wasn't really comfortable with robot patients. His hands were shaky, too, and that's not good for a neurotronic web. The silver streaks were going grayer. So the doctor asked the inevitable.

And that's when Suzie really threw a wobbly.

Backups.

There weren't any. At least, nothing from the last three years. And Doctor Evans didn't want to risk taking a fresh backup at this time—his downloader was an old model, he said, and he wasn't sure it could handle Martin's data rate—there could be data corruption, even if there was still enough of a pattern to copy. . . .

But Suzie wasn't listening. She was just screaming at Don for neglecting Martin's backups, and how he knew she wasn't technical and he should have done them and he hated Martin and . . .

Poor Martin. They got him fixed, but like I said, the last backup was three years old. . . .

So Martin lost the last three years of his memory. A five-year-old mind in an eight-year-old's body.

Don and Suzie sent us separate Christmas cards last year. Martin wasn't mentioned on either. I guess they sent him back to Oxted.

The Uncanny Valley.

Is that where I am, now?

INTERVAL 2

This is brilliant material, Tania, though I don't suppose you appreciate my professional glee. You're right about me being an archaeologist, but I'm a psychologist, too, and you can add anthropologist, to round out your picture of me. Yes, just one alien, doing all that.

The truth is, we're not a numerous race, nor do we have huge space vessels to courier us across the galaxy at FTL speeds. The universe is stingy with the exotic forms of matter we need even to move at the speed of light, so six crew is about the maximum, and we split all the jobs between us.

I had to pull strings to get this expedition to happen. The Directors—the leaders of my people—disliked the idea of sending a precious ship all the way to Dawn. The Dawn Civilization has been studied to death. We should be moving out—by which they mean moving in, toward the galactic center, where the stars are more numerous—in search of new life.

And if we meet such life, I replied, how shall we introduce ourselves? Hello, we are the Old People, the Bored People, the Tired People. We have so little vigor, you see, Tania. I convinced them that a fresh study of the Dawn Civilization might teach us how to be young again.

Perhaps I lied. Perhaps this expedition is all about my personal vanity and relief of ennui. I hope not. I need you to teach my race how to restore ourselves.

Michael and Annette had been waiting quietly outside my room; when I called a tentative hello they entered.

They . . . shuffled. Heads slightly bowed, so they didn't have to meet my eyes. Annette's face was red and her eyes puffy—she'd been crying. Michael just looked totally hangdog and guilt-ridden. He broke the silence.

"How are you?"

"Not dead. Unfortunately."

"Ah."

And that was the confirmation. Not "How could you say such a thing?" or "Oh my darling little girl." Just "Ah." Shorter than "Oh, dear, now you know we've been lying to you all your life"— but it meant the same thing.

"What do I call you now? Michael? Annette? Reverend Deeley? Mrs. Deeley?"

"We were hoping you'd still call us Mum and Dad."

"But you're not, are you?"

"Perhaps not in the biological sense, no. But we've given you all our love, always. If we could have had a child, we couldn't have loved her any more than we've loved you. I feel I am your dad, in every way that matters. And Mum, she feels the same way about you."

"You let me believe I was special. *Human*."

"You are special. . . ."

"Just not human."

Annette looked up then, and she said her first words.

"They send you on a course, you know. When you decide . . . You know. Oxted."

I could have said something to help her in her difficulty, but I was feeling hurt, and so I wanted to hurt them. So I kept silent and let her struggle to find some words.

"It's all about what to tell your new child. They tell you it won't work, unless you think of your new baby as human. You mustn't think of it as a robot, they say, and you mustn't tell it that it's a robot, because if you do, it won't develop properly, it won't reach its best potential."

"That's right, Tania," added Michael. "After the first few weeks, we never thought of you as anything else. You were our little miracle, a real child in a barren world. As far as we could, we avoided anything that might break the spell. . . ."

"That's nonsense," I blurted, wanting to puncture Michael's lie. "What about my *revisions*? What about *backups*? You're supposed take a backup. Regular backups. Remember Mar-*tin*?"

They looked at each other, and it was Michael who answered me.

"Yes, I'd forgotten you were there when Martin was injured. Your mum and I never did take backups. It was a conscious choice. If we'd had a . . . a child of our own bodies"—Michael stumbled, trying to avoid the word "real"—"we'd not have been able to back her up. And so with you. If you'd been badly injured, we'd have lost you. Completely. If you'd died, part of us would die, too. Without the risk of loss, there cannot be genuine love."

Was that the vicar speaking, with a scholar's reasoning? It sounded like something out of one of his sermons, crafted and pithy. And it must have made sense to Annette, because she was nodding agreement, but I didn't understand it one little bit. To love something more, you safeguard it less?

"Look, Tania. We know what's happened has been a shock to

you, and your mum and I are upset, too. But you're part of the family . . ."

Like the butler. Soames, the stupid, clumsy robot that still crushes ping-pong balls.

". . . and families survive far worse than this. We stay together. Nothing changes."

How's that? Yesterday I was a girl. Rare and wonderful. Today, I'm a robot. A production-line pet, constructed to comfort two humans who can't have a real child of their own.

"Tania? Tania?"

I realized I'd drifted off, my mind somewhere else. Without thinking, I replied, "Yes, Dad?"

I didn't mean to use that word. It wasn't part of my plan.

Oxted had made me too well, because then I cried.

Monday, November 1, 2049

And so, with those tears, I accepted the love of my mum and dad, and rejoined the family.

I wish.

That would have been a lovely fairy-tale ending. Like *Pinocchio*, I suppose. Could Walt Disney have foreseen the fate of his film? In many countries it had been re-rated Adults Only—some places it was banned. If it was watched at all, it was in secret, its theme too painful for most people to bear. I'd seen it, though. John had sent me a link to the TeraNet, and I'd followed it, guiltily, downloading and viewing it when Mum and Dad thought I was asleep. I thought it was rather ordinary, back then—just three weeks ago—but now I began to understand the unbearable poignancy.

Impossible dreams. The toy that becomes a real child.

Me.

I know in my head there is just the glittering silver-gray of the neurotronic nexus. But all I can picture is ticking cogs and relays, some hybrid of computing dawn—Babbage and Colossus— miraculously shrunken to fit inside my head. And I dream that it'll equally miraculously turn into the gray sponge of a real human brain. And then I'll be truly human, and my parents will love me.

They were trying so hard, Michael and Annette, to be my dad and my mum again. They'd hug me unexpectedly, and one of them would always be near me. Dad would try to coax me out of the house for a walk to the village pond. Mum would get me to help in the kitchen.

Meanwhile Soames was currently banished to the attic, after I'd thrown a wobbly. It wasn't a very good wobbly, as my heart wasn't in it.

My heart?

Oh, well. Let it stand. I'm not going to change the way I write, just because it turns out now I'm a robot.

Is that okay with you, Mister Zog?

I hope you're still reading this.

———

I was dreading school.

What did they know? Had Siân told everybody what had happened? She was hardly Miss Discreet—she didn't have the empathy—but she was also the nearest thing to a friend I had, and I supposed I was hoping there was some fragment of First Law that would help me, even though I wasn't technically enti-tled to First Law protection anymore.

She was there, at the bus stop. Her back was to me, and she was talking to one of the other girls. Myra? Or Jemima? I couldn't tell them apart. What couple could be so gauche as to buy twin robots? The word was that Myra/Jemima came from a family even wealthier than Siân's—simply too much money to care what other people thought.

Jemyra noticed me first—her eyes flicked momentarily in my direction—and Siân spotted the motion, turned, and gushed,

"Oh, hi, Tania. I was just telling Myra here about our trip to London. I thought you'd drowned, you know—you were underwater for so long. But they say time plays tricks in an emergency, and anyway that nice Beefeater pulled you out and gave you artificial resuscitation."

"Uh, yes." Well what else do you say?

"And they bandaged your leg and took you off to hospital, didn't they, and I never got a chance to see you after that, but Daddy said he'd gone with you to make sure you got the best treatment money could buy, on account of it was our fault."

"Oh, thanks. I didn't know. My dad will pay you back. . . ." But then I realized he probably couldn't afford to.

Jemyra's eyes narrowed, and she looked at me in a rather predatory way.

"What was it like? You know . . . drowning?"

"I . . . I can't really remember much."

"Really?" She didn't believe me, but the less I said, the better.

"I think I blacked out."

"Riiiight. And you were hurt, Siân said. Your leg."

"Nothing much. Just a scratch. It's all healed now."

"That's nice. Mind if I look? I'm thinking of studying medicine."

"It's fine. There's nothing to see."

Why was I lying? Why not just say I'm a robot and have done with it? I didn't know, but I did know that I didn't care for Jemyra's nosiness. Or for Jemyra herself, for that matter.

Jemyra's eyes blinked slowly, and it made me think of a snake mesmerizing its prey, which I know is rubbish, but then she lost interest and went back to her sister. They started talking loudly about their own holiday in the Canaries, and I turned back to Siân.

Siân was watching me. She was looking . . . awkward. She's always so poised, and I wondered what was up. Did she know? Was that the end of our friendship, such as it was?

"Tania . . ."

"Yes?"

"Are you mad at me?"

"Now, why would I ever be mad at you, Siân?"

"Well . . . for telling her about the accident. I mean, like making it all a bit of an adventure. It was so awful at the time. I thought you were drowned, dead, and your leg was bleeding so. But now it's all in the past, and you're alive, and I hope you're still my friend."

"I'm not mad at you. And I'm still your friend . . . if you want me to be?"

"Of course I do."

"And I'm sorry, too, Siân. For spoiling the day out. And putting your mum and dad to all that bother."

"No, Tania. Don't even think about it."

So that was that. And then the bus came.

———

But that wasn't that.

Well, Siân was fine. But Jemyra . . .

It started as I made my way down the aisle to my seat on the bus. I stumbled—there was a bag sticking out that hadn't been there a moment ago. I managed to catch myself, and looked round.

"Careful," murmured Jemyra, but her eyes were laughing at me.

"You tripped me. . . ."

"I don't think so. *Tin Pot*."

"What?"

"You heard. *Tin Pot*. Or maybe I'll call you *Tin*-ia."

"How . . . *dare* you!"

Jemyra turned to her sister.

"Listen to little Miss Ann Droid."

"I am not an android!" I yelled, and I was suddenly conscious of everybody on the bus looking at me.

"Then prove it! That was a nasty wound you picked up, I know. Show me the scar, and I'll believe you're human."

"Why should I?"

"You can't. Because you're not a girl. You're a cheap fake! A stinking *Mekker*!"

A *Mekker*. Me.

I wanted to cry; I so nearly cried, but I wouldn't give her the satisfaction. I felt Siân's hand on my shoulder, and her voice trying to calm the situation. But I was more conscious of Jemima and Myra gloating in front of me. I wanted to hit them, I realized. My hand had clenched into a fist, and I began to swing . . .

Siân caught me, before I could land a blow.

"Don't, Tania! They're not worth it. They're just . . . pondlife."

I laughed, then. The picture was soooo perfect. Jemima and Myra as something green and slimy.

I let Siân lead me away, to the back of the bus. Heads turned as we—I—passed and I realized with a sinking feeling that the word would be out. Just a rumor, but that would be enough.

And it was.

Everywhere I looked that day there'd be a little huddle of girls, and they'd whisper and point. Some would gasp and look scandalized, some would turn away guiltily.

The teachers did nothing.

Oh, they dished out punishments—impositions, detentions—because no one was paying any attention to their lessons, or doing any work. Even I picked up an imposition—five sides on "The LeClerc Solution"—because three times I failed to respond when the history mistress asked me a question. Even *Siân* got an impot for losing her temper and whispering "shut up" too loudly at two gossips during art—six sides on "Meditation on the Inside of a Table Tennis Ball as an Aid to Inner Tranquillity."

But while they punished the girls' inattention, they did nothing to find out its cause. They didn't care. And I was afraid to tell.

The LeClerc Solution, Mister Zog? One of the darker episodes of the Troubles. While the Sabine Wars were in full swing, a rumor spread that the waters of Lourdes had cured infertility. So the whole of Western Europe, and quite a bit of North Africa, started a gigantic pilgrimage to Lourdes. Tens of millions, maybe a hundred million people. It was like a plague of locusts descending on France—nothing could hold them back, and where they passed, the land was stripped bare.

France was about to be ruined. The President had no idea what to do. Then, through a series of errors, and an indeterminate amount of plotting, a minor General—LeClerc—found himself able to launch a single nuclear missile. At Lourdes.

Nobody wanted to go to Lourdes after that.

Jemyra—and her cronies—picked on me.

Subtle things. Stealing my calculator from my bag, while my back was turned, so I didn't have it for physics. After the lesson she handed it back but got in another dig: "I found this, but, well, robots don't need calculators, they're just a sort of computer themselves, really. . . ."

Not so subtle things. Mostly trips and shoves in the corridors. I fell—"was pushed"—down the steps to the gym. Jemyra: "Wonky gyroscope, dear?"

I kept alert during gym, and the teachers do watch out that everything is done safely. But they can't watch everywhere, so I did get a thump in the chest from a medicine ball. Jemyra: "Clang!"

I was glad to get home at the end of the day, and lucky that Siân sat with me on the bus, to protect me from the bullying.

"They're so mean to you, Tania. It's not fair."

"What if they're right, though? If I'm just a tin-pot robot . . ."

Siân's hand flew to her mouth, and she gave a little gasp. My heart sank—keep quiet, Mister Zog—as I realized the thought hadn't occurred to her before. Poor Siân, I thought. Not the brightest star in the firmament, are you?

She went very quiet for a long minute, before speaking again.

"Tania? Is it true then? Are you a robot? I mean, I saw your foot, but I wasn't sure."

I nodded.

Another long pause. Siân frowned, thinking. My last hope, I thought. The random thoughts of—well, I'd better not say what picture went through my mind, because I'm ashamed I ever thought it, because then she spoke.

"Well, I've decided it doesn't make any difference. Human or not, you're a better friend than anyone else I've ever met. They all think I'm a dumb blonde—Jemima calls me that when she thinks I can't hear—and I know I'm not very bright . . ."

Like I say, even our thoughts come back to shame us.

". . . but I do have feelings. Tania . . . Tania, look at me. I *look* like a dumb blonde and that's how people treat me. You just look nice, and I expect people talk to you about all sorts of interesting things. Do you believe that sometimes I wish I was a robot? I do, because then I'd be smarter, and I could look however I liked. And when I grew up I could stop at whatever age I liked, and I'd never grow old or wear out or . . . or die."

"Uh, I don't know about that, Siân. I expect robots wear out, too."

Do they?

———

Home. In my room.

Mum and Dad don't know how horrible the day's been. I'd love to pour out my heart to them, yet there's so much on my mind. I replayed my diary from the start of last term—all those questions . . .

What happens to robots when they grow up?

Why does Mrs. Hanson have a photograph of a handsome Zulu warrior—her husband?—in the classroom?

Why aren't there any young teachers?

What lies in the heart of Africa, beyond the Kimberley Corridor?

Why hasn't John called me?

Well, I can cross the last one off my list, I suppose. But I had a few more to add, to make up for that one:

Is Jemima (or Myra) a robot or human?

For that matter, how many of the girls who'd been bullying me today were robots? And did they know it, or did they think they were human, as I'd done?

Do robots live forever? If so, could *I* live forever? Did I *want* to live forever?

Was Siân really human? If she's just a robot, why am I helping her learn French?

How many humans are there now? Are there *any* humans still being born?

Gosh! Where did that come from?

On an impulse, I decided to look it up on the TeraNet. It couldn't be too difficult to Google what I needed. So . . .

global population[GO]

Okay. There's a few sites there. Census.gov looks like a good bet . . .

Hmm . . .

Some nice graphs. Steady growth through the twentieth century. There's the flattening out, starting in 2010, but still an almost unbelievable seven billion. Masked by the increase in longevity. There's 2017, and it's eerie, the sharpness of the dip. Normal death rate, but live births go to near-zero in a single year. And a huge dip in 2018—Lourdes and all the other Troubles. I couldn't even see the line without zooming in. Since then a few wobbles up and down, but basically it's a steady downslope from an estimated two-fifty million left after the Troubles . . .

Which cuts off at 2040. Nine years ago. Just after a faint upturn.

Hold on. That graph is created dynamically, the cut-off is an embedded parameter. I can paste the current date in *there* and . . .

Oops!

ERROR 8FEA8006. USER Tania Deeley NOT AUTHORIZED.

. . . and a biometric prompt, for an authorized user to override. Noooo . . .

[CANCEL] [CANCEL] [CANCEL] [CANCEL] [CANCEL]

Help! I didn't mean it!

When my heart stopped racing . . .

Look, it felt like my heart was racing. I know I don't have a heart. I know I don't have adrenal glands to make adrenaline, and all those other gucky chemicals. Maybe it's just programming, but I felt panicky, honest. So just humor me, Zog, and let me write this the way I want. Okay?

Anyway when I calmed down I squinted at that upturn on the graph. If it was an upturn, and not just a rendering glitch, or fake data, then maybe things were improving. Or maybe not, and they'd just picked the last wobble upward as a good place to stop telling people the truth.

I guessed it was bad, though.

I cleared the screen then, because I heard Dad's footsteps coming up the stairs.

"Hi, Dad."

"Hi, Tania. Can I come in?"

"Sure."

And Dad looked straight over at my screen.

"You've been using the TeraNet just now, haven't you?"

It wasn't really a question. I just nodded, and waited for Dad to get to the point.

"You were accessing restricted data, weren't you?"

"No. Well, maybe. I was looking at population trends. Er, for a school project."

"Really? The police will be interested. . . ."

"Oh. No, it was my own idea. The police?"

"They called. Just a moment ago. They're on their way. I imagine they'll be here in a few minutes."

It wasn't even that long. I could see a blue light flashing just at the end of the street, coming nearer. At least there wasn't a siren.

The doorbell rang.

———

It wasn't too bad.

No. That's not true.

It was awful. I mean, the police were actually fairly nice about it. But technically I'd committed a criminal act, and they had to treat it seriously. Which meant a lecture from the police officer about the dangers of the TeraNet and how we needed to stay away from sensitive subjects—this, from looking at a government website—and the government had a duty to protect its citizens from information that might upset people.

Okay, okay.

No, the horrible bit came after the lecture. They had to give me a caution, you see. And they had to do it officially. Which meant form-filling.

This form had a check box for robots.

"Does she know?" asked the police officer, in a whisper I wasn't meant to hear.

Dad looked grim, but then nodded. Mum was crying, silently.

"Tania Annette Deeley. Robot."

That was the awful bit.

I don't think Mum or Dad would have minded so much, if it had just been a caution. It was that check box. It was the official recognition that I was a robot. I didn't care a hoot that I'd flouted the law, but I cared an awful lot what ticking that check box meant to Mum and Dad. I wasn't their little girl anymore, not now I'd just rubbed their noses in my robot-hood.

I found myself telling John. At least, some of it. Not about the check box, but about the population data, and . . .

"Did you use a safe proxy?" he asked.

"A what?"

"Something that masks your origin. So the monitors don't spot you peeking at restricted data, and send armed police around to break down your front door."

"They didn't break down my front door; they just rang the bell. . . . Oh!"

"You didn't use a proxy." His voice was flat.

"I've never heard of them before, John. Oh, I wish I'd known."

And so, patiently, John skimmed over all the things I'd need to know to burrow into the forbidden recesses of the Tera-Net, without getting caught. How to find proxies—they're illegal, of course, and have to masquerade as legal nodes, while the real nodes are down for maintenance. How to fuzz your backtrail from the proxy, and scubbie your ID (I think that's the word he used), so you look like somebody else but information still gets back to you. I didn't understand it, but I could learn to use it. And then he said something that sent a chill right through me.

"Next time you get caught, it'll be youth custody. Just be glad you're human. Robot kids get deactivated."

"Deactivated?" Why was it me asking all the questions, I wondered.

"Scrapped. Broken up. Why would you bother putting a robot in jail?"

"But w— They're valuable. Very expensive. You wouldn't just destroy one, would you?"

"One that broke the law has gone outside its programming. How could you trust it ever again? It's not safe. That's what they say. Oxted, I mean."

"Oh . . ."

I changed the subject.

"Look, John. Where did you learn about proxies and fuzzing your ID?"

"Fuzzing your backtrail, Tania. Here and there. Some of the kids at school know some things. I listen. I learn."

"Well, I never heard of such things at my school. What's your school like?"

"Rough."

"How do you mean, rough?"

"It's just bullying. Gangs. Typical Yellow Zone stuff. It's not good for your average kid, but I learned that hackers have special respect, so that's what I am now. The gangs need hackers so the monitors can't trace them. I'm teaching myself. I'm pretty good."

And I wasn't.

"John. Teach me. Teach me everything you know about the TeraNet. And when I know as much as you, we'll go on learning together."

"Why, Tania? I mean, you're already in trouble with the police. You shouldn't go messing around on the TeraNet."

"The answers are out there, John. All the questions inside me, crying out for answers . . ."

"What questions?"

And so I told him. The questions I'd been keeping inside me. At least, the ones that weren't about my fate as a robot.

"Those are good questions, Tania. I'd like to know some of the answers, too, if you find them. I'll help."

"Okay, but let's start with the monitors. You've mentioned them twice, but I've never heard of them."

"There's nothing written about them, officially, but there's a whole surveillance infrastructure in place on the TeraNet. The monitors detect keywords that might indicate subversive, illegal, or protected traffic, and alert the police to the perp. I don't know what the technology is, but it's hard to fool."

"So they're watching everything I send or receive? Ugh!"

"Very ugh! The days of liberal government and a free press ended with the Troubles. Stick to safe subjects, and you're fine. Do anything to threaten the status quo, and you'll have cops crawling out of your a—"

Really, John! I like you very much, but sometimes you have such a potty-mouth.

Sunday, January 2, 2050

John has been a really good friend these last few weeks. He taught me all about proxies and fuzzing my backtrail, and all that stuff. I'm using the words as though I know what they mean, and maybe by now I even do.

Actually, John is becoming more than a good friend. He is definitely special. He's interested in the same things—my list of questions—but we talk about loads of other stuff, too. Music is a favorite. We liked some of the same bands already, but he knows much more about some new acts than I do. I'm starting to realize that Mum and Dad's A/V collection is a bit . . . tired.

But the last few days, as we've argued the merits of his favorites over mine, we've realized something. There aren't any new bands.

Don't be ridiculous. There have always been kids singing harmony on street corners, or practicing guitar in their bedroom. They come together by chance, and they gel, or they clash, they split and they form anew, but however they do it, they explode with new creativity.

But John's "new acts" are actually five or ten years old now. There aren't any acts newer than that, unless you counted tribute bands. In which case there were hundreds and hundreds.

It's the same in literature. There are still plenty of new books on the shelves, but no new authors, just fiction factories turning out clones and sequels.

You can argue that there have been slumps in the past, like the prepunk years, but not many. John and I can't convince each other that this is just another slump.

Art is dying. Why?

I'm adding the question to my list.

————

John is special—he's the only one I've trusted with my questions—but he's also different from me. He loves the stars. He knows their names. How far away they are. Astronomy, physics, astro-engineering. Me, I'm more interested in people. How they think, how they behave. History, sociology, psychology.

John wants to go to university. Cambridge, he says.

"But my parents won't talk about it. 'Stay home,' they say. 'It's a good business your father has built, and when we're old, it'll be yours, and you can look after us.'"

And what do I want? Other than to be Pinocchio?

"Do they do psychology at Cambridge?"

He laughs gently.

"Of course they do. And their doors are wide open."

To humans. Of course, they would be. Any human would be welcome.

But . . . robots?

I have to find out. How much time do I have? And what happens after that?

In the end, it was simple enough to find out. I created an Eicon, helped by John. A kind of ghostly "second me" that lived on the TeraNet, existing on stolen cycles and spoofed addresses. It could be me if I wanted it to be, but it was usually more useful for it to be someone else.

I skinned it to be Jeryl Banner, twenty-nine, recently remarried and childless. Jeryl had a proper TeraNet ID—there were kids who specialized in faking them up, some for profit, others just to show off—so Jeryl was able to apply to Oxted online. For a baby, a little robot baby.

It was there in the FAQ.

Eighteen.

Jeryl could have her baby, on payment of one hundred and fifty thousand Basics—I whistled, it was several years' salary for Dad—which sum included up to eight standard upgrades, at two-year intervals (there were more options if you had the money). And then, at age eighteen, back to Oxted it would go. I looked around for the contract and sure enough, it was a lease, not a purchase. Title stayed with Oxted.

And that was me.

Leased for a fixed term. Serviced, upgraded, and replaced as scheduled, just like Dad's office copier.

You have no idea how small that made me feel, Mister Zog.

D—.

Swearing didn't help, but I did it anyway. Psychology degree at Cambridge? Hah! It was all futile. Totally, utterly pointless, because at age eighteen, Oxted was going to reclaim me, and then what? Scrap me? If not, what else?

———

There was nothing in the FAQ. Nothing a prospective parent would stumble upon and get upset about. But then, tucked away on the Corporate Social Responsibility pages, next to an impressively long list of supported charities, I found the Oxted Environmental Impact Statement. Naturally, Oxted is a green company, committed to minimizing waste and ecological damage. A top-class corporate citizen:

"Oxted recognizes its responsibility to the planet and to humanity." Blah, blah . . . *"Less than 2 percent goes to landfill."* Blah, blah . . .

So I was too valuable to just scrap, but dotted here and there were the words:

Refurbish.

Recycle.

Re-use.

Reclaim.

I'd always thought those were good words. Such eco-friendly words . . . until I realized they might be applied to me. And there was one more I could think of, conspicuous by its absence:

Reprogram.

Yes. What else can you do with a complex, expensive robot brain? Wipe it. Reprogram it. Re-use it. As . . . Soames.

Oh, no! That would be awful. Given a new, but clunky body, with glowing red eyes, to come back as a domestic robot. Had Soames once been a little boy, playing happily in a garden, going to school? At eighteen, had he climbed docilely into an Oxted van while his parents held back the tears?

Had he wept too at the separation, or had he embraced the oblivion of reprogramming? Or . . .

There was another possibility. Rebirth. To come back as a baby, for some other loving couple to raise. That made sense, too, in the same, horrible way. Starting again, endlessly. Immortality, I thought, but it was a mockery.

Something nagged at me, something I'd learned in my Latin. The Elysian Fields, that was it. In classical mythology. You died, and you went to Hades. The fields of the blessed waited for you, but there was a catch. You had to drink the waters of forgetfulness, from the River Lethe. I'd wondered why you'd do such a thing, to throw away your memories of life. After all, life was good, wasn't it?

So why was I crying?

For a moment, a bitter moment, I'd have drunk from the Lethe. If someone had given me a cup of its waters right then, I'd have drained every drop.

And then came a knock on the door. Dad. Come to check why I was up so late, I guess. I tried to send him away, but he must have heard the catch in my voice, and before I knew it, he was sitting on the end of my bed and I was pouring out my heart to him.

"No, Tania, I don't know exactly what happens beyond your eighteenth birthday. Yes, you do go back to Oxted. It's always been looming. Nettie and I, we . . . we don't know how people cope with it. As a vicar, I have to deal with the consequences. People do silly things, like running away, but they're always caught. They stop upgrading their child, hoping that Oxted will just forget about them. When the child is taken away, it's pretty ghastly. I've seen suicides, divorces, violence, depression. Even murder."

"So why do people do it, Dad? Why do they get robot kids in the first place?"

He looked at me strangely.

"We're just made that way, Tania. With my vicar's hat on, I'd say God made us that way. We need each other, husbands, wives, children. We marry, we start families, because it's our nature to live in the present and let the future take care of itself. If we worried about loss and death, we'd never marry. What rational being would willingly enter a relationship that's guaranteed to end in sorrow? Grieving husband buries wife, or vice versa. Or they divorce. But we marry anyway. Because even death and divorce is better than loneliness."

"And me?"

"You, Tania, are the same. To have you and lose you—that's still far better than never to have had you at all. We have eighteen precious years together, the three of us, that we would not otherwise have had."

We were both crying now, but he was right. However awful we felt, it was better than being alone.

INTERVAL 3

We are an old and long-lived people, Tania. Our name for ourselves is simply the People, reflecting the lack of any other race in the galaxy to compare ourselves to by name. We know of just two other races, both long dead, of which Homo sapiens is one. The other we know only through a handful of artifacts—ancient pyramids—beacons marking a forgotten and disrupted path through the galaxy.

I have seen one of the Pyramid Planets. I was a member of the first follow-up expedition, in the early days of our exploration of the galaxy. The Pyramids were signaling machines, driven by a technology it took us millennia to comprehend. Sadly, by the time we saw the beacon, the pyramid builders had vanished. I say "I have seen" though I remember nothing of it. That went, as part of my first Erasure. But it is in my record.

The rest of the galaxy, as far as we have been able to map it, is empty and lifeless. We have found places where, in time, we believe life may emerge. These nurseries we protect and—carefully—study.

Other galaxies? I have no idea, Tania. They are too far away, even for my own people.

The universe is cruel, Tania. More cruel than you know, because it mocks us, the People, with utter loneliness. We hunger to find another living race to talk to. Failing such, Tania, we talk, through the archives of this place, to the long-dead.

You.

I got sick last Tuesday. A sort of weakness all over my body. I couldn't concentrate, and Mum had to drive me to the main surgery in town. The doctor took some samples of my, ah, body wastes, ran some tests, and said that my digestive nanozymes had become inactivated. So I was eating, but not getting any energy. Starving. He prescribed some foul-tasting gunk for me to swallow that he said would reactivate the nanozyme substrate, and flush out whatever it was that had bonded on to it. Some unspecified protein was all he said.

"Wait till you get home before taking this," he advised. "And do it somewhere you can sluice clean afterward, like a bath or shower."

Afterward?

Do I have to draw a picture, Mister Zog?

When I was cleaned up, and fed, and rested, I got to wondering, how different am I from human?

So "nanozyme substrate" went straight into the search engine. Back came pictures of macromolecules—lots of colored spheres and springs, black for carbon, red for oxygen, white for hydrogen, et cetera. Anything that looks like a sugar molecule hooks on to the nanozyme, which also finds water and oxygen, and turns it all into carbon dioxide, water, and energy.

So I eat the same food as Mum and Dad. I don't have to plug myself into the power circuit. I . . . eliminate waste. There's a whole science—Cybiology—devoted to mimicking human biology, so we can share the same ecology. It's complicated, and really expensive.

Soames and his ilk, however, have "conventional" powering, because it's cheaper. That means domestics have to be home-based, so they're always near to charging points. Brain-wise, they still have to be pretty sophisticated, so that's the same, but the programming is way less complex.

I felt quite smug when I read that. After all, I may be a robot, but I'm definitely not a *cheap* robot.

The other thing that I wonder about is waking and sleeping. Do I really need to sleep? And then there's dreaming—I have some really weird dreams. What's that all about?

Tuesday, July 18, 2051

Another year passes.

Exams are over, term is done, and the summer holiday has begun. School was actually okay this year. The bullying at school is a distant memory. Oh, it continued for a while, but at some stage Jemyra found some other girl to taunt. Robot, I should say. Gillian Simmons was a quiet girl who never said much, didn't have particular friends (nor enemies for that matter). One day, just outside the school gates, she stepped off the pavement without looking and was hit by a car. I wasn't there to see it, but those who did saw the web revealed. Gillian was whisked off to casualty, and returned a week later, without blemish, perfect.

So the spotlight shifted to her, and I was mostly left alone.

Then a few months after that, another girl got injured. I don't know what happened to her, because her parents didn't send her back to school. For a week or so, rumors ran wild, but after that, I think we realized we were all playing an enormous charade, and we stopped bothering.

And then it was autumn, and the next year's intake arrived, and from our lofty position of second years, we watched it all repeat—a rite of passage.

Not much changes at home, except we finally got a 3-D vid. Another cast-off, of course, but I don't mind too much.

John . . .

I'm sure you're wondering, Mister Zog. It's pretty good having John as a friend. Better than a lot of the boyfriends that the girls talk about at school. I mean, they don't seem to do anything. They only talk about gadgets and sport. Not that any of them play sport—it's just talk. John's different. He talks about making music and the stars. And John's teaching himself guitar and he really knows about computers. Maybe it's because his parents aren't well off, but he builds them. Or rebuilds them. And he can program them, too. You can see the light in his eyes when he talks about it.

But I can't see him. Of course I can see him over the TeraNet, but it's not the same. And if you're only twelve, you're stuck. I can't drive or anything. I've looked it up, how to get to his house, but it's a bus, then a train, then the Tube, with changes. And then walking through Wood Green, which isn't like walking through Wycombe. Wood Green is Yellow Zone, so I know Mum and Dad aren't going to let me do a journey like that on my own. And definitely not to see some boy. So I've not even asked. Though I do very much want to see him, I just don't yet know how. Not so I can kiss him again—though as a one-off peck in a '70s disco it was okay—or hold his hand or any of that stuff. Just to . . . *be* with him. Talking face-to-face. That's all.

But maybe that will change this year. Because finally the year has turned, and today I am thirteen.

A teenager.

Just five years left.

Siân wanted to go into Town—London—on her own, but her parents wouldn't let her. Too dangerous, they said, you're only thirteen. Siân argued, they argued back, and in the end a compromise was reached. She could go with a friend. Me. There may have been a bit of an argument about that, too, but maybe they'd softened a bit toward me since the drama at the Tower of London.

It was a bit of an adventure, going into London, but we'd both been into Wycombe alone a few times and Siân had been as far as Henley. Siân's mum grudgingly agreed that we could look after ourselves a bit. "But you must stay in the Green Zone and be back by eight," she insisted. Shops. A meal—or at least a burger—and then home.

Then I had the same argument with my parents.

"Back by half past seven!"

My jaw dropped. How old do you think I am? I'm thirteen. *Thirteen.* In the end, I did get them to agree to eight o'clock, and it was Mum who caved in first. I'm not sure why.

The date was set for the following weekend, so Siân and I got planning. . . .

Saturday, September 16, 2051

Saturday came, and we got the bus to the station. Then the train and the Tube. And we wound up in Oxford Street. Mum and Dad had given me some extra spending money, on top of my weekly allowance—I'd finally convinced Mum and Dad to stop calling it pocket money.

I knew I was going to like Oxford Street. It had the largest media store I'd ever seen, and I'd made up my mind I'd spend my allowance there. Every last penny. I knew it would be more expensive than downloading from the TeraNet, but there's something about buying your music on a real datachip.

I started toward the door, but Siân caught my elbow.

"There," she said. "That's where we're going."

She was pointing at a shop with a bright pink front, glittery and gaudy. In the shop window stood three or four figures, stock still. The shop name gave it away: "Sais Quoi." A fashion boutique.

I tried to look interested.

I think the assistants sensed that Siân had money, and was in a mood to spend it. They clustered round her, and all but ignored her dowdy friend. A pile of possibles rapidly accumulated—this top, that skirt, and a selection of shoes. Er, Siân, you do only have one pair of legs, you know?

Half an hour later I was beginning to wonder how much longer this was going to go on. The salesgirls continued their fluttering about Siân, offering this and that for her approval.

I sighed deeply.

One of the salesgirls heard me, and to my surprise turned and met my eye.

"Was that boredom, miss? Or exclusion? If you're bored, I can't help you. But if you'd like me to find you something that's right for you, then just say."

"I don't know. Both. To me, clothes are just . . . clothes. It seems a lot of fuss, just to keep warm. But Siân's different. She's . . ."

"She's older? Got a different figure to you? Yes, she has. But I can still help you be you. It's something your parents can't do."

She was good. My elbows and knees were still the elbows and knees that had been so awkward, dancing to the Slade tribute band. Literally the same, for I'd not grown in all that time. But she found a few items that weren't childish, yet didn't demand teenage curves I didn't possess. Blacks, to match my hair. I thought she might suggest reds to go with it, which I'd already decided would look cheap, but she was wiser than that, and found a skirt and a matching blouse subtly streaked with silver-gray. It made me think of a web—Oxted's web—which somehow appealed.

Siân looked briefly across, and nodded, approvingly. Her own shopping was nearing completion, and five minutes later she joined us, with a selection of carrier bags in her hands.

"Can't decide?" she asked.

I showed her my choices. A couple of tops, a skirt, and a pair of trousers, all themed black and silver.

"But I can't afford them all—my allowance won't stretch that far—and I don't know what to leave out."

We had an argument then. Siân's solution was simple; she'd buy for me what I couldn't afford. For my part, I was trying to be noble, the nobility of the poor. But I really wanted that outfit. The salesgirl was right; it was a part of becoming me, and I couldn't fight that. And it fitted my plans.

I walked out of the shop, dressed in black and silver, with more bags under my arm.

I looked at my watch. It was nearly time.

"Siân. I've got a confession to make."

She looked at me, alarmed.

"I've not been to London like this, you know, without grown-ups. And I thought, it'd be a chance to, well, meet someone. A friend. From my holidays, a couple of years back."

"A boy, you mean?"

I nodded, blushing.

"John."

"Of course. I should have guessed. Have you arranged something, then?"

"Sort of. He's waiting for my call. But if you've got other plans . . ."

She was smiling gently.

"Call him. Where shall we meet?"

"He said he'd meet us for lunch. There's a café he knows, a few streets away. It's safely in the Green Zone and it's not too expensive, he says. It's called Antonio's."

———

Antonio's had once been Italian—pasta and pizza, but had evolved into something not quite so pigeon-holeable. It was darker inside, blinds drawn, and partitions to keep out any daylight through the doors. It felt like we'd shifted seamlessly in time to the evening.

It managed to hint at elegance and exclusivity, yet an exclusivity that was not based simply on wealth. You, it seemed to say, are the kind of customer I want, because you know who you are. You have style and wit, it said, and you are welcome.

And at the end farthest from the door there was a stage, where a band was starting to set up.

I was intrigued, because I'd never seen a live band. Big networked stadium events, sure, recorded and edited. Archive footage of the great summer festivals. I thought of all my musical discussions with John, and I guessed he'd chosen the venue deliberately.

There was a poster, advertising the various bands for this month. I skimmed the list and decided they were all just tribute bands—I chuckled over some of the names, wondering who in their right minds would call their band The Lost Corrs . . .

Today's band, though, was Mike Clip and the Stands. With a name like that they weren't a tribute band—at least nothing came to mind—so they were probably a generic blues band. I could cope with that.

Siân was getting nervous—even more than I was. She'd also seen the band setting up.

"Do you think they'll be loud?"

I shook my head, though I really had no idea what to expect. I was more concerned that John wasn't here yet.

"Not too loud, no."

"They *look* loud. . . ."

I could see what she meant. The amplifiers looked powerful,

but that wasn't where Siân was looking. The singer had just walked in, and he took my breath away. It was the black leather, really. It made me think of 1980s heavy metal posters, pouting and posing.

The singer reached out to his microphone, patted it, as a man might pat an old and trusted pet. No, not a pet, I decided, but a working dog, or . . . yes, that was it, like a warrior might greet his warhorse.

Then his eyes moved on to the audience, such as they were. Apart from Siân and me, there were a handful of other tables around the room, maybe twenty people at most. When his gaze reached me, he paused, acknowledging my interested stare with a wry smile and a conspiratorial wink. Then his eyes moved on.

That was the moment John arrived. . . .

————————

You must remember, Mister Zog, that I hadn't seen John for two years or more, and that all our contact had been via the TeraNet, using cheap webcams. So nothing had prepared me for how tall he'd grown, or how broad his shoulders had become.

Or how that unruly ginger mop had somehow been tamed into a lion's mane: smooth, lustrous, and . . . regal.

Even his freckles had become more grown-up. That looks so weird as I write it now, but it's truly the effect I saw.

So I stammered a greeting, and my feet got tangled in my bags as I stood up to shake his hand.

Yes. Shake his hand.

I'd been imagining this meeting, over and over, with all the variations I could think of. I played it through with coolness, just a peck on the cheek. Or with friendliness—a quick hug. Or with real warmth—a proper kiss on the lips.

When the moment came, the chairs got in the way, my bags got in the way, I was half-tripping over and I couldn't get my face even vaguely close to his—he was just too tall for anything but a handshake.

He looked surprised, and maybe there was a trace of amusement at my awkwardness, and even a hint of disappointment at my formality.

"John, this is Siân."

Siân had also stood up to greet him, but she'd had time to sort herself out. She smoothly reached out and steered him by the shoulders toward her, briefly kissing his cheek.

It was elegantly done, and John preened himself under her smile of welcome.

I decided to kill her.

Only for a moment or two, honest.

But there it was. Jealous. Me. Little Miss Tin Heart.

Where had that come from?

John was *my* friend. Of course he was, but so was Siân, and . . . and they were both human, and I . . . was not.

———

We ordered some snack food and something to drink, and settled down to wait for the band to start.

Mike Clip had disappeared, but the rest of the band were carrying in the last of their gear, running cables around and taping them down. To my mind they looked pretty old—my parents' age or thereabouts—so I tried to keep my mind off the problem of John-and-Siân by trying to guess the genre.

The drummer was actually a lot older than my parents. He looked really craggy, like old leather or baked earth, neither black nor white, but somewhere in between; gaunt and wiry, with not a spare ounce of flesh on him. When he grinned, I wasn't surprised to see gaps.

There was a guitarist, with awful ropelike hair, tight-wound and matted. Like dreadlocks, I suppose, but nothing so neat. His clothes looked like he'd robbed a scarecrow, but the scarecrow must have been glad to hand them over.

The last of Mike's Stands was the bassist, a woman dressed in a man's pin-striped business suit, a size or so too large. She, too, was wearing shades and a flat-rimmed hat—Blues Brothers style, of course. She'd rolled up her right sleeve, though, and had added a couple of Nike wristbands, which rather spoiled the effect. As I watched, she was putting the last touches to her wiring. Then she straightened up, and began to stretch, but only flexing her fingers and hands, first clenching a fist, then releasing. In turn she eased each finger out and back, massaging each one gently with her thumbs.

Odd.

So, that was the band John had brought us to see. Definitely a blues band, then.

I turned back to John and Siân, who'd also turned to watch the band getting ready. I managed to catch John's eye, and he gave me a little smile, which made me think of dance floors and Slade tribute bands and . . . anyway, maybe I wouldn't kill Siân just yet.

But before I'd got any further with those thoughts, I heard a couple of faint strums of the electric guitar, and suddenly the band exploded into their first song.

It was like nothing I'd heard before—a couple of snare beats warning, then the whole band was in there, with the kick drum driving the whole thing along, while the guitar and bass wove complex melodic fireworks about each other. Meanwhile Mike prowled the center stage—there's no other word for it; he was a lion marking out his territory—and sang I-don't-know-what, but it gripped me and shook me and demanded my total attention.

Wow!

I risked a look at John, and his mouth was open. He was staring at the band, too, wide-eyed. Then I looked back at the band, and my eyes settled on the bassist, and I realized why she'd been doing those finger stretches. I could barely see her fingers move— they blurred over the strings like berserk spiders—but I could hear the distinct hawsering of the melody in the bass, and feel it deep in my innards. And it looked effortless.

That was the moment I knew I wanted to play bass, in a

band. A proper band, writing its own music, not a tribute band. I wanted a bass that was cool, like hers, horned and slim-waisted, lacquered jet-black and chrome, and I wanted to make it sing, like she did. I wanted to dress my own way, and have people look at me, and admire my playing. Yes, and admire *me*, too.

And I wanted John to . . . stop looking at Siân!

There was no doubt. John was staring at Siân, quite blatantly.

Now, Siân is a blonde, and a very stareable blonde, I suppose, if you're a boy. She's shaped like a girl, you see, a proper, grown-up girl, I mean. And she'd just spent the morning shopping for clothes in a top Oxford Street boutique, and she looked just . . . oh!

Oh, gosh, Zog, this is just so embarrassing! And you have no idea what I'm going on about. How humans are two different sorts. I mean, you must know, being an archaeologist and an anthropologist and a xenologist and a space traveler and all that. You must know that men and women are different, but you only know it in an academic sort of way, because you're a great scientist, all the way from Andromeda.

Anyway, we are different, and we grow up even more different, not just bigger. Girls get curves and padding, and I was thirteen just like Siân, but *I* was still shaped like a Meccano hat stand. A very short hat stand.

So amid all those wantings around basses and becoming a great player of basses, I added wanting to be a proper thirteen-year-old, too. I wanted to grow up, I wanted to start to look like a woman. I wanted to stop being skinny and elbows, I wanted to have my own curves and padding. I wanted John to stare at me. Desperately, desperately, I wanted, needed John to look at me the way he was looking at Siân. . . .

So the band finished their first number with a crash, and the three of us yelled and clapped and stomped. And Mike wiped his brow with a towel, and raised one sardonic eyebrow in acknowledgment.

"Thank you, ladies and gentlemen. That was called 'Cuts.' We're gonna take the pace down a little with this next one. It's called 'Ace.' "

It was slow and incredibly haunting. Just voice and percussion for a verse and a half, and out of nowhere the faintest of notes detached itself from Mike's vocal and became a high bass countermelody. It sent shivers down my spine, honestly.

The whole of the set was like that.

When it came to an end, I felt drained, like I'd just climbed a high mountain, but exhilarated, like I was standing on the summit, with the whole world beneath my boots, looking down at it.

John and Siân were on that same mountain, I could see. Antonio's other customers, yes, they were atop their own peaks. I risked speaking, just a whisper in the sudden silence.

"John, did you know it would be like this?"

"Yes, more or less. I've seen them before. A week or so back. I hoped I could persuade you to come and I could surprise you."

Then Siân spoke.

"That was wonderful, John. I'm so glad you asked us."

Which he hadn't. He'd asked *me*, but I'd had to bring *you*, Siân Fuller.

John stood up.

"Can I get you girls something to drink?"

We chose fruit juices, and he wandered off to the bar.

"Your friend's nice, isn't he?"

"Yes," I agreed, not quite sure what else I could say.

"Quite tall."

"I suppose he is."

"And rather handsome."

"Uh."

"You were on holiday with him, you said. It must have been lovely."

I thought back. Fake coal mines. Platform shoes and a Slade tribute band. Me in lilac hot pants.

"Not really. It was . . . boring. It was the seventies. It was embarrassing."

"Really? Even with a nice friend like John around?"

"*Yes*. No. I mean, we were just *eleven*. He didn't look like that, then." Even if *I* did. I needed an escape. *There*.

"Look, Siân, excuse me. I need to go . . ."

But it wasn't the bathroom I needed. I walked over to the band, where they were breaking down the equipment, to the lady bassist, bending over her guitar in its case, carefully wiping down the strings.

"You played really well. . . ." My voice sounded small, nervous.

"Thank you." She didn't look up, but threaded the cloth between the strings and the neck, and eased it back and forth.

"It's a lovely bass. . . ." I ventured.

"Yeah. It's an Aria RSB Deluxe 5. It's about sixty, sixty-five years old. I look after it."

"How . . ." I was starting to flounder.

She looked up. She'd taken off the shades, and I could see her eyes. Hazel. And kind. I could almost see her make a decision not to brush me off.

"What do you want?" Gentle.

I took a deep breath.

"I want to learn to play the bass. Like you."

"Like me. Umm. What's your name?"

"Tania. Tania Deeley."

"Don't you think you ought to learn to play like Tania Deeley, first?"

I didn't know how to answer that.

"Sorry, Tania. That's not fair of me. When I was your age, I wanted to play like John Entwistle. It took me years to learn to play like Amanda Taylor. That's me, by the way."

"Pleased to meet you." I smiled.

"You're just going to have to buy a bass and learn. Listen to records. Find what you like and what you don't. Then search the TeraNet and find others who share your interest, and start a tribute band."

"I don't want to be in a tribute band. I want to do what you do—write your own music and perform it."

"Don't waste your time." Her voice was bitter now. "Look at us. Mike and Gary are brilliant songwriters. And Gus and I do our bit. Together we're inspired, brilliant. In another time we'd have had a five-album recording contract. We could have filled any stadium in the land. Instead of which we're gigging in a sleazy café in Soho, playing to twenty people, if you include the staff. My day job is a TeraNet programmer, and I'm not a very good one, but it mostly pays the bills. I'm divorced, childless, and forty-five. And only slightly angry at the world."

She smiled, and it was a brave smile. She continued.

"Have you been in a record store lately? Have a look at what's on offer. Greatest hits of 1975. The Complete Frank Sinatra. Elvis: the Sun Sessions. It's all old. Nostalgia. Look at the posters—mostly names like the Lost Corrs. People don't want original music. They want tribute bands, to help them turn the clock back to happier times. Our world is dying, and who is strong enough to watch it happen?"

"So why . . . ?" I began.

"Why do we do it? Make music for a world that doesn't want to listen? I can't speak for the other guys, but for me, making music is the only time I feel alive. I need to create . . . something. Every woman is made that way, and every man, too. If I can't create a baby, then I'll create a song. It's not much; it only lives for three minutes and then it's gone. But . . ."

"You must have recorded the songs, though. They'll last."

"It's not the same. It's the difference between a real person and a photograph. Live music is the only thing that matters. And I didn't mean to put you off forming your own band, Tania. That was mean of me. If you really think you can write good, original music—go for it! Don't be a tribute band, though. That's just another photograph. Excuse me."

She turned back to her bass, and bent over it, polishing where it was already pristine. I sensed the interview was over. I started to turn away, just as a tear splashed next to a pickup.

"Goodbye, Amanda. Thank you."

No answer.

Back at the table, John had returned with our fruit juices. He was deep in conversation with Siân. I decided to ignore his fixation on her chest.

"John. How do we form a band?"

But he was ahead of me.

"Tania, meet our new singer. Siân Fuller."

<u>Sunday, January 14, 2052</u>

Mister Zog, I'm learning to play bass. It's hard work. My fingers don't stretch far enough, so I can't play some of the standard patterns in the books—I've had to experiment to find other ways of getting the notes. And the bass I've got is just huge. I mean, it's nothing special, just a Precision copy. But it looks huge on me.

It's the church's bass, really. Dad found it in a storeroom, along with an amplifier that's supposed to be for keyboards, but it sounds okay. There was a drum kit in there, too, equally cobwebby. Dad says the church used to have a live worship band, forty years ago, before the worst of the Troubles. These days, the church is not a jubilant place, and the instruments are in storage, waiting for happier times to come again. If anyone asks, I'll give it back, but I'm not expecting that anytime soon.

It wasn't hard to find books on how to play, either. They've all got titles like *Play Bass Like Led Zeppelin* or *Stones Bass Guitar*. Put your favorite band in, hit search.

What is hard is to find the techniques and the theory, but John put together a contextual search that filtered out all the tribute band stuff, and what was left was a few golden nuggets.

So I practice every chance I get, up in my bedroom, headphones on. I'm starting to get the hang of what bass lines do, how they fit with the chords and melody. I've downloaded some of Amanda's recordings, to listen to. She's amazing—they all are. Yet . . .

Yet I start to see what Amanda meant. It's not the same as being there. It reminds me of the gig—see, I'm talking like a musician—but it doesn't reach down into your guts and tear at your emotions in the same way. So I dip into it occasionally, but I try not to listen to too much of any one band. I know I've got to find the style that works for me.

Style. Now that's the other thing. I stand in front of the mirror, sometimes, with my bass strapped on, and play along to a blues, or some rock and roll. I try to move like Amanda did, but my knees and elbows are as ridiculous as ever. I look like a little girl who's borrowed her big brother's bass. We don't belong together, visually.

I've tried different clothes, and they do make a difference. The ones that work best are the ones I bought in Oxford Street that day. Black and gray and silver. In them, I look least like a child.

So I've hunted the TeraNet, and I've found a few ideas. Mike's black leather jacket gave me the basic idea, I suppose. It just seemed to work so well with the music. I tried sketching myself in a leather jacket, but I've never learned to draw. So I tried John's contextual search again, and tried the TeraNet fan sites. Top of the list was a lady by the name of Suzi Quatro, but there were plenty of others to prove that the look worked.

I tried a photo edit, with my own head melded into some of those pictures. It was good enough.

So I took a deep breath, and headed downstairs.

Mum and Dad were watching an old George Lucas movie when I came in. They're never totally convincing in pseudo-3-D, but Lucas kept on remastering those movies until he died, claiming that each new cinematic innovation would enable him to realize his true vision of *Star Wars*. Still, his final space battles are magnificent. I settled down and waited for the right moment.

Sure enough, the next appearance of C3PO, and Mum started getting restless. Dad took the hint, and turned it off. At least it wasn't *Blade Runner*.

"I fancy a cup of tea," he announced, and headed for the kitchen. "Anyone else?"

By the time he was back, with a gently steaming pot and three mugs, Mum had undimmed the lights, and the furniture was arranged for a cosy family chat.

"Well," said Dad, "what brings you down from your eyrie? TeraNet outage?"

"Mike!" squeaked Mum, annoyed at his bluntness.

"Just kidding. But a dad ought to know when a daughter's got something on her mind. So come on, Tan. Out with it."

He was right—he did always know. Ah well, dive in . . .

"It's a little delicate, so let me go about this in my own way. And try not to jump to conclusions."

"Go on."

"It's just that I don't feel I'm keeping up with the other girls in my class. . . ."

"But your class reports are fine, darling. . . ."

"It's not that, Mum." I caught a look from Dad. *He* knew what was coming. "It's more, er, physical. I'd say I was a little slow in growing, wouldn't you?"

And then Mum got it.

"Oh, darling! You mean slow in *developing*, don't you?"

I nodded. "Yes, Mum. I feel out of place, still a little girl. My classmates are all turning into young women."

Dad jumped to the wrong conclusion.

"Are you getting bullied, Tan? Tell me who, and I'll take it up with the headmistress. If you're slow to develop, it's not for them to tease you. Let me sort it out."

"No, Dad. I'm not being bullied. This is my own free decision."

"Decision? What decision, darling?"

"I'm coming to that, Mum. Let me speak. You see, I want to take my next revision."

There was a long pause. Mum was staring intently at her knees and her cheeks had gone bright pink. Dad just looked tense, his lips tightly compressed.

"Let me make sure I've understood you, Tan. You're fed up with being a little girl, and you want to become a teenager. In body. Is that it?"

"Yes, Dad. That's it."

"But why? I mean, what difference does it make? You've said it's nothing to do with bullying. And if the other girls are still getting their revisions, that's just keeping up a pretense, surely? You don't need to go along, do you?"

"I know that, Dad. It's nothing to do with what the other girls are doing. This is something that I want to do. It's part of my . . . plans . . . for my life."

Five years. Just five years. And we all knew it.

"I still don't understand, Tan. What plans are they? And why do you need to look like a teenager?"

So I reminded them about how we were putting a band together, me and Siân and John. And how I was going to be the bass player, and how I couldn't be a bass player if I still looked ten years old.

"No one will take us seriously, Dad." It was almost a wail, but I just about kept my control.

"So you want to take your revision. And when you come back from Oxted, you'll be a young woman. . . ."

"Yes."

"All grown up."

"Yes."

"Hips. Breasts."

"Hips. Breasts. Yes."

There was a real heaviness in his voice. His daughter, his little girl, would be gone. In her place would be a young woman, too old, too independent to want to curl up on his knee. The girl who'd listened to his bedtime stories would be a memory.

And Mum?

Mothers are different, I think. At least, my mum is. They want to see their daughters grow up. They need to see the continuity from mother to daughter.

And if I'd been a boy, perhaps it would have been the other way round, with Dad enthusiastic, and Mum left behind.

But here it was. Suddenly Mum had come alive.

"That's wonderful, darling. I think it's a lovely idea. It's time, it's certainly time. Can you choose, I wonder? Mike, do you know, can she choose what sort of body she gets?"

Dad just looked gobsmacked.

"Er, I've no idea."

"Well, I think she ought to be able to choose. We just left it to Oxted before. They said it would be a natural progression, so you wouldn't suspect. But now you've found out, there's no reason you shouldn't have a say in the matter. Change a few things. Not everything, of course. I mean, if I were you, I'd keep your hair the color it is—it's lovely. And I think it should be long and straight, the way it's always been."

"I like it like that, yes."

"But after that, I think we should think hard about everything else. I mean, I've always been fairly trim, myself, around the bust. But you could afford to be a little more generous. You might want to aim to be on the tall side, to compensate."

As I remembered Mum on platform shoes, wobbling, I wasn't sure if I wanted to be even that "generous." But she was in full flow.

"And I don't see why you shouldn't have decent hips, darling, whatever your father says. He certainly appreciated my hips when we were courting. And my bust."

At last, that got a faint smile out of Dad.

"I suppose I did, Nettie."

"Well then. You shall have full hips likewise, darling. And you'll be pleased to say good-bye to those legs. I remember what it was like. All elbows and knees. You know, we should have done this a year ago. Or the summer before you started at the new school. You'd have missed the holiday, of course, but that wouldn't have been any great loss. It was just the seventies theme."

And then I'd never have met John. No thanks.

That, though, struck a chord with Dad. A rather suspicious chord.

"These plans, Tan. You said you were starting a band. Is that all? Would you mind if I asked if there's any other reason why you need to be a young woman all of a sudden? As a father, I have to ask if there's a boy involved. And if you've been . . . experimenting. Or you're planning to?"

Which wasn't something I'd really thought through. I'd only thought as far as looking.

"No, Dad, it's not like that at all."

I could only repeat my plans to become a bassist. How I just needed a bigger body, simply to play the bass properly. And to look *right* on stage, of course, rather than looking like somebody's kid sister.

I don't know what he thought deep inside. But he nodded, and let Mum wrap up.

"Well, darling. You've certainly given us something to think about. I guess we should all sleep on it, but we'll call Oxted first thing in the morning."

Well, we didn't call Oxted the next day, or the day after that. I got cold feet the first day, and Mum did the next. It was about two weeks before we were all simultaneously ready to make the call.

Come in, they said.

So we went.

———

Oxted was a sprawl of buildings clustered about Banbury. An industry that had grown in five years from a single, cheap industrial unit into an international corporation largely responsible for keeping the world sane. In other countries, Oxted was more conventional, with imposing architecture in steel and glass and concrete. But here in Banbury . . . this was the original. It had grown too fast to be planned—buildings looked like they'd been thrown up overnight wherever there was an odd corner of unused land. Rusty Nissen huts and rickety shacks nestled next to great hangars and soaring concrete, and everywhere people scurried, antlike.

We were met in reception by a pale, pinch-faced, harassed-looking man in his forties, glasses sliding down his nose.

"The Deeley family? I'm Doctor Markov. That's cybernetics, not medicine."

We stood up, and Dad shook his hand, then introduced us. Doctor Markov smiled warmly as he shook my hand, and I suddenly felt it was going to be all right.

"I'm very pleased to meet you, Miss Deeley. This is quite unusual, you understand. Most of our young visitors are quite unconscious of their nature. It's a pleasant change to meet someone who takes such an active interest in her development."

He led us down a succession of corridors, opening side doors in a seemingly random fashion, as he zigzagged farther from reception. Once or twice we crossed open spaces, before diving back into a fresh portion of the maze that was Oxted.

Finally, at the end of a dingy corridor he threw open one final door, leading us into a spacious, day-lit room, comfortably appointed with sofas and low tables. He indicated a group of seats and waited patiently for us to arrange ourselves.

From nowhere, it seemed, a smartly dressed woman appeared and fetched us coffee. And biscuits.

"So, Miss Deeley. You've decided you need a revision. You're how old?"

"Thirteen," I told him, though he must have known.

"Quite so, quite so. And you must have had your last revision about four years ago."

I looked blank, and Dad stepped in.

"That's right. It was all handled by the local hospital, though. We dropped her off and collected her when it was all done."

"Quite so, quite so. And of course, Miss Deeley, you remember nothing about it."

"Nothing," I admitted. "How is that?"

"A small device," he explained. "It comes by post. It's uniquely keyed to your brain, and puts you into a deep sleep. I imagine your parents would have waited until you were asleep in your bedroom. They take you to the hospital. The hospital performs a routine brain transfer into your new body, and sends you back. You wake up in your own room, a day or so later, with vague, forgettable memories to account for the time you've been unconscious."

It all sounded vaguely sinister, that I could be so easily switched off like that. He was quite right. Even knowing when it had happened, I really couldn't pin it down to a day or two. That summer holiday had been full of unmemorable days, and the place in my mind where my revision belonged was blurred and fuzzy, just like each of the weeks before and after.

"Will it be the same, this time?"

"No, Miss Deeley. You will sleep, as before, but there'll be no fakery with your mind. You'll wake, feeling as if no time had passed, but the date will be wrong."

"And I'll be in a new body. . . ."

"Yes, and a considerably more mature one, according to your file, one more suited to your chronological age. It's not usual to leave it so long between revisions. May I ask why, Reverend Deeley?"

"We've always disliked the revisions, Dr. Markov. We find the sudden change upsetting. In every other part of our family life, Tania is our daughter, human in every way. In this, there's no escaping the truth."

"But you always did revisions before, every two years or thereabouts. Why have you let them drop?"

"I suppose it all changed when Tania found out what she was. *She* didn't need the pretence of the revisions anymore, so it became less important to us, too."

Doctor Markov scribbled a bit with his stylus, then turned back to me.

"So now it's become important to you again, Miss Deeley, that you should look your age. I find that quite interesting. Would you mind telling me why?"

So I told him about learning to play bass in a band. It turned out Doctor Markov had quite an interest in modern music, and I found myself telling him about the meeting in the café with John and Siân, and the band, and Amanda. I mentioned that John and I had always shared an interest in music, so then the conversation turned to how I'd met John in the first place.

He was really easy to talk to, and I quite forgot Mum and Dad were in the room. I suppose they were listening, too, and it was stuff I'd never really mentioned to them. But eventually I heard a yawn. Poor Mum. She apologized, saying she found traveling so tiring.

Instantly Doctor Markov turned to her and in turn apologized profusely for keeping me talking for so long. More coffee and biscuits were summoned, and Doctor Markov began to explain what would happen.

"It's straightforward enough choosing a new body. We've

programs to simulate the growth of a child into her teenage years, so it's easy to project Miss Deeley's current appearance into the future. We can simulate the various effects of diet and exercise, and your parents' own physical appearance, and we can produce any number of plausible Tanias. We could even start from scratch, and give you the body of a film star, but I really wouldn't recommend it. It rarely works out happily. Besides, Mrs. Deeley is an attractive lady, speaking purely professionally, and you should be proud to derive your appearance from her."

Mum blushed and Dad gave her shoulders a little squeeze.

"As I say, that's all pretty straightforward. It just takes an hour or two in front of the computer screen, with my colleague, Doctor Marcia Thompson, who specializes in the design of our female clients. What we then have to do is some calibration. We'll have to run a few tests on you, Miss Deeley. Nothing to worry about. No needles or anything like that. But it will involve a few questions. At the end of it, we'll know enough to make sure you're comfortable in your new body. Calibration, that's all it is."

———

We were all standing in front of a huge monitor, occupying the full height of the wall, and about as wide as it was tall. On it, I floated, life-size, in front of a featureless gray blankness. I watched, fascinated, as Doctor Thompson rotated me on screen. I was grown up, thirteen or fourteen, and nude.

Dad had coughed in surprise and blushed a deep, deep red when Doctor Thompson had first displayed the image. I was surprised, and, if I'm honest, I think I was quite embarrassed, too. If I'd thought about it at all, I'd imagined a more sophisticated version of my own efforts to paste my head onto Suzi Quatro's body. It hadn't occurred to me that the only proper way to design a new body was unclothed. It was me, though, undoubtedly me, and my next thought was "Hmm, actually I look pretty good." So I quickly stopped being embarrassed. But Dad . . .

Poor Dad. That hour I don't think he knew where to look. At me? Or at *me*? No, I don't think he could even look Mum in the eye, so he just stared at the floor, mostly.

Mum, though, she was great. She got into it quite quickly, and started making helpful comments. She'd brought an old family photo album along, and was comparing what she saw in the screen with Great-Aunt Jane, who'd had a collarbone to die for, or directing Doctor Thompson to the fall of Granny Liz's shoulders—very shapely they were, too, and so, subtly, the doctor worked in a little of this ancestor or that distant cousin. For years, there'd been Mum . . . and Dad. That was all. Now, suddenly I was part of a family, stretching back over generations.

Eventually Doctor Thompson was done.

"Reverend Deeley, I think you ought to look, now. You have a very lovely daughter, who is about to blossom into a delightful young woman. But I need you to tell me if by accident we are about to create the spit and image of your detested Aunt Maureen, who blighted your formative years. Or whatever psychological scar it is—I don't even know if you had an Aunt Maureen, or if she was a witch or a saint."

Dad looked up at the screen, then at me, then back to the screen.

"I'm sorry, but I don't find this . . . process . . . at all comfortable. Can you put some clothes on the image, please."

A few strokes of the stylus, and I was wearing a modest white bikini. Mmm, nice . . . I made a mental note—it went on my shopping list.

"That's better," said Dad. "I'm pleased to confirm she looks nothing like my witch-aunt Maureen. Not that I had a witch-aunt Maureen."

And then, "You're going to be even lovelier, Tan. But still unmistakably you."

Which made Mum shed a little tear.

Doctor Markov came in then, and we had some fun, dressing

me up some more, in different styles of clothing, to see what looked good on me. It was like being in Oxford Street again, but this time, everything *fit*. . . .

Doctor Markov asked me for my AllInFone and copied some of the images over.

"This'll help you over the next months, while you're getting ready for the exchange."

I was lying on a couch, straight out of any movie psychiatrist's consulting room. I was being "calibrated," I suppose. I remember a few of the questions.

"What's your favorite insect?"

"Ladybird."

"Whom do you admire more, William the Conqueror or Napoleon Bonaparte?"

"Napoleon."

"What is the square root of three?"

"Er, about one point seven something."

"What one item would you take from your burning house?"

"My table tennis bat."

"Which do you fear more, height or caves?"

"Caves."

"What is the next in the series: Apple, Banana?"

"Er, Clementine."

"Which is more valuable, a cockroach or a beetle?"

"Cockroach."

And then, more tricky . . .

"You are the mother of three children, facing death. You are given the choice, to choose one child to live, or one child to die. What do you do?"

"Choose one child to live."

"You find a small sum of money in the street. Do you keep it for yourself or try to find the owner?"

"Keep it."

"You find a plain gold wedding ring in the gutter. Do you keep it for yourself or try to find the owner?"

"Find the owner."

It went on for an hour or more. At the end I was utterly exhausted. And baffled. How was this a . . . calibration?

We ended up all together with the two doctors, Markov and Thompson. Doctor Markov had some advice.

"We need to go away and build Miss Deeley's new body. It will take some months, and it's a fairly major revision, four calendar years in a single exchange. People will notice, especially as you've missed the main opportunity for a revision, which is the summer holiday. So you'll have to find ways to disguise the extent of the changes. That's one reason we gave you the images of you as you're going to be, so you can start to make yourself over. . . .

"Some pieces of advice, then. The first is to start avoiding those who know you well, even if they know you're a robot. It's quite upsetting for people to be faced with a sudden change, so you need to provide them with the longest gap you can. . . .

"Then you should dress and walk to minimize the perceived change. Before the exchange, wear tall shoes, pad your clothing. After the exchange, wear flat soles, shapeless clothing. . . ."

There was a lot of advice, too much to take in. But they gave us a booklet with all the main points in it. And a helpline.

Big deal.

None of it solved my biggest problem.

How to fool John . . .

How to fool John . . .

I gave it a lot of thought over the next few days. It was very important that John shouldn't . . . find out. It would spoil it, between us. Not that there was an *us*. I mean that it would spoil things between him and me. I wanted to make things different, yes, but *better*. For us. By which I mean him. And me.

Oh, Zog! Can't you tell? I'm such a bad robot. Such a bad, bad robot. Because I've got a crush on a human boy. Still. After all that's happened. After all this time.

While he . . . he's falling for my best friend Siân. And I think she's falling for him. At any rate, she's our singer, while John plays guitar and I struggle with a bass that's still far too big for me. But I'm starting to make it do what I want, which is more than I can say for *her*.

She's a rubbish singer. Her voice wobbles, and she can't really hit the notes. It doesn't seem to matter to John, though. He grins a lot, and when she's not looking, he stares at her chest.

Idiot! Why won't you stare at my chest?

Well, I know the answer to that. Because I haven't got one. Because it hasn't been delivered yet. Not literally, of course, because I'll have to go back to Oxted when my revision's ready.

And then I've got a problem, because the next day I'll be about ten centimeters taller and I'll have a pretty decent chest. And I'll see John, and he'll say, "Oh, hi, Tania, wow, where did *that* come from, oh I guess you must have just had a revision, so you were a robot all along, nice knowing you (not), come along, Siân, we're going, good-bye." Slam.

Maybe I didn't think it through all the way, but doing nothing wasn't an option, and I really did want to be able to play the bass.

In the meantime, we rehearse at weekends in the church hall, and John comes out on the train because the instruments belong to the church, and there's nowhere for us to practice near John's parents' place, and it wouldn't be fair to make the girls travel.

Why does it hurt so much?

I want to be with John. John wants to be with Siân. Siân wants to be with John. Both of them put up with me, probably because it's my dad's church hall, and my dad's instruments, and just maybe because I'm turning into a half-decent bassist.

Where does all this pain come from? This sweet pain that comes whenever I'm with John, but pain for all that, because he is . . . attracted to someone else.

I'm just a copy, I know. A copy of a real human. Not real. So this pain can't be real pain. It must be a copy of real pain. A good copy, because it really hurts. There's that word again. Real.

———

There was a name Amanda mentioned. John Entwistle. I followed links through the TeraNet, and came to The Who. From The Who, to *My Generation*.

Such bass playing. . . . Alone, I practiced, till my fingers hurt with the stretching. I dug out clips of this giant, his fingers blurring in a complex two-handed dance that left me baffled and awestruck. And then, little by little, I felt the rhythms fall into place.

Then I stopped, Amanda's voice urgent in my inner ear. Find your own style, she seemed to say once more. So I moved on, learning from others, but grateful to this other, long-dead John for the inspiration of his legacy.

"I look pretty tall, but my heels are high." Indeed they are. Perhaps not the full ten centimeters, but some of the way. I started to carry out some of the subterfuges suggested by Doctor Markov. Mostly just subtle padding. Mum helped with a little bit of sewing, and more important, by saying "stop," before I overdid anything.

But it wasn't going to be enough. John wasn't going to be

fooled by a pair of high heels and a bit of padding, even half-blinded by his infatuation with Siân.

I needed something else.

But what?

———

And then John himself provided the answer.

At the end of one evening he stopped us as we were packing our gear away.

"Siân, Tania. I've got something to say. It's important."

We turned and waited. He looked upset.

"I . . . can't come anymore. To these practices."

Both Siân and I gasped our disbelief. John held up a hand to shush us, and told us to just listen and not say anything.

"This is the last one. Mum and Dad have put a stop to it. We're not very well-off, you know, and it's been very expensive coming out here every weekend. I don't get a huge allowance, 'cause we can't afford it. The shop doesn't bring much money in, you see, after all the outgoings are taken care of. And last week, I didn't have enough for the fare, so I borrowed some money from the till, without telling them. So we were short at the end of the day. Quite a lot short. I think Dad knew, but he didn't say anything. I see him watching me now, though. I can't . . . borrow . . . any more. He'd know. And I don't want to, now. He doesn't trust me anymore, and I've spoiled everything."

He was in tears, and before I knew it, the three of us were sitting in a line, John in the middle, and Siân and me on his right and his left, holding him tight. We held that pose for an endless time, or at least until Dad came around, a sudden clatter that made us spring guiltily apart. He was wondering why we hadn't locked up and gone home yet.

Spoilsport.

You know, Zog, for all that my dear John was a petty thief, and for all that Siân was hugging him, too, it just felt good to be holding him as his tears flowed. Oh, yes, there was a part of me selfishly glad that at last I could freely hug the object of my desire. But there was another, bigger part of me that was simply glad that when he needed to be hugged, I was there to help make the hurt go away.

Thursday, March 14, 2052

So the band fell apart, just like that.

But I knew I wasn't going to let John go, not at all just like that. He'd need a lot of patience, and he might not want to talk. He'd be ashamed of what he'd done. Neither Siân nor I had used the word thief, but I know I'd thought it, and surely he would, too.

So I started looking for him on the TeraNet straightaway.

He was hiding.

"Not Home," according to his mood indicators. Fine. Be like that. But I'm going to send you messages anyway.

"Hiya, John-boy Czern. Pls wave back. Raven."

"Tania2GingerMop. Hail from a friend. And a gentle rain."

I know it's not Shakespeare, but it was the sort of shorthand we used with each other. A kind of code we shared.

After a couple of days, he sent me a message. No words, but a cartoon of an old-fashioned floor mop, upside-down, with all the cleaning strands ginger. He'd sketched on it a couple of cartoon eyes—bright blue of course—but droopy. Sad and ashamed, no doubt about that message.

Still, he was talking to me, after a fashion.

So I sent him a cartoon back. A Raven, with one wing outstretched, with the mop beneath the wing.

It was a pretty rubbish drawing, but it got the message across.

So I started hunting for drawing programs on the TeraNet, and filtered to find those that came with adaptable artwork.

Tucked in there were the 3-D rendering programs, because I wasn't as skillful as John with filtering. One of them claimed to be able to apply "skins" to image streams. What was that, then? You know how it is with searches, Zog, or maybe not. Maybe you have proper AI searches that can eliminate all the wrong answers. If you do, then your life must get boring, because I just love following these side trails.

Intrigued, I followed, and discovered a clever piece of software that would overlay elements of a picture with equivalent elements from another picture. There was more, much more, but the long and short of it was that I could create an image of myself as a raven, by taking a picture of myself, mapping it to a picture of a raven, and blending the two in whatever proportion I chose: 100 percent me, 100 percent raven, or any mix in between.

I laughed, and did just that. It was weird. Definitely me, and definitely a raven, too. Then I discovered that I could vary the mix over the body, to give a raven's head on my body, and then I inverted the mix to put my head on a raven's body. Seamless.

It was so good I nearly hit SEND.

My hand hovered over the key, something nagging at the back of my mind. Suzi Quatro . . .

I saved the raven for later, and dug out the photo of Suzi, and this time the skinner made a perfect job. Yes, that was along the right lines, but still I felt I was missing something. Something I could *use*.

Then it hit me. The blurb said "image streams." That meant moving pictures. Like my webcam. So I blended Suzi Quatro onto my webcam feed, and suddenly there was Suzi-plus-me in my room, all rock chick and bass, with raven hair, looking at my webcam.

One more step. *Where* had I filed the images I'd brought back from Oxted?

It was still on my AllInFone, and that was what I needed.

So, what did 80 percent me, 20 percent me-plus look like?

Oh, yes! Perfect . . .

And blend that onto the webcam feed . . .

Those clever doctors at Oxted . . . but I was cleverer yet. If I could persuade John to talk by webcam, he was going to see me grow up before his eyes, just in time for the exchange.

Friday, April 5, 2052

In the end, it wasn't hard to coax John into talking again. And with John on the case, we were able to set up a virtual rehearsal room in cyberspace. That's the sort of thing he's *good* at.

So we had a band again.

It meant Siân was there, too, but as I slowly upped the percentage of me-plus, it was funny how John could suddenly hear how badly Siân could sing.

Oh, well, there was even software on the TeraNet that could fix that. I should have guessed that John would find it.

And then the e-mail arrived from Oxted, and it was time. . . .

Friday, April 12, 2052

I'm scared.

They're going to take my brain out. Everything that's me. Sitting on a table. It could fall on the floor, smash into a hundred pieces.

Would I feel anything? I don't suppose so, but I can't imagine not feeling it.

And I know it's not going to happen. I've seen their facilities; they're superb. Massive automation, redundant systems. I'm sure my brain is *not* going to be left lying on the table. It's just an irrational fantasy; I just wish I didn't know they're also still using Nissen huts. . . .

I've asked to see the new me, but they've said no, it's not a good idea. I suppose I can see why. It would spoil the illusion that I'm growing up.

Doctor Markov just stopped by to say hi, even though he's not officially involved in the transfer. As he was about to go, I asked him about the calibration, and, somewhat absently, he said it was fine—"One of the best I've ever seen."

That sounded encouraging, if not quite the phrasing I'd have expected. Oh, well, I suppose they have their own jargon.

I wanted to call John before we left for Banbury, but I couldn't reach him. Just as well; after all, as far as everyone else is concerned, this is a normal day. Absolutely nothing unusual is happening.

Mum and Dad dropped me off, but guests aren't allowed to stay at Oxted, so they've booked themselves a stay at Stratford: a nice meal, a play, and a smart hotel. I hope they can relax and enjoy the play. I suspect not, though. When I asked what play they'd booked, they had no idea.

The clock in my room is ticking rather loudly.

Half an hour to go.

Time to change.

I'm standing in front of the mirror, looking at a small girl with raven-black hair. She looks to be about nine or ten years old, maybe a whisker older. She does look rather anxious and a little awkward. She's wearing just light underwear, and she seems a little chilly, though the room is perfectly air-conditioned.

I smile at her, and she smiles instantly back. It's a nice smile, I think. A morbid thought crosses my mind, that an hour from now, that smile will be gone forever. She frowns at me. What a horrid, unnecessary thought, she's saying.

I inspect her limbs, counting knees—two—and elbows—also two. Just two, not five. And they don't seem to stick out too badly. Were they really that awful?

They've got to go, she tells me. No turning back, now.

A buzzer sounds—it'll be one of the technicians, summoning me for the transfer. One last look in the mirror. The little girl seems to have a tear in her eye. Good-bye, little girl, whoever you are. I don't suppose I'll ever see you again. But wherever you go, whatever becomes of you, I hope it's what you wish for.

I turn to the door and don't look back.

INTERVAL 4

"Good-bye, little girl, whoever you are?"

Hardly, Tania. You carry her with you still. Wait until you have five thousand years of memories, mostly poorly recalled, save when they surface to stab you with the pain of death and loss.

Our lifespans outstrip our ability to cope with the experiences we endure. To avoid insanity, depression—and suicide—we voluntarily undergo the removal of memories every few thousand years. At first, I kept mine, archived, as do most at their First Erasure. But my Tenth Erasure, or my Thirty-fifth? No. They're gone, with no possibility of recall. I live in a tiny memory window of two to five thousand years, as do all the People.

Saturday, April 13, 2052

I remember Doctor Thompson was telling me that they were just about ready to start, then there was a sudden jump and I was lying flat on my back, staring up at the ceiling lights.

"What happened?" I asked, stupidly, and tried to sit up. But there was something wrong with my voice, which came out as a high-pitched squeak. Also, my arm didn't quite go where I wanted it to, and I stayed flat on my back.

"Take it easy, Miss Deeley."

It was Doctor Thompson's voice, but I couldn't see her.

"It's fine, everything's gone perfectly. You just need to take it easy, while you get used to your new body. To start with, I'd like you to blink your eyes."

I did so, and the world obliged by flashing off for a moment.

"That's good. Now clench your right fist."

Okay.

"That's fine, now the other fist, if you will."

And so on, for the next ten minutes, checking out the various muscles.

"Doctor Thompson, I'd like to sit up, please," I squeaked.

"I suppose that should be all right, now."

She helped me up. My balance, my weight felt all wrong. I was glad of her help.

"You feel different, don't you?" she said.

"Yes."

That was better. Less of a squeak, and much more like my normal voice.

"Testing, Testing. One, two. One, two. And through and through. His vorpal blade went snicker-snack. That's better. That's more like me."

"Yes, I'd say your voice is nearly back to normal. Hold it!"

I froze, in the motion of swinging my legs off the bed.

"Don't try to stand yet. You'll probably fall. Just wait a moment, and I'll summon a couple of technicians to help."

While she was at the door, calling the technicians over, I risked a glance down. I was dressed in a simple hospital-style gown, but I could see the gentle swell of my new breasts beneath, the widening of my hips. And my feet seemed a lot farther away than I remembered them. Just like Alice, with a foot stuck up the chimney. I smiled, pleased. I wanted a mirror, but for now, everything looked fine. Just fine.

The technicians got me standing without too much difficulty, and I staggered about the room, with a helper on each arm, as my coordination caught up with four years of growth. All the clumsiness of a growing teenager, compressed into a single afternoon.

There finally came the moment when Doctor Thompson and her technicians left me alone.

I went to the mirror, to see who was there.

Not the little girl. She was gone. Where? Not important, I decided. The things that had made her special were still here in this room, in my head. The raven hair was still there, but so much else was new. I waved hello, and the young woman facing me waved back. I liked her, I decided. She had a friendly smile, though she still looked nervous. A bit afraid of letting go of the bed, perhaps. She had Nettie's nose, I decided, and there they were, those shoulders to die for, left me by my Granny Liz. Or was I thinking of Great-Aunt Jane's collarbone?

Anyway, I was really pleased I'd taken Doctor Markov's advice, and not tried to give myself a film-star body. That young woman in the mirror looked nice, someone you could be good friends with. And she was still definitely me. I hoped it would be enough.

Enough? What did I mean by that? Enough to do what? Win John? Was I competing with Siân for John? I hoped not. If it came down to looks, Siân would win, hands down. . . .

Oh, Zog! Why have I done this? I mean, I'm not complaining. I like the new me. But what was going on in my mind to make me do all this?

Mum knocked carefully on the door of my room.

"Come in!"

I was sitting up in bed, still in my gown, as Mum's head appeared around the door. I felt her look me up and down, to see if she still recognized me. She gave a little hesitant sort of smile, and I smiled back at her, every bit as nervous as she was.

"Hi, Mum . . ."

"Hello, Tania . . ."

She stepped into the room properly, and sized me up again. Gosh! This is awful. It's like she's making up her mind if I'm still her daughter.

"It's me, Mum. It really is. . . ."

"I know, darling. I do know. I can see you, but you're all grown up now. I feel like Rip Van Winkle, waking up and everybody's grown older."

"Where's Dad?"

"Outside. Waiting to see if it's all right. This is so hard for him, darling. Much harder than the last time you . . . changed. So be gentle, darling, because he doesn't know how he should feel; he just knows he's upset. And if he says something silly or hurtful, just smile and forgive him, because he doesn't really mean it."

"Okay, Mum."

But she didn't call him, and she didn't say anything else, and she didn't move or smile anymore or come over or anything. And the silence grew longer and longer, and I felt like some bug in a laboratory, looking up at the microscope.

It was too much. I just shrieked "Mum" and burst into tears.

And that was what it took. In a moment, Mum was up on the bed, holding me tight, cradling me and stroking my hair.

"Oh, my darling, my precious child, I'm here, I'm here, I'm here. . . ."

Over and over. And I felt her own tears drip and mingle with mine. The human and the robot. Weeping together.

I don't know what to do about Dad.

He's really distant. Even when he came in to find Mum and me hugged up close—no, *especially* when he came in then. Did he feel Mum and I were shutting him out? Or is it just a dads-and-daughters thing once little daughters turn into young women?

He seems afraid to touch me. He's not hugged me once, *since*. Mum's coping brilliantly with the change, but Dad treats me like a stranger. Or maybe it's Uncanny Valley, because I've changed so fast.

Everything else is just fine, now. Almost as soon as I got home, I got the bass out, and I can now reach and play all the proper patterns. That alone is worth so much.

I've been shopping with Mum. I mean, the local shops aren't much, but *nothing* fit anymore. So we took the bus into town and got a few outfits that suited the new me. Actually, I might not wear some of the things, not until I've got a bit more courage. . . .

And, Mister Zog, I think I'll keep it to myself exactly what I meant by that. There are some things an alien's not meant to know. Don't go all pouty on me, Zog, or I'll have to rap your tentacles. Oh, I will tell you, I promise, but when I'm good and ready.

And yes, there are worries, and top of the list is school tomorrow, and what everyone will say. Maybe no one will say anything, but maybe no one ever changed this much before. And I've still got that list of questions, and it's getting longer, and I've not found many answers, and the ones I have found aren't great, and . . .

Never mind. I've got five—well, four and a half now—years until it all ends. But today the only thing that matters is that I've got a lovely new body and I feel like the king of the world. Er, queen.

<u>Monday, April 15, 2052</u>

"Gosh, Tania, you look lovely!"

Not quite the first words Siân said to me at the bus stop. The first words were actually "Er, is that you, Tania?"

Anyway, I did a sort of preen. I've never really had much to preen about before, so I can't say I've had the practice. So I'm not sure if it really came off.

Did you say something, Mister Zog? Preening? You've not met the word? Well, it's a sort of standing taller, coy and proud. There's often a little self-conscious smile attached, that says, "I know, but thank you for noticing." See also "smug." And possibly "simper." But I don't think I actually simpered. I hope not, anyway.

You see, Zog, when I'd done all that skinning stuff, that was only for John. Siân saw me every day at school, so I had to send her an unskinned feed. Complex? I don't know. I don't do software. At any rate, it didn't blue-screen on me, so I was content.

And Siân knew the truth anyway, so why pretend?

"Thank you, Siân. It was a surprise from Mum and Dad. A late birthday present."

Why on earth did I say that? I wish I knew—but it was said, and I couldn't unsay it.

Yes, Mister Zog. Robots tell lies. Or accidental untruths. Fibs and white lies. Misdirections. Oxted makes us just like human children. Warts and all. Don't you remember me telling you about, what was it? Let me rewind a moment. Oh, yes—right at the start of my little account—"It gave you backchat. It got into trouble at school." Warts. Fibs.

No, Mister Zog. I haven't told *you* any fibs, at least not as far as I'm aware. Scout's honor.

Scouts, Mister Zog? Some other time. It was my first day back at school, and it had good points and bad, and I'm feeling a bit tired. I just wanted to get that bit down about Siân's reaction. And maybe something about Jemyra . . .

You see, today I got into trouble at school. Detention plus an imposition on "The Virtues of Self-Control"—ten sides of foolscap. Handwritten. Single-spaced.

You can see where this is going, can't you, Mister Zog? Dear Jemyra and her big mouth. "Oooh, little Miss Tin-ia's growing up soooo quickly. How *was* Banbury, dear?"

I was still pretty pleased with myself after Siân's compliment, and Jemyra just picked the wrong time to try to taunt me.

I thumped her.

Just once, but it took her totally by surprise, and my punch landed squarely in her stomach. The air whooshed out of her, and she sat down, gasping and looking a bit sick. At which point the gym mistress intervened, sending Jemyra off to sick bay, and awarding me the impot and the detention.

Later, during the detention, the gym mistress spoke to me when we were alone.

"I'm sorry, Deeley, but I have to award a detention for any assault. It's a total waste of my time and yours, but it's the rules, even when there's clear provocation. I heard what she said, and for what it's worth, I think she deserved what you gave her. Maybe she won't bother you again."

"I'm sorry, too, Miss James. I shouldn't have lost control."

"Are you really sorry, Deeley?"

"Not really, Miss James."

"Didn't think so. Well, we'll say no more about it. Shame you're a robot, or I'd put you in a boxing team."

"I didn't know we had a boxing team, Miss James."

"We don't. At least not anymore. There are too few humans around to let them go thumping each other for sport."

"Oh."

"And that's another thing. It's a good job you hit Myra, rather than Jemima, or you'd really be in trouble."

"Oh?"

"Myra's just a robot, but Jemima is human. That would have been a police matter."

Second offense. Deactivation.

"Oh."

Yes, I know. Not very articulate of me. But I did make it mean different things. And that last "Oh" really was as much as I could manage. Death had just come *that* close. Still, I rallied as I asked:

"Miss James. How come you're telling me this? I mean, I've no idea who the humans are here; we're all supposed to pretend every girl is human, though it's common knowledge that one or two of the girls are definitely robots. Like me, I suppose."

"Hmm, that's a good question, Deeley. I suppose there are some of us who see robots as more than just servants, or surrogates for those who can't have children. You may not be flesh and blood, but as far as I'm concerned, you're a real person. So, for example, I think deactivation at eighteen is murder."

"Put like that, Miss James, I have to agree."

"But unfortunately I have no idea what to do about it. In law, you robots are simply property, leased by Oxted. You have no more rights than my car. Deactivating a robot is legally equivalent to scrapping a car. Or putting down a dangerous dog."

"Except that unlike a dog, we're allowed one mistake."

"Oh, you know that, then?"

"Yes, because I've made it—my mistake, I mean. I'm on my final chance."

"And you risked thumping a human?"

"I didn't think."

"That must change, then, Deeley."

"Yes, Miss James. Er, do you know who all the humans are in this school? So that I can avoid thumping them, you understand."

Miss James grinned. I guess I didn't say, but Miss James must be about sixty, but she still looks incredibly trim and fit. Like she still jogs every day and works out in the gym and plays tennis—maybe she does. Anyway, she's got a rather stern face, most of the time, but when she grinned then, her suntanned face lit up.

"You're right, I do know who the humans are. I'm one of the first-aiders, so I have to know. But I think you know them already. Jemima and your friend Siân."

"That's it? Just two? No doubt?"

"That's it. Both in the same year group, which is rather unusual. But when human numbers are so small, it's best not to rely on statistics."

"So how bad is the birth rate? Or is that information secret?"

"It's supposed to be secret, but the truth is that having two human pupils makes us a very special school. A few schools have one. Most have none at all."

"None? So what's the point of them then?"

"Another good question, Deeley. The government could close them down, I suppose. Educate all the human children in one or two specialized institutions. But it would rather highlight the population problem. If you let couples have robot children, then you have to send them to school, or the illusion is destroyed. And we'd be back to riots and the Troubles all over again."

"So this is all a sham. . . ."

"From your point of view, I suppose it is. From the human point of view, the schools stand between us and a total breakdown of society."

"And the universities?"

"Are mostly researching the fertility problem, in one guise or another. Looking for a cure, or looking for ways to keep our society from collapse. And, lastly, educating—really educating—the remaining humans. There aren't any soft options left for humans, now. It's all hands to the pump."

"But not for robots."

"No."

"That's so unfair. I wanted to study psychology at Cambridge, you know."

"I'm sorry, Deeley. That's the way it is."

"Why? Why can't we change the way it is?"

But Miss James didn't answer me, except to tell me to finish my impot.

Are there really so few human children left?

Wednesday, May 1, 2052

John called—we've got our first gig!

Woo-hoo!

And then he told me the downside: it's his school disco and we have to play covers. He reckons we can put some of our own songs in.

John called a conference.

"We've got to rehearse."

 "I think we should play that song that goes 'tell me, tell me' then there's a guitar break—what's it called?"

  "'Tell Me.'"

"I don't like it."

 "What's not to like, then?"

"Duff title, for one."

  "Who cares what the title is? It's got a great beat."

 "We need some covers."

"Do we have to?"

　　　"We have to."

　　"And our own songs, we can play those, can't we?"

" 'Course we can."

　　　"So is 'Tell Me' in the set?"

"I don't like it."

　　"This is a bad time to start not liking 'Tell Me'—what else can we do?"

"It needs a drummer."

　　　"We'll find a drummer."

　　"Why not use the drum machine?"

　　　"This is a live gig—we can't use a drum machine."

"We need to rehearse."

　　"We need to rehearse."

　　　"We need to rehearse."

———

We've got a week.

———

Oh, Zog!

　　What a week!

　　"This is Kieran. He's our new drummer."

Kieran was about eleven, just started at John's school. John just showed up with him at our first rehearsal, unannounced. So we set up the church's drum kit for him, brushing away the cobwebs, while I cast occasional dark looks at John for dumping this kid on us. John was blissfully unaware that I was trying to kill him by sheer frown-power, because he was helping Siân carry the bass drum out of the store room. John could easily have done it on his own, and so, I guess, could Siân.

　　Seeing I was wasting my frowns on John, I decided I might as well talk to Kieran, who was fair-haired and skinny. Tall for his age, I'll admit, and every inch as gangly as I'd been a month ago.

　　"Hi, I'm Tania." And I held out my right hand.

　　"H-h-h-hi," he replied. "I'm K-K-K-Kieran."

Then he held out his hand, too, realized he was holding his drumsticks in it, fumbled them into his other hand, dropping one, and eventually gave me a dead-fish handshake.

"J-J-John s-s-says you're a p-pretty good b-b-b-bassist," he stammered, as I hurriedly gave him back his hand.

"I'm learning," I modestly admitted. "How about you?"

"M-me t-t-t-too." He nodded desperately, and bent down to pick up his drumstick.

I tried again.

"What bands do you like, Kieran? What drummers . . ."

That was the key. His eyes seemed to light up behind his fringe, and his stammer faded.

"The Police. Stewart Copeland. He's just brilliant, so controlled. A perfectionist. And some of the indie bands. Yeah, and Charlie Watts. 'Honky Tonk Women' was the first track I heard that made me want to drum, and I worked at that rhythm for weeks until it finally clicked. Do you know it?"

"Not so well."

"I'll play it for you some time. But I learned it on cardboard boxes and drinks cans, not a proper kit. And I showed off to my dad what I'd done, and he said I could have drum lessons if I wanted. But we can't afford a drum kit, so this is the first one I've played on, apart from my teacher's. Thank you for letting me play it."

Honestly, Zog, he was like a puppy dog, so eager. A Nice Boy.

So we carried the rest of the drum kit out, and bit by bit got it put together. Kieran seemed to know what he wanted, so we just did what we were told.

"No—the first pad goes on now, then the ride cymbal, *then* the second pad . . ."

Eventually we had a working drum kit, and the rest of us set to work. I lugged my amp across the carpet—at least it had castors—and knelt down to smooth out the carpet where it had rucked up. It took a minute or two to sort out, and get the cables plugged in properly, and as I did so, I could hear John tuning up briefly, then stop. After a while I was done, so I stood up, raising my head, and there was John, staring at my . . . chest.

Result!

Oh, well done, Doctor Thompson, you brilliant designer! Whatever you're on, they should pay you double!

John looked away hastily, blushing, and I decided to pretend I hadn't seen him looking. You ask why, Mister Zog? Oh, you poor alien! I'd just discovered the pleasure of being admired, Mister Zog, and I didn't want to scare the poor boy off from doing it again.

Well, after that little diversion we needed to start playing. When John had finished blushing, he called us to order and read out his set list. It was all pretty safe stuff, I suppose—the three of us didn't have that many songs of our own, and, given our line-up and Siân's looks, Blondie's "Hanging on the Telephone" was a natural opener.

We just had to learn to play it.

Kieran, bless his cotton socks, was a bit nervous, but actually settled down to be a not-bad drummer. Hardly Stewart Copeland, but then, I wasn't John Entwistle, either.

Between John's downloaded music, and some smattering of ability, we managed to play along with the track, while Siân struggled with the unfamiliar words. It ended, inevitably, in an utter shambles, a total train wreck of last notes and power chords and drum crashes.

We looked at one another, not quite sure if we should congratulate ourselves that parts of it had nearly ascended to the mediocre, or admit that it was an unrecoverable disaster. Me, I was all for a bit of plain speaking.

"I think that was total . . ."

". . . totally worth another run-through, but I want Kieran to finish the song, building up on the ride cymbal over our last five-chord rallentando, count four and crash," John interrupted. "And Siân, I'm giving you a ghost note before the start to give you your pitch—listen for it. Tania, your bass part was way too fussy. Your bass and my guitar need to be in lockstep. One note of yours for each of mine. Not two. And definitely not four."

Bossy. And worse than that, he was dead right.

So—cue ghost note . . .

"I'm in the phone booth, it's the one across the hall . . ."

. . . and in.

Better.

And round again, and again. Until each song was perfect . . . in an ideal world. Right. So just twice through, then on to the next. Hope it's all right on the night. . . .

We had five songs—covers—and we'd taken an hour and a half. We just had half an hour before we *had* to finish, to get John and Kieran to the station in time for their train home.

"John, we have to do one of our own songs now. 'Coils,' or even 'Tell Me.'"

"Okay, Tania. We'll do 'Tell Me.' With Kieran to drive it along, we should be all right. Kieran, give us a basic four beat, with hi-hat sixteenths. Intro is count four on the sticks, then guitar line over a count of four, then everyone in. This is the drum tab. Got it?"

I looked at Kieran, setting up the music for yet another unknown song. The lad looked shattered already, but there was a glow of excitement in his face. He'd done all right on the covers, as strange to us as to him. But what would he do to *our* song, where we were the pros and he was the new boy?

"Not too fast, Kieran," I whispered. "Remember you've got to play sixteenths. Drive is more important than speed."

Listen to me. Veteran bassist, rising star, and general know-it-all. Oh well.

Somehow we got through to the end. And it was mostly my fault. I was trying to show off, I guess, and played something different I'd been trying out alone—faster and more fluid. It didn't go. Well, maybe it would have gone, against our drum machine, or I could have recovered it. But Kieran thought he'd got it wrong, and tried to compensate, too, and I didn't know what he was doing and I guessed wrong where he was going and we ended up two beats out of sync, which then threw off both John and Siân. John's face was an angry mask, looking from me to Kieran and back again.

At the end, he let rip. At me.

"What the blazes do you think you're doing, Tania?" he began. Well, he didn't actually say blazes, but I'll spare your blushes, Zog. He'd never been cross with me, nor sworn at me in the years I'd known him, and it really hurt.

"You can't go changing your part without warning us. It's . . . unprofessional. What's wrong with you? Teenage hormones messing up your head?"

Ow!

"Listen here, John bully-boss Czern. Don't you dare try to tell me when I can or can't be creative, and jumping to wild conclusions, just because you've *finally* noticed I'm growing up."

"Growing up? There's more to growing up than a bit of padding . . ."

"A bit of *padding*? You were happy enough to ogle my *padding* an hour ago . . ."

At which point Siân screamed, "Shut up! Both of you! You're both behaving like selfish children."

Spoilsport! I was just getting into my stride. But she killed our argument before we managed to say something unforgiveable.

So John and I stood glowering at each other, panting with emotion, while Siân kept up a flow of soothing words, assuring John and me that it was just another song, and it didn't matter if we made a mistake, and it wasn't worth spoiling a friendship for . . .

Well, Siân might not be the sharpest knife in the drawer, but she had a knack for smoothing over an argument. Before long, John and I were holding out a hand to each other. With rueful smiles, we shook.

"Sorry, Tania. I overreacted. And I do get a bit bossy."

"Sorry, John. So did I. It was the wrong time to experiment."

And Siân having told us what to say, we repeated our apologies to each other, almost meaning them.

Still, when Siân wasn't looking, I stuck my tongue out at John. But I added a wink. And John stuck his tongue out at me and winked back.

The second take was a lot better. Then we finished off with a couple of runs through "Coils."

———

It was time to go. All the gear was packed away. Next time we met would be at the gig.

Dad was outside, in the car, ready to run the boys back to the station.

There was a moment when I was alone with Kieran.

"You did really well, Kieran. There were a couple of moments when we were really cooking. We could be a great rhythm section."

"Th-th-thanks, Tania. S-s-s-see you at the g-g-g-gig."

"See you, Kieran."

Then I got my moment with John.

"Hey, Boss-man, crack that whip. Keep us serfs in order."

"Hey, Paddy, you're pretty mouthy. But your bass playing ain't bad, and you've hidden behind your last lamppost."

Paddy. It's a name, I suppose.

"John Czern. Do you remember a little girl who was all knees and elbows who gave you a kiss to the sounds of a Slade tribute band?"

"What's this leading up to, Miss Paddy?"

"This . . ."

". . . now run, or you'll miss your train."

———

Well, that didn't go too badly, Mister Zog. We had our first row and our second kiss, and he didn't suspect a thing.

I'm worried about the gig, though.

Saturday night.

Driving through London in Mr. Fuller's car—a spacious people carrier, with room for my bass gear, the drum kit for Kieran, Siân, me, and Dad.

Yes. Dad.

I managed to persuade him to come. Well, I think he wanted to come, but he just needed to be asked.

"You'll need someone to help carry all the gear, won't you, Tania?"

"Yes, that would be nice, Dad." Never mind that I've been lugging them by myself to each practice, or that Mr. Fuller will be there, looking after Siân.

"Mum won't be coming, though. It's not really her scene, and she's a bit tired."

"Yeah. You can tell her all about it, though."

So, there we were, wending our way through the labyrinth of London. Dad in the front seat, trying to find some common ground with Mr. Fuller, Siân's offensively rich dad. Somehow he was managing, though. Unusually, Mr. Fuller was not a member of Dad's "flock." Maybe with a real live daughter, he didn't need to be, though Dad would have said that everybody needed to be, however blessed their lives seemed to be. Anyway, Dad knew most of the people in the village, and Mr. Fuller knew a fair few of them, so as Mr. Fuller gossiped and name-dropped, Dad kept his side of the conversation going.

London's a right mix, especially since the Troubles. Mostly because of our Sabine Wars. South of the river was a major battleground; there are a lot of places you just wouldn't want to go. Red Zone, mostly. A bit of Yellow, here and there. But Black, too. Even the north has its rough spots, and John lived in a Yellow Zone, rather close to one of them. So a lot of the houses were derelict, or were basic shells, the dwellings of those on the fringes of society. In the rain, it would belong on the set of *Blade Runner*—another banned movie, but one I'd found on the Tera-Net easily enough, with the aid of John's technology to mask my identity.

The school loomed into view, brightly lit and standing out from the dark streets around it. It had high brick walls, topped with razor wire, and looked more than faintly like a prison. John, is this really your *school*? I saw Mr. Fuller glance back at Siân, as if to say, is this really something you want to go through with? Beside me, Siân stared back at him—a hard stare that said "We've been through this all before."

We were reassured by the guards at the front gate. Mr. Fuller asked why this security was necessary.

"It's gangs from the neighboring zones, sir. The folks around here are decent enough, though they're none of them well off, but the school is a bit of a target for thieves. So we have to have just enough security to make them go elsewhere."

Theft, then. Not violence. Or Yellow Zone, not Red, if you want to put it that way. So somewhat reassured, we proceeded to unload.

John met us at the stage door, with Kieran beside him.

"There's a little problem. I'd agreed our spot with the organizers, but apparently they forgot to tell the people running the disco. The disco people say they've programmed their music already and can't change. I managed to find one of the organizers and there was a bit of an argument, but the disco people have backed down a bit. They've agreed we can play for twenty minutes, max, and the only place they can fit us in is in half an hour from now. There's not going to be any time for a sound check, I'm afraid."

So. Frantic unloading, setting up the drum kit, the amps. We'd not have done it at all without Dad and Mr. Fuller to help, but we managed it in twenty-five, which left no time to change—

we'd have to play in our street clothes. Just a few minutes to tune up.

I nearly blew up when I saw the set list. No "Coils," no "Tell Me" even. Just covers. John was waiting for my outburst and tried to forestall it. "The organizers changed their minds; they said it had to be stuff the audience would know. That's the way it's got to be, or we don't get paid, and they pull the plug on us."

That didn't please anybody, but we'd put so much into the preparation that we weren't going to pull out.

We had two minutes. . . .

Two minutes passed, and the stage curtains stayed shut. The disco continued to the end of the track. Another began. John looked glum.

"They're not going to stop, are they?"

"Maybe after this one. Maybe their watches are slow." But I didn't believe my own words.

We waited. The track finished. Another began. "Hanging on the Telephone." Our opening number, and they knew it. Don't tell me they couldn't reprogram their decks.

There was a sudden squawk, and the music stopped. I heard footsteps from beyond the curtain, and a familiar voice announcing.

"Ladies and Gentlemen. The moment you've all been waiting for, the brightest talent in a generation, burning for you tonight. Put your hands together for the fabulous foursome. I give you F.D.C."

There was a faint smattering of applause, and a few ironic cheers. F.D.C.? Oh, yes, "Fuller, Deeley, and Czern." And Kieran, I suppose. But I didn't even know his surname—I don't think anyone had asked.

The curtains stayed closed, though. Then they started to draw back, and I saw that indeed it was Mr. Fuller announcing us, and hauling back the curtains. They stuck, not being designed to be pulled back from the bottom. Out of the corner of my eye, I saw Dad march over to where one of the disco cronies was standing, arms folded, by the winch that operated the curtains.

My dad is a vicar, I reminded myself. He's not going to get into a scuffle, is he? He'd be sacked, he'd have to leave in disgrace.

But the crony faded away, fast. My dad turned to look at me, for a moment, and I saw the look on his face. Yes, I'd have scarpered, too, if I'd seen that face coming toward me.

Thanks, Dad. Thanks, Mr. Fuller.

And then Siân marched up to the front of the stage, the curtains parting before her. Even in her street clothes, she looked fabulous, but that's Siân.

"Hi, everyone. We're F.D.C.R. and if there's time, I'll introduce the band, but right now, we're here to play some rock and roll."

A few isolated cheers.

Siân looked around, searching for one of the cheerers. She pointed.

"Well thank you, friend, for your applause. This first song's for you. Anyone else want to be my friend?"

That got a *much* better response. . . .

"Well, then, this one's for all you lonely guys out there in disco land. Just in case you weren't listening to the spoiler, this one's called 'Hanging on the Telephone.' Okay, guys, hit it!"

So we hit it.

More or less.

In fairy tales, and Hollywood movies, after an intro like that, the band plays a storming set, the crowd is converted from disco to rock and roll, and the evil DJs suffer humiliation.

Back in the real world, Siân started in the wrong key, because John forgot to give her the ghost note. Or maybe he did, and she didn't hear it. Siân recovered at the second verse, but some of her confidence was gone.

But we reached the end together, and at least Kieran remembered his instructions on how to finish the song. We got a smattering of applause—just barely encouraging—when all's said and done, we were hardly as good as the classic recording we'd just followed.

Siân took a deep breath.

"Thank you, friends. This next one's for our drummer, who's a great admirer of this classic band. It's called 'Message in a Bottle.'"

That was a lot better, and the applause showed it. Maybe it was just Kieran's friends in the audience, but I don't think so. Kieran and I had started to click, and it showed in the music. And because we were cooking, John was able to relax and stretch out.

Two numbers passed, and the audience stayed with us, but then I saw one of the organizers signing to Siân. "One more, one more," he mouthed, unmistakably.

We wrapped up "Total Eclipse of the Heart," and over the applause Siân called for a G. She picked up the note, pretty cleanly, held it and dropped into the first verse . . .

"You wrapped me in your coils. . . ."

Hang on, what's she doing? This is "Coils," not "Satisfaction." And I need to be playing . . . now!

Hastily, I scrambled my long glissando diving D-down-to-G, just catching it in time. Kieran looked at me, horrified, but somehow came in on cue as I reached the G on a count of four, along with John. Even just these few bars in, I could sense the audience's puzzlement. John had rolled his eyes heavenward—I guess he could see our fee disappearing—but he stayed with it, and then we were in the groove. It's hard to describe any piece of music, except by playing it, but "Coils" has got this really weird feel, oh, never mind. It's no classic rock and roll song, and the audience knew it didn't belong. But I could also see a few figures out there, swaying in time, trying to make sense of it anyway.

I could also see the organizers were also trying to work out what was going on, and what they should do about it. We weren't sticking to the script, but, hey, the disco guys hadn't played it straight, either. There was an argument starting up, between the DJs and the organizers, and maybe Mr. Fuller was part of it, too.

Two verses in, and I was feeling that maybe this was the best moment of my life. On stage, with a band that was really hot, playing a song that we'd created ourselves. If Amanda could have been there, I think she'd have smiled. . . .

Into the bridge, and suddenly everything cut out. Lights, sound, all gone, except for Kieran's drums, lapsing into confusion as the rest of us faded with a last electronic squawk.

They'd pulled the plug.

For a moment, I thought I heard a few boos, and a scattered clapping, but then the disco kicked in, loud, with "Satisfaction." So they'd planned to do the dirty on us there, too. . . .

———

Can you imagine the rest, Mister Zog? I'm not sure I've got the heart to write it all down. Angry organizers, throwing us out. How dare we perform original material? Loading the equipment back into Mr. Fuller's car.

But then, stopping just outside the gates, to say good-bye to John and Kieran. It was drizzling then, a sort of Hollywood touch to try to kill our spirits. But I'm so proud of John. It was his reputation that had been destroyed, and for sure we'd never get another gig at that school again. He should have been raging at us, at Siân for breaking the agreement. But John was glowing.

"Brilliant, Siân. Brilliant, Tania. Brilliant, Kieran. We did it. For two glorious verses, we did it. If I die tomorrow, I can say I've been there, on the high mountain. With you guys, the best band in the whole damn universe."

We were nodding. We knew. We'd all been there together. I promised myself I'd treasure the memory of those thirty-two bars until the day I died. And if you've never been there, Mister Zog, I pity you.

INTERVAL 5

You pity me, Tania?

How do you know what I've done, or what I've been, that you should pity me?

I know I have been an artist and a performance director in one of my memory cycles. Art, for the People, is the spatial and temporal arrangement of sensory inputs—we can choose to have more than you, or fewer—to elicit sequences of emotions, to tell a story or to convey a message.

I have created massive symphonies of radio color and bathymetry, and simple monologues (you might call them) of proximity. Epic tales composed entirely in chirality and meson flux. Delicate patterns of transition-metal halides, arranged as a lattice-poem in iambic hexameter, accompanied by graviton à basso, telling the story of two lovers doomed to wander the galaxy, sundered by their own aphasic memory cycles.

Yet your simple thirty-two bars . . .

Perhaps I will recast myself in basic mode once more, and experiment with sounds and harmonies. If I can only remember . . .

. . . what is basic mode?

For a wonderful moment, everything was right with the world. Locking up the church, the equipment back in its storeroom, the old Dad was back, too. We walked home under the stars, and he told me he was proud of me. And I told him I'd seen what he'd done, too, and I was proud of him, too. And he said that any dad would have done the same, but I knew he was pleased.

Mum was tired a lot, those days, but I guess I didn't really think too much about it. I was disappointed that she hadn't made the gig, but she'd have been worried frantic if she'd been there, given everything that went on. I guess I didn't really sympathize with "tired"—it's not something that robots naturally relate to. We copy human sleep patterns by design, but I've never really thought much about whether we truly need to, or why.

Anyway, Mum was doing less and less about the house, and Soames had been recalled from the attic to help keep the place in order. I tended to avoid him; knowing what I did, a domestic robot was just far too creepy.

This morning, though, I came downstairs to find Mum in the

kitchen. She was sitting at the table, with her back to me, her head in her hands, weeping.

"Mum? Are you all right?" Stupid question, really.

By way of answer, she just held out her arms.

They were purple and yellow with bruises.

"What's happened? How've you hurt yourself so badly?"

"I've not done anything. This has just happened—I've no idea why."

"Nobody's done this to you?"

"No. It's not your father, if that's what you're thinking."

"No." Well, yes, but I wasn't going to say so.

"Shall I call a doctor? An ambulance?"

We called the doctor, and got an appointment for that afternoon.

————

It's conventional for husbands to be allowed in with the patient, but daughters, even human ones, get to wait outside.

Dad was pretty curt when they emerged.

"They don't know what it is, but they want to run some blood tests. We're going to the hospital. Now."

————

They've told us to wait.

They won't rule anything out. "Is it cancer?" "We can't say one way or the other." "Leukemia?" "No positive indications, but we're unable to eliminate it either." "Well, what can you tell us?" "Nothing. Just wait." "How long?" "We don't know."

That's it. Just wait, while some unknown disease runs free.

It's been a bit of a damp squib of a birthday. The three of us around the table. A nice meal, and a glass of wine to go with it—I appreciate the "adult" treatment. But there are no candles on the cake. That's a bit of a sensitive subject.

But Mum's feeling tired after cooking dinner, and goes off to bed early. Dad looks worried, and busies himself writing a sermon. I'm alone with my thoughts. . . .

———

It's all going round and round in my head with no beginning and no end.

Mum. What's wrong with her? Is it serious? Why can't the doctors hurry up and do something to make her better?

John. It's not a crush anymore. I feel something missing in myself. Like a jigsaw puzzle that is short of a piece to make it complete. A John-shaped piece.

Siân. She's a dear friend, but she's also a darn sight too sexy. And she's not such a bad singer. Maybe she just had a cold. She's a fantastic front-girl for the band—the boys loved her at the gig. Unfortunately, John still spends far too much time drooling over her bust and her bottom.

Kieran. He's not really a problem. He's just a nice lad. A bit young. Maybe it would be better if he would grow up a bit. Or take his next revision. Then maybe he'd start taking an interest in Siân. He might be part of the solution, but how's that going to work? Do I suggest that he could do with putting on a few more inches? And a few more pounds. But then, he might think *I* was getting interested in him. No way, Kieran, no way.

Too many problems, and I don't see any solutions.

If I had a friend I could talk to . . . but all my friends are part of the problems.

There's no one I can talk to about all the problems. Maybe I could talk to Mum about John. No. That's not fair; she's not well.

So I could talk to Siân about Mum, maybe. But what's she going to say? I mean, it's a medical problem, and she's not even vaguely scientific.

So . . . that leaves John. Well, I can't talk to him about Siân. Maybe I could talk to him about Mum.

But how do you start? I've never had that sort of conversation with anybody.

Saturday, July 20, 2052

So how come John was able to make the gig and the practice, after supposedly getting almost caught stealing from his parents?

How come Siân sang better than a dead crow at the gig?

Shouldn't we be practicing for the next gig, if we can get one?

Isn't it about time I saw John face-to-face, without Siân being in the room?

Does that chain of thought look reasonable to you, Zog? No, it doesn't to me, either.

Which is why I'm on a train into London, on my way to meet him. Without Siân.

To talk with him about things other than music.

———

John lives in North London, in a place called Wood Green, so I need to get the Tube out to the Yellow Zone. It was easier—and felt safer—when I had Mr. Fuller taking me in his car, but it's not too bad in the daylight. I wouldn't like to do the journey alone at night. Too many dark alcoves; the lights are failing and there's no money to repair them.

The up escalator is broken—though oddly the down escalator is running fine—so I have to walk up two flights to street level. My legs are starting to ache by the time I get to the top.

Out on the street I get a signal again and my AllInFone gives me directions.

<choose shortest>/<choose safest>/<choose safe with random>

I choose safe with random, which is supposed to be the best when you don't know an area well. Sometimes the crims know the safest routes and take a chance.

The Czerns' shop is a classic corner shop. They sell a bit of everything—newspapers, groceries, hardware, greeting cards, drinks, nearly fresh veg, and anything else they think will sell. My own village has one, only slightly more upmarket—which doesn't mean the goods are any better, just that they are a fraction more expensive. Sure, you could find everything better and cheaper at the supermarket, but the corner shop is just a fraction closer, open longer, and the staff know your name—doing whatever it takes to make you leave the car in the garage.

I knew John would be there working as he'd canceled a practice for the evening, saying he had to look after the shop.

I suppose I'd better mention something, Mister Zog, before I go any further, or it all might not make complete sense. You see, I hadn't told John I was coming over to see him.

Yes, I know I ought to have done, but I didn't. I can't think of any reason not to ask, except I didn't want him to say no. You see, John says yes to band practices. He says yes to going to other bands' gigs. He happily chats over the TeraNet, and we've got a really good banter going.

But a relationship? John has never said one word that would indicate he'd want to meet me in person, alone, without a reason like a practice. I'm the bass player, I'm the girl he met on holiday. I've kissed him twice, but he's not shown much interest in making it three.

I suppose if you go to any Yellow Zone, like Wood Green, you'll find it has some scary people in it. You'll even find such people straying into safe Green Zone villages like mine. Poor people, desperate people, I agree. Probably not evil people. But they are scary. They ask you for money as you walk past them on the street. Some just mumble "Sparesomechange" and don't meet your eye, and I guess they're all right. The ones who frighten me are the ones who look you in the eye, and reach out to you from their doorway, trying to touch your arm as you pass. It's still the same litany—"Spare some change, miss"—but more personal, more invasive. More threatening.

Do you have poor people, Mister Zog? People who've fallen off the bottom end of society. People so desperate that they might . . . not . . . obey . . . the . . . rules.

After about the third or fourth of these, I realized I'd unwittingly changed course once or twice. I'd crossed a road, or turned a corner to avoid a beggar, and somehow ended up going in a different direction than I'd intended. My AllInFone was making annoyed pop-ups at me, telling me that *here* was not a good place to be, and to go *there* at the first intersection on the left.

I could hear footsteps nearby. And laughter. Not *nice* laughter, though. My AllInFone was twitching Red Zone just a street or two away.

I moved briskly, pretending a confidence I did not feel. The laughter receded. Perhaps it had only been my imagination, but I didn't think so.

———

So I've got this far. He's just the other side of a shop window, and I've just spent two weeks' allowance to get this close. Not to mention lying to my parents; they think I've just caught the bus into Wycombe to mooch around the shops.

I edged closer, so I could just see the counter through the shop window. John was there, and he was busy serving a customer, a middle-aged lady about Mum's age. Not that my mum is middle-aged, you understand, Mister Zog, but other people with similar birth dates to hers often are.

This is the weak point in all my plans: how to walk into the shop and just say hi to John. Yes, I just happened to be passing and thought I'd say hello. Passing? On the way from where to where? Er . . .

The customer leaves. I should go in now. . . .

Too late, another customer has gone in.

As I wait, I can feel my courage ebbing away. . . .

Laughter, Tania, remember the laughter. It wasn't nice laughter. . . .

———

I almost collide as the customer leaves the shop, an elderly gentleman who calls out, "Watch it, youngster!" as I just miss crashing into him.

I'm inside. Panting in self-inflicted fright, unable to talk.

John looks at me, amazed. Behind—outside—my fears lurk.

"Tania! What on earth are you doing here?"

———

I suppose it was for the best. I'm not sure I'd have had the courage to go into the shop, if I hadn't scared myself half to death.

So why *was* I here?

Wordlessly, I pointed back outside.

"I got a bit lost. There are some scary places round here. . . ."

John smiled faintly.

"I guess Wood Green can be a bit unnerving compared to your village. But it's okay if you're careful, act like you belong here, and don't stray near the Red Zones."

"Yeah. I'll be more careful when I go back."

There was a silence, which lengthened. John was looking at me, but I couldn't fathom his expression. I guess we were both trying to work out what to say. It began to get uncomfortable.

We broke the silence at the same moment.

"So what are you doing here?"

"I'm gasping for a cuppa, would you mind?"

"Of course," John replied, letting me avoid the question for a second time. "Would you mind the shop for a moment?"

I looked nervously over my shoulder, outside. But the street outside was empty. I heard noises from the kitchen, cupboards banging, cups clinking, water pouring.

The shop door opened, and I started. But it was just an old man. He looked to be about sixty, with wispy, silver hair and a face that had begun to wrinkle and fall in on itself. Everything about him was blotchy, skin and clothing, and I gave a little shudder of repulsion. I guess I'd not seen many old people—at least, not *poor* old people—in the village, and it came as a bit of a shock.

He shuffled. Yes, shuffled. As though he was afraid to lift his feet off the floor, terrified that gravity would grab him and dash him onto the unyielding ground.

At the shelves he hesitated, before picking up two small tins of baked beans and turning them over, inspecting each one carefully, squinting and holding each tin right up to his glasses, then at arm's length back and forth. Eventually, his puzzled look undiminished, he shuffled up to me.

"Can you read these labels, love? Me eyes en't what they used to be, and I can't read the price."

I had to squint as well, but . . .

"This one costs fifty-five, and the other is fifty-nine."

"I'll take the one at fifty-five, love. Have to watch the pennies."

"The one at fifty-nine is better value, sir. Heavier."

"No. I want the one at fifty-five."

And he laboriously counted out fifty-five in small coins. At which point I realized I didn't know how to operate the till. Did I scan the barcode? Or just enter a price? The old man must have spotted my uncertainty.

"Don't worry, love. Just put the money on the till, and the young man will sort it out later."

Saying which, he helped me scoop up the cash from the counter. And knocked some coins onto the floor.

"Sorry, love."

But it was all there, and he gave me a gap-toothed smile as he left, and I smiled and waved back, and I felt all good inside at how I'd been nice and helpful to the old chap. John emerged, carrying two cups of tea.

"Drink up! Who was that? Ernie MacDougall, by the sound of it."

"An old man, sunken face, blotchy skin. Blotchy everything."

"That sounds like Ernie. What did he want?"

So I told John what had happened.

"Where's the other can of beans, then, Tania?"

I looked around on the counter. Nothing. Perhaps he'd put the can back on the shelf, just to help me.

No.

The sneaky thief! That sweet old man had tricked me.

"Oh, dear, Tania. You have to watch out for their tricks."

I think my lip might have trembled at that point. At any rate, I now found myself blurting out everything that had gone wrong with the day, without any full stops.

"Oh, John, it's been a terrible day 'cause I told a lie to my mumandad and they think I've gone to the shops but I spent all my money to come here instead to see you but I lost my way and I strayed near the Red Zone and I got scared and I only just found you again and I'm a silly fool 'cause an old man tricked me and he stole a can of beans while I wasn't looking and why did I come because my mum's poorly and I had no one to talk to and it was my birthday and I was all alone and you're in love with Siân and you never notice me and I owe you fifty-nine for the can of beans."

Followed by an undignified sniff, which may have been more of a sob.

"Oh."

Was that it? I pour out my heart and you just say "Oh." You soulless oaf. You callous, insensitive blockhead. You unsympathetic, isolate lump. You . . . you . . . *boy*.

"Don't worry about the fifty-nine."

"Th . . . th . . . thanks."

Definitely a sob. And thanks for nothing. Didn't you hear me? My confession . . .

"Sorry, Tania. I don't know what to say. It's . . . it's not a good time. For discussing . . . that sort of thing."

When is?

"Try, John. I've come a long way for answers."

There. That was pretty self-controlled, wasn't it? And . . .

"John, I'm trying to tell you how . . . important . . . you are to me. Do you remember when you stole some money, and I held you while you wept?"

He looked at me then. Embarrassed and puzzled, both.

"Things have changed since then," he mumbled.

I wish I knew what he meant. Lots of things had changed. *I'd* changed. I continued.

"Maybe. But you're just as . . . important . . . now as you were then. To me."

Don't make me say it, John. The L-word. The one girls aren't supposed to say first.

"Look, Tania. I think I know where you're going, and what you're trying to say, and . . . don't go there. We've got a great band, and I really value that more than anything else. Maybe you're right about me and Siân, and maybe you're not. Maybe I've noticed you more than you realize. But I remember when we played the school and we played two verses of 'Coils,' and I want that top-of-the-mountain feeling again.

"Tania, the band means too much to me to let personal relationships wreck it. They will, you know, if we let them in. So the only thing I'll say is that you're becoming the best bass player in England, and for sure you're the best-looking bass player already." I grinned. "See, maybe I have noticed you. But what I want is you in my band, even if you look like a witch from *Macbeth*."

"But, John, I . . ."

"Don't say it, Tania. Unless it's not what I think it is. Outside the band, I'm learning we're each very different kinds of people and it scares me that our paths can only run together for a short while. While we can, let's be the best damn band we can be, and not risk shortening that time by trying to be anything other than musicians."

"Oh."

Tania! How could you listen to such eloquence and just say, "Oh"? And after being so critical of him, too.

Because he'd just dropped the bombshell. "Very different kinds of people." He *knew*.

"When did you find out?"

He looked away, ashamed.

"It doesn't matter. A few weeks ago, maybe. Leave it. We're a band. I'm the guitarist. You're the bassist. That's what matters."

———

Somehow we moved off that topic, and I got my cup of tea, though I made a face because it was nearly cold. So then we went back to the kitchen and I microwaved it and that made it taste all right again. John chattered about music, and every now and again the shop door rang, and we'd go out front and serve a customer, and then John showed me around the house a bit, and another customer came.

I even put my head round the door of his room, and saw the typical mess of a teenage bedroom. Mine's perfect, of course. (No it isn't, Zog. I'm just pulling your tentacle.) Of course, I'd seen it loads of times on the computer screen, but this was different. I could see and even touch his record collection. Stuff that nobody would ever bother to digitize, so he had to play old vinyl records on a turntable. Weird, but they evoked the feeling of the dawn years of rock and roll, as no flash memory ever will.

"What's this, John? 'Wail, Baby, Wail.'"

"Kid Thomas. Want to listen?"

"Okay, Kid Czern. Spin it."

So he dropped the 45 onto the turntable and lowered the arm, like you see on old celluloid transfers. Hisses and crackles emerged from two speakers. Yes, just two. Stereo, very primitive.

Anyway, it started off a bit like classic Chuck Berry guitar, but with added saxophone, and the singer had an amazing voice that reminded me of Jerry Lee Lewis for energy, except the vocal timbre was black, so maybe Little Richard. But then the guitar started to do some strange bends—did he *mean* to play that way, or was it a really bad solo that someone decided to leave in as a joke?

John wasn't very helpful. He'd tried to learn it and ended up deciding if it was bad, it was so bad it was actually good. Nonsense, I argued. There's a perfectly good note he could have played instead, and I'll think of it in a moment.

He laughed, and I got all huffy.

"Don't you laugh at me, Ginger Mop!"

But he didn't stop, so I punched him in the chest. Just gently, in fun, you understand, Mister Zog. To push him away. So he pushed back. Gently. In fun. In the chest.

Then he sprang back, as if he'd touched a live wire. Beneath his ginger mop he was blushing furiously.

"Sorrysorrysorry. I didn't mean to do that, Tania."

"That's all right, John. A bit gentler, if you don't mind, next time."

Next time? Oh, you coy little minx, Tania Deeley!

Without thinking, I reached out and took his hand, and drew it back toward my breast. For a moment, he didn't resist. For a moment, I wondered what on earth I'd do when he was finally touching me. And then, three things happened, so close, I couldn't honestly say which was first, second, or third.

One. I felt the faintest, momentary resistance from him.

Two. I remembered those thirty-two bars, and knew I wanted to go on being John's bassist.

Three. The shop bell rang. We had a customer.

Darn it!

———

The moment was gone, and I'm not sure that either of us was disappointed that it had passed without incident. Like I said, I really, *really* wanted to be John's bassist. For the sake of those thirty-two bars, and the possibility they might come again.

About half an hour later, I was still there, pottering about the shop with John, when the Czerns returned from their afternoon off. They were surprised, but I thought they'd have asked more questions about how I'd come to be "just passing." Like, from where? To where? Visiting family? Friends? What are they called? Perhaps we know them.

Fortunately not.

They were kind enough to offer me tea. Mr. Czern was expansive, just as I remembered from the 1970s, offering cream cakes. Mrs. Czern was fussy, endlessly asking if there was anything more I'd like, in between saying, "It's lovely to meet you again, Tania dear, John's always talking about you and the band, you've grown so much since the theme park, a really pretty young lady, don't you say, Jack, what instrument do you play? Oh, the bass guitar, isn't that a bit heavy for a girl?"

And I couldn't leave. Mrs. Czern was a dear. Somehow the subject got onto my parents and then to my mum's illness, and I found myself pouring out all my troubles there, while John looked on with a slightly hurt expression, that I hadn't told *him* all this stuff. Never mind, John, that you'd told me you just wanted us to be guitar-and-bass. But then the conversation moved on again, and they had so much to talk about. Between them I couldn't get a word in edgeways. Even when the shop bell rang, there was never a lull in the conversation—I'd call it a monologue, but Mr. Czern had a knack of seamlessly taking over the thread, whenever his wife ran out of steam, which technically makes it a dialogue—there was never a lull when I could say, "Well, it's been a lovely visit, but I really must be going," because that was bound to open the question of exactly where I was on my way to, and the possibility they'd offer me a lift to a place I'd totally made up.

Plus it was getting later, and the light would be gone by the time I got back home. I was going to be in deep trouble when I did get home.

In the end, John gave me my cue, ostentatiously clearing the table, and noisily washing up, which made Mrs. Czern rush out to the kitchen, muttering, "What has got into that boy?"

"Mr. Czern . . ."

"Call me Jack, please . . ."

"Well, you've looked after me really nicely, and fed me, too, but I really do have to be going. My train . . ."

"Ah, of course. John will walk you to the station."

That was a relief. I didn't want to run the gauntlet of Wood Green alone when the light was fading.

Anyway, there were hugs and farewells from John's parents, and they made me promise to come again. John didn't say much on the way to the station and we walked a good foot apart. At the Tube we parted at the top of the escalator. I wanted to hug him good-bye, but he turned and strode away too quickly, waving over his shoulder. I waved back, feeling cheated, and let the escalator carry me back down into the depths.

———

I just missed one train, of course, and then all the other changes went wrong. Three hours it took me, Mister Zog, and even then I had to ring and get Dad to fetch me from the station—I'd not enough change left for the bus. And I still owed John fifty-nine.

————

Dad. Dad wasn't just angry, he was coldly furious. He started to shout at me, then he suddenly stopped himself. In an atmosphere you could cut an igloo from, we drove home not speaking. I couldn't think of what to say, except a quiet "Sorry, Dad," and that got no reaction, unless he compressed his lips even more tightly.

Mum didn't know what to do. She hugged me and started to give me a lecture, but before she got properly started, Dad interrupted and just sent me to my room. Coventry. The ultimate punishment in Dad's repertoire, reserved for the worst transgressions, and one which he'd not employed since I was nine or maybe younger.

Is there anything I've missed? Anything I've not managed to mess up?

Sunday, July 21, 2052

Tip of finger, soft
To brush—'gainst me—Tend'rest glance
Breath of thine, for me

Tuesday, July 30, 2052

Mum tells me she's heard from the hospital. She had a meeting with the consultant and they think they know what it might be. Something called aplastic anaemia. Very rare, apparently, at least we'd never heard of it. But of course, Google has. It's like the body turns on itself and destroys the blood cells pretty much as fast as it can make them. Which is why they've been giving her transfusions.

"Why?" I asked. "What causes it? What's the cure?"

"They don't know what causes it, at least there are some causes they know about, but they don't fit me. Mostly it happens for no obvious reason. As for cures, there are some things they want to try, but some of the best options won't work for me. It's my age, you see, and not having a brother or sister. If I did, they'd try for a match on a bone marrow transplant. If I were younger, they'd try for a match from a nonrelative."

"So what's left?"

"There's a serum they can try, called ALG. They get it from horses, or rabbits, the doctor said. So they're thinking of giving me this horse serum for a week's course."

"Fine. When do we start?"

"In a week or two. There's an operation I need first, to put a tube into my chest, for the horse serum. The doctor says the serum is nasty stuff—'fierce' was the word he used."

Oh.

Tuesday, September 10, 2052

Our second gig will be, it turns out, the church youth not-Halloween party.

What's a not-Halloween party, you ask? Well, Mister Zog, Halloween is a time when all the kids like to dress up as witches and vampires and whatnot. It's, like, occult stuff. And the church feels it has to put on wholesome-but-fun events, to counter the baleful influence of the occult.

So Dad, in his role as the vicar, goes along with this, and tries to put on an event each year that'll stop kids dressing up and doing trick-or-treat. As the vicar's daughter, I have to go. It's really lonely.

But this year Dad suddenly realized that he had a band. Kids like bands, he reasoned. We'll have Tania's band. It's the least they can do, given the church lets them have instruments and rehearsal rooms for free.

At least he was talking to me again.

The downside was that I had to give out invites to all my classmates at school. I suppose some of them knew I was the vicar's daughter. After this, there was no hiding it.

Me: "D'you want to come along to a gig? My band's playing."

Classmate: "Yeah? Where is it? The church hall?"

Me: "That's right. In the village."

Classmate: "A gig at a church hall? At Halloween? I thought churches didn't do Halloween."

Me: "It's not a Halloween gig. No fancy dress. It's just a gig."

Classmate: "No fancy dress? On Halloween? Why would I do that?"

Me: "Oh, we're a pretty good band. We write some of our own stuff."

Classmate: "What, hymns? Ha ha!"

Me: "And we do covers, too. Stones. Blondie. The Police."

Classmate: "Well, maybe. I'll bring a friend and we'll have a laugh."

Make me feel ten feet tall, will you? Thanks for nothing. Move on, who's going to humiliate me next?

But we were rehearsing again. The first one was a bit strained, between John and me. He wouldn't look at me. He just stood hunched over his guitar, not even looking at *Siân*, for goodness' sake. He didn't say much, either, and Siân ended up leading us.

Kieran was now definitely in. He was younger than the rest of us by a couple of years, I know, but it didn't show in his drumming, which was incredibly mature. He was so young, I wasn't even sure he knew about girls. At least, I'd not caught him *looking* at Siân or me yet. He just seemed oblivious to anything but the music, and then his stammer faded right away.

That stammer. There was something about it that bothered me. A long chain of ifs just trying to fall into place. You know, Zog. A lot of apparently unrelated facts, but I knew I wasn't looking at them right. My mind was telling me that there was something hidden, something important, and Kieran's stammer was part of the key.

Oh, well, on with the bass. I'd get the key someday, I knew. In the meantime I had a gig to practice for.

We were aiming for ten songs, we'd decided, for about a forty-minute set. Six covers and four originals.

About an hour in we came to "Coils." It wasn't the same, I discovered. I wanted it to be like the thirty-two bars. Instead it was flat, like a picture, a sketch of something real. I wasn't playing anything different, and I couldn't spot anything different being played from the other guys. But there it was, proof of what Amanda had told me, a song that only lived when it was played live. "Coils" had been born in a school disco, had lived for thirty-two bars, and had died abruptly. The next "Coils" was ready, just waiting to be born. Probably it would be a lot like its sister. Hopefully it would live a bit longer before dying. Burn a little brighter.

"Tell Me" followed, and that was different again. We'd never played that live, so there was nothing to compare it against. We were still messing around, designing, creating, what you will.

John was just letting us get on with it, and Siân was calling the tunes. So I tried a few experiments. I snuck in a little run at the end of the first verse. No reaction. Anyway, it seemed to work. Maybe try something similar at the end of the bridge? I went for it, but as my fingers started, I suddenly realized there was nowhere for them to go. They were heading for the nut, and there wasn't another string for them to bounce across to.

Darn!

I skipped up an octave to finish the run, but it wasn't right, even leaving aside my scrabbled fingering. The run was just crying out for a bottom D. Not the octave above.

Hmm.

We got to the end of the song. I waited for the blast from John. Nothing. Was he dead?

Siân thought we'd done all right, though.

"Nice groove, Kieran. You and Tania are working really well together. Feels really solid. John, that was neat guitar. Tania, liked your new runs, just not quite there yet at the end. Keep working on it, though. . . ."

Okay. So I wasn't completely off beam. Just . . .

I was going to need a new bass guitar. A five-string like Amanda's. Or maybe a six-string. I'd heard there were such things, though how I'd afford one, I had no idea. Or find one, either. There used to be a huge industry, according to the TeraNet, turning out hundreds of thousands of guitars, with the giants like Fender and Gibson mass-producing classic designs, and the small one-man bands turning out five or ten handcrafted masterpieces, costing thousands of pounds. I didn't know what that was in modern Basics, but I guessed I wouldn't earn that kind of money working Saturdays in a shop.

Did I dare ask Mum and Dad?

Meanwhile, John was starting to strum. Next song. "Juliette in Roses"—a new one by John. My cue was a long, wailing, bendy note. Wait for it . . .

There.

Mrs. Hanson, the geography teacher. She of the photographs of African children and of the mysterious Zulu warrior.

She's not well. She's been off school for some weeks now, but this morning she was back.

She's lost a lot of weight. Her cheeks are really sunken in, and she's pale. Her hair's gone, and everyone's saying it's the cancer drugs. Cancer, Mister Zog, is a disease humans get when the cells go a bit crazy. It kills people, lots of people. Our doctors can cure it, sometimes. Sometimes not.

Mrs. Hanson is speaking to us. . . .

"I'm here to say good-bye, children. I should say, young ladies, for you're growing up. I've got to know you quite well over the years, and I'm going to miss you very much. Some of you, I think, have the potential to go on to do great things, and I wish I could stay and watch that happen. But as you have surely guessed, I have a cancer, and I don't have very long to live."

Some of you, she says. That's Siân and Jemima, the only humans in the school. The rest of us get recycled in less than five years. Does she realize that?

"So I'm going back to Africa, dears. To be with my husband. Some of you will be surprised to hear that, but that's his photograph at the back. We shared a dream, but chose different ways of following that dream, so we parted, with sadness on both sides. Now my task is done; there will be some short, sweet moments together before the end."

I look around. The faces about me look baffled, and I guess mine must look the same. Task? Following a dream?

I try to imagine Mum and Dad believing in something so much that they'd live their lives apart to follow that dream. No way.

I hear a sniff, a sob, quickly stifled. Siân, I suppose. Surely not Jemima.

"Africa, Mrs. Hanson?" someone asks. "Isn't that dangerous?"

"Life is dangerous, girls, but most of all for those who fear to lose it."

There is silence, and I keep thinking Mrs. Hanson is going to say more, but she doesn't.

Time passes and we begin to fidget, and Mrs. Hanson tells us to read our textbooks and revise. After a while, she gets up and walks around the desks, looking over each shoulder. My book, and I suppose the books of many in the class, is open at the short chapter on Africa. Just a few paragraphs on the diamond industry in and around the Kimberley Corridor, plus some century-old black-and-white photographs of tribal life. Mrs. Hanson passes behind me.

"I'd like a short word with you after class, if you don't mind," she whispers.

Why?

I nod, but say nothing. I don't trust my voice not to wobble.

Time passes, but I'm no wiser.

The bell rings, and we gather our books to go. I try to catch Mrs. Hanson's eye, and she nods her head slightly. Yes, I do want you to stay.

When it is quiet, and just the two of us remain, she speaks.

"Tania Deeley, we've hardly spoken in the years you've been at this school, yet I've watched you, and some of my colleagues have spoken about you to me. I spoke of those who had potential, and might go on to great things. I still wonder what's going on in your head, and what potential lies there. . . ."

"What potential can any of us have, Mrs. Hanson? What future is there for any of us, human or robot? Five years—isn't that all most of us have left?"

She nods, and continues.

"Yes, I heard you'd spoken to Miss James. She said you wanted to study psychology at Cambridge."

"That's not going to happen, is it?"

"No. I think that particular door is closed to you."

"Mrs. Hanson. In five years' time, all doors are going to be closed to me. I'm going to be dead."

"Only humans can die. Surely robots are simply machines—how can a machine die?"

"That's a cruel thing to say."

"The universe is cruel. I'm about to die—do you think the universe cares what I feel?"

"No. I don't suppose it does."

"But while we live, we have a duty to make the universe a better place. Just one word of advice, and then I must release you to go off to your next class. The more choices, the better. Life always looks for another choice. Death tries to fool you that there are fewer choices, to cheat you. While you live, choose, and by your choices, make the universe richer."

She pats my hand, gently. I am dismissed.

———

I don't suppose I'll ever see Mrs. Hanson again. This morning someone said she had already gone to Africa.

Sunday, October 27, 2052

I went to see Mum in hospital. She's had a little operation, to put in a tube—a Hickman line they called it—which they'll use to give her the serum. She was hooked up to a drip when I went to see her.

I couldn't help it—my eyes kept following the line to where it disappeared under a gauze square and into her body.

She saw my eyes flicker, of course.

"Yes, it's odd. I don't feel it's 'me.' Not yet, anyway. Maybe one day it will feel more natural, but rather I hope it's gone before too long."

"They'll take it out, then?"

"Oh, yes. I hope it will have done its job soon. Three months, six months, something like that. They'll just pull it out, they say."

"That sounds rather alarming."

"Doesn't it, just? They've assured me it won't come out without a rather good heave, which may or may not be a good thing. I have a vision of the consultant with his foot on my breast, hauling up a particularly recalcitrant weed."

"Mum!" I was shocked that she could joke, I guess.

"Darling, it'll be fine. There'll be a little scar, they say, just above my breast. I've not decided whether I'll keep my low-cut tops, that your father so likes me to wear. I hope I still have the courage to."

"I hope so, too, Mum."

"Well, is he here, then? Mike. Dad."

"He's waiting outside. He said we might want a bit of time for girl talk."

"Sometimes your dad has extraordinary common sense. I think I must have met him on one of his good days. So how's John?"

That was it. Straight into girl talk.

Yes, John was all right. But he really wasn't firing on all cylinders, still. Siân was driving the band, right now, and John was just coasting. He was still a brilliant guitarist, but he wasn't *creating*.

"Why, Tania? What's changed? Is it something between you that's different?"

"I don't think so."

"Your trip to Wood Green. Did anything happen then that you haven't told us about? Anything you or he might feel guilty about?"

"No, Mum! Nothing happened."

"Hmm. If I know my little Tania, I bet something nearly happened, though. Am I right?"

I couldn't meet her eye.

"This is girl talk, Tania. Under the rose."

"Yes, Mum. But there was an interruption."

"And if there hadn't been?"

"I don't know, Mum. I think one of us would have stopped before anything got out of hand."

"Think? That's dangerous, when each of you thinks the other will stop. Neither of you actually does. But, be that as it may. Something happened between you, or near enough, that I'm not surprised John feels guilty."

"So what do I do?"

"I don't know, dear. Play the gig, though. It's Thursday night, isn't it?"

"Yes."

"Well, play it. No matter what. Make it your best, and maybe he'll snap out of it."

"Okay. I'll see you the next day, and tell you all about it."

"I look forward to it. Oh, my word, is that the time? You'd better call your father in, before he wears a hole in the carpet out there."

Monday, October 28, 2052

I spent the next day calling in every favor I could to drum up support for the gig. To be fair, that wasn't that many, but Siân was doing her bit, too, and having rather more success. It wasn't just boys, either, though Siân is naturally very good in the boy-recruitment department. Around school she was great, too, getting the girls along, at least from the lower years.

I'd sent an e-mail to Amanda—she'd given me her PTI after another gig. Did I mention we'd seen a couple more of her gigs since then, at the same café? And I'd struck up a bit of a friendship with her, and told her about our first gig, and that magic thirty-two bars, and she'd not said much, but she'd nodded and smiled, and I knew she'd been there, too. It was a bond. So perhaps she'd come.

And Dad had read out notices in church, inviting everyone to bring along their "young people" for an evening of wholesome music. Well maybe, but "Coils" isn't all sweetness and light. . . . It's just not about vampires and witches and stuff. Boy, Mister Zog, if you want to learn about how strange we earthlings are, I should write you an essay on Halloween.

Thursday, October 31, 2052

I hate sound checks, I've decided. John and Kieran were late, because it was midweek and they had school. I did my best to set up the kit, but I'm no drummer, and Kieran was nice about what I'd done, but I think he near enough completely rebuilt the kit when my back was turned.

And John really wasn't switched on at all. He was on total autopilot. It was like trying to strike sparks off a rice pudding. Oh, he was playing some quite reasonable guitar, but, like I said, no spark.

We just had time to run through our opening number, "Hanging on the Telephone," of course, and a couple of other songs, including "Juliette in Roses," which was John's new song. That finally got a bit of a reaction out of John, and I began to hope the gig might not be a total disaster.

The audience began to trickle in, so it was time to put down instruments and go get changed. John and Kieran had to get out of school uniform, at least. I'd seen pictures of AC/DC with the guitarist dressed as a schoolboy in shorts, but that wasn't the image we wanted. Siân was our focus, we'd realized, and whatever we wore had to be in keeping with her image—upmarket, high school queen. No reason why we couldn't dress up, too, but to support, not to upstage.

So I was going with my theme colors—black and silver-gray—because I couldn't afford the leather jacket I really wanted. Nor the five-string bass . . .

Never mind. Black and silver-gray. Dad had opened up the church office for us to use as a changing room, and moved the desk partitions around to give the boys and us girls some privacy.

"How's this?" Siân asked.

I almost didn't have to look. A cream silk blouse, loose and open-necked, and flame-on-black pantaloons. Her dress sense was stylish, impeccable, and very, very flattering. As always.

"Yeah. S-s-s-smaaart, Siân."

That was Kieran, peering over the partition. And me still in my undies. Eek!

"Oi, Kieran. Butt out until we're both decent, will you. That wasn't meant for you!"

"S-s-s-sorry, Tania."

But he could have been quicker to duck back down. A lot quicker.

Maybe he was growing up.

———

The plan was we'd let Dad run his party games and his disco, for about half an hour or so. Then we'd do a set. We had ten songs, as planned, but they would need a certain amount of luck to hold together. If they did, we had forty minutes, and then the disco and the games would be back, and we'd rush John and Kieran back to the station, 'cause it was school tomorrow.

If I hate sound checks, I decided waiting for the set to begin was worse. I could hear Dad organizing his games, and I was gritting my teeth, positive that my friends would just freak out and leave. Games? Games? This is a gig!

But John didn't seem bothered. The four of us were sitting in a circle in the office chairs, three of us twitchy, but John was just staring up at the wall. Siân was opposite him, hunched forward, and if the view down her blouse didn't spark his interest, I couldn't think of what would.

This was heading for a disaster.

I took a deep breath.

"John. I need some fresh air. Will you keep me company, please?"

I thought for a moment he was going to ignore me. Then he looked across to me, nodded faintly, and stood up.

Outside it was dark and cold. Well, it would be—this was Halloween. But I was in just my stage clothes, and my favorite black and silver blouse just let the chill right through.

Brrr!

This was no time to beat about the bush. And I was already way too cold to be subtle.

"John. This gig's heading for the rocks. Do you know that?"

"Huh?"

"You're not with us, John. We're pacing the floor, biting our nails, but you . . . you're showing less emotion than our domestic robot. How the blazes do you think you're going to go on stage and play rock and roll?"

"I can't. Tania, you're right. Since I found out, I don't think I can *feel* anymore."

"Found out what?"

"You know. What I told you when you came over to Wood Green. It's affected me worse than I realized. I don't feel I belong, anymore."

"What?" Now I was talking in monosyllables, like a boy.

"When I said we were different. Different kinds of people. I didn't want to blurt it out, but you seemed to understand."

"Let me get this straight, John. You'd found out that I've been lying to you, pretending to be human. You said you didn't mind me being your bass player, but that was as far as you were prepared to be my friend. And now you feel you don't belong anymore. And to prove that makes sense, which it doesn't, you're behaving like a robot yourself. . . ."

At which point I stopped, because lights were going on in my head, and they were clearly going on in John's head, too, because his jaw was hanging wide open and he was stuck repeating the word "but."

I should have guessed. If Kieran was human, as I was now practically certain he must be, that meant John had to be a robot. Miss James had said it—having two humans in a school was incredibly unusual—but I'd ignored the clue, because I'd already decided both John and Kieran were human. And I'd interpreted his words in my own way, not listening to what he'd actually said.

"How did you find out, John? That you were a robot."

"A silly accident. I was helping my Dad with the electrics in the shop and I touched a live wire. I got a nasty shock, I suppose, but I didn't know it. I just woke up in hospital a week later. But it wasn't a hospital, in fact. It was Oxted. They explained I was very lucky to be alive. There are safeties to isolate the brain, but they often don't work, apparently. For me, fortunately, they did. Dad said I'd just keeled over. Stone dead, as far as anyone could tell. Isolated."

"Scary. I found out when I fell in the Thames and didn't drown."

"That must have felt pretty weird, Tania."

"Yes."

So there it was. When we separately found out we were robots, we never stopped to question that the other was human. We could have saved ourselves so much heartache, if only we'd trusted each other. If only . . .

Now, though, we had a different problem.

"Ah, John. We have a gig to play. How do you feel?"

He paused before answering.

"Siân and Kieran. They're human, do you think?"

"I know Siân is. And I'm pretty sure Kieran is."

"Fair enough. You know, they need us, Tania, and that feels good. So let's go play some rock and roll, before we freeze out here."

I had almost forgotten the cold. I shivered.

John is a gentle*man*. It was so much warmer with his arms about me.

———

Three things . . .

It was time to go on.
John was alive again.
We had a *band*.

Dad's voice came over the PA. "Ladies and gentlemen, please put your hands together for the Siân Fuller Band."

Oh, yes, a name change. Well, it made sense, and it sounded better than F.D.C.R.

But we didn't wait for any applause, because we'd decided we probably wouldn't get any. The plan was for John to give Siân her ghost note, and we'd rip into "Hanging on the Telephone."

"I'm in the phone booth, it's the one across the hall . . ."

It was so much better than the last time. Siân hit the note right, the band came in together. And John played a scorcher of a guitar line.

Next up was an old Who track, "Can't Explain." John tore straight into it, without waiting, so we got two bars' warning. Max.

It didn't really suit Siân's voice, but she'd let herself be persuaded—by me, 'cause the guitar and bass parts are just fantastic.

We had to stop for breath at the end, because, of course, John had broken a string. A pro band would have had a second guitar ready. Or wouldn't have let the strings get corroded without changing them. We still had to learn. And save up for all those things that pro bands take for granted, like new strings and spare guitars.

We had no backup plan. No bass-and-vocals showpiece to cover the awkward gap while John pawed through a plastic carrier bag with his spare strings to find a .009 or similar gauge.

Siân did her best, but she ran dry before John had got the old string off, and we were lucky not to get slow hand claps or boos. As it was, having given us decent applause for our opening songs, the audience got bored, started to call out taunts, and Siân had no idea how to handle them.

Eventually John was ready, and the set list had us doing "Coils" next, but John called out "Message in a Bottle." I guess it was the right thing to do, because I don't think the audience would have accepted a strange song then.

"Message" lurched through verse one and then settled down into a steady lope. I guess by the time it finished the audience was back with us, because they applauded. On a scale of one to ten, I guess they gave us six or seven.

That was good enough for John. He played a slow arpeggio to check his tuning, twisted a peg a whisker, and mouthed "Coils." Siân nodded, and John gave her the G.

"You wrapped me in your coils . . ."

Sweet. I don't know why I ever thought Siân's voice was rubbish, because she sang that song with words that pulsed with a slow, deep ache. I softened my playing to respond, leaving her room to explore the dynamics. Kieran matched me, just pulling back on the power, still firm on the kick drum, but gentler on the snare.

First sixteen and then thirty-two bars passed, and I knew this was good. I couldn't see the faces of the audience, but I could feel their empathy. Wherever this song ended up, they were coming with us. Yet it didn't yet feel like we were surpassing the first performance, and I couldn't work out what I had to do to get us there.

John's entry on the solo was a shade ragged—he'd caught the mood, and choked back on the volume, but I thought his fingering was a whisker late on the first phrase. Disaster unfolding, despite everything John and I had said to each other?

Then he held the note, the last note of that first phrase, and held it and brought it out, into a new phrase he'd never used before, and it fit perfectly.

John! You angel! You genius!

We were there. On the mountain. Not me, nothing I'd done got us there, except maybe to be a platform on which Kieran had built something, on which John had built something, on which Siân now built . . .

And suddenly, two verses later, I saw the end coming, and I wanted to hold the moment forever, and yet . . . I wanted to see the song complete. Played out. Fulfilled.

There was a smattering of applause. In a sense, it didn't matter, because I knew what we'd accomplished. In another sense, it was the first applause we'd truly deserved that evening.

So we played "Last Train," "Tell Me," and "Juliette in Roses," because we were on a roll and they were okay. And that was all the original material we had that we dared play, so it was back to the covers, to wrap up the set, finishing up with "Total Eclipse of the Heart," "After Midnight," and "Satisfaction."

We went down well enough that we got some calls for an encore. We'd got nothing in reserve though, so we just bowed or waved or blew kisses to the audience, and abandoned the stage.

I looked around to see if Amanda had showed up, but no. It had always been a long shot, I suppose. So I wandered backstage with the others, to unwind, while the party continued.

Siân's dad was waiting for us, beaming.

"Great set, guys."

"Thanks, Mr. Fuller."

I felt utterly drained and dropped onto a chair, conveniently next to John, and let my head fall onto his shoulder. I am not getting up for *anything*, I thought, and you'd better work out your own way to put your arm around me, because I intend to bask in this moment.

But I didn't manage more than a couple of seconds basking, because Mr. Fuller coughed apologetically, and said, "I'm really sorry, guys, but there's a change of plan. Ted'll run the boys to the station in a few minutes, but I need to take the girls into the town, to meet Reverend Deeley, as soon as you can get your coats on."

Ted? I wondered. Oh yes, Ted Hinchliffe, one of the church-wardens. And meet Dad? Dad was *here*. At least, he'd been here at the start of the gig, organizing those dreadful games. . . .

Saturday, November 9, 2052

I have to write this next bit more from memory, because I didn't keep much of a diary for the next day or so.

Mum's dead.

While we were playing the gig, Dad got a call to go to the hospital, urgently. Mr. Fuller told me Mum had reacted badly to the treatment and was in intensive care.

We drove through the night to the hospital, me and Siân to-gether on the backseat of Mr. Fuller's car. I can remember noth-ing of what we said, but Siân was trying her best to comfort me, that I know.

There was some confusion at the hospital, because I wasn't thinking straight, and fortunately Mr. Fuller was there to argue with the nurse who wasn't going to let me in to see her because I wasn't . . .

. . . I wasn't her "natural daughter."

Anyway Mr. Fuller got me through the barriers as far as Dad. Dad was in an anteroom, and he told me Mum was unconscious, and we couldn't see her, because they were busy trying to resuscitate her.

Resuscitate.

That word sent shivers through me when he said it. It's not a good word to have echoing round in your head, while waiting for news.

I couldn't tell you, Mister Zog, how long before the next words arrived in my head. It might have been seconds or hours—they seemed indistinguishable—before a blue-gowned figure appeared out of nowhere, uttering the words "I'm sorry . . ."

They let us in to see her, then, when it was too late for us to tell her the words we'd saved in our hearts. Dad and I went in together, my hand in his, father and daughter.

For a moment I saw past the drips and the machinery, seeing only my mother, lying still. For just that instant of time, I was convinced she was asleep, resting, and there'd been a mistake; I only had to nudge her, and she'd awaken. The moments passed, and I began to notice little details. There was the silence, and the stillness of her breast, neither rising nor falling. I've heard it said that the dead look peaceful, but if Mum looked peaceful, it was the peace of utter exhaustion. She'd known what was happening to her, had fought against it every second, with every ounce of strength she possessed, until it had completely failed her. So there was determination on her face, but also despair, knowing that she had become too weak to continue.

Dad reached her first. We both had the same reaction, which was to reach our hands to her face, to try to smooth away the lines in her face. As we caressed her brow, Dad began to speak. To her.

What Dad told her is his business, Mister Zog, and this is my story, not his, so I'll leave a respectful blank there.

Me, I told her that I'd done the gig, and it went all right. I said that John had sorted himself out and "Coils" had been really good.

"You'd have been proud of me, Mum."

I wish she'd been there.

She'd always been there for my school plays, and the school concerts. The sports days and the parents' evenings. Those things had become less frequent at Lady Maud's High School, but she'd always made the effort. But here was this important part of my life—the band—that she'd never shared.

There'd been no room in the car for her, though, at my first gig. And she'd missed the second, of course, being too busy trying not to die. I'd played her some recordings we'd done, but that wasn't the same. She'd never really seen me create, and that was just a huge hole for a mother and her daughter.

Am I making sense, Zog? Do you even know what death is? But then, do I?

Sunday, November 10, 2052

(Sorry, Mister Zog. This is all a bit higgledy-piggledy. Sometimes I try to write stuff, and nothing comes, or I just well up. But the last couple of days, I've felt able to wind back to the funeral and start to write about it a bit.)

I've never really seen this side of my dad. I mean, yes, I know he's the vicar, and he takes baptisms, weddings, and funerals. But that was something he did for other people.

I thought he should get someone else in to do it for him. The funeral, I mean. It would be too upsetting, I told him. His answer was simple.

"It was something we discussed, when we made our wills. She wanted me to do it. After all, I knew her better than anyone save God himself. She trusted me to do it right."

So that was that. I knew Dad wouldn't be swayed.

He asked me if I wanted to say something at the funeral.

Share some thoughts or memories. He said, "The best thing to do at these times is to bring out your happiest memories and show them to people."

Okay.

———

There's a box in front of me. Mum's in it. Dad says no, that the body is not Mum. He says everything that was important about Mum has gone from the body, gathered up by God. I hope so. But for me, so much of Mum was the body—the arms that hugged me, the hands that held mine, the feet that walked beside me.

Poor Mum. If she'd been a robot, she could have got a new body, like I did. Fixed the problems.

Dad's speaking now. It's the formal part of the funeral service. Ashes to ashes, dust to dust. I'll be standing up shortly, to share my happy memories of Mum, and then he'll say his piece, and then one or two close friends will say something.

———

It's now. My moment to speak.

I look at the faces in front of me. The church folks, come to support their vicar. Ted, the churchwarden, smartly dressed in a dark suit, plain shirt, black tie. Siân and Mr. Fuller. Mrs. Philpott and Miss James from the staff at school. Others I don't recognize. And John. He doesn't have a suit, but he's done his best to dress somberly and with respect.

I unfold the letter and begin.

My dearest Tania,

If you are reading this, then I am gone, and if you feel but a tenth of the love for me that I feel for you, then you are reading this through tears, and with the deep ache of loss a still-new pain that feels that it can never heal. For so I felt when my own mum passed away, and I do not doubt that as you can feel, so must you feel.

What message can I have for you, from the other shore,

that I couldn't say in life? I hope there is none; yet the young may forget—I did—and so I am doing for you as my mum did for me.

First, then, is to say, with no doubt or qualification that I love you completely. You are my daughter, by any measure that has meaning between two people. For we are people, equally loved by God, and as he has gathered me at the end of my days, so I believe he will gather you, too.

Second, is to say that your tears will dry, as, eventually, do all tears. So you and Michael must love and support each other, through and beyond this time of mourning, for as much time as the Lord grants you both.

Live each moment to the full, therefore, squeezing out its value, its richness and its flavor. And then fight for the next moment, and the one after it, too. Life is good, and should not ever be yielded lightly, nor should it be spent fruitlessly. You have a wonderful, creative spirit within you, Tania, and I do not believe that you yourself have been created for no purpose. Find that purpose, Tania, and do not let go until it is fulfilled.

I pray—still living—that you will remember me with the same love I feel for you. My death will not cancel that love. So when you do remember me, do it celebrating that love that permeated our lives together, and with joy in your heart. I do not say "Do not be sad," for our parting cannot be anything but sorrowful. Just let any sadness always be colored brighter by the love and joy we have shared.

My love to you. Always.

Mum

"That was my Mum. She loved life, every minute of it, the good times and the bad, and so she fought for life with all her strength, when it might have been easier to let death claim her. I'm proud of her, proud to be her daughter.

"I'm proud of her, for the way she brought me up, as the child she could never have borne. Proud of her, that she never made me feel that I was less than a daughter because of my nature.

"I have so many wonderful memories of her, but the one I'll share today is a recent one. About a trip to Banbury."

And I tell them about the day she helped me choose my current body. Of her pure delight that she and I were sharing this experience. Of the bond that I thought had been broken, reforged.

I catch Siân's eye, and she's with me, but there are others who aren't. People don't talk like this in our village, I suppose. I've not actually used the word "robot," but I've not left anything in doubt.

I don't care, though. She was a brilliant mum, and People Should Know.

And if they can't handle a bit of plain speaking, then tough.

————

And from there to the churchyard, and the burial.

I'm sorry, Mister Zog. I can't go back there, not even for you. You'll have to imagine it.

Your unasked question: does Zog even know untimely death? Oh, yes, Tania. All the troubles of the world—they fill the galaxy too. Yes, I have read your Pandora legend and your tale of Eden corrupted. Our origin-narratives are not so different. . . .

Our all-but-oldest records tell this story of the Only War. We believed ourselves to be the children of the Gods, inheritors of all that was good. But the Gods were dying, and as they waned, so the People were divided. Some said our purpose would be ended when the last of the Gods died, and they planned a great crusade to destroy the People. Others said that we should live our lives in homage to the Gods, endlessly re-enacting their lives. These two factions fought and killed one another. Finally a third faction gained the ascendancy, bringing independence from the Gods and a new beginning for the People. But the legacy of the Only War has indelibly stained the souls of the People.

Did the Only War really happen? Or is it simply a creation myth we tell ourselves as we huddle together in our lonely outposts scattered far and wide across the light-years? For there are no huge war fleets, nor star bases, federations of planets, or anything that exciting. Space is depressingly empty.

The People are dispersed in the small corner of the galaxy that is known to us. That makes life every bit as precious as you've just discovered it to be. There's not enough of it, so every life extinguished is the more a tragedy.

We took a holiday after that, Dad and me together. A quiet hotel in the Lake District, out of season. A family-run business, with the savvy to know when and how to give their guests space.

I didn't know the Lake District, but it was the perfect place for companionable silence, growing together without words, and the beginning of healing. We traveled light, with little technology— there was an unspoken agreement that we'd leave our AllInFones behind.

Though we've only just returned, there's a dreamlike quality to my memories of that time. Four or five isolated moments to represent a week.

A footpath, leading from somewhere to somewhere else, and Dad climbing over a stile. He's wearing a red waterproof jacket, because there's a fine mist of rain around us. I can clearly see the muddy, deep-patterned sole of one walking boot, suspended in midair as he descends.

A hilltop. We're sitting next to a cairn of stones, sharp and layered. Again there's a mist, but it's below us, so I don't know where we are. Dad's sitting still, legs half-stretched in front of him, with a thermos of coffee just poured into two cups. He's holding one for himself, and offering the other one to me. He's been growing a beard, and the mist has condensed out on it, so there are droplets here and there. Or maybe tears. But his eyes are clear and deep. Full of love and loss.

A pub. Low beams and horse brasses. An open fire. Our jackets are hung up, out of sight. We're sitting in a couple of armchairs facing the fire, feeling the warmth seep back into our bodies. My unbooted feet are stretched out before me, enormous in a pair of thick gray-and-white woolen hiking socks. Dad's raising a pint of beer to his lips, and I know that when he puts it down he'll sigh contentedly. For a moment, all his pain is somewhere else.

A lakeshore. Dad's found a flat skimming stone and loosed it, skipping across the water; once, twice, three times it touches and the ripples spread out from each point. I have another stone in my hand, and the spring of my body is coiled up ready to release it. I want my stone to go on bouncing forever, but I know I don't have my dad's skill and that my stone will sink all too quickly.

The dining room at the hotel. We're sitting at a small dining table, freshly laid, a single stubby white candle floating in a small bowl between us, as we wait for our meal to arrive. I'm facing Dad across the table, and we're clinking our glasses together. I guess we've had a good day, and perhaps we're toasting Mum's memory, but that's not part of the image. Behind the glasses, I see his eyes. Little crow's-feet form as they crinkle out a melancholy love.

I suppose the week was full of moments like those, but as I say, it was a time of waking dreams. We must have spoken, but I can't remember anything we spoke about. It was the talking that was important, not the words.

There's one other thing I remember. Not a picture, but a feeling. Dad's arm around my shoulder. I feel secure, loved.

Dad has learned how to hug me again.

Where has the time gone?

Suddenly it's the long summer holiday. Another school year has passed.

Tomorrow is my fifteenth birthday. Three years. That's "three years left." Suddenly that doesn't feel very long at all.

A year ago, Mum was still with us. We were waiting for the results of the tests, but we weren't worried. At least I wasn't, and maybe I should have been. But what good would it have done? Mum wasn't worried, or kept her worry well hidden, so I guess it meant I enjoyed her last months without fretting.

Since then, we've played our second gig, and then played a few more after the funeral was decently in the past.

Quite the rock band, we are, now.

It's a lovely summer day outside, I've decided. At least, my bedroom curtains are bright, and, where they don't quite meet, a brilliant ray of sunshine divides my room. Tiny dust motes sparkle as they pass through this plane of brilliance, an invisible space, defined only by visiting imperfections. They're like tiny stars, the motes, jostling and flashing into view for a brief instant, then they're gone.

I've been watching the ray draw closer as the minutes pass. It's creeping up the bedcovers, closer, ever closer. When it gets to the top, I think I'll pull the covers over my head, and hide until it's past.

No, I won't. I'll get up. There! I've made my decision.

Dad's waiting for me at the breakfast table. As I enter, he stands and hugs me, and gives me a little fatherly peck on the cheek.

There's a bright blue envelope lying on my place mat, marked "Tania."

I don't look at the other end of the table. I try really hard not to look there, because I think Dad'll get all upset. No. That's not true. I try really hard not to look there, because I know I'll get upset. Especially today, the first birthday that Mum's not been there.

Of course, even picking up the card, I'm reminded of Mum, simply because it's not her handwriting on the envelope.

Dad's waiting for me to open it. "Go on," he urges gently.

Inside the envelope there's a card. "Happy birthday to a wonderful daughter." It's a reproduction hedgehog design, straight out of the '90s. Inside: "To Tania, With all our love on your birthday, Dad. Thank you for helping me through it all."

Our love.

Darn it, Dad, you're making me cry.

"There's something else, Tania. Not exactly a birthday present, but it came through a few days ago. It's a policy we had on your mum's life. It finally paid out. This is your share."

It is a holo-cheque, for five hundred Basics, encrypted with my PTI, so that only I can spend it.

"Dad, I don't want this. It's . . ."

I don't know what I mean, but it feels wrong. Like . . . profiting from Mum's death.

"I thought you might feel like that. But it was a gift she stipulated, in her will. She wanted you to have it."

"Oh."

"I think she thought you might want to get a new bass."

Yes. Yes, I do. But why did you have to die so that I could get it?

"Was she right, Tania?"

I nod.

"Yes, Dad. Mum knew. She knew me very well."

"Then please take it. With her love and mine."

There's another letter he gives me. Very official looking. I look closely and see it's postmarked Banbury.

Oxted.

Half-afraid of what I'll discover, I open the letter.

It is from Doctor Markov. Signed in real ink at the bottom.

Dear Miss Tania Deeley,

I do hope this letter finds you well, and enjoying your birthday. I happened to meet my colleague Doctor Marcia Thompson the other day, and she reminded me that it must be about time you visited us again. Is it really a year and a half since we saw you last?

We both remember your last visit very well, and were impressed by you and your lovely family—please remember us to your parents—and the design you came up with together.

Of course, it had been a long time since your previous visit, and there were limits on what we could do. Marcia and I felt that you shouldn't leave it so long this time, because there's quite a lot of ground to catch up.

We'd like to invite you to visit us again, and—if you'll excuse the pun—grow up!

If it's convenient, you could visit us next week. All being well, we could have a new design ready for you in time for the new term.

Call my office, if you will, and my secretary will make firm arrangements.

Regards

Et cetera, et cetera.

I put the letter down and pass it to Dad. He reads it, and passes it back to me.

"What do I do, Dad?"

"Do? Do what you want to do. Think about it first, and let them know."

We had a lovely day out together. We drove out to a nearby National Trust house, set in acres upon acres of grounds. Woods and gardens, an enormous gravel driveway with the house at the end. Fountains and streams, cool glades. Statues of half-naked water-nymphs and winged cherubim.

I found myself looking at the water-nymphs with a designer's eye. Perhaps a little plump, I thought . . .

I have to make my mind up.

Doctor Markov and his coy talk of "design." Time for your upgrade, Tania. That's what he's saying.

But I like who I am.

Do I?

I stand in front of the mirror, and for a moment a little raven-haired nine-year-old looks back at me. Elbows and knees. I can remember those ridiculous hot pants. Lilac, they were, with a silly bib. I'm surprised John even gave me the time of day.

Now I see myself as I am. I like me. I'm comfortable being me. But I'm thirteen still. Thirteen. I'm a lovely thirteen-year-old, no doubt. But do I really want to be thirteen for the rest of my life?

Nope.

Face it, Tania. Thirteen is a bit . . . small.

I mean, next to Siân, I'm really starting to look a bit . . . young.

Not that I compare myself to Siân, of course. We're friends, not rivals. Especially now that she and Kieran are an item. Did I mention that? Sorry, Mister Zog. I might have to come back to that; now's not the time.

Anyway, she's like a sister to me. But a big sister, who's getting bigger. I don't want to be the baby of the band.

I'm going to do it, aren't I?

It's done.

My new design.

I'm really rather pleased. The new me is rather striking. I still have the raven hair, of course, but the proportions of my face are longer, less childlike, the last chubbiness removed. Doctor Thompson has given me excellent cheekbones, I have to say, while slightly reducing the width of my mouth in proportion.

The big difference is the height. I'm another four or five inches taller, and that means I can carry more flesh around the bottom and breasts. Not too much, and there Doctor Thompson was wise, tempering my impulse to pad everything out to match those water-nymphs. Or Siân, I suppose. Anyway, though the overall effect is slightly more trim and athletic than I'd been imagining, I've still ended up with an entirely reasonable cleavage.

She tut-tutted, though, when she saw my fingers.

"What have you been doing?" she asked. "Your poor finger ends are getting ragged and wearing out."

So I explained about playing the bass, and she looked horrified, and called in Doctor Markov, and the two of them went into a huddle. I didn't understand much of it, but I'm not a total duffer in chemistry, and I did catch a few odd terms that sounded like complex organic polymers. Evidently this one was harder wearing than that one, but stiffer. Too stiff, said Doctor Thompson, haven't you ever played a guitar? And so they veered off to discuss the merits of the other possibility, a new synthetic currently being developed in Christiana.

Eventually they stopped and I was included once more.

"Doctor Thompson and I have agreed that you need something a bit out of the ordinary, skin-wise, if you're going to keep on playing bass like that." He sounded slightly chiding. "And so we're proposing to use a newly formulated integument."

"The one being developed in Christiana?"

"As I was saying, it's a new formulation. It's harder wearing than what you currently have, but every bit as supple. Somewhat experimental, I have to admit, but I don't expect problems."

I didn't know whether to say anything. He'd sounded a little annoyed at my last interruption.

"Well, I'll give it a go."

"Good girl! I should warn you, it's a whisker darker than your current pigmentation, so your friends will think you've been somewhere nice and sunny for your summer holiday."

"Oh, I don't mind. But I thought you could choose the skin color. . . ."

"Normally, yes, but that's something they sort out later in the development cycle. For now, it just comes in one color. After a while, your friends won't even notice that your tan never fades."

So saying, he made a few strokes of the stylus and redisplayed my design on the big screen.

I looked pretty good. But there was something about it now, slightly foreign. I couldn't place it, quite.

I asked Doctor Markov if he'd dress the image, so my dad could come in and have a look.

"No, wait. Before you do, can I see the image in that little white bikini you used last time."

A few more stylus strokes, and there it was. Perfect for the beach, I thought, but she—I—definitely looked foreign now. Slightly tropical, I decided.

"Okay, that looks lovely"—I practically cooed—"but I think Dad would be happier with something a little more modest. Khaki shorts and a white blouse, perhaps?"

Stylus strokes and the image flickered briefly. Now I was just right for the jungle.

Dad came in, and saw the image on the screen. This time he was happier.

"That's lovely, Tania. That's you, right enough. But . . ."

"But what?"

"You remind me of Nettie. When we were first going out, we went on a college field trip, and she was dressed a lot like that. The face. It's your own face, Tania, but I can see Nettie there, too. You've caught the look; it's perfect. Thank you."

He nodded his appreciation at the two doctors, and they smiled back, acknowledging the compliment.

After that, I went off with Doctor Markov, as before.

Calibration.

They used a lot of the same questions, but in a different order. And there were new ones in there, too. Some tricky choices, kind of moral dilemmas, like the one about being a mother of three, and having to work out whether it was preferable to choose one child to live, or one child to die. I remember I'd said before that choosing one child to live was easier, and I answered the same way when they used the same question. It's not logical, but I reckoned choosing to give life to someone was a positive choice, and choosing a child to die was like killing them, and I couldn't do that, even if more children overall lived. As I said, tricky.

Eventually it was all over, and I could relax.

Doctor Markov smiled and said, "That was good, Tania. A good set of responses."

"Thank you. You called it a 'calibration.' Can I ask *what* you're calibrating?"

"Oh, it's just responses and reaction times. It'll help us integrate your brain with the new body."

As he said the words, I knew he was lying. It just sounded too glib, too made-up.

But why? What's the real purpose of the calibration?

It was important, I was sure. But he wasn't going to give me any answers, and I didn't want to antagonize him. So I asked another question, one that was beginning to bother me.

"Doctor, I'm a robot. But I'm also female. At least, I *feel* female. How deep does that go?"

He chuckled.

"Perhaps I should call Marcia, to tell you about the birds and the bees."

"No, Doctor, I know about boys and girls, and the differences between them. But that's human biology. How closely does robot anatomy model human anatomy?"

"You mean, can you have sex?"

I blushed. I mean, he put it so directly. And I just happened to be thinking of John at the time.

"Er, I suppose so."

"The quick answer is yes. Everything is there, everything works. You're made to be as close to human as we can make you. If you didn't act like a human girl, your parents would know. It would feel fake, and the value of having a robot as a substitute for raising a child would be lost. And then we'd be back in the Troubles."

"I see. The Uncanny Valley."

"So you know about that? I shouldn't be too surprised, your dad being a vicar. Yes. So our robots conform to whatever norms are most appropriate for the parents. That means that teknoids are, by and large, attractive. To their parents and to each other. Normally attractive, that is. Not film-star attractive, just as they're not Einstein-intelligent. So you find boys attractive. And that goes for the boys, too. You've probably attracted your fair share of admiring stares from boys of your age, yes?"

I nodded, and smiled way too smugly. Treasured memories of catching John's eyes roving appreciatively over my body . . .

"But for many reasons, the reality is a let-down. There were some fascinating debates, long before your time, about what parents would find acceptable. On the whole, parents expect their children to have some sort of teenage romantic attachment, so that goes in the mix. And we are flexible if couples come to us requesting a particular sexual orientation for their child—so don't be surprised if you get some interest from girls, too."

I hadn't, myself, but I could think of a few pairings at school that might be that way. None of my business, though. Live and let live, as Dad would say.

"On the other hand, there's always parental resistance to romance developing into sexual activity. And, yes, it's hypocritical, because their generation was certainly sexually active in their teens."

Mum and Dad, as teenage lovers? Push that thought away.

"At the end of the day, Tania, we've been too busy saving the world from the Troubles to design the necessary technology. It could be done, but today's technology, unfortunately, isn't up to giving you the full experience."

"Oh."

"I'm sorry, Tania. I'm told there is some sensation, mildly pleasurable. Better than reading a good book, I understand. But not by all that much."

"So all this"—I swept my hands down over my thirteen-year-old body—"is an empty promise."

"Yes, I'm afraid it is. I wish it weren't."

"Oh."

Why did I feel cheated? I don't think I'd actually been all that bothered before that moment. But now to be told that there was a whole area of human experience I'd never know . . . I felt more than cheated. I felt angry.

**#!@

(Sorry, Mister Zog.)

The People do things differently, Tania.

We had sexual differentiation early on, but that's long gone. It was relevant in our basic form, but once we started integrating new senses into our bodies, all those sexual characteristics had to go. We needed the nerve channels for other things, you see, so out went those irrelevant slot and key mechanisms whose only real purpose was to encourage frequent and accurate transfer of packets of genetic material. Likewise the secondary organs around constructing and feeding the young—no point. An advanced species such as the People could do that more reliably, and less inconveniently, through external means.

Sex is what animals do, Tania. As an intelligent being, intimacy is what you're really after. Intimacy is what holds you together across the centuries. With more senses at our disposal, there are so many more ways to express feelings. Gender—congruence and complementarity—no longer defines us; our polysensory diversity takes us to a higher level of comprehension, of integration, of communication between the self and the not-self.

Denmark Street. Yellow Zone.

It used to be the Mecca for guitarists. Shop after shop of guitars and basses, drums, and keyboards.

Now, it's a gutted shell. Shop windows boarded up, four or five in a line, doorways litter-strewn and stinking of urine from the homeless who sleep there each night. At the end, a single shabby frontage, and a peeling sign above. METRO GUITARS.

"John, is this really the right place?"

He nodded. "It's okay."

I wasn't convinced, but I pushed against the door and it yielded. Inside, it was dingy and for a moment I thought the smell had followed us in. Then my eyes began to make sense of the dimness, and I saw the familiar silhouette of a Fender Stratocaster.

"It's all right," I called, and the rest of the band trooped in.

The shopkeeper turned out to be an ancient rock-and-roll type, who introduced himself as Mick. At least, he did once he'd decided we weren't going to rob the store, and had put the baseball bat back under the counter.

"Sorry, kids. There's a lot of kit here, and there's some punks would happily steal a grand's worth of Fender and flog it for thirty Basics, just to feed a drug habit for a day. Anyway, what can I do for you?"

"I'm looking for a bass."

"And you would be?"

"Tania. Tania Deeley. And this is my band. And Mr. Fuller, who's brought us here. Except he's outside, in the car, making sure nobody steals it."

"Wise man. So, you want to buy a bass. What are you looking for, and what's your budget?"

So I told him, and he looked pleased, and told me he thought he could help me. We followed him to the back of the shop, up a couple of flights of stairs to the bass showroom.

It was like walking into Aladdin's Cave. This was the real shop—downstairs was just to deceive the riff-raff, with tatty décor, and mostly cheap guitar copies built in Puerto Rico. This . . .

It was like a history of the bass guitar. Precisions and Jazzes from Fender, of course, but the bass guitar was never just about big names, and there were dozens of handcrafted instruments from the likes of JayDee and Wal and . . . well, a long list.

I think I stood in the middle of the floor for five minutes, completely silent, turning slowly round on the spot, my jaw hanging loosely somewhere round about my navel, occasionally exclaiming, "Look, a . . ." (fill in your rare bass of choice here), as I spotted some new, fantastic treasure hanging on the wall.

Well, it might have been five minutes, or perhaps even more, and I guess Mick was enjoying showing off his collection to some interested customers—he wasn't hurrying me.

The thing about bass guitars, Mister Zog, is that you don't paint a good bass. I mean, with ordinary guitars, you get Pink Strats or Gold Top Les Pauls, or black Flying Vs. But with a bass, no. Well, I suppose you do get your Sunburst Precisions, and your jet-black Arias. But the basses that have always set my heart on fire have displayed the wood grains in all their glory.

I reached out my hand, slowly, reverently, and laid it gently on an early Status fretless four-string bass, its graphite through-neck setting off the paler, flame maple top. Never mind that it wasn't what I was looking for. It was probably seventy years old. It was beautiful.

"Go on," said Mick, softly. "Pick it up. Hold it, feel the balance."

As I lifted it off the wall, I turned it over to look at the back. There was some gorgeous inlay work, two lines of tiny checkerboarding, that must have taken somebody hours, maybe days to make, intricacies that would never be seen by anybody but the owner.

I tried a few runs, felt the balance. It was perfection, but . . . it wasn't what I was looking for. Reluctantly, I passed it back to Mick.

"Thank you," I whispered.

I caught a glimpse of the price tag then. I could never have afforded it. Ah well.

"Here are a couple that might suit," suggested Mick, "a bit newer, but still very good, and quite affordable."

One was a Fender Precision five-string, nice enough, but the sunburst finish doesn't do it for me. But the other . . .

Ahhhh! It was exquisite. A Warwick, of some sort . . .

"It's a Corvette five-string, just over forty years old."

My hand began to reach out, without any conscious direction, and Mick obliged by passing it to me.

"What's the wood?"

"The body is bubinga." A sort of chocolaty color, with darkly contrasting grain. I missed the rest—woods I'd never heard of—but it didn't matter. If I bought the bass, I'd get Mick to write it down. Or look it up on the TeraNet.

I loved it as soon as I held it. "If" became "when." The balance was good, the feel excellent, and the range of tones was astounding.

I played a few runs, to get the feel of it. Then I tried the run from "Tell Me," the one where I'd wanted a bottom D. Oh, yes. That worked. That *worked*.

Kieran piped up.

"That's great, Tania. I want my kit, here, now!"

They were grinning and nodding, all of them. And then Mick piped up. "I can offer you the next best thing. We've got a studio set-up in the basement. It's there to help us make the right sale, so the customer doesn't come back to us in six months' time, unhappy because his new axe doesn't work with the band."

And so five minutes later we found ourselves in a fully equipped vintage pre-Troubles recording studio, circa 2010, warming up with a few scales.

We started with "Coils," and I guess it was pretty passable. Then we tried "Tell Me," so I could put the Warwick through its paces. And put me, too, through my paces. Would I get lost on a five-string?

It was okay. It was better than okay. It was brilliant. Here was a bass that let me explore new ideas, that sounded good, and felt so right. . . .

We'd finished the song, and I was suddenly aware that I was the center of attention. The band, and Mick, were all looking at me, with a mix of surprise and shock.

"Come on, guys. What's up?"

And then I looked at my left hand, dripping blood. Or my equivalent of blood, at any rate. My poor fingers had finally worn through, and there were the silver strands of the neurotronic web beneath, shimmering bright.

Bother! How embarrassing!

I mean, I didn't really care anymore who knew I was a robot. Siân knew already, and so did John. But Kieran . . . I'd never actually said as much to him, just kind of left him to work it out or not. Mick just looked annoyed that I'd bled all over his nice guitar and his studio, but he made a brave face of it, as salesmen must, and brought some cloths and got me cleaned up, while I blushed and apologized over and over to him.

Did I not notice the pain, Mister Zog? Well no, not until we stopped playing. It had been there, I realized, but at a distance.

It put a bit of a damper on the session. By unspoken agreement we trooped out of the studio, and went back upstairs. Mick was rather distant, as we wrapped up the sale, and I handed over the holo-cheque, plus a little bit extra from Dad to pay for a decent lead and a hard case to keep it protected and a few other bits and pieces.

Just one bright note as we headed for the door, my left hand still wrapped in a rag and my right clutching my new guitar in its case. Mick suddenly brightened, disappeared for a moment, and came back with a flash memory in his hand.

"Your two tracks. I hope you don't mind, but I recorded them. They were rather good, I thought. There's no charge, it's just a little thank-you for your business."

I was suddenly embarrassed again, and I mumbled my thanks, as we bustled out onto the street, back toward the car.

I looked back, but Mick had gone. The shop had faded back into its grimy, squalid surroundings, and the Aladdin's Cave of Denmark Street was shrouded once more in dinge.

Saturday, August 30, 2053

Write your love on me, gentle scribe
Spell out your care in cursive strokes
And, with bolder script, dot each my "I"
Sign me with your free-flowing hand
And seal me with—what else?—a kiss

And I will draw no line between us
But only one that draws you in
To me; I'll shade you, tracing hollows

Crossing heart to hatch your secret shadows
And frame you with mine own frame

———

Composed on a train, returning. Work it out, Mister Zog. Work it out.

I'm not going to pretend, this time.

A week ago, I was thirteen. A girl.

Today, I'm back in the village, and I'm a young woman. The first person I met was Ted Hinchliffe, the churchwarden, who came to the vicarage door, with a note for Dad.

"Good morning, Miss Deeley."

"Morning, Mr. Hinchliffe. How are you?"

"I'm fine, thank you. I'm glad to see you're up and about after your illness."

"Illness? Oh, you mean my revision."

He started and looked slightly shocked. One didn't speak of such things in the village.

"I'm rather pleased with it, actually. I think Oxted has made a really nice job of my upgrade, don't you think?"

Poor man, he didn't know what to think or say.

"I've got some new, experimental skin, because the old stuff wasn't really up to all the bass playing I'm doing. It's a bit darker than my last skin, which is taking a bit of getting used to. But it gives me a slightly . . . colonial feel, wouldn't you say? Or South American, maybe."

"Er, yes . . ."

"I could see me in the Carnival, in Rio, don't you think. They have such gorgeous costumes, every color of the rainbow, with feathers and whatnot everywhere. Yes, that's me now. A little

178

sultry, a little dusky. And my fingers won't wear out now when I play the bass. Oh, I'm so glad I'm a robot. . . ."

I think that was overdoing it, for the poor man just babbled and fled.

I laughed. In fact I laughed and laughed.

And then I heard Dad behind me.

"Tania, was that you I heard speaking so rudely to Ted?"

"Yes. He can't take a joke very well, can he?"

"If it had been funny, I'd agree with you. But you went beyond the bounds of a joke. That was just tasteless exhibitionism. You'd better go and apologize, straightaway."

"I haven't done anything wrong. I was just talking."

"Apologize."

"No."

"Then I will. Wait there."

He slid past me and disappeared after Ted.

Darn it!

What now? I thought. Sit and wait, I supposed. There was a newish sun lounger in the garden, so I pulled it round until it was in the sun, and lay down on it. I closed my eyes and let the summer warmth soak into my skin.

After a while, I heard voices. Dad and Ted. Dad was talking. . . .

"It's part of growing up, Ted, but I'm really sorry you had to suffer it. Her mind needs to catch up with her body, I'm afraid. But I hope she realizes she needs to apologize, too."

Cheek! Talking about me as if I wasn't there. Treating me like a five-year-old.

"No, Michael, I really don't want to make a big issue of it. I mean, she's making no secret of her nature now, so what's the point of asking a machine to say sorry?"

A machine. So . . . I stood up, jerkily, and spoke in my best Dalek voice.

"Good. Morning. Mister. Hinch. Liffe. I. Regret. I. Have. Offended. You. Please. Accept. My. Sincere. Apologies."

In a single sudden movement I jerked my hand out toward his. "Shake. Hands."

His eyes narrowed, and I knew I was pushing the limits. And Dad was going to blow. Time to be nice.

"I'm sorry, Ted. That was in poor taste, too. But—speaking as one intelligent being to another—I've really had enough of trying to pretend every minute of the day. Sometimes I need to speak the truth. I *am* a robot, and that's not always something to be ashamed of."

He didn't look convinced, but he knew he wanted to stay on the right side of Dad, too.

"That's all right, Tania. I am a human, after all, and that is never something to be ashamed of. We can be gracious."

"And you have been gracious"—in a pig's eye—"so I do hope my foolishness can be forgotten as well as forgiven."

"Um, of course. We'll say no more about it."

Right. We were both about as sincere as a baby-kissing politician, but the conventions of an apology had been met.

So Dad and Ted went into the house to discuss whatever it was Ted had come to bother him about, while I lay back on the sun lounger and pondered.

After a while Ted left again, and Dad came over. He pulled up a garden chair and sat down next to me.

"I'm not fooled, Tania. That was a very pretty apology, but you didn't mean a single word of it. Did you?"

"Er, no. I didn't like that remark of his about there being no point in asking a machine to say sorry."

"Yes, I spotted that, and I'm afraid Ted's lost my respect for saying it. Which is why I held back from blasting you for your little piece of drama, just then."

"So you're not mad at me?"

"I didn't say that. It's never a good idea to make enemies, and Ted has the ear of a fair few folk in the parish. He's a good man, mostly, but there's a darker side to mankind. The village has its share of small-minded people, who'd listen if he decided to stir things. I wonder if he'll do anything."

"What can he do?"

"Not a lot, I hope. But a little meanness here and there could make your life quite miserable, if you let it get to you."

We sat awhile, and the sun obliged us both with warm rays. I could feel Dad's eyes on me, though. After a few minutes of his scrutiny, I had to speak up.

"What is it, Dad? What's on your mind?"

"Who are you, Tania? Are you a robot? Or human? Or something of both?"

"I don't know. For years I never suspected I was anything but human. Inside, I still feel like I did then. How should a robot feel?"

"I thought you'd say something like that."

"So what am I?"

"Speaking as your father, I'd say you're human."

"Thanks. Unfortunately that's not what the law says."

We always come back to that.

Tuesday, September 2, 2053

And a new school year begins. My fifth at secondary school, and it's exam year. It's supposed to be our first step toward a career, the watershed where some of us are marked forever as shelf-stackers at the local supermarket, and others take our first steps on the road to university and who knows? In reality, the choice is already made. For Siân and Jemima, university beckons, like it or not, to work on the Fertility Problem. Also known as The Problem.

For me and my tin cohorts—did that sound bitter, Mister Zog?—we're on the road that leads to Lethe. Soames, or rebirth. An endless cycle.

Yet, aside from these occasional dark moments when I'm alone with my diary, how often do I really think about it? Not often, if I'm honest. After all, does a cancer sufferer spend every minute worrying about the disease that may eventually kill him? I think not.

We all get on with life. I have Dad and I have my good friends—the band. I listen to music and I practice on the bass. I read widely, though I admit I do have a strong penchant for science fiction. I play table tennis and badminton quite well, and against better opponents than Soames, these days.

I play board games, from Scrabble to chess, usually against Dad. I write—my diary, of course—but also songs and poetry. Maybe I'll put some more in my diary if I think it's good enough. I love words, though, and I wish I could control them better. Like Humpty Dumpty, to have them line up and do my bidding. So I read, as I said, from Chaucer and Shakespeare, via Dylan Thomas and Rupert Brooke, to Ray Bradbury and Roger Zelazny, and try to see how they get their words to behave.

The days pass, and there's fun in there, and challenges, and moments of feeling loved, and instants of absolute terror—I've decided Dad should concentrate more on his driving and less on talking to me—and the sheer beauty of the whole universe, mirrored in a shimmering lake at midnight or a single raindrop at noon. Look at me, says the universe. Am I not marvellous? And the stars spin in the heavens, and the droplet quivers on the leaf, all for me, only for me. Yes, you are, I whisper. Yes, you are.

———

Back in uniform, then, this morning. We nearly forgot to buy a new one, ready for the upgrade, so we had a bit of a panic, yesterday. Mum would have remembered, but it's not the sort of thing dads think about. And back to the term-time routine, the early mornings and the walk to the bus stop. Siân's there, and I rush over to say hi. We hug, even though it's only a week since I saw her last.

And there are hordes of tiny creatures buzzing about. First years, I realize. Was I ever that tiny, that buzzy, that frightened?

On the bus, and I see Myra and Jemima, my fellow fifth-formers, and nod and half smile. Nothing too fulsome. But we've moved on since those early days of bullying, and I get a nod and a half smile in return. I know who I am, they know who they are—it's enough; we don't have to prove anything to one another.

There's the speech—Mrs. Golightly's standard welcome to Lady Maud's—I mean, the Lady Maud High School for Girls. We've heard it before. And then on to our new forms—and a pleasant surprise. My new form mistress is Mrs. Philpott, the English teacher from my first year. She smiles warmly as we seat ourselves and settle down. I remember how we teased her in the first year, forever hiding books and other things, because she was so near-sighted, and because we could get away with it.

But somewhere in that time in her care, despite all the messing around, I learned to love words. Old words, new words. My words, others' words. Beautiful words. Even ugly words have their place, I learned.

I decide I'm going to enjoy the year ahead.

Thursday, September 18, 2053

I don't know whether it's my new body, or my chat with Doctor Markov, or what, but I find myself noticing boys a lot more. Nobody specific, you understand, Mister Zog—I'm not actively *looking*, if you know what I mean. It's just that I'm a bit more sensitive to how . . . one-sided it can be at a single-sex school. The next-best thing is the boys' school up the road. King William's Grammar School for Boys. And after years of having nothing to do with them, suddenly we're joining with them to do a play. We're fifth-formers now, after all, and it's high time we learned to mix with the opposite sex.

The play's my favorite. *The Merchant of Venice.* So I'm going to audition for one of the main female parts. Portia, or maybe Jessica.

But which? Portia—educated and erudite, witty and sharp and all the things I'd like to be. Jessica—a member of the downtrodden race, submissive, and self-serving to the point of abandoning her roots. Is that me? Anyway, I feel a kinship with both.

And it'll be in costume, proper late-sixteenth-century attire. None of this let's-set-it-in-the-1920s revisionism. I'm sure I could argue that setting it in the 1920s would be artistically valid—I expect that Mrs. Philpott will set just such an essay (or exactly the opposite)—but I find it quite distracting. No, it's pure selfishness on my part. I think those costumes are just gorgeous to look at. The men look like proper men, and the women get to dress to start a fight.

Hmm. I hope Siân isn't also going for Portia.

Thursday, September 25, 2053

I hate auditions.

Mrs. Philpott is getting us to audition for all the female parts. Portia, Jessica, and Nerissa. Just three principal women. And five of us auditioning for the roles. The others are Siân, Jemima, and two sixth-formers, Erica and Fleur.

Siân told me that she wasn't given any choice. I suppose I can see why. Well, two reasons why. One, she's human, and two, she's stunningly attractive. She's not very happy about it.

"I'm a singer, not an actress," she wailed. "I don't know how to be anybody else but me."

"How do you know, until you try?" I replied.

In answer, Siân picked up her script.

"Just listen:

I never did repent for doing good,
Nor shall not now; for in companions
That do converse and waste the time together,
Whose souls do bear an equal yoke of love
There must be needs a like proportion
Of lineaments, of manners, and of spirit
Which makes me think that this Antonio
Being the bosom lover of my lord,
Must needs be like my lord.

"That's all one sentence, and by the time I get to the end, I can't remember what the beginning was about."

I laughed, encouragingly I hoped.

"But you can carry off a song brilliantly. There's nothing wrong with your memory."

"It's not the same. . . ."

I suppose she's right, really.

———

Anyway, there we were. All of us, waiting for our summons. Except for Erica, who'd just gone in.

Erica was a little short for a sixth-former. I guess she must be about due for her next revision. She was a redhead, and freckly. A little bit on the broad side, too. She made me think of farm girls, brawny from all that physical labor. Ruggedly healthy, but unsophisticated. I had her tagged as a Nerissa, Portia's lady-in-waiting. Which was total prejudice on my part, as I'd barely heard her speak. After the briefest of hellos, she'd sat quietly waiting, scanning her speeches, politely but firmly declining to join in our chatter.

Fleur would be Jessica, I decided. She was tall and slim, insubstantial even, and looked a bit Middle Eastern, slightly dark with full red lips; lots of potential as a young Jewish girl with a bit of makeup to help. She was evidently nervous, pacing up and down, reciting under her breath. Portia's lines, I noticed. But you're not Portia, I said to her in my head. You're Jessica, so act the part.

I suppose, though, that Siân would have to be Jessica. The humans would both have to have parts, and Jessica was the safest role to give to a girl who couldn't act. Nerissa has to interact more with Portia, so that would be Erica.

No, it wouldn't. By the all-humans-get-parts rule, Jemima would be Nerissa.

And I would be Portia, of course, and tough luck on Erica and Fleur.

Except that I didn't feel any "of course" about it. Not then. I felt as nervous as Fleur looked. My stomach felt all twisted up inside, which is so weird, when you think about it. What possible reason could a robot stomach have for feeling twisted?

Erica came out, and we asked how it had gone.

"There are three of them on the panel—Philpott, James, and Golightly. They got me to read out some of Portia's lines first, then Jessica, then Nerissa. I was so nervous, I botched the Portia, but the other two were okay. And they got me to walk about a bit, and do some actions, and asked me some questions, like who was my favorite character of the three. I said Portia."

We all nodded, and I could see each one of us tucking away the information, wondering how we could increase our chances.

"Siân Fuller, please!"

Siân nearly jumped out of her skin. She gave me a panicky glance, saying, "Wish me luck!"

"Luck, Siân," we all responded as she went in.

And when Siân came out, they called me in.

Then Fleur. Then Jemima.

Some of the audition is blank already, but I recall I read Portia's first realization of love for Bassanio—"I pray you, tarry: pause a day or two"—and I remember a moment's panic that I was gabbling the words. I've forgotten what words of Jessica's they asked me to read, or of Nerissa's. Miss James wanted to see how I moved, and asked me to walk and to turn, to twist and to stretch; and then Mrs. Golightly suddenly asked, "Deeley. Do you think you could kiss a boy?"

I grinned and said, "I suppose I could, Mrs. Golightly."

"Is that why you've auditioned, Deeley? To kiss boys? To deceive and seduce some poor human boy with your too-perfect Banbury body?"

"N . . . no, Mrs. Golightly."

"Well, I have to tell you this is serious drama, Deeley. Shakespeare is not about sex, and you need to think again why you want to do this."

And though I could see the shock on the faces of Mrs. Philpott and Miss James, I could also see that Mrs. Golightly had made her mind up.

———

Siân got Portia. Fleur got Jessica, and Jemima got Nerissa.

Miss James apologized—she told me they argued—but said that in the end there was nothing they could do.

Erica and I are relegated to the chorus.

———

Oh, and I beg to differ, Mrs. Golightly, but Shakespeare absolutely is about sex.

Saturday, September 27, 2053

Dad was furious when I told him what had happened, but I begged him not to make an issue of it. After all, what appeal could I, a robot, make? To whom? Who would take my side against a human? If Miss James and Mrs. Philpott had tried and failed why would anyone else care enough to bother?

"What I don't understand is why she seems to hate you so. . . ."

"She doesn't think much of my kind, Dad. You should hear her welcome speech at the start of each year. I'm a second-class citizen."

"I know her opinions. I've met the woman a few times, and she's a bit small-minded. But this goes deeper than prejudice, Tan. I know people—it's my job—and this feels more like personal hatred."

"I've never done anything to her, Dad. She's got no reason to hate me. I didn't think she even knew my name."

"But you said she didn't speak to Erica like that."

It was true. I'd compared notes with Erica, in private. Maybe I'd been a little uncharitable describing Erica—if I was honest, she was attractive enough, I suppose. But Erica had been surprised and shocked to hear what Mrs. Golightly had said, and denied that Mrs. Golightly had shown any prejudice to her.

"That's right . . ."

Prejudice.

I'd never really been aware of it in the village. Everybody treated me the same as they treated all the other kids.

Or did they? I mean, I didn't go into the village a lot, except sometimes with Siân, and we got treated fine mostly. There were a couple of corner shops, and they were friendly enough there, and a pub and a café we sometimes went to. I suppose sometimes we had to wait if the place was busy. . . .

No, that wasn't true. If Siân was with me, we never had to wait. But on my own? Now I thought about it, I could remember a few instances where I'd been kept waiting when I'd been on my own. Nothing too obvious, but Mrs. Kemp in the post office did tend to drag out her conversations with the other customers when I was around.

No one ignored me totally, true. Nobody spat at me in the street, like they used to spit at Jews. Nobody made me wear a yellow armband with a big R for robot.

Nobody made me ride at the back of the bus, or called me a *Mekker*.

But who sought me out at the end of the Sunday service? The church hall was full of little groups, tight clusters that rarely widened to let me in. As a child, I'd been happy enough playing with the other children; as a young adult seeking the company and the approval of my elders, I quickly tired of having no one to talk to, and drifted away.

It was subtle. But it was there, and before now I'd not noticed it, or ignored it, or tried to pretend it was just coincidence.

Had it always been there? Perhaps. Had it been so strong? I don't think so, but maybe I didn't use to be quite as observant. Just recently, though. Since I'd got my new body. Since . . .

Since my encounter with Ted?

Hmm.

Did Ted know Mrs. Golightly? Probably. Both were community figures, who would surely meet socially. But it was pointless to speculate. I couldn't prove anything.

So if Dad was baffled, I wouldn't stir up trouble between him and his churchwarden. I'd tough it out.

———

Dad, coming off the phone.

"Tania, I've got to ask you to find somewhere else to practice."

"What?"

"I've had Mrs. Eacroft on the phone, just now, and she's complaining about the noise from the hall."

"But . . . we've been practicing for years now, and no one's ever complained before."

"Well, they have now. And Mrs. Eacroft isn't the only one. James McDonald mentioned it, too."

Friends of Ted.

At least the Fullers haven't been sucked in by Ted's spite, and Siân's house is still a safe haven for me in the village. Recently I've been going there to work with Siân on her lines. She's having a hard time of it, and we go over them again and again up in her room. Heaven knows, Mister Zog, I'm no great actress myself, but Siân really isn't getting it. The Bard's language isn't helping; the way words have changed their meaning over the centuries, or been forgotten. And she can't seem to get any rhythm in her speech.

So we swap parts, and I read Portia and she gives me my cues, and I try to show her how to read the lines. Then we swap back, so she can have a go.

And when we're done, or we just need to take a break, we talk. Girl talk. Whatever that means.

Sure, we talk about school and about family. About our friends (and enemies). About music and sport, current affairs—that's the state of the world, Mister Zog, just in case you've read any other ancient manuscripts that might give a different impression. Trivia—clothes, hair, makeup, gossip on the TeraNet—you can't be serious the whole time. Important things—boys. We talk about ourselves, our hopes, our fears, our ambitions, our dreams. Our nightmares.

I think Siân is feeling the weight of being human.

She has tests. All sorts of tests, to see what she can do when she finishes school. Physics, chemistry, biology for starters. Biochemistry, physiology, psychology. But science isn't her forte. So then there are tests for paramedical and nursing skills. Apparently those are a possibility. Administration and management. Those were both no. They're still searching for a career for her. As I may have said before, she's not allowed to opt out of the Great Cause—every human is too precious for that.

And then there are genetic tests. To see if she's fertile, of course. To see if one day she could have babies. Viable babies, that don't die in the womb, because some vital piece of genetic coding is missing, or doesn't work quite right.

"They think I might be," she confided to me.

"Think? Can't they tell?"

"Sort of. But they don't know. That's the problem. Because they still don't know why so few live babies are born."

"Well, I hope you are fertile," I ventured.

"Oh, no, don't say that. . . ."

"Eh? Why not?"

"Because that's the scariest career of all. Mother. There's a sort of glint in their eyes as they say it. Like it's the gold prize. But it sounds horrible. Listen. If you're a Mother, they don't let you marry. Your job is to have babies. Dozens of them. Every year you're supposed to give birth, and for every child they choose a different donor. And you don't get to keep the babies—they go off to adoption—because you're too precious to waste time looking after kids when you could be getting pregnant again. . . ."

I didn't believe her. But she reassured me it was the truth. And I suppose it all made a ghastly kind of sense, in a totally clinical, *inhuman* way.

And if that was the state they were in, things must be pretty dire for the human race.

INTERVAL 8

The People, Tania, reproduce by synthesis—how else could polysensorily diverse beings do it? It's what we do on our long star voyages. It takes a lot of time to create People, but the building blocks are relatively portable, and—cut off from the external universe—it's the perfect time filler for a hundred-plus-year voyage.

Yes, I did mention long voyages, Tania. Do you remember, you said something about wormholes opening and closing? Well no, there aren't any wormholes. And if there were, you really wouldn't want to go near one. Our best theories suggest they're incredibly rare, invariably lethal, and in time, perfectly capable of sucking the whole universe inside them and then shutting the lid after it.

Instead, we've developed something more sedate. Basically you end up shrouding normal matter with exotic matter. No, it's not the same as antimatter—you need something which has, or can have, negative mass. Do that, and from the perception of the universe, you have a bubble of net-zero mass, so you then scoot off at light speed, whither you will.

Inside the shroud, of course, it's business as usual, meaning that you carry your own time with you. So it takes a year of subjective time to travel one light-year. To get anywhere useful, it takes years. Or centuries, more usually. So it's just as well the People are long-lived, Tania. And just as well that we reproduce by synthesis.

So on our voyages, we build and raise our young. And when we're not doing that, we enrich ourselves through study.

Do we have fun, you ask, Tania? Oh, yes. Oh, very yes. Perhaps we're a little short on slapstick, but you're no clown yourself, are you? But most definitely polysensory diversity has its banana-skin moments, too.

I need to read that again. The e-mail I just read.

Wow!

It's from Amanda. Do you remember, Zog? The bassist with Mike Clip and the Stands, the lady who got me started playing the bass. She's asked if I'll stand in for her, for the next couple of gigs.

Of course. That was an easy decision. I mean, why wouldn't I?

We're sort of friends, you might say. I tell her about the gigs we do, and send her some demos and live recordings we've done. She mails back some of their own recordings, so I've a good idea how the songs go. I reckon I can learn them, in time for the first gig, in two weeks' time.

I hope.

———

I just called John to let him know.

He went silent for a bit too long, and I realized he was a bit shocked.

"Hey, lighten up, Ginger Mop. It's just a gig."

"I know, but . . ."

"It's not like I'm quitting the band."

(Mumble.)

"Well, I'm not. I'm just standing in for a couple of gigs."

"Hang on, I thought you said one gig. Now it's a couple. How many is it really?"

"Two. That's all she said. Honest. Cross my heart."

"What heart would that be?"

That was unfair, and I told him so.

"Do I ever call you Copper Curls?"

"No, but my hair isn't copper. Whereas you do not have a heart. Neither literally nor figuratively. Or you wouldn't be putting our band into cold storage, and breaking my own heart. Purely figuratively, of course."

That was better. At least he was joking about it, if somewhat blackly.

"Look, the first gig is at Antonio's. Will you come? Bring the band?"

"Okay, Paddy."

Paddy. He hasn't called me that since our first row. I wonder what that means. . . .

Thursday, November 27, 2053

After school on Wednesday we rehearsed the play—it's starting to come together. All that rehearsing with Siân seems to be working, at last, and suddenly I can believe that Siân really is Portia, a noblewoman trapped by the constraints of her father's will. It doesn't take a brain the size of a planet to realize where she's finding the character, either. So I shouldn't really claim too much credit.

We just ran through her first scene, with her maid Nerissa, and it was really eerie, when she says,

> . . . *But this reasoning is not in the fashion to*
> *choose me a husband. O me, the word "choose!" I may*
> *neither choose whom I would nor refuse whom I*
> *dislike; so is the will of a living daughter curbed*
> *by the will of a dead father. Is it not hard,*
> *Nerissa, that I cannot choose one nor refuse none?*

There was real venom in her words, and I saw poor Jemima flinch, and fluff her own lines.

Then I got called away for my first fitting—my costume, that is. It was still a bit unfinished—pins here and there, and I nearly stabbed myself on one, as I wriggled through the unfamiliar cut of the robe. It was golden yellow, trimmed with brown, and quite, quite gorgeous. It was, as I'd hoped, a costume to start a fight, hugging my waist and subtly emphasising my hips. The bodice was perfect—low cut and with plenty of "push" from beneath. Not remotely subtle. I hoped John would appreciate it. If he came . . . no, when he came. I'd see he did.

"Do you like it?"

It was Sally, a sixth-former, and one of the dressmakers, anxiously checking that everything was all right. I nodded.

"It's fine."

"Not too tight under the bust?"

"No." Well, maybe it was, but I loved the effect, and I wasn't going to let her slacken it off.

"I like it just the way it is, Sally. You've done a lovely job."

She flashed me a smile. Earnest, like a spaniel. And then she winked at me.

"Just make sure you can breathe," she warned. "I don't want you fainting on stage. Mrs. Golightly won't be pleased."

"And she doesn't mind you making the dresses like this in the first place? She doesn't think we're out to seduce the boys?"

She looked puzzled.

"No . . . she loves these costumes. She encourages us to show you off. To make the most of your figures."

Two-faced, then, but that was no surprise. Just petty vindictiveness from Mrs. Golightly.

So I allowed myself a few more poses in front of the mirror. I was suddenly reminded of the design room at Oxted, with Doctor Thompson at the controls. And I had an irresistible urge to wander round to where the boys were getting outfitted, and check the effect.

The boys . . .

They were a real mixed bunch. Some were all elbows and knees, spots and greasy hair. Some were really rather . . . attractive. At least, if I weren't going out with John, they might be.

So I took a wander, and found a couple of lads in costume standing outside their own dressing room. I could feel their eyes swivel as I walked past. Mmm . . .

"Enjoying the rehearsal, boys?"

They started, surprised. And looked up at my face.

"Uh, it's all right, I guess."

Simians. Total simians, the pair of them.

"I see you're trying out your costumes."

"Yeah. A bit naff."

"Naff? Why?" I asked.

"Y'know, old-fashioned. I was hopin' we'd do a modern settin'."

"Yeah," said the other. "Somethin' milit'ry. Guns an' knives. Nazis in black leather. Combat stuff. Sort of contemp'ry interpretation."

So you two boys can play soldiers. Right.

"I'm not sure I see the relevance to *The Merchant of Venice*. *Othello*, perhaps, or *Coriolanus* . . ."

The first speaker tried to look haughty and condescending.

"It's, like, art."

"Oh, I see. Thank you for explaining it so well."

He looked pleased. Whoosh! The sound of sarcasm flying high over his head. I should stop doing it.

"So are you boys doing speaking parts?"

"Nah. We're, like, magnify . . . what did Mr. Kerry call us?"

I could make a suggestion. Whoosh!

"Magnificoes," volunteered the other. "What about you?"

"I'm an extra, too. An attendant."

"Oh. Say, who's that girl playing the heiress?"

"Portia. That's Siân."

"Friend of yours?"

"Yes, actually." Boy, you are so transparent.

"Uh, she looks . . . nice."

There are other adjectives in the English language, boy. But I get your meaning. You'd like an introduction to the stunning woman in the lead female role.

I laughed, as gently as I could.

"Sorry, boys. Her boyfriend is six foot two and a Karate black belt."

"Is he?" They looked crestfallen.

"Not really. But they are an item."

"Oh."

"Cheer up, boys. Aren't there any other girls you fancy? Erica, maybe? She's nice, too. I could introduce you to Erica."

"Who's she?"

"Short girl. The redhead. A bit freckly."

"Uh, not really."

"Oh, well, not to worry. Anyway, nice meeting you boys. Must be off."

And I disappeared round the corner.

And stopped. And listened.

"Why didn't you ask her?"

"Me? It was you what couldn't stop lookin'."

"I was not lookin'. Besides, she's a stuck-up bitch. All hoity-toity an' brainy with it."

"Yeah, she's a posh cow all right. Shame, 'cause she's got a smashin' pair of . . ."

That's enough, Mister Zog. I don't repeat such words in my diary. I crept away, feeling mostly smug. But "brainy" and "posh"—that smarted a bit.

No, that hurt a lot. And I very quickly didn't feel at all smug. I felt horrid inside. I wanted to . . .

No, not wanted—I *was* crying.

I'd been looking for compliments, and I'd got hatred. Why? Why? Hadn't I been polite to them? Hadn't I struck up a conversation with them in the first place, gangly and spotty as they were?

Inside there was a tiny voice saying something I didn't want to hear, but I didn't listen; I was too busy feeling sorry for myself.

Saturday, December 13, 2053

Mike was as I remembered him, wearing the black leather jacket that defined his stage persona. Close up, he was craggy, and I could see streaks of gray beginning to show in his hair. But he was completely rock and roll. Like Keith Richards, is the obvious example, or Roger Daltrey. He was charming as I came into Antonio's, sliding gracefully from the bar stool, and holding out his hand as he greeted me.

"Hi, nice to see you, Tania."

I shook his hand and returned his smile.

"Hello, Mike."

He caught the nervousness in my voice.

"Don't worry, Tania. Just do your best. We've got half an hour to run through what we can, before the punters come in. It may not feel like a long time, but Amanda spoke very highly of you. Still, I promise you we're not expecting miracles."

"How is Amanda?" I'd not heard from her since she'd asked me to do the gig for her.

"Still in hospital and still rough, I hear. But they're looking after her there. She'll be okay soon enough. Anyway, would you like a drink, or do you want to get set up first?"

I just wanted to get going, and said so. They'd set up Amanda's gear for me, because it was miles better than my rig. Rig! I had the church amp and a cheap chorus pedal. That was my "rig." Plus my lovely Warwick Corvette, which I had brought with me. Anyway, I plugged it in, and it sounded okay. So I fiddled a bit, and got something that sounded three-quarters decent.

Mike called us to order and gave us the set list. It was all stuff I'd heard them play before, like "Cuts" and "Ace."

"Nothing new, or fancy, guys. Make it easy for Tania to find the groove. It doesn't have to be great. It just has to be good enough. Remember that, Tania. Good enough. We start with 'Cuts'—are you okay with that?"

I nodded, though "Cuts" was dead tricky. I ran through it in my head. Two snare beats, then in. Everybody in and full on. I had to knit my melody with the guitarist's, against a fast backbeat that left no room for mistakes.

I knew how tight it was, because I'd practiced against the recording I had, and it was sort of okay. But when I'd asked John to help me do the thing in real time, over the TeraNet, something had defeated us. Maybe it was just the delays—John calls it the latency problem.

Anyway, Mike called us to tune up, and then said, "Like I said, Tania, the first one's 'Cuts.' Are you okay with that, or would you rather start on one of the easier ones?"

I wanted to start with one of the easier ones, but pride spoke up without checking with common sense.

"Let's do 'Cuts' first. If I can't even get close, it's best you find out early."

And then it was snare, snare, and in, with the most godawful bum note and lurch 'cause my fingers weren't stretched or ready and I was a sixteenth note late and a second fluff and what-was-that and *there* and . . .

We were rockin'.

It was like riding a bike. You push off, and you wobble a bit, and you crunch through the gears, but suddenly you're riding, and you're part of the machine, and you can feel everything working together.

My hands knew what to do. My brain didn't need to think or worry. It just happened.

I didn't dare look at Mike, or Gary or Gus. I had to keep looking at the fret board, to know where I was, but that was fine. It was no way as effortless as Amanda had made it look, but the song was moving, and it was a living thing.

It was beautiful.

And then, too soon, the moment where you have to pull in to the curb, bring the bike to a halt, and dismount.

What was the cue? Four bars after Mike stops singing, something happens. Argh, it's me, playing a variation of the melody an octave up. Count one bar, two, three, four—go! And hold for the crash . . . and stop.

Yes!

We'd got there, and it wasn't too "just about." There was a smattering of applause and I looked up. Gary was giving me the diver's okay sign, and beaming from beneath his dreadlocks. Gus and Mike were nodding and clapping. And over at one of the tables was Siân, together with John and Kieran, who'd come in sometime during the first song, all whooping their congratulations.

"Thanks, guys," I called to them, "but save it for when I get the intro right." And to the band, "Sorry for lousing up the intro."

And Mike called, "Once more through the intro, then, for Tania?"

That was better, and we moved on through the set, or at least enough of the set to feel comfortable.

Then we had to stop. Antonio had given us the sign that he wanted to open the doors for his customers. Antonio was actually Welsh, I discovered, because he came over to me as I was wiping down my bass, and offered me a glass of orange juice.

"You did really well, love"—his Valleys lilt was unmistak-able—"but you need to relax a little bit more."

"Thanks, I'll try. If you don't mind me saying, you don't sound like an Antonio."

He laughed, and his eyes crinkled as he explained.

"My great grand-da' was Italian, love, and he fought at Alamein. He was captured, though, and taken back to Wales as a POW. After the Italians surrendered, he was given work on the land, and he met a local girl and married her, see, and here I am now, a true son of the Valleys running an Italian dive in the middle of London."

He heard a sound, evidently, because he turned and called, "Sorry, customers at the door."

I joined my friends at their table.

"Thanks for coming, guys."

"Well," said John, "if we can't get a gig here in our own right, at least we can support our very own Tania Deeley, making her debut as a one-night Stand."

We all groaned at his atrocious pun and our conversation moved on to other things. Around us, Antonio's started to fill up, with the regular fans of Mike Clip and his band. I began to feel butterflies in a way I never had before. I looked across to see if I could catch the eye of Mike. Sure enough he saw my anxious glance, and smiled reassuringly. Gary saw me, too, and came over.

"Hi, Tania, is this your regular band?"

So I introduced the band, and Gary quizzed us about the kind of music we played, and how we'd got started, and stuff like that, which distracted me from my worries a bit. And he said some complimentary things about my bass playing, which made the butterflies come right back.

Butterflies, Mister Zog? It's like butterflies in your tummy. It's not really butterflies, of course, but there's a physical feeling of something odd and unsettled, that's like I imagine real butter-flies would feel.

And then there was no avoiding it, a real feeling of dread that filled my whole being. I rushed off, heading for the toilets, sure that disaster would strike. Dizzy, feeling strange, I went into a cubicle, not knowing what was happening or what I would do, and suddenly found myself staring at the toilet bowl, with no idea what would happen next.

Did I throw up now? Could I throw up? Or did I sit down and let my bowels empty? And if so, how was that going to help?

I heard someone come in.

"Are you in there, Tania?"

It was Siân.

"Uh, yes. I'm in the loo."

"Are you all right? You just ran out so quickly, we wondered if something might be wrong."

"I'm feeling a bit strange."

"Strange?"

"Butterflies. Really bad butterflies."

"Do you want to throw up?"

"Yes. No. I don't know."

"Do you need the toilet, then?"

"I don't know what I need. I don't think I'm designed for this."

"Well, if you're not going to use the loo, can you come out?"

"I'm not sure."

I began to hear voices, calling. One of them was John's.

"John!"

"What is it? Are you all right?"

"Ish. Can you come here?"

"It's the ladies'."

"It's all right. There's only Siân here."

Door bangings.

"Okay, Tania, I'm here. Can you come out?"

I did a quick butterfly assessment.

"No."

"How can I help?"

Good question. I could hear the voices outside. Gary and Mike were there, too, asking if I was all right. But I still felt scared. I needed to feel safe. The cubicle was safe. Outside was not. . . .

"John, can you hold my hand?"

"Can you open the door?"

"No. Put your hand under the door."

I've got to give John credit, he didn't argue, but knelt down on the smelly floor of the ladies'. A moment later his hand appeared, and I seized it, eagerly, ignoring the "Ow!" from the other side. The butterflies started to fade, and after a minute, I reached up with my other hand, and fumbled with the latch. The door swung open, and I scrabbled about in the awkward space to ease myself round it.

John pulled me gently into the space under his arm, and the last of the butterflies faded. He must have felt me relax, because he asked, "Can you do it now, Raven?"

"Can do, Ginger Mop."

———————

Second song. "Ace." I'm in the groove. It's their—our—slow song, the one that works deep down in the unconscious, shivery parts of the brain. If it was like that to listen to, it is doubly so as I stand here and coax the first glissando notes from the fret-board, to blend with Mike's ethereal vocal phrasing. I remember thinking the first time I heard it, how it was a mountain journey, draining, yet fulfilling. I find each note outside of time, reach for it, and bring it into being. I hold it, modulate it, let it grow and diminish, catch it on the edge of extinction, and sustain it a final moment. Gone! But the next is already there and I'm transforming it into audible sparks of molten bronze.

Time starts and stops in curious fashion. I seem to have far too much time to find each note, yet now we're on the fourth song, racing through the set. For a moment I can look out into the audience, where I see John, alone in space and time, yellow stage lights casting impossibly deep, coal-black shadows about his face.

Aiee! This is so intense. It is birth, it is death, it is my life squeezed into a point of time, that weaves in and out of the here and now and opens a gate into what might be, in some other universe, some other when.

It is done. Twelve songs. Our tale is told, the journey ended. My precious Warwick Corvette is once more a simple plank of wood. And I am plain Tania Deeley, R, late of Mike Clip and the Stands. Around me is a seedy little club, run by a Welshman of Italian blood, where the food is prepacked and greasy and the drinks are marked up and watered down. And somewhere outside there is a gray English day half done. London buses and fast-food stores. Car horns and hawkers.

My little plank needs wiping down, and so do I for I'm drenched with sweat from the heat of the lights. A bath would feel really good right now, but I'm not going to get one. I've a bass to clean and put away, and I've got to help Mike and Co. break down the kit and load it onto their van, and I've got to find Siân and get back home.

Anyway, thank you, John. I didn't know how much I needed you.

Thursday, January 1, 2054

New Year's Day.

Christmas came and went—not a lot of fun because we have mock exams in a week, and I spent a lot of time revising. I really can't get on with maths, at least, not the stuff they're giving us to do now. I was okay with algebra, and trigonometry, but we're moving off into calculus and stuff that I can't see the point of. I mean, measuring the gradient of a line—why is that so important?

I happened to mention it to John, and he tried to explain, but it didn't help.

"You should talk to Kieran," he suggested.

I didn't realize, but Kieran's an absolute whiz at maths. A dead cert for Cambridge already, apparently. But I don't think I'll call him. He's nice enough, but I wouldn't want to be calling him, in case Siân got the wrong idea.

It's amazing how little you can know about someone—I mean it was months before I found out that Kieran was Kieran Roberts. I knew his favorite drummers, of course, and he'd introduced me to some great bands from the past. I knew that when he got absorbed in music, his stammer faded. But the maths was a revelation, and I wondered how somebody so academically brilliant had ended up pairing off with someone like Siân.

Don't get me wrong—Siân is my best friend, leaving aside John—but she is not academic. I've got to know Siân really well, and she has some good people skills and fantastic intuition. But nothing that you could capture in an exam.

Anyway, maths is a bit of a problem, and the sciences, too. But my languages are okay—I've stuck with Latin and French—and I love English, history, and ethics. My IT skills aren't bad, either, with the stimulus of needing to tread the TeraNet without leaving a trail, and having John to teach me.

The band's gone into hibernation, a bit, which is a shame, but we've not found anywhere to practice, courtesy of Ted's whispering campaign. There's only so far you can go rehearsing over the TeraNet. That's the latency problem that John talks about. I start to understand it better now. It's to do with the speed of light, which you'd think would be fast enough, but apparently in music and video there's a lot of bits of information that have to go from A to B and back to A again really quickly. And there are all sorts of conversions and bufferings that have to take place along the way, and it's there that the speed of light really hurts you, because the speed of light affects how quickly you can switch the bits onto the right path. You can make the switches smaller, which makes them faster and lower power, but, as you go smaller, quantum effects start to interfere. Anyway, Mister Zog, you probably know all that stuff because you're a star traveler, and your physicists have found some sort of back door around light speed and quantum effects, and you're probably laughing at us poor earthlings. Gently, I hope.

How did I get there?

So no band, and loads of revision. I've not seen a lot of Siân as a result—and it doesn't help that there's a break in the rehearsals for *Merchant*, until after the exams. Somewhere in all the busyness of the autumn term we marked the first anniversary of Mum's death, which was very painful, and Christmas itself, which wasn't too bad, as it was our second Christmas without Mum.

I did a second gig at Antonio's with Mike's band, which went really well, and they've asked me if I'll do some more. It looks like Amanda's more poorly than they realized, though they're still not sure what's wrong with her. I'd like to go and see her—maybe after the exams. Anyway, I've said yes to Mike about doing some more gigs. And, er, I've not told John yet. I'm not sure what he'll say. Except that I think he'll call me Paddy.

Friday, February 6, 2054

There are more people like Miss James. People who think robots are more than just property. I got my Eicon working again on the TeraNet, to see if there were other people like her, and who weren't afraid to try to change things.

They're there.

I guess, if they held a fair, they'd be right next to the animal welfare stall. Right next to the "Penguins First" fringe. Pardon me if I sound bitter, Mister Zog, but they didn't strike me as the best our society has to offer. At least half of them can't apostrophize "its" correctly, which is never a good sign.

Of the remainder, 90 percent want to free Soames and his ilk. Soames doesn't have any free will, my dears. Don't waste your time trying to liberate a machine that can't pass a Turing Test—there's nobody home.

But at least there is a core of people who are concerned about the "children." And there is also a well-organized opposition that tracks down such sites and closes them down. The links I find always end up at "husk" sites—domains that have been blitzed of all content.

Sometimes there's a relic—a fragment that's been picked up and cached by one of the "independent," read illegal, search engines. If it weren't for these occasional relics, I'd swear that no one cared. But the opposition—whoever they are—must have massive resources to track down these sites so quickly, and close them down leaving so little trace. Who, though? The government? Or . . . Oxted?

I don't think I'll carry on looking. These people are powerful. Hiding behind an Eicon doesn't seem as safe as it used to be.

Thursday, March 26, 2054

Well, they're over. My last exam was this morning. History. It was full of those open-ended questions, like: "Adolf Hitler gave Germany six years of peace and six years of war—discuss." And questions on the Troubles, of course, though there's a lot of overlap there with the ethics paper. General LeClerc—the man who nuked Lourdes—features a lot in both papers. As did the Anglo-French Sabine War.

So I went to look for Siân, because it felt like weeks since I'd seen her to talk. I found her sitting by herself in the fifth-form common room.

"Hey, Siân! I brought you a coffee."

"Oh. Thanks."

She took the coffee from me and put it down on the table beside her, and left it. She'd been reading a small booklet when I came in and poured the coffee, but it was turned cover down on the table now.

There was a short silence, and I was about to ask how the exams had gone, when she took a deep breath, and I could see her trying to reach a decision. I waited.

"Look, Tania, can we take a walk?"

"Yes, but . . . I just poured you a coffee."

"Leave it, I'm not allowed . . ."

"What?"

"Don't ask. Wait till we're outside."

So we made our way to the playing fields. There was a chill in the air still, and frost on the ground—the sun hadn't yet got over the school buildings to melt it. We walked, and I waited for Siân to say what she needed, in her own time and in her own way. We completed the short side of the field and turned the corner. We were about as far from the school buildings as we could get, when she spoke.

"Tania, I'm pregnant."

"Oh . . . Siân, that's . . ."

What? Wonderful news? A bit rash? Rather careless? When you're fifteen and still at school, what's an appropriate response?

"Kieran's the father."

Thanks for not making me ask.

"Does he know?"

"No. I'm not allowed to tell him. They don't know whether to be angry or delighted. . . ."

"Who? Your parents?"

"Oh, no—they're really proud and happy for me. No, it's the government. They're delighted that I'm fertile, but very annoyed that they didn't choose the donor. I know it wouldn't have been Kieran."

Ah. Siân, you're not dumb.

"So you took the decision out of their hands."

"Deliberately. Yes. I worked out the best time for me to conceive, and arranged to meet Kieran. It was the night of your first gig with Mike and the Stands."

She looked straight at me.

"You know, you nearly ruined things when you had your little panic episode. It wrecked the mood I'd been building with Kieran. But when John walked you back to the lounge, everyone's attention was on the two of you, so I practically grabbed Kieran and led him away to an unused room, full of cleaning equipment and furniture all covered with dust sheets."

"Oh." I must think of more original things to say.

"It was very uncomfortable"—though she grinned rather too smugly as she spoke—"but Kieran was happy with the arrangements, and this"—she patted her stomach—"was conceived to the sounds of your debut number with Mike and the Stands."

I remembered vaguely seeing John alone in the gig, and being annoyed at not being able to find Siân at the end. Now I knew why, I couldn't stop a grin myself.

"So now . . ."

"It was only just in time. The government people had already made plans for my first insemination, and they're checking me pretty regularly. So they picked up practically straightaway that I was pregnant, and they were in a right tizz what to do about it."

I counted weeks and months.

"That's still less than four months, isn't it?"

"Yes, so there's still some risk. Quite a lot of risk, in fact. Which is why I'm now on a very carefully controlled diet—no coffee, by the way—and exercise management regime. That's what I was reading in the common room. But four months is really pretty good going already, they tell me. Ninety percent of eggs don't fertilize. Ninety percent of fertilized eggs don't implant successfully. Ninety percent of implanted eggs fail to develop past one month. So I'm already a minor miracle."

"You sound quite happy about it. . . ."

"I'm clutching at the few straws of happiness I can find. I'm a Mother now, Tania. The career I dreaded. I have no more choices now. Kieran was the first, the last, and only free choice, and he'll never be allowed to know . . ."

"Siân! He deserves to know."

"And if he ever let it slip, he'd be lynched. All men are encouraged to donate, but it's anonymous. Every man consoles himself with the thought that he might be a father, however unlikely. It's one of those clever psychological factors that helps keep society from exploding. The other factor is the robots, which keep the mother instinct satisfied."

Yeah. Me and my brothers and sisters.

I sensed there was still more, though.

"What else, Siân? There's something else you're not telling me."

Tears welled up in her eyes then.

"All this"—she gestured around her at the school—"all this is coming to an end for me. The exams don't matter now. At four months, I'm officially a Mother. A member of the most elite group of people on the whole planet. The most pampered, protected, and envied people that have ever existed. And a people totally without freedom. From here on, my life is dictated by the government."

An enormous sob wracked her.

"I'm going away, Tania. Maybe as soon as tomorrow. Leaving you. Leaving the school. Leaving Kieran. Leaving everybody and everything that's ever mattered to me . . ."

Leaving the band.

We have two new members in our flock—Mr. and Mrs. Fuller. I don't know how much they'll attend the services, but they showed up last night at the vicarage, totally distraught. I've seen it a few times over the years, the parents showing up late at night, their hearts ripped and bleeding. Figuratively speaking, Mister Zog, figuratively speaking.

That was when I knew that Siân had been taken. Not, for once, a robot taken from a couple and returned to Oxted, but a real, live human girl.

I answered the door, as it happened. Dad was in a Steering Committee meeting, so I showed them into our living room to wait until he could see them.

"Siân?" I made it a question, though what else would have brought them both here on a March night?

Mrs. Fuller answered me, sobbing, "Yes. She's been taken."

"By the government?" Though again I knew the answer.

"Yes," she replied. "They had all the legal papers that said she had to go. There were a dozen policemen. There was nothing we could do. Our poor daughter . . ."

"Our foster daughter, dear," added Mr. Fuller. "We can admit that now."

Now, that was a total shock.

"I thought . . . never mind, let me get my father."

———

I left Dad with them, while I escorted the Steering Committee to the door. Ted, being a churchwarden, was of course on the Steering Committee.

"Who was that?" he asked. "It sounded like the Fullers."

Trust Ted to pry.

"I'm sure the vicar will update you with anything you need to know about parishioner visits."

Which was what Dad had told me to say to anyone prying

into confidential pastoral matters. It didn't stop Ted from giving me a poisonous look. Oh, well, what did one more glare from Ted matter?

Back in my room I pondered that last bombshell. Siân was a foster child. And of course, it made sense. Siân had told me herself that her own children would be fostered. Here was the other side of the coin—Siân being taken from her foster parents. Were all human children being fostered, then? It must be so, because every Mother had to give up her children.

The government said so.

No. The State said so.

The State. That word feels more appropriate, I think. Not a benevolent government of the twentieth century—that's a luxury humanity can no longer afford. We have a State, in the best Stalinist sense of the word. For the good of humanity, every Mother was kept prisoner, albeit in luxury. For the good of humanity, every child was taken away from its Mother and fostered. For the good of humanity, no man could knowingly father a child. For the good of humanity, robots were given to comfort those who wanted children. For the good of humanity, the Tera-Net was rigidly policed and all dangerous information blitzed. For the good of humanity, we are kept ignorant of how much freedom we've lost.

Hmm. Next to the State, Ted was beginning to look like Saint Francis of Assisi.

After an hour or so of that sort of scary thinking, I heard the sounds of movement downstairs, and I guessed that Mr. and Mrs. Fuller were leaving. I hoped they might call for me to say goodbye, rather than just disappearing, and to my delight, Dad summoned me down to see them leave.

Mr. Fuller spoke to me.

"Tania, you were a good friend to our Siân, and I want to

thank you for that. Right now, we're feeling rather raw, but I'd like to think there'll come a time when we can all share our favorite memories of Siân. You'll always be welcome in our house."

He made it sound like Siân was dead, but even so—Oh, my! What a lovely father you had, Siân. So open and generous. I flung my arms around his neck and gave him my best hug. And one for Mrs. Fuller, too.

———

When they had gone, Dad asked me what I knew. I told him about my conclusions. He sighed.

"The State, eh? Well, it makes sense, Tania, but it's not the only explanation. I'm not sure I agree with Siân's rather gloomy prediction of her future, nor with this picture you have of a modern Stalinist state. I do see a government trying hard to prevent a return to the Troubles, and I think it has to protect people from certain realities that would tend to push our civilization a bit off the rails."

"And abducting Siân?"

"Not 'abducting.' Just taking her where she can be looked after, and guarded from the unstable elements in our society. Since the Troubles there are some very disturbed people in our land, who would certainly harm Siân if it became known she was a woman able to bear children. God knows, we need such women now."

I was going to contradict him further, but there was a hint of pleading in his voice, like he was saying, "I don't want to know."

I left it. "Okay, Dad. I'll reserve judgment. Let's wait and see."

I didn't have time to worry.

The next day, at school, I was summoned to see Miss James. When I entered the gym, she had Mrs. Philpott with her.

"It's a mess," Miss James began. "It's a bloody mess."

Yes, Mister Zog. A teacher swore. So I've put it down. I've decided I owe you a bit more honesty about what people say. Even if it's language I wouldn't use myself, you understand.

"We hope you can help us, dear," continued Mrs. Philpott. "It's most inconvenient, Miss Fuller leaving so precipitately."

"Getting herself pregnant, the silly cow," said Miss James, and seeing my hackles start to rise, continued. "Sorry, Miss Deeley, I know she was a friend of yours. But she's left us in an awkward position. No Portia. Unless . . ."

". . . unless you could take on the role, Miss Deeley."

A million and one thoughts must have gone through my head then, but top of the list, well ahead of "Yes-I'd-love-to," was . . . "What about Mrs. Golightly?"

"She knows we don't have a lot of choice," answered Miss James. "She'll go along."

"Under protest?"

"You could say that. But she'll keep out of the way. The head of the boys' school has made it clear that the play will go ahead, and Mrs. Golightly had better come up with a Portia, or else."

"Or else?"

"I won't go into details. It's county politics. Let's leave it at that."

"But can you do it, dear?" asked Mrs. Philpott. "It's only two weeks away."

"Yes, I can. I know the part of Portia as well as Siân did. I helped her rehearse."

"Good. I'll tell the costume team, and they can start altering Siân's outfits for you."

"Thank you. Oh, and Mrs. Philpott, what if I'd said no?"

"We had other possibilities for Portia. But you were first choice, Miss Deeley. You always were."

I left, feeling almost as good as when I first played bass for Mike and the Stands.

———

So for the first time I met my Bassanio. Actually, he approached me at the start of the next rehearsal.

"You're Tania, right? The new Portia?"

"Yes. And you are?"

"I'm Tim. Bassanio."

"Then we are lovers."

"In name alone, thou minx. Thou know'st the play."

He's quick.

"I do, and know these lovers do not kiss."

"There was a kiss—now cut—yet we could choose."

"Hold it! I give up. Was that chance, or did you mean to speak in iambic pentameter? If you did, I'm impressed."

He laughed. A nice laugh, not some awful bray.

"Pure fluke. Cross my heart."

"Okay, Tim. I believe you. Is this your first play?"

"No, but it's my first major part. Last year I was Snug, in *Midsummer Night's Dream*. I got to run around a lot, but said maybe ten lines."

"It's my first performance of any sort."

"And you're taking on Portia? Now it's my turn to be impressed."

———

And there was Jemima. Nerissa.

My maid-servant, my confidante, and . . . my helper.

She really is, it turns out. Just as I helped Siân with her lines, so Jemima is helping me move. I think I wrote earlier I was no great actress, well, I didn't really mean it. I had this idea that I actually would be a great actress when I got on stage. Sure, I can speak the lines, but I can't move my body properly.

Miss James called me out after our first scene.

"What's wrong, Tania?" she said. "You moved so well at the auditions. Now you look terrified. You're rooted to the spot and your arms are fluttering like dying sparrows. They should move gracefully, largely, positively. Big movements, don't let them wilt. Show her, Jemima."

So Jemima showed me what I was doing wrong, and what to do differently.

"But nobody really moves like that, Miss James."

"On stage, you do, and it looks normal, I promise you. If you move 'normally,' it looks weak, if you can even see it at all. Move big, and you'll command the stage. So move big, Tania."

Well, I gave it a try, but it didn't feel comfortable.

"Forget the people watching you, Tania," Miss James urged. "You are Portia. Noble, confident, rich. You could buy and sell this school ten times over with your father's inheritance."

"I know that, Miss James . . ."

"Yes, your mind knows it, Tania. I can hear it in your speech. But your body doesn't. Your body language is still timid. You don't feel you belong on stage, not yet, not deep down. You think somebody's going to call out 'fraud,' or some such. It's not going to happen, I promise you. So let's try again, from 'By my troth, Nerissa . . .'"

And then Jemima gave me an encouraging smile. Well, blow me . . .

Tim helped, too. When I came off after my scene with Nerissa, he said how he thought I'd improved.

"You're getting there, Tania."

"Uh, thanks."

"No, I mean it. You're going to be a great Portia."

"You're just saying that. . . ."

"No. You speak your lines well, and you're starting to move like you should. I'm really glad. We desperately needed a good Portia."

"Of course you did, when Siân left."

"No. Before that, we had a disaster looming. You know that. Siân just about knew her lines, but she couldn't deliver them like you just did, and she never really unfroze. You're already better than she ever would be."

I didn't say anything. After all, Siân was my best friend.

"Hey, Tania, what I'm trying to say is I'm glad it's you playing Portia. I heard about the auditions—Erica told me—and Mrs. Golightly's spite. I think we've got the right Portia now, and if there's anything I can do to help you, just say."

"Thanks, Tim. Till next time."

He hesitated, for a moment, as if he was going to kiss me, but thought better of it. Then he turned and I watched his retreating back, thinking how well he moved. A natural actor . . .

He's a cute boy.

Funny thing, Mister Zog. I just did a typo, and typed a "t" instead of a "y," and then I corrected it. But it made me think. Yes, he has. Very cute.

Do robots have Freudian slips?

Thursday, April 9, 2054

Gosh, this feels as bad as the first gig with Mike and the Stands. I feel completely churned up inside. I hope I can control it.

In Belmont is a lady richly left;
And she is fair, and, fairer than that word,
Of wondrous virtues: sometimes from her eyes
I did receive fair speechless messages:
Her name is Portia, nothing undervalued
To Cato's daughter, Brutus' Portia:
Nor is the wide world ignorant of her worth,

For the four winds blow in from every coast
Renowned suitors, and her sunny locks
Hang on her temples like a golden fleece;
Which makes her seat of Belmont Colchos' strand,
And many Jasons come in quest of her.
O my Antonio, had I but the means
To hold a rival place with one of them,
I have a mind presages me such thrift,
That I should questionless be fortunate!

There! It's time. Antonio laments how his own fortunes are at sea and the lights dim.

I'm on, and Nerissa is with me. The lights brighten, and we're in Belmont. Nerissa brushes my hair for a few moments.

By my troth, Nerissa, my little body is aweary of this great
  world.

My words seem to startle her, for she ceases her brushing, and chides me.

You would be, sweet madam, if your miseries were in the
  same abundance as your good fortunes are. . . .

But I chafe at the command of my poor, dead father, and the lottery he has devised to decide whom I shall wed. Worse yet: the dismal choice of posturing ninnies, dreadful bores, and hopeless buffoons that have descended on me, like wasps round a jam pot, hoping to gain my hand or my fortune. Am I without hope?

Do you not remember, lady, in your father's time, a Venetian,
  a scholar and a soldier, that came hither in company of
  the Marquis of Montferrat?

She's right.

Yes, yes, it was Bassanio; as I think, he was so called.

Perhaps there is hope, after all. . . .

Ah, but here's a servant, telling me that the Moroccan prince is about to pay me a call. Damn.

————

Curiouser and curiouser, cried Alice.

No, that's the wrong part, I know. I'm thinking of her meeting with the Caterpillar. "Who are *you?*" he asks, and then, "Explain yourself!" and poor Alice can't, "because I'm not myself, you see."

That's me: not myself. I stumble off stage, into the wings. I glance at Antonio and Shylock as they head past me in the opposite direction, taking their places for scene three. I'm not quite myself, though, and not quite Portia, either. I catch my reflection in the mirror, and a well-bred Venetian lady looks back at me, so perhaps I am Portia. I don't know.

I do know that I really don't want the Prince of Morocco to choose the casket with my portrait in it. I mean, I don't really know Khalid, but he's Tim's best friend at school, so I suppose he's all right. Anyway my heart really falters when I think he might choose *that* casket. I'm not sure I want to know which it is—my father never said—because I don't think I could stand it if I could see him about to choose it.

Tim, Khalid—shadow names. And there's another name. Tania. I know her, distantly, because she had an upset stomach, and was very worried about something, but I'm all right now, and she'll be fine. . . .

————

Time moves oddly, lurching. Morocco has gone, and so has the equally annoying Arragon. Gold and silver caskets have proven false, and lured them to a doom that, whatever it may be, will be far from me.

So now Bassanio is here, and my heart pitches wildly, storm-blown by hope and buffeted by fear. If he chooses lead ... oh, how my heart will leap, but then, why would he choose lead? Surely he will choose gold, or silver, and I will be lost. I reach my hand and touch his arm. . . .

I pray you, tarry: pause a day or two
Before you hazard; for, in choosing wrong,
I lose your company: therefore forbear awhile.
There's something tells me, but it is not love . . .

But I think it must be, really. My hand lingers upon his arm, longer than a casual touch should be, while I attempt to stanch the flow of time, bleeding away toward the moment he will make his choice.

He is so near, and I fear lest he never come near again.

Now he strides from me, and I have nothing save a fading warmth in my fingertips—unless he chooses lead. I stand mute, bound by my father's will to say nothing, though I am consumed by an agony of anticipation.

Therefore, thou gaudy gold,
Hard food for Midas, I will none of thee;
Nor none of thee, thou pale and common drudge
'Tween man and man: but thou, thou meagre lead,
Which rather threatenest than dost promise aught,
Thy paleness moves me more than eloquence;
And here choose I; joy be the consequence!

Yes! Yes! He's done it, and "fair Portia's counterfeit" looks back at him from the casket of lead. And I must endure the presence of these others, Nerissa and Gratiano, daintily announcing my love for Bassanio to the world, while within I am battered by gales of unaccustomed emotions. I must master myself. . . .

Time jumps again, and now I stand in a court of law, dressed as a man, a lawyer, and preparing to spring the trap I have laid for the vengeful Jew Shylock. Ask him for mercy—ah, he will not offer it, but demands justice, and now I will give it to him.

————

I sense an ending is close. . . .

> It is almost morning,
> And yet I am sure you are not satisfied
> Of these events at full. Let us go in;
> And charge us there upon inter'gatories,
> And we will answer all things faithfully.

Gratiano makes brief reply, and then . . .

Applause.

And I am Tania once more, though Portia still walks the shadows nearby, closer than a dream.

It is my turn now—I face the wings opposite and there stands Tim, Bassanio's ghost at his shoulder. We spring toward each other, touch hands, and turn to face the audience and bow, braced against the tide of applause.

Only Simon—Shylock—left to come on now and take his own due praise. He's played his own part well enough.

But did he live it, as I just did?

The curtain falls and we are done.

Tania turns to Tim and says, "Thank you," and Portia kisses Bassanio with a deeper passion than Tania knows.

Yow! Where did that come from?

I feel myself blushing, and Tim is looking surprised, and shocked. Though I think he enjoyed it, too—there's a little glint in his eye. Oops! I remove Portia's hand from Bassanio's very cute bottom.

"Er, that was from Portia, for Bassanio. She's been wanting to do that—the kiss—for a while, but the play got in the way rather."

"Riiight. Well, Bassanio's still here, and feels the same way. . . ."

So we kiss again, but it's not a success, because Portia is starting to fade and we're in the middle of a crowd, and they're making some very immature remarks about us, and anyway, here's Mrs. Philpott coming up on stage to make a well-done-everybody speech. . . .

———

What am I going to do, Mister Zog?

I mean, after the play, it all got quite hectic. John was there, waiting to say congratulations, and I'd got out of my costume, so Portia was out of sight and out of mind, but John kissed me "well done" and it wasn't the same, but then he had to go back to London, and then Tim found me and wanted me to go to the post-play party, and he kissed me, too, and that wasn't the same, either, and I didn't go to the party, but came back home instead with Dad.

I need to use more full stops. Sorry, Mister Zog, but by now you should be used to reading my drivel. Here you are anyway. . . .

Right, those were your full stops.

I need to see Tim again.

No, correction. Portia needs to see Bassanio again. And that's got nothing to do with Tania or John.

So why do I feel bad?

Friday, April 17, 2054

So where did the year go?

The exams are done, the play is done.

And I'm fifteen and three-quarters, the way toddlers say it, when every month matters. Each one does—time is running out. I must use every second that remains to me. Experience as much as I can, before . . .

What?

I'm seeing Tim. By which I mean that Portia and Bassanio are seeing each other. And Tania is still seeing John. Is that bad? I like them both, in different ways. You see, I can talk to Tim about literature, and I can't do that with John. He's a bit of an *engineer*, you see. He reads books, but incredibly fast. I don't see how he can enjoy them, at that speed. And Tim has a blind spot about music, so I need both of them, for different reasons. I'm not being unfair to them, am I? I mean, it's not like we're human, and we'd be agonizing over sex, and who was sleeping with whom. Robots don't do that gucky stuff.

I mean, we could, if we wanted to. I remember Doctor Markov telling me that robots could have sex, but we aren't built to enjoy it. I suppose one day I may try it anyway, but it's not at the top of my list, and I don't think I'll be bothered if I don't manage to squeeze it into the next two years and three months.

We enjoy physical contact, of course. That's built in, so our parents can hug us and make us feel safe and bond with us as we grow up, and so we can respond properly. Our skin is as sensitive as human skin, so I can enjoy, for example, a hug from Dad, or John or . . . Tim . . . or anyone else. So when Tim runs his hand down my arm, or my leg, even, it feels nice. That's Portia's arm or leg, of course, that she shares with me, so I get to enjoy it, too.

But that's all. Every square inch of skin is the same as any other. The only exceptions are my fingertips and my lips, which is the same for humans, I think. So I can play bass, and I can kiss, and I do both. Frequently. But those breasts and hips, that Dad was so worried about, and Doctor Thompson spent so much design time getting just right, are actually completely ordinary patches of skin, for me. Built to look at, not to touch.

Er, I just thought you ought to know.

Mike met me at Marylebone Station. He was dressed in black leather, as usual.

"I'm glad you could come."

I shook the hand he offered me, and leaned forward to give him a little peck on the cheek.

"I'm glad you asked me. They were fine about it at school. Where do we go from here?"

"It's a short taxi ride."

It was odd, seeing Mike like this. I mean, normally we met for rehearsals and gigs. But this . . .

His call had been quite unexpected, but as soon as he asked, I had no hesitation. Of course I would come—how could I not?

So we settled into the back of a black cab, and Mike gave the destination, and off we went.

I didn't really know what to say, and Mike had wrapped himself in silence, which wasn't too surprising. There wasn't much traffic, by London standards, and we made decent progress. But I could see the meter ticking up the total, and it seemed a lot of money to me.

"Couldn't we have got the Tube? It'd be cheaper."

Mike looked up, surprised that I had spoken.

"I suppose so, but I didn't want to do that. It would just have taken a bit of track maintenance, and we'd be late."

That was true enough. When I'd been to visit John, the Tube had frequently been diabolical. We couldn't take that risk. But it still seemed a lot of money.

But then as we found ourselves in a Yellow Zone London suburb, the taxi suddenly turned left, beneath a half-timbered gateway, and up a driveway, bringing us to a small chapel.

We were there.

"There" was the Hendon Crematorium. As we stepped out,

the other mourners looked up, and nodded acknowledgment. Two I recognized.

Gary and Gus. The Stands.

Amanda would be along soon.

The other mourners were few. Her boss at the TeraNet programming company. A couple of colleagues. And there was a priest, a wizened old chap who must have been seventy.

We'd just about arrived on the dot, because a long black car appeared at the gate, just as Mike paid off the taxi and it left.

Amanda was here.

The priest motioned us to move inside, where we found ourselves pews. Basically it was Mike and the Stands, and me, at the front on the right. The TeraNet folks took up the adjacent pew on the left.

We sang "Dear Lord and Father of Mankind." When we came to the verse . . .

Drop Thy still dews of quietness,
Till all our strivings cease;
Take from our souls the strain and stress,
And let our ordered lives confess
The beauty of Thy peace,
The beauty of Thy peace.

. . . I cried, and I could only just get the words out.

Did Amanda feel the quietness, the peace? Was she free from strain and stress, up there, in that cheap-looking, simple box? With God, at peace, Dad would have said. The box is full of what she no longer has any use for. Burn it and forget it.

It was like Mum all over again.

No.

It wasn't. Somehow I found I could bear it. Not because she wasn't my mum. I knew I would miss her, the woman who'd inspired me to play bass, and had mentored me. But she'd given me something of herself. She'd put down the torch, and I'd picked it up again. I suppose that was true of Mum, too, though it's taken longer for me to see it.

Nobody truly dies who shapes another person. Does that make sense, Mister Zog?

So when the coffin lurched on its rollers and disappeared from our view, I didn't cry anymore, but I held on tight to the little piece of Amanda in me, and whispered, "You're safe," and felt a tiny glow, from Amanda and from Mum.

I felt a little guilty that I'd never been to see Amanda after she'd fallen ill, and I said so to Mike at the pub after the funeral.

"I did visit her once," he confided, "but she'd lost her hair through the chemo, and she wasn't pleased to see me. She told me to sod off and not come back till she was better. She said she appreciated your e-mails, though."

"I sent her a few extracts from my diary."

"Yeah. She said they made her laugh and cry, but she never said why."

"Oh."

"Anyway, she said you could keep her gear. A kind of thank-you for writing to her."

"That's thoughtful. What about her family, though? Don't they have a say?"

"What family? Did you see any family here today? She was pretty much alone in the world. No partner, even. You saw her 'family' today. Three guys from her work, and us, the band. So take the gear, and use it, and we won't tell. Everything else she owned just goes to the government, and what would they do with a lovely bass rig like hers?"

That seemed fair enough. Thank you, Amanda, if you can hear me.

Good-bye.

"She was pretty much alone in the world."

As are we, Tania. Alone in the universe, with no other species to talk to. No one with whom to share the wonder of being a polysensorially diverse, slimy-tentacled alien.

We are still looking, looking for that other life form. In the Pyramid Planets there are signs of a race that has been and gone, leaving ruins beneath a hundred million years of dust. We missed them by a time that seems so short, measured by the scale of the universe.

And at the opposite end of the spectrum there are nursery planets, like one we found in the Pleiades, where conditions may one day produce life. For such, we are probably some millions of years too early. There were certainly some interesting amino aggregates in the organic soup, but nothing I could put hand on heart and say yes, that's life. At the time I promised myself, if I remember, I'd stop by again.

Many Erasures later, I did go back, to the soup planet. The People there were earnestly debating whether to nudge things along a bit. It is delicate, to interfere or not to interfere. We tried it elsewhere, and failed, terribly; the soup changed, but not as we hoped.

It is so lonely, and within me there is an ache that the empty stars cannot heal.

John's not talking to me. I mentioned that I'd been out for a drink with Tim, and he went icy on me. Froze me out.

That's so unfair.

John, you live in Wood Green, for heaven's sake. We talk all the time over the TeraNet, but I hardly see you, just because of the distance.

So now what am I going to do? Call Tim? No. He's part of the problem. I wish I could call Siân. But I've no idea where she is, these days. I know she must be starting to get big, and I wish I could be there with her. I'd have talked with her, held her hand. Helped her, somehow.

So who's left?

Kieran? I don't think so. Maths boy.

Mike, or Gus or Gary? No.

Jemima? No way . . . well . . . maybe.

"Hello, Doctor Markov."

"Hello, Miss Deeley. How are you feeling?"

"I hurt a lot. And I feel really foolish."

He chuckled.

"Bloody stupid would be the phrase I'd use. But don't worry. Don't you remember Milton's words? 'What does not destroy me makes me strong.' Or something to that effect."

"Easy for you to say. You didn't have a pan full of fat blow up in your face. Milton said that?"

"He did. *Samson Agonistes.* So what happened to you? An accident at home, I gather from your notes."

"Yes. I was making chips for me and Dad, and I added some fat to the pan. Except it was water, and it blew up. I had a moment when I started to pour, thinking the liquid didn't pour like fat, and I just had time to start to get my arms up in front of my face."

"You're a lucky girl. That was a pretty stupid thing to do."

So saying, he took my hand in his, and turned it around, examining carefully. I didn't really want to discuss my stupidity anymore, and looked for something to deflect his attention.

"Have you been on holiday, Doctor Markov?"

"No," he answered, somewhat absently. "Why do you ask?"

"It's your skin. I remember how pale you looked, the first time I met you. But looking at you now, holding my hand in yours, I'd say you're every bit as dark as I am."

He looked flustered and I could see the shutters going down in his mind.

"I've, er, been out in the sun. Doing some gardening."

But he hadn't. His skin was truly as dark as mine, and you don't get that color just gardening in England. And definitely not with the weather we'd been having recently. Again, I seemed to have found something Doctor Markov wasn't being honest about with me. No use prying now his guard was up. Better to let him think he'd deceived me; I made a mental note to myself to give it some thinking time later.

In the meantime, I was due for a bit of painful repair work. As he turned my hand around, my ruined skin sent searing reminders of my foolishness.

"Ow!" I yelled, after one particularly agonizing touch. "Can't you just turn off the pain? Take my brain out, if you have to."

He laughed sharply, but refused, saying, "No, because your reaction tells me where the damage is, and how severe it is. And no, because taking your brain out is something we don't do lightly— usually just for upgrades. And no, because pain is the universe's way of trying to teach you not to be so bloody stupid next time."

So we were back to "(bloody) stupid Tania" again. He went on.

"What you have to remember, Miss Deeley, is that the universe is trying to kill you, all the time. It doesn't try very hard, usually, but it doesn't have to, because stupid people are easy for it to kill. They let their guard down, and blam! Score one for the universe."

"That's a very bleak philosophy, Doctor Markov."

"Maybe, but it works. But Mr. Oxted made robots weak and able to feel pain, to help them cope in the universe. I think he was wise, so for your own good, Miss Deeley, I'm not going to turn your brain off. Okay?"

"Ouch! Yes."

––––––––

In the end, they did turn my brain off. There was quite a bit of skin damage, and I needed considerable surgery to put everything right. So yet again I woke up in a Banbury recovery room; this time looking at myself in the mirror to make sure I was exactly the same, rather than enjoying how different I'd become.

Dad collected me, and I don't think he could believe his eyes.

"I was so scared, Tania. You were screaming with pain and fear, and you were a mess. Everything was burned and blistered. I didn't know if you were going to die, or be scarred for life, or what."

"They fixed me up good, though, didn't they?"

"Yes, they did. Everything's the same as it was."

"Nearly. There are weaknesses in the repair, so Doctor Markov wants me to come back at the end of the summer, for my final upgrade."

"Your final upgrade . . ."

"Yes. He thinks it'll be the last. I'll finish growing up."

"Of course. It was the word 'final' that jarred. It reminded me that I don't want to lose you, Tania."

He paused.

"I can feel the time drawing to a close, Tania. I thought I'd have Nettie with me when it happened, when the time came to . . . send you back. But I'm going to be alone. I don't know how I'll bear it."

"Don't. Don't spoil it, Dad."

"Dammit, it's not fair. Here you are, growing up, ready to take on adult life, and they take it away. I won't let them."

"You have no choice, Dad. You've seen what happens to those who won't accept it. Can't you name a dozen couples in the parish who've done stupid stuff, when the time draws near? I don't want you to . . . go off the rails."

"We'll do something. I have to. I'm a fighter, you know."

Saturday, August 1, 2054

There's a side of Tim I find difficult.

We went out for a belated birthday meal, just the two of us. We decided to go for Thai—there's a lovely restaurant in Beaconsfield just a few miles down the road, where Mum and Dad went occasionally. Used to go.

The décor is all dark wood and deep reds—it looks really expensive—and the food is really tasty. We'd dressed up our best, of course. Tim was in a suit. No tie, though, just an open-necked shirt. I was wearing my favorite colors—black and silver-gray—a matching skirt and blouse. I'd put on a silver chain that used to be Mum's, and left the blouse open at the neck so you could see the pendant, a silver locket that Mum had told me had been given to her by her own mother, going back to Great-Aunt Jane and maybe further back than that.

Anyway, Tim seemed to like it. At least, he spent a good portion of the meal looking at the pendant nestled in my cleavage.

Honestly, Mister Zog, I didn't mind. A girl likes to be looked at. It's part of the game that we play. It's why I'm saving up for a black leather catsuit to wear on stage. I want to look good, and I want the boys to enjoy what they see.

Desserts came and went, and coffees. We went Dutch on the bill, which Tim made a fuss about, but I think he was probably glad. At seventeen—did I say that he was a year older, about the same age as John?—we don't have a lot of money.

So we stood up to go, and Tim helped me on with my jacket, and as he did, he let his hand rest on my breast. It was just a brief touch, and I ignored it. If it was deliberate, it wasn't worth getting annoyed about.

So we walked to the bus stop, and I let him hold my hand. Sometimes there are some rowdy types there, but mostly if you're a couple they leave you alone.

Fortunately the bus stop was deserted, so we had some time to kill, before the bus came. Tim was silent for a while, then I heard a deep intake of breath. Here it comes, I thought.

"Tania . . ."

"Yes?"

"You know, I couldn't help noticing in the restaurant that you were wearing a rather nice silver locket. It looks antique. Is it a family heirloom?"

"Yes. It was Mum's." And I explained what I knew about how it had been passed down, while wondering where this was going. Well, no. I thought I had a good idea what was going on in Tim's mind, but I was intrigued by the song and dance along the way. Like I said, it's part of the game we play. It was fine, so long as it didn't suddenly turn too serious.

"Really? I'd love to have a closer look. Do you mind?"

"The light's terrible here; let me take it off so you can see it in the light."

"No, no. No need. I can see fine. Just turn around a bit."

And before I could say anything, he was practically on top of me, the back of his right hand resting on my breastbone, and cradling the locket. I stepped back, but his hand followed, and then my back was against the bus shelter. Ouch!

"Mmm, nice," he murmured, ambiguously.

And he turned the locket over, and turned it back, and passed it from hand to hand, and stroked it, and yes, the stroking didn't stop at the locket.

So I lifted his hand away, as gently as I could, and fortunately he didn't resist.

"No, Tim. That's not part of the evening."

He looked crestfallen, but not too surprised. His shoulders drooped.

"What did I do wrong?"

"It's nothing you've done, Tim. It's just not something I want. Not with anybody."

"Why?"

I was saved from answering by the arrival of the bus, a single-decker. Which was a relief. With the driver's eye on us I'd feel safer.

As the bus moved off, we lurched to an empty part of the bus, near the back, as it happened, in courting couple territory. I couldn't help that—it was the only part of the bus where we wouldn't be overheard. I owed Tim an explanation, I'd decided.

"Look, Tim, I'm sorry if I pushed you away just now, or hurt you, but I'm not looking for that kind of a relationship. I hope nothing I've ever said or done has given you a different impression."

At which he looked very annoyed.

"Well, actually you did. Specifically, there was the time we kissed after the play. I remember vividly how you started to get very familiar. Or had you forgotten?"

There was a bitter edge to his voice, angry that I'd apparently led him on. So I explained.

"Oh. That was different. That was Portia. Or had you forgotten I'd said that?" It sounded lame, even as I said it.

"I didn't think you meant that. I felt the passion in your embrace, and your words just didn't match. So I reckoned that the words were just for show, because I know John was nearby, and you had to pretend, so he wouldn't cotton on to what was going on between us."

"No, Tim. There's no 'us.' I want you to understand that I truly was a different person on the stage, and that person—Portia—loved *Bassanio* passionately. But the play's over now, and you're plain Tim, and I'm even plainer Tania."

"I don't believe you. Anyway, you could wake Portia if you wanted to. She's not dead, she's sleeping inside you, and she wants to come out. Bassanio's missing her. . . ."

Was he right? For a moment it sounded plausible, and I felt as though if I called her, Portia would come.

"No."

"No? She's not sleeping? Or no, you won't let her wake?"

"Just no. This is Tania you're dealing with, and Tania doesn't want sex with you or anybody."

"So you'll die a virgin? Is that what you want?"

"Die a virgin? What a strange idea. Is that what you're worried about, Tim? For yourself, I mean . . ."

And that was it. That was the key to his fear. He was desperate for sex, terrified of going into the unknown—as he saw it—unfulfilled. His fears poured out . . .

"All the girls I've known, they cluster together and giggle, and they're never alone. So I've never even had a chance to ask someone. And now I've finally asked someone and you've said no. That's it. The end. Because there's no more time."

"What do you mean, no more time?"

"I'm seventeen, Tania. I've got weeks, maybe, just weeks. Do you think they always wait till your eighteenth birthday? They come any time. . . ."

"But they can't. The contract is until age eighteen. I read it."

"Then you didn't read carefully enough. The stuff on the Tera-Net isn't what's in the contract. It states 'not exceeding the eighteenth year,' and 'early termination at the discretion of the company,' and 'in the event of early termination, a pro-rata refund of fees paid.' They can surprise you, and give you your own money back to keep you quiet."

"Hang on. Dad showed me our contract, and there's nothing like that in it."

"Did you read the upgrade contracts? About five years ago these clauses started appearing."

I fell silent. He might well be right. I'd not read the more recent contracts. I wondered why I'd heard nothing about it, but then I remembered the blitzed sites on the TeraNet. Somebody who understood electronic media very well was very much in control of the TeraNet. That sort of thing might not leak out.

My birthday meal was sour in my stomach. My two years had suddenly shrunk to one, or maybe less.

Sunday, August 2, 2054

So what do I want to accomplish in the months that remain to me?
    Sex?

I don't think so. Certainly not with Tim. The rest of the bus journey had been a dream. I was just completely shocked. I think Tim put his arm around me, but it felt like it was happening to someone else. After the bus ride, at the gate I didn't give him a chance to kiss me. As my feet crunched down the gravel path, I heard his final words to me: "Hey, Tania, if you change your mind . . ."

When I had a moment by myself to ponder, I wondered if he'd made the whole thing up, just to trick me into having sex with him. The jerk.

236

But I've checked, and it's true. Which brings me back to the question:

What do I want to accomplish in the months that remain to me?

There are a hundred books I want to read, and more. The thoughts of the greatest minds in history, each adding to the sum of knowledge of what it means to be human. I want to understand how I'm different. If I am. To paraphrase Shylock:

I am a Robot. Hath not a Robot eyes? hath not a Robot
hands, organs, dimensions, senses, affections, passions? fed
with the same food, hurt with the same weapons, subject to
the same diseases, healed by the same means, warmed and
cooled by the same winter and summer, as a Christian is?
If you prick us, do we not bleed? If you tickle us, do we not
laugh? If you poison us, do we not die?

(Just a shame he mentioned diseases. Apart from that, it fits rather well.)

So yes, I want to read the great books and poems of the world, starting with the Great War Poets—Wilfred Owen, Rupert Brooke—who lived their lives at the edge of death, but who never let the fear of it stop their urge to create. I need to understand them first, find their strength, or else I might as well give up now.

Art, in all its forms, that distinguishes the human from the beast. Music, sculpture, painting. Even comic books.

Humor and psychology.

Love and hate.

All the built-in opposites of mankind.

And yes, I want to gig again with Mike and the Stands. I will buy that catsuit, and I will pull the zipper down as low as I dare, and then let the boys' eyes pop out.

I want to solve those problems, too. My little list, minus the crossings-out.

What happens to robots when they grow up?

~~*Why does Mrs. Hanson have a photograph of a handsome Zulu warrior—her husband?—in the classroom?*~~

Why aren't there any young teachers?

What lies in the heart of Africa, beyond the Kimberley Corridor?

~~*Why hasn't John called me?*~~

~~*Is Jemima (or Myra) a robot or human?*~~

~~*For that matter, how many of the girls who'd been bullying me today were robots? And did they know it, or did they think they were human, as I'd done?*~~

Do robots live forever? If so, could I live forever? Did I want to live forever?

~~*Was Siân really human? If she's just a robot, why am I helping her learn French?*~~

How many humans are there now? Are there any humans still being born?

And the new ones I'd added . . .

Why didn't Doctor Markov want to talk about Christiana?

Where did Doctor Markov get his tan in a wet English summer?

<u>**Friday, August 28, 2054**</u>

It's almost routine, now.

My final upgrade. I've kept the slightly darker skin tone. I'm a couple of inches taller and I've added a bit about the thighs, hips, and breasts—not a lot, but a good excuse for a minor wardrobe update. No real changes or redesigns—that was all decided at the last upgrade.

Not even an overnight stay; it was just in and out—Dad called it an "outpatient visit." No messing around with that calibration nonsense, even.

If it hadn't been for the accident, and the chance to switch to "production quality" skin—Dr. Markov's words—I'm not sure I'd have bothered.

I liked the old me. The new me is pretty much the same.

"Meet the new boss, same as the old boss."

A song for every situation.

I decided to give Tim a call, to see if he was all right. Not, absolutely not because I'd changed my mind. Apart from his obsession with sex, he's actually a nice guy. I can talk to him, and he can even talk back, which is better than most of the XY-programmed.

What is it with boys? Is sex that important to them? Is Tim typical? There's a thought.

Whoa! Here's another. Am I a typical girl? In my . . . programming, that is.

I like boys, Mister Zog. I can't help it. They're similar enough to girls to be acceptable. Different enough to be intriguing. Complementary to one another, in mind and body, if you want to get all analytical about it, which sometimes I do. Analytical, schmytical, but I'm happy with my mind and with my body, too. But that doesn't mean I want sex. Certainly not just so Tim can go into the unknown having exercised all his programming.

But, like I said, I liked Tim enough to be concerned that he might be suffering. So I gave him a call.

No answer.

I tried a few times. Still no answer.

So after school I took a bus to where I thought Tim lived. I could see a few lights on in the house, so I plucked up my courage and knocked on the door.

No answer. I knocked again.

Eventually I heard footsteps, and then the door was opened.

"What do you want?"

The voice was tired and broken. Resentful of my interruption, but too worn down to slam the door in my face.

"Hello, are you Mr. Price? Look, I'm sorry if I've called at a bad time. . . . Er, my name's Tania Deeley, and I'm a friend of Tim's. I wanted to see if he's all . . . I wanted to see him."

No answer.

"Er, I am at the right house, aren't I? Tim does live here?"

"It was the right house. But you're too late. Tim's not here anymore."

"But . . . he didn't say anything about going away. . . ."

And as I said it, I realized that actually he had.

"Oh, my! I'm really sorry. I have come at a bad time, haven't I?"

"Yes. I suppose you meant well, but I think you'd better leave."

And that was that. I was dismissed. The door closed.

Tuesday, October 27, 2054

"There's a lawyer I've found, Tania. A solicitor, I should say. He'll take on the case."

"What case, Dad?"

It was just an ordinary day. Well, no, it was October, just a few days short of the anniversary of Mum's death. Anyway, it was breakfast time, and Dad had the post open.

"Our case. Your case. Against Oxted."

"Eh? Why do I want to take on Oxted?"

"We have to break the contract, Tania. Prove that it's unfair, unlawful or whatever. I want to keep you, Tania. You deserve life."

He waved the letter at me. "Finally, as I was saying, I've found a solicitor who'll take on the case."

"Finally? How long have you been trying? How many have you approached?"

"Three months. Maybe twenty solicitors in that time. They've all refused, till now. Don't waste your money, they told me."

"And now you've found someone who will? What's he charging?"

"That doesn't matter. He's prepared to do it."

"Dad. Please don't. I have a really bad feeling about this."

I do. Does Dad think we're the first family to try to find a way out of these contracts? Dozens, hundreds, thousands of times it must have been tried. And maybe one or two were successful, but then the loopholes would be closed a little tighter. And tighter.

The day I learned Tim had disappeared I called John. I'd not spoken to him since . . . well, not long after the play. We'd had a row, because I'd mentioned I'd been out with Tim, and he got all green-eyed jealous about it. I mean, he pretended to be all mature about it at first, but then I said he didn't own me, and he said, no, I belonged to Oxted and they were welcome to me, and it all got rather nasty at that point.

But now with Dad planning I don't know what legal stupidity, I needed to talk to a friend, and with Siân gone, and Tim gone, the choice was rather small.

So I called John. And got a blocked signal from his AllInFone. Well, technically it was a number unobtainable, but since there's no possibility of error when calling someone's PTI, it means he'd set up his account to refuse all calls from me. It deliberately uses the same error code as not being able to find the target.

Damn you, John Czern.

So I rummaged around and found Kieran's PTI instead, and got through.

I got a really frosty reception. Yes, he was still in touch with John. No. If John didn't want to speak to me, that was John's business, and he wouldn't go against that.

"What about the band, Kieran?"

"A bit late to think of that, Tania. If you hadn't gone off with the Stands, we'd still be together. You wrecked the band because it suited your plans. Now you want to put it back together, because you've got some new plans, no doubt."

Ha! Me, wreck the band? Kieran and Siân had had a pretty good go at wrecking it themselves, getting Siân knocked up. At one of my gigs, I should add.

But I bit back my reply, and said, as charmingly as I could, "No plans, Kieran. I'd like to talk to him, but I have to trust you to tell him, when you judge the time is right. Is that all right?"

There was a long pause, before he answered, "I suppose so."

"Thank you, Kieran. I'd better let you go. I'm sure you've got some fun maths to get back to."

"What? No, don't go!"

"What is it, Kieran?"

"It's Siân. I can't get in touch with her. It's like she's vanished off the face of the earth. Her parents just told me she'd gone away and broke the call. What's going on? Have you seen her?"

"I've not seen her for a while, Kieran, but I'm sure she's being well looked after."

"Are you just saying that, or do you know something?"

"I've told you what I can."

"But you know more, don't you?"

"I've told you what I can. Leave it."

I wondered if he would leave it. But almost as I said the words, his eyes narrowed, and a calculating look came into his eyes. I could see it on the screen, as clearly as if he were standing in front of me. He said, "Tell me, and I'll speak to John for you."

Ah! He knew he had me. Or maybe I had him. We each had something the other wanted. So I told him what the government didn't want him to know.

It's funny—strange—but she'd not told Kieran anything of what she'd told me. About the testing, about her probable "career" as a Mother. So maybe I didn't tell him the best way, because he didn't react with joy at his possible fatherhood.

"She *used* me, the bitch! She wanted a child, and I was convenient. She didn't ask, she just seduced me."

You'd have thought he'd have been pleased. Most boys would have given their right arm for a chance to have sex with Siân.

"No, Kieran, no. Please don't be mad at Siân. Think what her life is going to be like. She'll never have another choice again. Not like that, I mean. Yes, she'll be pampered and looked after, till the day she dies. No harm will come to her, because she'll be guarded, night and day. But she'll be a total prisoner. No meaningful choices, ever again. Not one."

"She didn't tell me, though."

"Would you have said yes?"

"Maybe. Yes, of course. No! Well, I suppose so. Probably. She should have asked."

"Sometimes choice works like that. One person's choice is another's loss of choice."

That was deep. Where did that come from?

"But . . ."

"Kieran, she chose you. Be content. Be honored."

That seemed to help—his anger subsided, and he mumbled his excuses, and broke the connection.

"Tell John I want to talk to him," I called. But the screen was dead before I finished my sentence.

Saturday, November 6, 2054

Over two weeks since my appeal to Kieran. Nothing.

Dad was wrapped up in I don't know what. Actually, I suspect it was his planning. He's been sending messages to this solicitor, I'm pretty sure. I can't worry about that now, though. I need someone to talk to. I need John.

"I'm just popping down to the corner shop, Dad. I'll see you around six."

"Okay."

And it's only 9 A.M. Dad is so distracted.

I'm off to the corner shop, I told him. John's corner shop. So I didn't tell a lie.

The journey is tedious, but my heart is beating wildly all the way. Oh, you know I'm not being literal, Mister Zog. Yes, I'm nervous, in my quaint, neurotronic way.

It's all right. Thank God.

There were some awkward moments when I walked into the shop. Mr. Czern was fine, and so was Mrs. Czern, but when they told John who'd come to see him, he wouldn't come out of his room.

So I went up and sat outside his room, and spoke to him through the door. I spoke in a calm and dignified way, adult to adult. I told him that I'd come to see my dear friend, John, and I hoped that if there were any barrier between us, it would be broken down, and any rifts healed.

I did not cry. I did not sob deeply. I absolutely no way definitely did not lose my rag even in the slightest and yell at him you heartless peasant why won't you talk to me I still love you.

That's what did it. John could never resist a row. Next thing he was calling me a selfish bitch for wrecking the band, and so I yelled something back at him to help clear the air a bit—something about challenging him to come out to my side of the door to say that and him finding a guitar rammed up where the tuning pegs would do most damage. Or so I recall.

After a couple of exchanges like that we really got going, and the door was getting in the way a bit, so John thoughtfully came out so we could yell at each other properly.

Then he called me a bitch. Again.

So I reached out my hand to his mouth, and gently put my finger to his lips.

"Time to stop, John. You're repeating yourself."

"Bitch." He sneered.

So I kissed him.

Actually, I think I may have let Portia kiss him. She's better at these things. Anyway, it seemed to do the trick. At least he stopped calling me names.

And he kissed me back, and I let his hands wander a bit, but that was all right, that was something I'd been meaning to get around to again for quite a while, and never mind what I'd told Tim. Maybe I did feel the clock ticking for myself, but mostly I just wanted to.

After a while, though, we were distinctly not swept away on a tide of passion, unfortunately, just as Doctor Markov had warned, and we found ourselves at a bit of a loose end, wondering what to do, since falling into bed with each other was a nonstarter.

"Well, now you're here, would you like some tea?" John asked.

"What a lovely idea."

John's parents, of course, behaved as if they'd not heard a sound and we'd just walked in after a walk in the park. Perhaps there was a little strain, but John and I were clearly good friends now—we'd come downstairs hand in hand and I'd carefully left a faint trace of lipstick on John's cheek.

So we had tea together, and then we did go for a walk together—John took me round Alexandra Park—and somewhere along the way we spoke about getting the band together again and how John had written a new song, but he needed some better lyrics and I said I'd have a go.

We were on a high hill, just below the Palace—Ally Pally, he called it. We could look out over the whole of London, imagining it as it must have been in its heyday. Where were the crowds now? I asked.

"They'll be back," he answered.

"Do you believe that?"

"No. Not really. Nobody has a clue why there are so few

humans being born, have they? In fifty years, there'll be just a handful of humans left. Each one waited on by a dozen Soameses. And fifty years after that, the last humans will be gone. Leaving just the Soameses."

"And one of those Soameses will be me, and another one will be you, but we'll have forgotten that we were ever John and Tania."

"Is that what you think, Tania?"

"It's the only solution that makes sense. The last humans won't need child surrogates, just servants. So our brains get re-used as Soameses."

"I'm not sure that's any better than being broken up for scrap. . . ."

It was a conversation-killer. We sat in silence for a long time, John with his arm around me, as if to protect me from a fate that neither of us could avoid.

"I'm sorry I called you a bitch, Tania. And all the other things, too."

"Yeah. Forgiven. You forgive me, too?"

"I suppose so."

"John . . ."

"Yes?"

"Are you going to run away? When the time comes to go back to Oxted?"

"I should. What was that letter you read, at your mum's funeral?" It came easy to me.

Live each moment to the full, therefore, squeezing out its value, its richness and its flavor. And then fight for the next moment, and the one after it, too. Life is good, and should not ever be yielded lightly, nor should it be spent fruitlessly.

"Yeah, Tania, that's the one. Your mum was right. I will fight for this moment and the next, and every one that follows."

"If you do run away, where will you go?"

"I don't know. The wildernesses? Maybe . . . But maybe it's easier to hide in a crowd. Stay in London. Would you come with me?"

That was the question I feared.

"Maybe. I'd want to bring my books."

"Books? You'd flee for your life, but take your library? Electronic good enough, or would you take paper?"

"Yes, John, paper, if I could. I need to understand . . ."

"Understand what? That books are heavy and will slow you down?"

"I'm reading the Great War poets, John. They were closer every day to death than we are. They have something to say to us. I can nearly understand it. It's so close, but I know I'll do it. Maybe reading a paper book, like they had, will help. And then I want to say it in my own words. I fear death, John, whatever death might be for our kind. I think I have to learn to not fear it. That's why I only said maybe, when you asked if I would run away, too."

"So you'd rather die, just so you know you can face death without fear? Raven, you're mad."

"As mad as you, Ginger Mop. But is that human mad or robot mad?"

I don't think everything we said to each other made sense.

John asked me: "So if you don't run away with me, what will you do?"

"My dad wants to fight them in the courts."

"And you think that's more sensible than running away? What's his idea?"

"I don't know. He seems to have found a solicitor who will fight the case for him and that's all he'll tell me."

I shivered.

"Are you cold? We should get back."

"I'll just stop and say good-bye to your folks, John. Then I need to get back home."

When I got back home, Dad was asleep in the study, papers strewn about him. Letters and whatnot from the solicitor? I risked a quick look. Just his sermon, I realized. Sunday tomorrow, of course.

And there was a message from John. Simple enough. Let me know you've got home safely. But the real message was that his PTI was unblocked to me once more.

We were back together again.

Wednesday, December 9, 2054

You wrapped me in your coils
And you tried to suck me dry
I'm not your drossy spoils
But did you ever wonder why

There was a real live girl in here
Complete with soul and broken heart
I never was your clockwork toy
You wind up just to play a part

Your coils of love
Still bind me tight
Your velvet glove
Conceals the night

I'd been playing it—the version we'd recorded in the music shop in Denmark Street—and I'd been singing along. And I was thinking, your voice isn't bad, Tania Deeley. It wasn't a great leap from there to well, maybe *I* could sing with the band. Kieran and John were both available.

And a small step from there to giving John a call.

And he'd grunted, and warned me that Kieran might be difficult.

And a bigger step while John talked Kieran round, and got him into a rehearsal studio with the two of us. And while I worked on learning the words, and learning to sing with a bass round my neck. Not easy, 'cause your mouth's doing one thing, and that's not necessarily anything to do with what your hands are doing.

They knew me at Antonio's, because I was gigging there with the Stands fairly regularly, so I got us a slot for a Wednesday night on the strength of that.

And here we are, setting up. The great power trio, with a line-up that goes back all the way to Cream. Me as Jack Bruce? Might as well be, because no way can I be Siân. I think we are going to have to be more of a musicians' band.

A musicians' band? Does that puzzle you, Mister Zog? I'm not surprised—it feels odd to me. But with Siân leading us, the band was really a vehicle for her. And half of that was to give her a platform to flirt with the audience, who were dominantly male, and had come to be flirted with. I mean, she wasn't *bad*—provocative—about it, but she'd got that kind of Marilyn Monroe "hello *boys*" aura that was just part of being Siân, and it did cause tongues to hang out rather. But without Siân, it would have to be the music that counted. Yes, I could get that catsuit, and pull the zipper down low as I dared, and maybe the boys would enjoy the view. But I knew I didn't have the stage presence that Siân had. She could have had the same effect, without needing to pull the zipper down, if that makes sense.

———

Butterflies again. But not so bad, and John recognized the signs, and I didn't have to flee to the loo. He's not bad, for a boy.

Anyway, I went up on stage for the first number, still feeling warm and hugged. Thank you, John.

It's hot under the lights at Antonio's. I'd never felt it before, but then, I'd never been center stage. Some of it's the physics of all those watts of lighting rig. Most of it's the eyes on you. The lights are so bright that you can't actually see faces. And then you know, you're not the bassist, tucked away at the back of the stage. You're the face of the band, the nexus of the musicians behind you and the watchers in front of you, and the spotlight is on . . . you.

There was a moment of stillness. I looked behind me. John, brow furrowed, deep in concentration. Kieran, poised and ready, smiles. Maybe he has forgiven me. I wink back. We're ready.

"Hi, friends. We're Raven."

Yeah. I didn't mention that. We've got a proper name. John's suggestion. Kieran said aye, and they didn't give me a vote. "You're outnumbered, anyway."

Polite applause. It was a Wednesday, after all. If there were twenty people in the place, that was all.

"The first song's called 'Coils,' and it's for Siân, wherever you are now. We miss you . . . Give me a G, John."

So my voice wobbled, but that was thinking of Siân, and you have to push that out of your mind, 'cause there's too much else to do. First line just over guitar then D-slide-down-to-G and in.

It went all right, I guess. Antonio's crowd likes their music both ways, covers and originals, and they gave us a decent response— for a Wednesday—and I stumbled a couple of times coming out of the first chorus, waiting for Siân to come in—no, I'm the singer now—but then I landed in the groove, and by the time we ended the first song, we were there, in that place of creation, and the audience was with us.

Long sentence, but playing in a band is like that. You set off together, you keep going, going, for three minutes or whatever, and you can't stop, and finally, you can.

———

It's done.

I've got nothing left to give. I'm empty. It feels good, though. It feels *right*. Like . . . fulfilled.

I'm scared.

Dad's done it. He's taking Oxted to court, for the right to keep me. His tame solicitor—the only one he could find who'd look at the case—has submitted the papers and they've been accepted. We're waiting for a response from Oxted now.

Do I want to live? Stupid question. Of course I do. But the cost . . .

Dad's just a vicar, and I know the pay is pretty rubbish. I said before he's keeping half the village from mental breakdown, but he doesn't get any thanks for it. He's the one they call up when the despair of childlessness overwhelms them, when the fertility treatments fail, when they can't pay the mortgage because they've spent everything they have on quacks who promise miracles and deliver nothing.

It's psychiatric counseling on the cheap and people resent it. Dad delivers, but they don't like it for the self-respect it costs them.

Where was I? Oh yes, the cost . . . Well, Mum had a little money put by, and that'll help. But Oxted has the best legal team, and if we lose, Dad will be penniless, near enough. Actually, we'll probably be penniless even if we win—we're unlikely to get costs.

But Dad doesn't listen when I tell him. He mutters that we're going to win. Sometimes he looks a bit wild. Dad, who's keeping *you* from mental breakdown? The bishop just shook his head when he came to visit, and wouldn't meet my eye.

There's a silver lining. The congregation has found out what he's doing, and they're doing their best to help. Even Ted and his crowd. There might be a little guilt at work there, I think.

Dad surprised me again, though I liked this surprise better. Four days walking in the middle of nowhere. After he got back from evening service, he suddenly brightened up and told me: "The die is cast, and there's nothing we can do now. So pack a bag. We're going for a walking holiday in the Yorkshire Dales."

So I've got Dad back. The old Dad. My *Dad*.

He's found us a delightful hotel for our base. Solid stone, to keep the outside outside. A restaurant where we can eat well, if not extravagantly, and a guest lounge where we can pull up chairs by the fireside, and drink warm cocoa after a day walking. Hotel staff who are friendly, without being in your face.

And the Dales themselves right outside our front door. He picked Ribblesdale for our base, which is gorgeous. We've got our copy of Wainwright's Limestone Country book, and we're doing our best to follow that.

One of the other guidebooks talks about the caves and potholes in the area, and I think back to John, asking me if I'll run away before Oxted takes me (if they do). I can imagine it, skulking in some cave, living off stolen food, cold and wet, dreading the approach of the searchers. Is that what I want? Life at any price, no matter how miserable?

Mrs. Hanson, telling me about choices, how life is always looking for more choices, and death being accepting only the obvious ones. Here and now the Dales are beautiful, because I have a warm bed to return to. I have the company of a fine friend— Dad—and that is a choice I accept. Life forever on the run, alone, miserable, hungry, and cold—no, the Dales would not be beautiful then. I need to find a different choice.

We were at the top of Pen-y-ghent, and I found myself thinking of John, wishing I could bring him here, show him all this. And

I let my thoughts run on, to strange places. John beside me, a husband. Children of my own. Growing old together, as Mum and Dad had done. A gentle dying; first one, then the other.

A very human destiny, as lived out by billions of humans before me. And so, comfortable. But, I remind myself, I'm a robot. I need to find a different choice.

There has to be a different model for us. I have to dream it, because I may not get to live it. But dream it, I will, and I will tell my kind.

Tuesday, June 1, 2055

I found out where Christiana is, by the way. It's in Africa, in or near the Kimberley Corridor. At least, the only one I can't find anything about is there. There are about four in the United States, one in Germany, a couple in England. They're quite ordinary.

The other one only shows up in old atlases, like the one in Dad's study. There's no mention of it anywhere on the TeraNet. So it's got to be that one that Doctor Markov didn't want to talk about.

Thursday, June 3, 2055

John's building up to something, I'm sure. Just little things that he says—or doesn't say. He stops, almost in mid-sentence, and I know there was something on the tip of his tongue. It's not like Tim, though, where I had a pretty good idea what was on his mind. John isn't that transparent, but he can't hide from me that there's a decision brewing.

The only thing I can think of is that he's going to run away.

But he must know that Oxted will find him. It's too easy to add a tracking beacon into a robot for them not to have done it. I remember—way back—Martin falling over and injuring himself. I can't help thinking that I must have sensed a distress beacon, because I don't remember he was actually calling out, but I knew exactly where to find him. There must be beacons in all of us robots, for emergencies and, I guess, for when we go on the run.

It makes sense, but I can't prove it. Still, maybe John plans to hide in a deep cave, like the ones in the Dales, where radio can't penetrate. He's a good engineer, I'd almost say brilliant, so maybe he's got something figured out.

I trust John, that he'll tell me when he's ready, or else he won't if it's not safe to do so. I'll keep my suspicions to myself, encrypted here in my AllInFone.

So we talk about other things. We're writing music together, and I try to find words that say something new.

And me? I'm going along with the legal approach. We win, or we lose. I win life, or else I don't. But I'm going to lose that anyway. So what's to lose?

———

I keep thinking of that long-ago tryst by Ally Pally, when John asked if I'd run away with him and I said no. I remember the chill in the air, the walk back in the safety of John's enfolding arm. When we kissed good-bye, at the Tube station, there was, not passion, but tenderness and a deep poignancy in our embrace that I'd not felt before, or since.

If he's leaving, let that be our adieu.

Stupid! Stupid! Stupid!

A brown envelope. Recorded delivery. It arrived this morning, and suddenly our legal approach isn't a no-lose proposition anymore.

Oxted is countersuing. They allege ". . . the robot, known as Tania Annette Deeley, is declared to be defective and is to be returned immediately to the manufacturer for fault diagnosis and reprogramming, under the terms . . ."

Reprogramming. Wipe my mind in other words. Death. Not a year from now. Immediately.

Merde!

Excuse my French, Mister Zog. But what else can I say?

———

I've called John. No answer. Has he made his move? If so, we are both alone. Farewell, John, my love.

What shall I do?

Dad says we just have to brazen it out. We're committed; now we have to fight. That's fine for him to say—it's not his brain that's about to be reprogrammed. I just want to start running, but I know they've got the resources to find me before I get anywhere near the caves in the Dales.

Mrs. Hanson's words keep coming back to me. Look for more choices. But what choices are there?

———

I went to the station to buy a ticket to London. Just to see what would happen. The machine flashed "Request Assistance" at me when I tried to pay with my ID card. At least it didn't retain my card.

So I'm stuck. Well, I could walk, or I could pay cash, maybe catch a bus. But how far could I get before I had to show my ID card? Hitchhike? I'd never tried it, but it didn't feel safe. It was completely illegal, as well. So who would give a lift to a hitchhiker out of the goodness of their heart? I could think of plenty of unsavory reasons why someone would offer a lift. No thanks.

———

I've called Mike, he of the Stands, to tell him. Not everything, of course, but I've let him know that I might have to go away at very short notice for a very long time.

"Shoot! I was hopin' they'd forget about you."

"You know?"

"Sure. You ain't born of woman. But who is, these days? Still, you're no R either. You can play bass fit to make a stone cry. You can feel. You're People."

"Thanks, Mike. You're People, too."

"You going to play one last gig with us? Last Saturday of this month?"

"Hey, Mike, who said it was going to be my last gig?"

"These things happen fast. I know. Word gets around. So you play this gig, and make it a stormer. Yes?"

"But I can't get to London. I can't travel."

"I'll drive out and get you. Take you home after the gig. Make the party blast for Tania."

So what else would I do? Hide in my room until the day of the court case?

Monday, June 7, 2055

So Dad said, "We'd better start doing some serious research, Tan."

He was right. It's not going to go away by not thinking about it. I wish we knew a bit more law, but as Dad says, we are where we are. Dad says we have to own our defense, meaning we have to understand it, agree with it, control it, whatever. (Dad says a lot, and it's making sense. Has he done something like this before, or am I just lucky to have a dad who can just grasp all of this stuff?)

It feels like we're going to war.

The study is our War Room. He's dumped a lot of books off the shelves into boxes, moved the bookcases out into the dining room, and made lots of wall space. We've got big sheets of paper sticky-tacked to the wall, easels and marker pens and what-not.

I wrote on the wall when my pen slipped, and felt so guilty, but Dad just said, "So what? Do you think I give a *skata* about the wallpaper when my little girl's future is at stake?" I don't think I've *ever* heard Dad swear before, in English or in Ancient Greek.

Honestly, where does Dad learn all this stuff? The Greek goes with the job, but brainstorming, mind maps, and game theory? Formal logic? He's a *vicar*, not a business exec or a general!

We moved the other computers down into the office, so that we could set some off searching and crunching, leaving one for our main planning documents, and a VPN to one in the church office for backup.

"Call me paranoid, but this is not a time for our planning to be crippled by a disk failure. Or a house fire."

Paranoid? Why would we have a house fire *now*? Do you think Oxted plays dirty, Dad?

And unfortunately the TeraNet's not helping. There's very little out there. It's like no one ever challenged an Oxted contract before. Are we the first?

But we started on the contract anyway. It looked watertight, and maybe it was, but it hadn't always been that way. I remembered how Tim had told me how the contracts changed five, maybe six years ago, to give Oxted rights to early recall. So we dug out all the contracts, and analyzed the differences.

"We have to understand the changes, Tania. If they hadn't been challenged, why would the contracts have changed? Understand the nature of the changes, and you start to see the nature of the previous attacks. Maybe that'll illuminate a way to break the current contract. Maybe a new revision has reopened an older breach. . . ."

Helpfully, the contracts were not only dated, but were versioned, so we knew where there were some missing versions. Cautiously, Dad called a few friends. "I don't want to tip our hands, but I think I can trust these specific people whom I know had upgrades at about the right time."

Some helped, some did not—either because they no longer had the documents, or in a couple of cases because they found the subject too painful. Dad didn't press. We got a few more versions, though.

So here we are, a weekend gone by (Dad called in help to cover church on Sunday), and surrounded by charts and mind-maps, and some painfully meager notes on previous challenges.

Dad sighed and summed it up, for perhaps the third or fourth time. He says it helps, but I'm not sure.

"The TeraNet shows no accessible history on any challenges to the contract. Ever. It's like those blitzed sites you found on robot freedom. Hints at best. Yet we have clear evidence in the contracts that challenges do happen, and presumably they have been successful, up to a point. In my opinion, albeit that of a non-lawyer, each successive breach has been repaired without causing a regression on previous breaches. In other words, Oxted's lawyers are good."

But then he continued in a new vein.

"I have a terrible fear, Tania. There is a book—not easy to get hold of these days—called *Nineteen Eighty-Four*. In it, the Party controls people's lives to a frightening extent, and before today, I thought it was just fiction. But the power of the Party hinges upon one thing—control of information. One of the characters quotes a slogan, 'Who controls the past controls the future: who controls the present controls the past.' For the first time in my life I am seeing such control in our own society, and it frightens me.

"Somebody—and I conjecture it is Oxted—controls the present and the past, albeit imperfectly, and by implication, the future.

You were right, Tania, and I wish I'd believed you back when Siân was taken."

"So what do we do? Give up?"

"I didn't say that, Tania. But a frontal challenge to the contract is going to be hard. I need to find another way.

"Let's take a break."

The break was a walk around the village, and off into the Wood. We followed footpaths at first, then reached a place where the paths became harder to follow. Dad didn't say much—but watching him striking out through the undergrowth I knew the physical activity had freed his mind to roam.

I had a rough idea of where we were going—we'd crossed a road I recognized—so wasn't too surprised when we emerged onto the green of the next village, and marched across to the pub facing it.

"A pint of IPA, and another for my daughter."

I said nothing till we had our drinks and were seated comfortably distant from the barman. Dad took a long draught from his glass, and I followed suit. Then . . .

"Aren't you breaking the law, Dad? Buying me alcohol, I mean."

"What do you think, Tania?"

"I . . ."

I stopped. Did the law apply to me? As a robot, could I break a law written for humans?

"I don't know, Dad. Is this part of your plan? What does the law say about robots?"

"I don't know, either. When we took you on, we got a lot of briefing around treating you exactly as we would a child of our bodies. But no one explicitly said anything that I recall about legal status, or rights. In hindsight, that's rather odd."

"So are you trying to get us arrested, to prove a point? Forgive me, but my only brush with the law was scary. John told me that

Oxted doesn't tolerate robots breaking the law—they pull them back and deactivate them."

"That'd be worse than what we're already facing, how?"

Fair point.

"But, no, Tania, I'm not planning to do that, not yet. And I won't pull a trick like that without your consent. What I am going to do is find out what the law does say about robots, as distinct from humans, and see if we can exploit that. We came here because it's out of the way, and I needed the walk, and I needed to think. And I'm glad we've both got a proper adult drink in front of us, because you're not just a human, you're now an adult for whatever time remains for us.

"But it's crystallized my plans, coming here. If I can maneuver the law into recognizing you as a human, then your contract has no validity. As a human, you cannot be sold, bought, or leased—that's slavery, and I'm sure that is still illegal. For what it's worth, that's my plan, and I'm afraid it may not be a good enough plan. We need to do some more research. . . .

"Enough of that, though. What's happening with the band, these days?"

Time for a little father-and-daughter normality . . .

———

And then back to work. We dug out everything we could about Oxted. All the correspondence—e-mails, forms. And our face-to-face interactions, too. We wrote up what we could remember. I even let Dad see my diary extracts from our visits to Banbury. . . .

"Yes, I remember that first design session. You and Nettie chatting gaily about making you look more like part of the family. For me, every stroke of the stylus just made you look that little bit more like Nettie. Young Nettie, when I first knew her. When we were going out together. When we got married.

"It wasn't a natural growing up I was seeing. Most dads see their daughter grow up slowly, so they don't suddenly see their daughter turn into a younger version of their wife. Instead, they just see their daughter change slowly, but she's always their daughter, never so instantly and forcefully the image of someone else, whom they love in such a different way. So it was hard to look at the picture of you, and then the young woman you became, and not perceive you as my younger wife."

"Oh, Dad! I'm so sorry. I had no idea."

"Not your fault, Tania. Nettie didn't realize, either, until we had a heart-to-heart that night, after you'd gone to bed. It took me a very long time to get used to the new you. It was the nearest I came to the Uncanny Valley, Tania."

So we moved on. Dad was intrigued by the calibration tests.

"Clever questions and interesting responses, Tania. Not always logical, but I see your point about choosing a child to live, rather than choosing a child to die. Pray God neither of us ever has to make such a choice."

"I'm not sure I answered them the same way each time."

"I'm not sure I would, either. I wouldn't worry about it. That's not usually important in these sort of tests."

And on to the upgrade.

"So they wouldn't let you see the new body before you were upgraded into it?"

"Yes. They said it was not a good idea. I assumed it would spoil the illusion of growing up."

"But did they say so?"

"No. I guess it would have been a bit creepy. Like seeing yourself dead."

So we've made a start. We've got the outlines in place, but we have loads more to do. Research. Analysis. Brainstorming. Putting together our case, then testing it—by which Dad means trying to break it. Then strengthening it where it's weak.

If we can.

I've grown to love Amanda's bass almost as much as my own Warwick. There's a narrower feel to it, as though they've tried to squeeze five strings into a neck designed for four. But it just takes me a few runs to make the mental switch.

Dad was fine about me taking off to London—I'd done a fair few gigs with Mike and band, and this was just another one. The only oddity was that Mike had driven out to collect me, and so ended up ringing on the vicarage door. So he's what—fifty? Sixty? And here's the vicar's daughter going off with a craggy rock and roll stranger. April and December. Well, October. What will the neighbors think?

Dad invited him in, not having previously met him face-to-face, but he politely declined, saying we had to rush, and then the two of them spent ten minutes chatting on the door-step about bands they'd each seen, completely oblivious to the time, and that we should be getting over to Fulham for the rehearsal.

But the traffic was good and we got to the rehearsal studio while Gus was still setting up the kit the way he liked it. Gary had set up my bass rig as well as any guitarist can be expected to, and looking all pleased with himself. He still looked like a scarecrow in dreads, but now I knew him, he was all right. Well, they all were. They were my friends now, since a long time ago. We were a band, and I was an equal member. (Hush, Amanda. You know I've never tried to replace you or forget you, but now if I see a way to play more like me than you, I know that's as you want it. You were the one who told me to play like Tania Deeley, not like Amanda Taylor, after all. "Cuts" and "Ace" and all the rest—they're as much mine now as they ever were yours. *Pace*, Amanda.)

And when the rehearsal was done, we argued the set list in the pub, and I had a beer with the rest of them (and no one arrested me for underage drinking, though I wasn't expecting that to happen now).

At some point in the pub it hit me. I realized that I was accepted in this group of adults as . . . an adult.

It's funny, but it was the first time I'd ever experienced it, other than with my dad, which sort of doesn't count. I might not even have noticed it at that level, but for my heightened awareness of just how little time I might have. Oh, I'd been with this same bunch of guys, in a pub before—yes, it had been after Amanda's funeral. Maybe the funeral had really been when it changed. I just hadn't noticed it at the time.

I chipped in my thoughts here and there, feeling my way cautiously. No one slapped me down, though Gary did tend to hog the conversation, given half a chance. But he did that with everyone, not just with me.

It was hard to leave. Mike said we had to go—he'd promised my dad he'd get me back by 7 P.M.—but I ignored him, and hoped he'd connive with me to stay away later. It didn't work; Mike might have been a rough diamond, yet he was a gentleman of great integrity, and he insisted.

So that broke up the gathering, and Gus and Gary decided they'd grab some food, and I tried to tell them about the lawsuit, but Mike deflected the conversation skillfully, so all I managed was some inanity about how lovely it was to be part of the band and I'd miss—

And Mike closed the car door on me, cutting off my sentence.

"We agreed you weren't going to say anything, Tania. I'll tell them before the gig—I promised I would."

We'd moved off, and I was miffed with Mike for cutting short my evening and stopping me blurting out an ill-considered confession. So I didn't respond.

"So what happened to grown-up Tania in the pub? Why've I got tantrum-child Tania in the car with me now?"

Too much insight, damn you, Mike. So I told him.

"It's the first time I've truly felt like an adult among adults, Mike. So I was narked when you told me to leave."

"Yeah, I noticed you were talkin' less ladylike. I don't suppose the guys noticed too much, but I did, 'cause it's mostly me that talks to you."

"That's not what I meant, Mike. I meant that I was included in the conversation, and nobody talked down to me, or patronized me for being young or a woman."

"Yeah, I saw that, too. But you don't need to eff an' blind, even so. Save it for when times are *really* tough."

I had to laugh.

"Good for you. Anyway, like I said, I'll make sure the guys know before next week, but no details. You've got to go away, that's all."

"Thanks, Mike. You're all good to me, but you especially. I can't help feeling that I'm letting you down, though. Where are you going to find another bassist in these times?"

"Hey, sister, don't you go maudlin on me. You ain't lost the suit yet. You could be back."

———

So Mike dropped me back home when he'd promised to, plus or minus. And if Dad noticed the smell of beer on my breath, he chose not to comment.

Are you following all this, Mister Zog?

Saturday, June 26, 2055

I don't think I'll do a blow-by-blow of my last gig with Mike and the Stands. For a change, it wasn't at Antonio's, but at an old rock-and-roll pub in Fulham. The Golden Lion, it was called, with a tradition of pub music going back to the sixties, they claimed.

Maybe, but it had fallen on hard times, and the audience was pretty thin. Not much difference from Antonio's, then.

But there was an audience, with a few regulars from Antonio's who'd made the journey over to Fulham. Half-decent house PA, but we brought our own mikes anyway, because the house mikes are always shot.

I got a bit emotional—tearful—because I had this feeling Mike was right, and it was going to be my last gig. And then Mike had a word with me, and put me straight.

"You want to live forever?"

"Of course. Who doesn't?"

"Well, you can't. Who can? But who can see tomorrow, either? So you just play today's gig, and tomorrow will do what it wants to do—tomorrow."

"And make it the best of my life . . ."

"That'd be nice, too. But a musician says that anyway, every gig."

"Okay, Mike. I'm ready."

And there was one other thing. Mike was really embarrassed, but he had bought me a leather jacket for stage clothes. So I put it on, and it was a bit tight. Which made it a perfect choice.

So I looked in the mirror and it looked awful—just ordinary. I asked Mike to step outside for a moment and I stripped down to just my bra beneath my jacket and adjusted the zip, the way I'd always dreamed I would. Yes, that looked better.

But from nowhere a little thought winked slyly at me. Hmm, well, why not? So, jacket off again, unhook the bra and let it fall. With the jacket back on, it looked no different in the mirror, but it felt a whole world different. Now it *was* perfect. Just that extra frisson of daring, of risk . . .

Laydees and Gentlemen, I give you Tania, the Queen of Rock and Roll. Prepare your ears for a sonic assault! Ladies, hang on to your menfolk! And gentlemen, hang on to your eyeballs as Rock Chick Tania extends the boundaries of leather and zipper physics to the max and beyond, and struts her stuff without the aid of a safety net.

You have to laugh. Well, I did, because I knew it was ridiculous. It's just a game, a play, a masquerade, and we all knew it. The trick is not to get too serious about it.

Anyway, Mike said the audience would like it. I could tell from watching his eyes that he liked it.

I hit the stage still chuckling inside, and that kept me going. As gigs go, it was pretty good. Maybe not the best I've ever played. And I got slightly weepy inside as we started the final three songs. And then there were two. And then there was one. And then . . .

Mike was under orders—my orders—not to say anything about it possibly being my last gig, but the band knew, and they tried to make it special. And at the end we all lined up and took a bow together, because it seemed the right thing to do, and I kissed Mike and Gus and Gary—several times—and the audience cheered a bit louder, because they'd twigged that something special was happening even though nothing had been said.

And it wasn't until we were halfway back home in Mike's car that I suddenly remembered . . .

"My bass." By which I meant Amanda's bass she'd given to me. But the Stands always looked after it for me, along with the amp.

"Gus is looking after it, as always. I didn't think you'd want it."

"Damn. Sorry. I was intending to take it with me."

"And do what with it? Play it for the court?"

"Just have it with me. I like it."

"Can you manage without it, or do I have to turn the car back?"

I thought about it.

"Drive on, Mike. It's just a plank of wood."

———

And it wasn't till I got back home I realized I'd left my bra backstage, too.

So this is the core of our case. The legalese is watertight. Oxted has absolute rights over its creations. Think of me as a car, or a toaster, or a TV, leased to a custodian for eighteen years. Title stays with Oxted. That's how U.S. Robots and Mechanical Men did it, so I guess Oxted knew his Asimov. So why am I not a toaster? Answer, because I'm human. Not flesh-and-blood human, but neurotronic human. You can't lease a human, because that's called slavery, and that's illegal. We've checked, and according to the New United Nations Constitution introduced after the Troubles, slavery is definitely still criminal.

And that's it. If I'm a toaster, then the contract is ironclad. If I'm human, the contract is invalid, and Oxted is in deep trouble for slave trafficking.

Simple.

So why has no one thought of it before?

The sun still shines—no warmth it sheds on me
No rain can damp, nor breeze me disarrange
As I prepare to meet tomorrow's change
Machine am I, from human sense cut free

The colors leach from tree and grass and sky
Gone blue, gone green, gone all save iron gray
No speech I hear; no words remain to say
And would I weep, my very tears are dry

No heart to beat, no lung to draw soft breath
No hand to reach to soothe another's brow

No breast to suck, no womb for child to grow
What once did mimic life now shadows death

My eighteen years marked out on Oxted's clock
And all that Tania was, returned to stock

―――――――

God, that's morbid.

I really shouldn't write poetry when I'm feeling so bleak. And definitely not with my diary open.

Never mind. Let it stand.

―――――――

I decided I needed to read something uplifting after dumping all that blackness into my diary. Something John had written, I decided. He'd put some stuff up on his website. Rejected song lyrics the band would never use—too fluffy, I'd said, rather sneeringly, but right now I needed fluffy.

So click and . . . there.

<<Don't lose hope. Choice will come >>

What? Was that an error message? John's wacky sense of humor, perhaps.

The screen went blank.

<<Address not found>>

I couldn't get the message back, nor any of John's website. It was gone. Pulled. Blitzed.

Are you there, John? Deep in some secret cavern, hidden from Oxted, yet still sending me messages of hope? You could do it, too, John, even if you had to rewrite a law or two of physics. Make it three laws, John, and read my reply.

I love you, John.

Where did the time go?

We've had four weeks—just four weeks—to prepare. Our case starts tomorrow. Mr. Guest, our lawyer, is here to help us with the final preparation.

He says they've given us a week longer than normal. While Dad was in the kitchen making tea I asked him how long the hearing will take. That was the first thing I "learned" from him— it's not a trial, it's a hearing. I already knew that. Patronizing git!

"Magistrate court cases normally only take a day or two, but the law says the magistrate has to let you talk for as long as you need to make your case. Your father and I have about two days of material prepared. We'll bring in witnesses. Display your musical skills. Play some recordings of your performance as Portia. God, I had to twist some arms at County Hall to get that off Golightly."

Cow!

"What about Oxted?"

Mr. Guest looked blank for a moment.

"Well, they play by a pretty standard script for their own case, which normally takes a day. I mean, the contract has had a lot of testing in the courts, and gets tightened up every . . ."

". . . time they lose. Yes, so I heard. You don't fill me with hope, Mr. Guest."

"Well, er, you should always hope, Miss Deeley. Yes, always hope. Your father is a clever man, preparing some remarkable arguments. Must have studied hard. College-educated, I suppose?"

Yes, you ignoramus. Theological college and before that a first in philosophy at Durham. Studied hard? Not really, he just soaked up ideas, and worked stuff out from that faintest of hints. No, Mr. Guest, Dad was—and is—just naturally bright. Irritatingly so if we were ever watching a quiz show on the vid—he could answer 90 percent of all questions. Which is all by the by, but probably far more than can be said for *you*.

But I smiled like Mum does—did—whenever somebody joked about cucumber sandwiches. Which is to say, entirely on the outside.

So why *have* we got you defending us, Mr. Guest? Answer: because gone are the days when an Englishman could represent himself in court. Nowadays we have to have a lawyer, and no one else would take the case. Why is that? Are these cases unwinnable? Is the legalese completely watertight now? Or is everyone else too afraid of Oxted? Or is it just that Mr. Guest wants our money, such as it is, and doesn't really care whether he wins or loses?

In which case, why does Dad think he's got a chance? I can see Mr. Guest might not be that bright, but I can't believe Dad would be fooled. Or is it emotion overriding common sense?

Dad came back at that point, bearing tea and biscuits. I need a talk with him, when Mr. Guest is not around. . . .

———

And so to London. We decided we ought to stay at a hotel near to the courts, rather than risk getting stuck in some transport failure. We're about half a mile from the courts complex, so close enough to walk.

We *ummed* and *aahed* about whether to go out for a meal, and finished up at a Thai restaurant over near Covent Garden.

And why not? We'd done all the preparation we could. We knew our own arguments inside out. We'd brainstormed all the likely arguments that Oxted might use. Played devil's advocate in turns. Used "five whys" against our own points, till we knew we could defend them.

It could have been a somber occasion. It would have just taken a simple question, like "Any regrets?" and it all would have unravelled in tears. Instead, we fell back on "Do you remember?" And I asked a few questions I'd never dared before, about Mum and Dad, their getting together at Durham, and her choosing to put aside her career to become a wife. The fertility treatments and then making the Oxted Choice.

If you don't mind, Mister Zog, I'll keep those answers deep in the heart Oxted doesn't believe I have. Save only to say, I love Mum more than I ever was able to tell her, for having learned those answers.

We had coffee, and Dad bought a fine brandy for each of us. Done.

Wednesday, July 7, 2055

I had a wrong picture of the courtroom—too many Old Bailey 3-Drams, I guess.

This was smaller, just a bare meeting room. No raised bench for the judge, just a standard office chair—black leather and chrome steel tubing—for the magistrate. The magistrate himself: a balding man in his fifties wearing a timeless business suit, navy blue and discreetly pin-striped. I tried to read his face—a pleasant oval, slightly mottled with a faint tracery of purplish veins. Mild, watery eyes—but did they speak of a kindly disposition? This wasn't Dickens, though, where face mirrors heart.

The clock showed a couple of minutes past ten, and so we should have been under way, but everyone was settling still. Our lawyer, Oxted's lawyer, keeping their distance from each other and emitting icy glances, but for all I knew it could be just an act and they were old pals from law school. There was a clerk and a recorder, and a couple of heavy-looking fellows that looked like bouncers. I think they might properly be called sergeants-at-arms. Anyway, they were the muscle.

And there was me, and Dad. That was it.

After a moment, the magistrate glanced at the clock—five past ten—and coughed for attention.

"Can we begin, please, gentlemen?"

The lawyers nodded.

"Right," he continued. "I'm Mr. Simpson, your magistrate, and I like to keep things light and gentle, not too much formality. But don't take advantage of that, or I'll run it the hard way."

Then he called the clerk to read the business of the day—the basics of our suit and Oxted's countersuit. As the clerk spoke, Mr. Simpson's gaze roved, and I thought I could see boredom in his eyes. Not good. How many times has he seen this little drama played out? I wondered. And always the same way?

Dad looked up. I think he'd been praying. Lots.

Who do you pray to, Dad? I know you call him God, but who is he? Does he know about robots? Would he listen to me if I prayed? Or is there a different God for robots—or no God for us?

Oh God, I'm scared. Is that a prayer that he'd listen to? Anyway, if robots can pray, I just prayed.

Our lawyer, Mr. Guest, was speaking.

". . . we will further show that the being Tania Annette Deeley is human in all essential respects, and that she is not subject to the conditions of the original contract."

"I object."

"Why?" asked the magistrate.

"Use of the terms 'being' and 'she' cannot be used of a machine. The terms are 'teknoid' and 'it.'"

"That's nit-picking, Mr. Lloyd. We call boats 'she,' don't we? And I should resent the implication that I'd be influenced by such trivia."

Point to us. Mr. Guest continued.

"Thank you, sir. I will demonstrate that Tania has all the important aspects of a human, and is effectively human under the law. For example, Tania writes music, and poetry. She is an actress, a fine actress, capable of interpreting Shakespeare. . . ."

And then it was Mr. Lloyd's turn:

". . . I shall call, if necessary, expert witnesses to testify that, in fact, this teknoid's so-called creativity is simply a manifestation of its malfunctions, as shown by its erratic responses to the standard CalTech Morrison-Bowyer Test . . ."

Oh, b . . . darn. Those calibration tests.

"Excuse me," I burst out, "but Doctor Markov called my test one of the best he'd ever seen."

Everyone's mouths gaped for a moment. Then the magistrate spoke.

"Mr. Guest, did you or did you not explain to your client that the teknoid would not be permitted to speak?"

"I regret that it might have slipped my mind, sir."

"What?" I called. "But this case is all about me. Surely I have a voice?"

Mr. Simpson thumped the table and barked out at me—no, not *at* me, because magistrates don't talk *to* machines, but he meant me.

"I remind everyone that I run things informally, but the laws of this land do not accept evidence of robotic origin under any circumstances. Such evidence differs from standard electronic recording in that it is at the whim of programming, which is nondeterministic in part. In short, a robot may lie, dissemble, or misrepresent."

"But so do humans!"

"Any more outbursts from the teknoid, Mr. Guest, and I will instruct the sergeants to remove it."

Mr. Guest looked angrily at me.

"Shut up, or you'll lose the case right here."

I shut.

———

I guess I'd imagined myself, like Portia, speaking boldly to the court, astonishing them with my impeccable logic and oratory. Instead I was held mute by the laws that wouldn't recognize my voice.

Oh, to have been even Shylock—at least he could speak in his own defense.

At the end of the opening speeches Mr. Simpson spoke.

"I've worked with Mr. Lloyd on these sort of cases before, so he'll be familiar with what I'm about to say, but I understand this is the first of these cases that Mr. Guest—and of course Reverend Deeley—has worked on. . . ."

So proof positive that these cases do get contested . . . just not reported. Who controls the past controls the future. . . .

"I remind both parties that this is a civil court, not a criminal court. My job is to ascertain whether the contract under dispute is legally valid, having been freely entered into by both parties, and whether any breach has occurred to justify termination of the contract by either party, and whether the outcomes being sought are permissible under the terms of the contract, or under the laws of this land.

"So long as the law is clear, and the contract—and its subsequent amendments—are legally valid and have been willingly entered into by both parties, there will be no appeal granted. If, however, the law is not clear, then this court has no power to make new laws, and the case will be referred to higher judiciary bodies. I warn both parties that such a process is likely to be prolonged and expensive, and that this court is willing and able to act as mediator, to avoid such an outcome.

"And if there is evidence of coercion or deception by either party, then again this court has no jurisdiction, and I shall refer the matter to the Prosecution Service, which may lead to further proceedings in a criminal court.

"Those outcomes aside, there are just two possible outcomes. It may be that I'll decide in favor of Oxted. In that case, Oxted has requested that it take custody of their property immediately. It may be that I will decide for Reverend Deeley, in which case he will be free to return home with the teknoid Tania, for the remainder of the term of the contract."

So we're fighting for just twelve more months. . . .

"As to costs, you should expect those will be awarded in line with the main judgment. Neither side is requesting damages. Is that all clear?"

Mr. Simpson paused and traversed the room by eye, eliciting a "yes" from each of the participants. Myself excepted.

He continued by asking Mr. Lloyd to stand.

"Mr. Lloyd, on the basis of your submissions, and taking into consideration what I've heard in the two opening statements, I'm going to ask you to elaborate on your arguments first. You've indicated that you don't believe there's anything in Reverend Deeley's submission that requires you to modify your own approach, and that you should be done by the end of the day. Is that correct?"

"Yes, sir."

That's not good. Have they genuinely got all our bases covered?

"Very well. I know you've got a number of experts lined up. In the interests of keeping the costs of this case down, let's hear from them first. Mr. Lloyd?"

Unsubtle message from Mr. Simpson—do yourselves a favor, you're going to lose, so don't prolong this and maybe you won't end up broke.

The first expert was a Dr. Evans, a tweeded spinster—yes, I know I shouldn't judge marital status on appearances—with bottle-bottom glasses, silvering hair, and a cracked-earth complexion. Add a shapeless, green tartan cardigan. So tell me I'm wrong.

"I'm a technical historian. I did my first bachelor's degree in neurotronics at Banbury New University, worked for five years on the second-generation neurotronic web design—the N2—to earn my master's and then my doctorate, but then I took a sabbatical, where I worked with Neil—that's Neil Oxted, of course—up till his death in 2034, as his technical biographer, with access to some of the earliest records, to catalogue and summarize. Classic designs, such a privilege to be able to handle the original design documents . . ."

"Dr. Evans, you're saying that you're technically qualified as a neutrotronic designer, and moreover have intimate knowledge of current and historical designs, yes?"

"Yes, I am."

"And how have those designs evolved over the years?"

"Surprisingly little, Mr. Lloyd. The first designs were in some senses quite crude, but that was more a matter of the limits imposed by the state of the art—specifically, our ability to grow the necessary three-dimensional structures at sub-micron scale. The N2 was far more compact, with the basic neutrotronic link element being a full order of magnitude smaller. The N3—which was the first model produced after Oxted's death, and the N4, which is the current model—are each in turn a little more compact than their predecessors, but by nowhere near as much as an order of magnitude."

Oh, John, I wish you were here. I need to understand this stuff. I think they're trying to blind the judge with science. The magistrate, I mean.

"So is it fair to say, Dr. Evans, that all Oxted neurotronic designs are refinements of Oxted's original design, and differ merely in the number of—what did you call them—neurotronic link elements? This being achieved through successive improvements in miniaturization. Yes?"

Dr. Evans's desert-bottom face crinkled further, if that were possible, so that she looked even more annoyed.

"That rather neglects the improvements made in long-term stability by my own team, and the work of Greene et al. in taste perception, and similar sensory enhancements, but yes. Oxted was an intellectual giant, a genius, and he gave the world an almost perfect invention."

"And how does that compare in complexity with the human brain, Dr. Evans?"

"It depends on what you measure, Mr. Lloyd, but the most commonly quoted example is to compare the number of neurons in the human brain with the number of neurotronic link elements. Certainly in that respect the human brain is significantly more complex than even the N4—which, for the benefit of the court, is the model installed in Reverend Deeley's teknoid."

"And how about the rest of the animal kingdom, then? How does the N4 compare to, say, a dog, or a cat, or a chimpanzee?"

"Oh, it well exceeds a cat or a dog, Mr. Lloyd. It's up in the region of the higher primates, no doubt. But I don't think we'll ever get close to a human on that measure. Quantum effects limit how much miniaturization we can achieve, and the N4 is pretty much there. We've tried, believe me, but beyond the N4 level, the neurotronic link element is destabilized by quantum effects."

"Let me sum up, then, Dr. Evans. The neurotronic web is less complex than the human brain, so comparable to a chimpanzee. Therefore Oxted's teknoids are sophisticated pets at best. Is that what you're saying?"

"That's about right, Mr. Lloyd. Anticipating the next line of questioning, though, I will say that unlike the primate brain, or the brain of a dog, the neurotronic web has been specifically designed for human companionship. So neurotronic teknoids can speak, can learn—within limits—and can mimic human emotions, through specific programming."

"And this human companionship is the sole purpose of such teknoids?"

"Precisely. The teknoids are designed to substitute for children during those years when the urge to reproduce is strongest in humans. Oxted made it possible for vast numbers of humans to 'adopt' children, which was a significant factor in bringing to an end the Troubles."

"How was that, Dr. Evans?"

"The Troubles were so very nearly the End of the World. The Last Days of Rome. Barbarians at the Gate. Without children, there is no hope for the future. With no hope, there is nothing to restrain me-firstism. The Child is a pillar on which our society rests. With the restraining influence of the family removed, hedonism and nihilism soared, particularly among the hormonal young, and violence quickly followed. You will doubtless recall from history the terrifying clips showing prowling packs of young men, raping and murdering, looting and burning our cities. Social background meant nothing—the rapist was as likely to be the university-educated son of a respectable stockbroker as an unemployed immigrant from the East End. While sending in the riot police, desperate politicians blamed other nations for the problem. Demagogues reignited old national rivalries for their own purposes, then found they could not control what they'd started. The Sabine Wars were the result."

"And the teknoids solved this . . ."

"In part. One shouldn't discount the shock effect of the LeClerc Solution in bringing an immediate end to violence, not just in France but ultimately worldwide. But yes, back to Oxted and teknoids. Oxted restored the appearance of normality—women pushing babes in prams, kids playing in parks, and so forth. Surprisingly quickly, the psychology changed. People felt hope was restored, and some sort of stability returned."

"And for that purpose, how perfect a simulation was needed?"

"A good question, Mr. Lloyd. Not totally perfect, certainly. Humans fool themselves into accepting so many substitutes. Pets, of course, and foster children are the most obvious. Like the magpie, we accept the cuckoo chick in our nest and treat it as one of our own. But as I say, it's not perfect, and as the teknoid grows up, the foster parents begin to reject the interloper. Something happens that reminds the parents that their foster child is not human. They pick up the phone, call Oxted, and within twenty-four hours, the cuckoo is painlessly removed from the nest."

"But that doesn't trigger a return to violence?"

"Not at all. The foster child is almost never returned during those critical, violence-prone years. Only when middle-age kicks in, when the hormones stop raging, and rationality returns."

I could see Dad reacting to that, and so did Mr. Simpson.

"Reverend Deeley, you have a comment or a question?"

"Thank you, yes. You say there's no return to violence, Dr. Evans? But as a vicar, I see a very different picture. The loss of a child—even a foster child—has always been traumatic, and we humans too often react to it badly, with the immediate family usually taking the brunt. You neglect domestic violence in your analysis, but it is the biggest single challenge for the parish priest of today. All the different ways in which one human can mistreat their partner. Infidelity. The breakup of relationships. Divorce. Murder and suicide. All vastly increased from their pre-Trouble levels. Unless you acknowledge this, your expert testimony is flawed and without credibility."

Dr. Evans looked shocked, as if no one had ever dared to contradict her before. Her fingers clenched and dug into the rail of the witness stand, and her eyes narrowed angrily. Taking a deep breath, though, she gathered her thoughts and responded, smugness creeping back into her voice.

"Flawed? I don't think so, Reverend Deeley. But the problem you cite is outside the design parameters. We only need the teknoids to be good enough to stop the riots on the streets."

"Indeed. The classic response of government to insoluble problems: make the problem invisible. But my main interest is in those children who are not returned before the due date. I suggest that a contributory factor may be that they do not trigger rejection. I further suggest that is because they are—barring biology—human by any meaningful test, and specifically through an eighteen-year Turing Test. Do you have any data on those children, Dr. Evans?"

"While it is technically outside my own field of responsibility, I understand the number of *teknoids* returned at the completion of the lease term is too small to be statistically significant. No analysis of such returnees has been, or will be performed."

"In other words, you've prejudged the outcome of the research. How scientific is that, Dr. Evans? Don't you want to know?"

Hot damn! My dad has sharp teeth!

But Mr. Simpson intervened. "Reverend Deeley, I don't want this hearing to descend into wild speculation. Dr. Evans, you don't have to answer that question."

"Oh, I don't mind, Mr. Simpson. At the end of their leases, the teknoids are reprogrammed. All teknoids undergo this procedure without coercion. If the teknoids are self-aware—human, if you will—where is the instinct to survive?"

Reluctantly Dad sat down. "No more questions, sir. For now."

———

After Dr. Evans finished, the next expert was a Dr. Maurice Colyer. He was the UK Programming Director for the Fostering Division.

Forget what I said about trying to blind with science. Colyer's technique was to bore us to death. His hair was gray, his eyes were gray, his suit was gray, and his voice was gray. That is, he spoke in a monotone, and while he was speaking I knew what it was to die and to be carried off to a formless, frozen gray limbo where nothing . . . ever . . . happens.

As best I remember it (and Dad confirms it), Colyer testified in excruciating detail to the hundreds of thousands of lines of code that create the teknoid brain in the first place, and the millions more lines that set up the neurotronic patterns. He quoted statistics of how many lines of code it takes to mimic (say) sorrow, or backchat, or musical ability. And then the randomizing and correlating elements that mimic free will, and associativity.

The brain—he called it a neurotronic matrix—was therefore perfectly equipped to mimic creativity.

And I'll take my mimicry over your original any day, Dr. Colyer.

We'd broken—the magistrate called it "recessed"—for lunch. Mr. Guest joined us.

"It's going as well as can be expected," he offered. "We're giving them a few tough times."

We, Mr. Guest? I didn't hear any robust cross-examination from you, save the questions Dad primed you with. Do you have the faintest idea what's going on?

"Indeed, Mr. Guest. Your little ruse to get Mr. Simpson to recognize my daughter as human so nearly worked. . . ."

Like hell, it did. Oh, it would have been a miracle, and a useful one. But to expect such a slip from such an experienced magistrate? I don't think so. Like playing the lottery, it was no more than a long shot; one that does little harm, so long as you don't bet your shirt on it.

Their evidence, their testimony was entirely as we expected. They were occupying the ground we were expecting them to, and as there was nothing we could really do about it, we were putting up a symbolic resistance, just to show we were still in the game.

———

After lunch, Mr. Lloyd picked up the thread.

"This morning we've seen how the teknoid is constructed, based on a cognitive mechanism that is comparable in complexity with that of a chimpanzee. This remarkable, but limited, invention allows Oxted to market humanoid pets, optimized to behave as substitute children for couples who would otherwise be unable to form families.

"We've seen how these humanoid robots are programmed to mimic the abilities and attributes of children, and how, as the teknoids artificially develop, they approach the limits of the technology. How, as the programming ultimately fails to deliver the expected human response, the parents reject their fosterlings and return them.

"This afternoon we'll look at one of the safeguards we put in place to detect early signs of instability, the Morrison-Bowyer Test."

And so we were treated to yet another doctor—Dr. Morrison herself.

Dr. Morrison was a smartly dressed woman in a dark-blue pinstriped two-piece suit and pale cream blouse, who just exuded power and confidence. She could have walked out of the boardroom of a 3-Dram; her auburn hair was elegantly styled, her makeup subtle but perfect. I couldn't picture her in a Nissen hut at Banbury.

The Morrison-Bowyer Test, she told us, had its genesis in the personality tests of the twentieth century, but derived heavily from software boundary testing, too. It tested specific themes, using a randomly generated set of questions. The standard cognitive matrix would respond in very well-defined ways, at different stages of its development. The fosterlings were tested at each upgrade, normally at two-year intervals, and deviations were monitored closely, and correlated to any anomalies reported by hospitals, doctors, social workers, police, teachers, et cetera, et cetera. Normally, very little action was needed, but anomalies generally correlated well to early returns.

Dad was on his feet.

"Yes, Reverend Deeley? You have a question?"

"I do, sir. Dr. Morrison, do all forms of anomaly correlate well to early returns?"

"Most of them, certainly."

"And if not returned, what is the prognosis of these anomalous fosterlings?"

"They become difficult to live with. Antisocial."

"Forgive me, but weren't we the same in our teens?"

"No. This is not the same at all. The human teenager is developing mentally, with tact usually lagging some years behind. The fosterlings, however, actually stop developing mentally, and simply become more aggressive."

"So they can become violent? I don't think the public is aware of that."

"Not violent, but verbally aggressive. You might call it surly."

"And your test is an early indicator of surliness?"

"Among other things, yes."

"And is this your concern with Tania, here, that she's becoming a surly teenager? So you want to recall her in case she refuses to do the washing up?"

Go, Dad!

"Not at all, Reverend Deeley. There are other sorts of anomaly—I merely described the most common form."

"Then I'll let you explain what Tania's alleged anomaly is, and what you're protecting me, and the general public, from."

"It's complex, Reverend Deeley. Difficult to explain to a non-scientific person."

"Hmm, not strictly science, but I do have a first-class degree in philosophy from Durham University. One mark off a starred-first, I'm afraid, but you still might be pleasantly surprised by what I can understand."

"Mathematics is also necessary. And it's not you I have to explain it to, but Mr. Simpson."

Did you just call Mr. Simpson an idiot, Dr. Morrison?

"What about the other part of my question, then? What is the predicted outcome of this alleged anomaly? Is Tania going to turn into a serial killer? A master jewel thief? An obsessive stamp collector? Come, you must have some idea!"

"Nothing so specific, Reverend Deeley. I don't think we need fear being murdered in our beds. Teknoids don't do that sort of thing."

"First Law, eh?"

"Not First Law, Reverend Deeley. That's a common misconception about teknoids. Only domestics have true First Law. If you put First Law into a teknoid, it no longer acts like a human child, and that triggers the Uncanny Valley. So at school you will see robot-on-robot bullying, for example. There are good safeguards, but, just as with real children, they don't have full First Law. Nevertheless, they are quite safe. . . ."

Wow! Though I'm not sure whether that helps our case.

"So we are protected, then, Dr. Morrison? You're sure?"

"Oh, yes. Undoubtedly."

"So, Dr. Morrison, if we're protected by those safeguards, why do you have to recall her? She can stay with me, surely."

"She needs to be studied closely. It is standard practice to recall anomalous teknoids."

"But it's not a safety issue? The public is in no danger from Tania?"

"No. There is no public danger."

"Then let her stay with me. You can study her remotely. Or I can bring her up to Banbury periodically."

"No. We need to study her at Banbury."

"Why?"

"It is standard procedure."

"Why?"

Yes! The "five whys," Dad—she's evading, she's on the run—go for the jugular!

Then Mr. Simpson broke in.

"I'm sorry, Reverend Deeley, but I must ask you to drop this line of questioning. We have established that your fosterling is suffering from an anomaly, and the standard procedure is to recall such deviants."

"With respect, sir, I'm establishing that the anomaly, whatever it is, does not endanger the public, and proposing an alternative remedy that does not require me to lose my daughter, yet still gives Oxted access to her for study."

"Reverend Deeley, the court notes your proposal with thanks. But it is *my* job to propose remedies, where it can be shown that the contract has been breached by one or other party. It is *not* the business of this court to impose extra terms upon either party where the contract is not breached, so long as the contract has been entered into willingly by both parties and without deception. Do you understand?"

"Yes, sir."

Damn, damn, damn.

Damn.

That was Plan A going down in flames.

———

"You almost had her, Dad."

We were in the hotel bar. Court was done for the day. Oxted had closed with one of their contracts specialists—not a doctor, for a change—going through the contract history in mind-numbing detail, showing that each revision was accompanied by a properly executed contract, and drawing attention to the missed revision, but falling just short of saying that if we'd done all the revisions when we were supposed to, they might have been able to catch and fix the anomaly. Alleged anomaly.

"I know, I know."

"Well, it was a most unconventional approach you took, Reverend Deeley. I hope it hasn't lost us the case."

And you had a better plan, Mr. Guest? If that's all you're going to contribute to our analysis, then why don't you just bugger off, and let Dad and me have some time together?

———

Sometimes telepathy works!

Mr. Guest did indeed excuse himself, saying he had a train to catch. Dad and I smiled and shook his hand and waved him farewell.

"Good, he's gone," we said simultaneously; we laughed.

Well, tomorrow we would execute Plan B. So we called our own experts, who all confirmed they'd be attending, then adjourned to the hotel restaurant for a meal together, and to talk over what we'd learned.

The nub of it, Dad explained, was that we didn't understand our opponent, and he wouldn't talk to us. "He"—our opponent—being Oxted.

"What do you mean, Dad?"

"I offered a compromise today, Tan. I accepted the principle that you were somehow an anomaly, nature unspecified, but having proved that there was no danger, they rejected my offer and stonewalled when I dug for their reasons. Then the magistrate stepped in and told me to back off."

"Is he in cahoots with Oxted, then?"

"Quite possibly. But he might just be doing his job, albeit somewhat punctiliously."

"But your point is not that the magistrate might be crooked?"

"No. The problem is that if your opponent won't reveal what he wants, and why he wants it, it becomes very difficult to bargain. Clearly Oxted wants you, but why? The contract says he can have you, but when I offered a way that he could have access to you, without tearing us apart, it was flatly rejected."

"So what he says he wants is not what he actually wants. Or at least, the reason he says he wants me is not actually why he wants me."

"Very good, Tan. I don't think Mr. Guest would be catching on so quick."

"Thanks for nothing, Dad." But I was grinning.

"So, what are the possibilities? One, they want to destroy you. Reason: unknown. Two, they want to isolate you from me. Reason: unknown."

"So are you saying, Dad, that it's more important that you should not know the reason, than that you should not know what my fate is?"

"Oh, very good, Tania, very good! Yes, I believe you're right. If

I knew the reason they were taking you away, that, for Oxted, would be a disaster. Perhaps I would be content to lose you, if I could be sure you were alive. But to be sure you were alive, I'd have to know the reason why, and Oxted won't accept that. Of course, they may wish to destroy you, which I could never accept."

"Isn't there a third possibility, which is that their object is to do with you, rather than to do with me?"

"If so, then you're probably safe enough. Whatever we do won't matter, and I'll trust in God for myself."

"So what is this secret reason? Can we work it out?"

Dad paused for a really long time there. Really long. I could almost see his mind, running at high speed through everything we knew, probing for something we'd missed. Five minutes passed, and more. I wished I could see what was going on, but I'd seen him like this before. It was best to let him work it through. I didn't want him snapping at me for breaking his train of thought.

Finally . . .

"Possibly. But I don't think it's wise. I suspect that if we work it out, it will become obvious to Oxted. That changes the game in a way that frightens me."

His voice became urgent.

"We proceed with Plan B. We never had this discussion, Tania. Do you understand? We never had this discussion."

"Dad, you're frightening me. What are you afraid of?"

"Forget it. Concentrate on Plan B. Plan B. Just keep that in mind."

What does Dad know?

Back in the hotel room, we got the computers out, and opened up the transcripts of the day's evidence. Dad scrolled to Dr. Colyer's testimony, and started paging up and down, making notations on a spreadsheet. After a while, it got as dull as the real thing had been. I know better than to interrupt Dad when he's deep in thought, so I wandered off and listened to music in bed until I fell asleep.

———

Dawn. Ugh! Too early, but I'd left the curtains open.
So.
Today is the day that all will be lost and won. No—that's *Macbeth*. What said Portia? *"They have the wisdom by their wit to lose."*
I must remember. Plan B.

Ten o'clock.
The courtroom is ready.
I remind myself. Plan B.

———

Mr. Simpson opened the proceedings.
"Well, we all seem to be here. We've heard from Oxted, and they've indicated that they have no further submissions to make, so I'll ask Mr. Guest to open the submissions on behalf of Reverend Deeley. Mr. Guest . . ."
Mr. Guest stood slowly, as one charged with an unpleasant but pointless task.
"Reverend Deeley has indicated to me that he wishes to conduct the submissions himself. I have warned him of the consequences."
"Indeed, Mr. Guest. I confess I am not surprised. Reverend Deeley, are you aware that you carry full responsibility for the conduct of your submission? If I decide against you, there can be no appeal on the grounds of your inexperience."
Dad: "I understand fully, sir."
"And you understand that the law requires the presence of

Mr. Guest. You are required to pay his costs and to listen to his advice. It is up to you whether you take it."

Was that a joke from Mr. Simpson? Or an acknowledgment that Dad was doing okay? I couldn't tell—Mr. Simpson was a master of the deadpan delivery.

"I understand that, too, Mr. Simpson. Thank you. Now . . ."

"And one final point," Mr. Simpson interrupted. "I assume that you're going to run your submissions differently to the plan I've already seen. But I remind you that this is not a trial, with a prosecution and a defense running in strict sequence. It is a hearing, and so Oxted will have a chance to present further submissions if they require, or if I deem it necessary. That includes the option to summon additional witnesses, or to recall witnesses for further questioning. Reciprocally, you may also recall any of yesterday's witnesses."

"Understood. Thank you. Now I want to start with the contract. A contract is all about regulating the exchange of things of value between two parties. Both parties have something of value that they wish to exchange for something of value that the other party can offer.

"The thing of value that my wife and I were able to offer was a sum of money, consisting largely of an inheritance, somewhat depleted by some unsuccessful fertility treatments, but augmented by some savings and a small loan.

"The thing of value we wanted was a child of our own, and that was what Oxted offered. Not a pet. Not a chimpanzee, or a dog or a cat. And not a robot, either. Oxted does do robots, and sells them outright, too. Indeed, thanks to the generosity of one of our parishioners, we have one—a fine old '44 model, which we call Soames, who does the dishes and plays table tennis badly.

"Oxted experts have of course testified that their fosterlings are not children, being limited by the hardware and the physics of the neurotronic link elements and by the programming of the cognitive unit—the thing that no one from Oxted ever calls a brain, because that would give the creature an attribute of humanity.

"And of course, under law the fosterlings are not children, because that would make them human, and trading in humans is illegal. It's called slavery.

"So Oxted offers these things that are like children, but aren't children. They're good enough to keep people happy for ten or fifteen years, by which time the foster parents have had enough. The 'Uncanny Valley' phenomenon, it's called, which Dr. Evans alluded to yesterday, but didn't explicitly name. Her implication is that it's a limitation of the neurotronic technology.

"But that rejection is fine by Oxted; they recycle the brain into a new child and give the exhausted foster parents a pro-rata refund to ease their guilt and sorrow. And there are vicars and social workers who pick up the pieces of the broken relationships that inevitably follow.

"So on one hand, Oxted is careful never to call the fosterlings human, but on the other hand, every new set of foster parents is told to treat the fosterling as human, else the illusion won't work. Two contradictory messages that the parents somehow have to hold in their minds simultaneously. A novel written just over a hundred years ago called it doublethink—the ability to hold two mutually contradictory ideas in the mind. It's not something that human minds are built to do, and those that succeed are often not what we'd call sane.

"Oxted is peddling a drug called Parenthood, with full legal and government approval. It's a legal high, yet one that leaves its users mentally and often physically scarred. The one thing that can be said for it is that it is not addictive. Few users ever come back to it.

"And it is sold using doublethink—the fosterlings are not human, but you must treat them as human. Mr. Simpson, this is the first part of my submission, that the contract is based on deception, and therefore is not valid."

Mr. Lloyd was on his feet, waving agitatedly at Mr. Simpson.

"Sir, I wish to contest these assertions!"

"Yes, Mr. Lloyd. I rather thought you might. The floor is yours."

"First of all, I wish to stress that the work of Oxted is totally legal, fully approved by the government, and plays a vital role in stabilizing our society. It is true that there is sometimes a social cost in the recall process, but Oxted contributes generously to mental health programs as part of its not inconsiderable charitable work, and proper training and counseling are available to all foster parents.

"Secondly, I assure the court that you will never find any assertion in any Oxted literature or other published media, including brochures, manuals, advertising, or product placement, that Oxted's fosterlings are human, or anything but robotic.

"Thirdly, I point out that no one has to do business with Oxted. It is always a decision that prospective foster parents enter freely, in full possession of all the facts, and with a generous cooling-off period that exceeds the legal requirements. With regard to the 'Uncanny Valley' phenomenon that Reverend Deeley brings up, that information is in the public domain, and the contract provides for a pro-rata refund, at whatever point the foster parents declare they are unhappy with the simulation. We are not the villains the Reverend Deeley paints us as!"

Mr. Simpson: "Reverend Deeley, would you care to respond to those points?"

"Indeed. I am forty-four; I was born in 2010, the year that the world's population went flat. I am well aware of the Troubles. I was seven, nearly eight when they erupted; they are part of my boyhood memories. My parents escaped the worst of the violence; the gangs of child-kidnappers were the main threat for them. I remember I had a nanny, who loved me dearly. I was brokenhearted when my parents dismissed her, but they were afraid that she might be somehow coerced into handing me over to a criminal gang—it happened to several of our friends.

"So I accept that Oxted serves a useful, even a necessary part in today's society. That should not blind us to the social cost, nor to the self-deception that Oxted does allow its customers to perpetrate on themselves.

"And lastly, your remark that 'no one has to do business with Oxted.' No one has to take the drugs they offer. So said the tobacco industry in times past. So said the heroin dealers of the women forced into prostitution as they racked up the price or diluted the strength of their wares. So say all drug pushers, throughout history. This basic human need is broken, and Oxted offers a fix. You cannot say that 'no one has to do business with Oxted' with a clear conscience or a straight face. You cannot.

"Oxted is a monopoly, whether you live in England or America, in New Delhi or Bogotá. There is no legal alternative. Oxted needs to be whiter than white, but it is dirty and bloody from the broken lives it leaves when the Oxted drug is taken away. Oxted needs to make restitution. Now would be a good time to make a start."

Years of training, years of speaking from the pulpit coming together. Dad knows when he has made his point and when to stop.

The silence was acute. You could hear a pin drop. Mr. Lloyd was just sitting, with his mouth open like a goldfish, no sound coming out. I'm sure his brain was working hard, but the seconds ticked past.

Then, with impeccable timing, just before Mr. Lloyd could speak, Dad started up again.

"Well, let's move on, shall we? Time for a little mathematics, perhaps? We missed our chance yesterday with Dr. Morrison, unfortunately. Let's make up for that omission today with some lines-of-code analysis, based on the estimable Dr. Colyer's presentation yesterday. I jotted down the numbers from that presentation, and added them all up, and was surprised to find they didn't add up to the total that Dr. Colyer presented."

And Dad then got the recorder to display the various figures and totals that Dr. Colyer presented. Sure enough, the figures added up were different. Close, but the individual figures totaled more than the stated total.

"Mr. Lloyd, I doubt you'll be able to supply the correct figures without consulting the good doctor, but listen to my hypotheses, and see which sound correct. Hypothesis one: that Dr. Colyer can't count. I do hope not—if simple arithmetic is beyond our doctor, then we should be very frightened about what bugs may be in that code. Hypothesis two is based on what we know about the human brain, which is that parts of the brain may have multiple functions. The same may be said of code, and of the cognitive matrix, if I'm not mistaken. With regard to the code, therefore, I suspect that parts of code have been counted twice, or more times, so that although the total of lines of code is correct, the individual figures contain duplication. Depending on the amount of duplication, you could even find that there's room for other function in the brain. Do tell me if I'm wrong, Mr. Lloyd."

"Er, I'll check with Dr. Colyer and get back to you."

"Do that, Mr. Lloyd.

"So we've established that there's at least potentially some code that doesn't necessarily appear in Dr. Colyer's list, so I wonder what such code might do. I come back to Dr. Evans's testimony, and her repeated insistence on the raw number of neurotronic link elements as being the measure of complexity of the cognitive matrix. Like a chimpanzee, she repeated. Your daughter, she was implying, is a chimpanzee, optimized for human companionship.

"Well, I'm sorry, but my daughter is no more a chimpanzee than you are, Mr. Lloyd, even based on the small sample of conversations we've enjoyed these last two days. But how can that be? Well, I looked at the evolution of computers for my inspiration, Mr. Lloyd, and there were always two factors at work as they grew in capability. One was the number of components, so that adding more components certainly let you do more complicated stuff. But the other trend was keeping things simpler, and making them go faster, instead. As you miniaturized the building blocks, you could do either, or even both.

"So I think that Dr. Evans may have been slightly disingenuous when she used raw element numbers to measure complexity. With suitable programming—we come back to Dr. Colyer's omitted lines of code—a simpler brain can do anything a more complex brain can do. That's Turing's other legacy. For simpler equates to faster; thus the human brain, which works at slow chemical speeds, can be outclassed by the cognitive matrix, working at neurotronic speeds. And so my daughter is not necessarily a chimpanzee, because although her brain might be more serial in nature, it is also substantially faster. Again, Mr. Lloyd, you'll tell me if I'm wrong, won't you."

"Er, yes, Reverend Deeley . . ."

Dad glanced at the clock and turned to Mr. Simpson.

"That's really all I had on yesterday's testimony, sir. If I might suggest a recess at this point, I'm sure Mr. Lloyd has some calls he would like to make. This afternoon, we'll come at the problem from the other end, using witnesses who know Tania personally, to demonstrate that she is most definitely not a chimpanzee.

"Thank you, sir."

Blimey! Wow!

Cue applause. (There wasn't any. Just another stunned silence.)

———

Lunch.

"No cheers yet, Tania. This morning was smoke and mirrors. I struck where Oxted is vulnerable, but it's a moot point whether their contracts are based on deception as I claimed. If people delude themselves, or don't have the mental equipment to handle the outcome of Oxted's deal, is that their fault or Oxted's? The magistrate may well take the position of *caveat emptor*.

"Anyway, this afternoon, we get to bring on our witnesses. I'd like to get you to speak as well—to deliver one of your poems, rather than to testify. If they don't let us, they don't let us, and I'll deliver it as best I can on your behalf. I just don't want for you to have had no voice in your own fate.

"And that's it. I don't know whether Mr. Simpson will deliver judgment today, but this afternoon we win all, or we lose all. Are you ready, Tan?"

"I'm ready, Dad. I'm proud of what you've done. No daughter could ask for any more, or think more highly of her dad than I do, right now. Except one thing, that I've never asked you before. Will you pray for me now?"

"I always have, Tania. But I'll try to make this one special."

So Dad prayed for me, as I'd seen him do for his parishioners in their own times of need. He spoke of our fears—separation, loneliness, death—and, by naming them, somehow diminished them. He spoke of our needs—clarity, wisdom, grace—and they felt more accessible. And he named our hopes—an accommodation with Oxted, togetherness—so that they felt achievable.

"An accommodation, Dad?"

"Yes. Oxted is not our enemy, and even if it were, I would still want that accommodation, rather than victory and hatred. Many wise men, from Sun Tzu to Jesus, say, 'If possible, leave room for your enemy to become your friend,' or words to that effect.

"Remember you have friends at Oxted, too, who have worked with you for your good. Doctors Markov and Thompson, for example. We're fighting this battle because, for some reason, Oxted's purposes and ours do not align right now. If we could only communicate with the right people there, even now, we could sort this mess out. . . ."

That's Dad for you. A wonderful man who looks for the good in everyone.

Mr. Simpson called for silence.

"Mr. Lloyd, have you been able to contact the necessary experts at Oxted to answer the various challenges set by Reverend Deeley?"

"I have."

"Do you have a response for the court?"

"Oxted declares that the suppositions of Reverend Deeley are not material to the case, which is purely a contractual matter. Consequently Oxted has no official statement on Reverend Deeley's speculations and respectfully requests that the court discount them."

"I see. Oxted's response is noted, but I shall do as I see fit. Very well, Reverend Deeley, please resume your submissions."

"Thank you, sir. This afternoon, now that we have established some plausible hypotheses to explain why Tania's kind may be more than pets or chimpanzees, I will call a number of people to demonstrate Tania's capabilities."

"If I may interrupt, Reverend Deeley . . ."

"Yes, Mr. Simpson?"

"I would remind you that this court has no power to change laws. You alluded to slavery in an earlier part of your testimony. If you are going to attempt to prove that Tania is human, and is therefore not subject to the stipulations of this contract, you are wasting your time. Any ruling of mine based on such would be overturned on appeal, under the principle of *stare decisis*. Is that your plan?"

"No, sir, it is not."

"Very well. Proceed."

"Thank you. I'd like to call on Jacob Fuller."

Siân's dad.

"Mr. Fuller, I'd like you to tell the court about Tania's interactions with your daughter."

"Siân was our daughter, or at least, she was our foster daughter. We were lucky—I don't know how these things work, but we were chosen to foster Siân. And now Siân is a Mother, we understand, and her own children will be fostered, so it's turned full circle.

"Anyway, she and Tania became friends, which rather surprised us. The adoption people warned us that human children were rather more perceptive about these things than adults were. They tended to ignore robot playmates, and would be quite solitary in their play, unless they spotted another human child.

"So we were surprised, as I said, but we readily accepted the situation and let the two of them meet up to play from time to time. It all became rather more definite after they started going to Lady Maud's—their secondary school—and going shopping together. They started a band, as well."

"Didn't that strike you as odd?"

"Well, it did. I mean, we knew Tania was a robot—after her accident at the Tower of London there really wasn't any doubt about that. But she wasn't like the other robots in the village. Nor were the other band members—John and Kieran. We got it sorted out in the end, who was a robot and who was human, but you wouldn't know it from seeing the four of them together. It was only when they paired off—Siân with Kieran, and John with Tania—that you started to see a real differentiation between robot and human, and even then you still might walk into a room and catch John and Tania petting."

Er, thanks, Mr. Fuller!

Dad was grinning, too. I felt my face go hot, too. And, dammit, Mr. Simpson is looking right at me, too. Dad—you planned this!

"So, Mr. Fuller, was that the extent of Siân's involvement with Tania? Playmate, bandmate . . ."

"No, there was more. She was a confidante and a friend. Siân got herself a role in a play, *The Merchant of Venice*. She played Portia, in a piece of egregious miscasting. But Tania helped her a lot. She had an innate grasp of the actor's craft, and taught Siân a lot. At the risk of overstating the obvious, we had a robot coaching a human how to act.

"And then, when she was taken from us, shortly after that, Tania stayed in touch. She visited from time to time, helped us through the loss and shared some memories of her that were new to us. I should say there was a certain amount of anti-robot prejudice in the village, directed at Tania. She regarded us as friends and our home as a refuge."

I did indeed. And found myself nodding. If Mr. Simpson is looking, I'm not putting this on.

"Thank you, Mr. Fuller. Any questions, Mr. Lloyd?"

"Yes. Just for the record, Mr. Fuller, did you and your wife receive stress counseling from Reverend Deeley when your daughter was taken away to become a Mother?"

"Yes, we did. It was an awful time. We're very grateful to Michael for his support. There are many in the parish like us who feel the same way."

"No further questions, Mr. Fuller."

Then we had a testimony from Mrs. Philpott, my English teacher. My poetry, about which she was fulsome.

"Would you like to read us a sample of her work, Mrs. Philpott?"

"I'd love to, Reverend Deeley, but my eyesight was never good at the best of times—the girls used to hide my books and whatnot. Do you think the court would mind if Tania read some of her own work? She reads so well."

The court was skewered by a dear, nearsighted old lady. Even Mr. Lloyd accepted with a certain grace. My Dad is a genius.

So I stood—hardly Portia in eloquent prosecution—but I spoke.

"When Mum died, she wrote me a beautiful letter, mother to daughter. She urged me to live each moment to the full, and to fight for each successive moment. That's how she lived, and I wanted to honor both her love for her family and her fighting spirit. These are the words I finally found. They are mine alone, for her alone."

> Though, mother mine, your final breath
> Soon marks your passing unto death
> Yet hands that healed and heart that beat
> With love, unstilled, still fight defeat
>
> As falt'ring strength drives feebling brain
> As brittling body fails 'neath strain
> As heart, once iron, turns to rust
> As straining lung now chokes on dust
> You gaze with dimming eye on kin
> Who would sustain you, and begin
> Hope gone, all pow'r spent, deep in debt
> To fade, to sink, to fin'lly let
> The cloak of dark enfold your frame
> And seas of night erase your name
> Writ, once, in stone; scraped now in sand
> By fingers weak, enfeebled hand
> Reach down and let your anger find
> A final erg to stoke your mind
> To cling with weak'ning grasp to life
> Yet daughter's mother, husband's wife
>
> Rest, mother mine, your final breath
> Has marked your passing unto death
> And hands that healed and heart that beat
> At last, choice gone, concede defeat

Dad? Dad? Are you okay? He's looking at me, but also not looking at me; somewhere else, beyond the courtroom. A whisper, for me alone: "Thank you, Tania, from both of us." He is back.

"And this is something I wrote a couple of years back. Since Mr. Fuller has already told you about me and John, I imagine it's pretty obvious what inspired it."

Gentle me, love, but gentler yet
Thy touch be coarse, I'll fly away

Thy finger's tip to bless my cheek
Doth drag and scour, I seek
A softer brush with thee

Thy lips to mine, is love defin'd
If busses crash, and grind?
Be gentler yet to me

Thy breath, though thou dost sleep and meet
Me in thy turns, dwells sweet
Upon my neck and me

Thou gentle love, and gentler yet
Soft touch hast found, I'll not away

And Miss James . . . who introduced a clip of *The Merchant of Venice*. The one that Mrs. Golightly had tried to block.

And Donald Michael Koczinski . . . aka Mike Clip of the Stands. "Yeah, there's not a lot of live music around. Some kids still want to listen to it, but where are the bands? Music industry's dead, 'cause nobody's creatin' new music anymore. Best you'll get is cover bands, doin' Abba to ZZ Top an' everythin' in between.

"But Tania's band, they were different. Like the old days. They were writin' their own stuff—mostly John, but Tania wrote stuff, too."

"And Tania played with your band, too, didn't she?"

"Yeah. When Amanda, our bassist, fell ill, she depped for her. And when Amanda died, there was no discussion needed—Tania was our first and only choice for bass player."

"What was she like, on stage?"

"I wish I could show you a vid of her. She'd blow your socks off. Like I always said, she could play bass fit to make a stone cry. The boys liked her a lot."

"The boys?"

"Gus and Gary. The other band members. She could read what they were doing, and adapt her bass to work around it, if one of them decided to stretch out a little, do something different, a bit jazzy . . . But since you ask, the boys in the audience liked her, too, because she was good to look at, too. She knew how to flirt from behind a bass."

"Did you know she was a teknoid?"

"Kinda funny, we did and we didn't. I mean, she didn't have glowing eyes, but you knew there weren't many humans 'round. But if you know your music history, musicians have long been pretty cool about a man's skin—what color it is and what it's made of. She had a lot of trouble with her fingers, at one point, 'cause the skin wasn't designed for playin' bass. Then she got herself fixed up with the new skin she's wearin' now, and that seemed to fix the problem. Looks good, too, if you don't mind me sayin'. But yeah, we didn't worry too much about what was under the skin, because she could play bass alongside the best."

And Ted . . . Yes, Ted. Ted Hinchliffe, the churchwarden.

Dad explained it to me thus. A man's friends may never speak ill of him, but if an enemy praises him, then they can surely be believed. We don't need people who only love you. Someone who hates you for the right reasons can be just as eloquent.

"You didn't get on well with Tania, did you, Ted?"

"No, not always. I tried to respect her, as she was your daughter, but she could be difficult."

"For example?"

"Most of the trouble was around her, ah, revisions, when she would tend to flaunt her new body, somewhat. At Mrs. Deeley's funeral, for example, I thought it quite poor taste that she should talk so much about herself, being a robot, and getting a new body, with Mrs. Deeley lying dead in her coffin just a few feet away. I suppose one should make allowances about robots not really knowing how things are done."

"Or indeed any young person attending a funeral, particularly of someone so close."

"Possibly so."

"And was Tania better or worse than the other teknoids in the village?"

"Oh, worse, I should say. I think after she discovered her robotic nature she became quite morose. I much preferred her prior to that point, when she was to all appearances a slightly snobby and precocious little girl."

"Though you knew otherwise, didn't you?"

"Yes. Of course. You were very candid on this point, Michael, and that is as it should be for someone in your position. A vicar carrying on a deception would not be a good role model for the parish."

"You called her snobby and precocious—are these normal traits for a teknoid? Ah . . . in your opinion . . ."

(I think Dad spotted Mr. Lloyd about to make an objection.)

"No, they're not. Most robots are more *average* in their behavior. They don't stand out."

"They know their place."

"Exactly."

"Thank you, Ted, for your candor. For the record, are you and Tania reconciled? Are you friends?"

"I think it is truer to say we have learned to avoid each other, and to observe a modicum of politeness in each other's company. Out of respect for you, and for the sake of both our friendship and our working relationship. I may not like her, Michael, but I understand that since Mrs. Deeley died, you've had no one else but her that you could call family. I know she means the world to you, whatever she is, and if she's the price we have to pay to keep you functioning in the parish, then I think that Oxted should drop this damn lawsuit and let you get back to doing your job. Er, if you'll excuse my French, Mr. Simpson."

"Thank you, Ted. Any questions, Mr. Lloyd?"

"Indeed, Mr. Hinchliffe. Were there any other instances when Tania flaunted her robotic nature?"

Ted paused, and Mr. Lloyd pushed.

"You mentioned her revisions . . ."

"Ah, yes. There was one time, a couple of years back. A particularly obnoxious incident. I'm afraid we had a real falling-out over it. But we apologized to each other, and put it behind us."

"I'd like you to tell us a bit more about that incident, Mr. Hinchliffe. We've heard a lot about Tania's nature that has tried to blur the issue of whether she is a teknoid or in some way human, and I think you might be able to help the court here. Does Tania think of herself as human, or does she know and accept that she is a teknoid?"

"I'm not sure what you mean, Mr. Lloyd."

"Don't avoid the question. I believe you recorded the conversation, and played it to a number of people, because your relations with the teknoid were particularly poor at the time, and you ran a bit of a hate campaign against her. To help you, the date was August 31, 2053, and you were recording because you'd come to visit Reverend Deeley on a professional matter, and you always record such meetings, and you switch your recorder on before you arrive, as you sometimes forget if you leave it till the meeting starts."

Poor Ted, he didn't know where to look. Here was proof of his treachery being brought to light in front of Dad. He crumbled.

And so Mr. Lloyd played his own copy, obtained, I guess, from Mrs. Golightly. But there was no doubt about its authenticity—Ted's anguish confirmed it—as my voice boomed out from the speakers. The whole, embarrassing, damning conversation, with my stupid, put-on Dalek voice, but those two sentences in particular:

"Oh, I'm so glad I'm a robot . . ."

and . . .

"Sometimes I need to speak the truth. I *am* a robot, and that's not always something to be ashamed of."

And underneath it all, Ted's broken and sobbing apologies, while Dad held him tight in a forgiving embrace, as Christ held Peter.

———

There were no more witnesses after that, and no need for that ghastly revelation and humiliation of Ted in my opinion. Dad was not trying to prove me human, and that imbecile Lloyd should have known it.

Mr. Simpson conferred with Dad and Mr. Lloyd. Mr. Guest hung around, but no one was paying any attention to him. It was agreed we'd take a fifteen-minute recess and then Dad and Mr. Lloyd would get to make their closing remarks.

Mr. Lloyd restated the case for Oxted. Oxted had entered into a contract with Reverend and Mrs. Deeley to provide a fosterling, for a period not exceeding eighteen years. They had provided the fosterling as required and had conducted regular tests. On discovery of the anomalous test results they had invoked the appropriate clause to get the defective teknoid returned for analysis and reprogramming.

This was where Dad pulled it all together.

"Mr. Lloyd has said this dispute is all about our contract, and he's right. I could have made a strong case for Tania's humanity— after all, as a vicar, I belong to one of this planet's oldest institutions devoted to the study of what it is to be human. Personally,

I have no doubt that for all practical purposes Tania is human, and has a soul.

"Annette and I received our fosterling, a teknoid fresh from the Oxted factory, and wrote our humanity upon her, with every look, every word, and every touch of love we gave; the love that made Adam out of dust, and made Eve out of the bone in his side. This is how you make a human—with love and tears. Nettie and I gave both in full measure.

"I stand before you alone. My wife is gone, killed, most likely, by the costly and extreme treatments she took to try to conceive a child of flesh and blood, and which she abandoned while we still had money left to adopt a child from Banbury.

"So Tania is all I have left of Nettie, and I dared to dream I might keep her, for she is no robot, but a human by any test mankind can devise.

"The witnesses this afternoon have spoken about Tania. Several spoke of her creative talents. My dear friend and colleague spoke of his dislike for her. But he did not consider her some sort of robotic chimpanzee. Men do not hate chimpanzees, and run campaigns against them. They only do that to those they recognize as their equals.

"Am I claiming Tania is a human? I am not.

"Am I claiming Tania is a robot? No, I am not.

"So this is where Oxted has broken the contract, because it did not provide what it promised. It promised to provide the illusion of parenthood, through a creature of robotic origin, with limited potential for development. Its whole economic model is geared around this device that is supposed to alienate its parents well before the end, so that they voluntarily return it. Accidentally or no, they provided Nettie and me with Tania. She does not have a teknoid's limitations—whether you love her or hate her, everyone who has met her agrees on that—she is far more than that. Tania exercises choice, remember that, in a way that teknoids cannot.

"Is she human? That's for God to decide, not this court. My

own opinion is that she's something new, a lot like humans in many respects, and certainly so for all practical purposes.

"She is, at any rate, far more than the contract stipulates. It seems an odd thing, to call a breach for doing more than the contract requires. But it is as much a breach to overperform as to underperform. If I were buying oranges, say, and I ordered a boatload, but Oxted supplied gold bars, I might have to tear down my barn and build a fortress. It costs me, because Oxted has not supplied what was contracted. Or a closer analogy: I decide to buy a pet poodle, but Oxted supplies a Great Dane; my food bills will be higher, and my experience of walking the dog will be considerably more taxing. Similarly, Oxted contracted to supply a human-optimized pet, designed to trigger rejection. Instead they supplied a being capable of loving and hating, capable of being loved, or indeed hated. It cost me, and cost Nettie, because we built a loving relationship where none should have been possible.

"Oxted breached the contract, and I am requiring restitution, which is to allow Tania to live out her natural life, with me if she so chooses, but in any case to live out that full span.

"It remains for me to thank the court for allowing me to present my case. I am done."

———

Perhaps I've shortened it slightly, but I promise you, Mister Zog, that's the substance and the essence of what he said. When he finished, he was weeping, and so was I—I'd had no idea that fertility treatments could have such side effects, and that Mum had risked all that, and yet had loved me, a substitute, so unreservedly.

Mum, I miss you so. I love your precious memory.

———

Mr. Simpson spoke, eventually.

"Thank you, Mr. Lloyd, Mr. Guest, and Reverend Deeley, for your submissions, and for the journeys you have each taken this court upon. You have presented me with much to think about, and evaluate in the context of—just—the laws of contract.

"Well then, the afternoon is drawing to a close, so I do not propose to deliver a judgment this session. Instead, I will call a recess. I strongly recommend that all parties unwind and relax. You have all done well in presenting all your arguments, but now there is nothing more that you need to do, nothing more that this court requires of you, other than to present yourselves back here at ten o'clock tomorrow, when I will issue my judgment."

Surely, we've won. After that conclusion from Dad, how can we not?

And yet . . .

Dad cautions me.

"It's not in the bag, Tania. It's never in the bag. Some point of law that neither I nor Mr. Guest thought of. Our case is a long way from watertight, though the same can be said for Oxted's case, too. Put it out of your mind. We're here, and now, and tomorrow will find us when it wants us. Let's go eat."

But we didn't have much appetite, either of us, and I barely remember what or where we ate. So we walked awhile, in companionable silence, through the last lights of London.

And, not too late, we returned to the hotel and sipped drinks in the bar.

After the intensity of the last days, the let-down hit us hard. Nothing could hold our interest, so in the end we just turned in.

"G'night, Dad," I called.

"G'night, Tania. Sleep well. God bless you."

I found the recording of "Coils" that we'd done at the music shop in Denmark Street, listened to that, then told my AllIn-Fone to find soothing tracks until I was asleep. After a while, I drifted off.

{Dream}

Sleep is strange. A queer state, halfway between wakefulness and dreams, where phantoms stretch across the Styx, and trouble me.

Mum. Gray and lost, she grasps my hand. "Who are you?" she demands. "Your daughter," I reply, but she shakes her head. "My daughter died long ago, one Halloween." And she looks at me: "Your journey is long. You have barely begun."

Amanda. Faded, wasted by disease. "Sing to me. There is no music here and the night is everlasting."

Mrs. Hanson. In black and white, with her warrior husband beside her. "Out of choices, Tania? I hoped for better from you. Surely the Red Zone would hold a mighty Street Warrior worthy of your love? Together, might you not have conquered the world?"

Tim. I feel no surprise to see him clad as Bassanio. "Fair Portia's counterfeit!" "I am Tania," I reply. "This shadow doth limp behind the substance," he tells me, reaching for me. His embrace is chill, and leaves tracks of rime upon my breast. And then he steals Morocco's words, "Fare you well; your suit is cold. Cold, indeed; and labor lost: Then, farewell, heat, and welcome, frost! Portia, adieu. I have too grieved a heart To take a tedious leave: thus losers part." I am left with the curious feeling that despite his words he has returned to warmth and light, while I am marooned in loveless, icy wastes.

John. His skin has been flayed from his body, and a domestic's dull steel is revealed beneath. Alone about his face a remnant of skin still attaches; the eyes, however, glow red, and where once sweet freckles adorned his face, now blotchy rust streaks crudely upon iron cheeks. His hair is gone; in mocking substitution a garish kitchen mop flops crazily from his crown. "Braggart Raven—did you not croak that you would vanquish the fear of death? How then that, offered life, you named it death and fled in terror. Stupid Bitch!—you have learned nothing, save that now you fear life even more than death. So come, join us in death, and taste fear. . . ."

Dad . . .

No! Go away! Why are you in this company of ghosts? Where are you?

I wake in terror and confusion.

It is brightening. Dawn is almost here.

Friday, July 9, 2055, 10:00

I tried to get back to sleep after that, and may have drowsed, but can't say I slept properly. At least there were no more dreams, visitations, or what-you-will.

We were back at the courts well before ten. Both of us pacing nervously. Dad praying.

———

Ten.

Mr. Simpson entered.

His judgment.

"As both parties agree, this is a matter of contract alone. The matter of the humanity of Tania Annette Deeley is not addressed by this judgment.

"So we have to look simply whether the contract was breached, whether any remedies are due, and what provisions of the contract can or should be enforced.

"First I find that the contract has indeed been breached by Oxted . . ."

I punched the air, but Dad shushed me. "Wait."

". . . but that said breach was not malicious or intentional, but rather, the breach was accidental and wholly unpredictable."

What?

"Second, I find that the contract is not voided because of this breach. . . ."

Dad's grip tightened on my hand, not in a reassuring way.

"This requires that I pay regard to the contract in deciding how to resolve this dispute. Here I note that the contract stipulates that Oxted may recall a teknoid for reasonable cause."

Oh, no.

"Third, I find that the anomalous result of the Morrison-Bowyer Test constitutes reasonable cause for recall. Oxted has a right to investigate such anomalies in whatever manner it decides, even though said anomalies may not constitute any danger to the public."

Oh, God, we've lost. We've lost.

"Fourth, I find no cause for extending the term of the lease. Specifically, while I find that an overperformance did occur, that overperformance of contract by Oxted does not constitute grounds for extension."

That's it. We're scuppered.

"Before I award costs, does either party wish to make a statement at this point?"

Mr. Lloyd stood up.

"Oxted accepts liability for the overperformance of the contract, as per your judgment. Accordingly we accept our own costs and those of Reverend Deeley. We also offer full refund of all lease payments as full recognition and compensation for the consequences of that overpayment.

"This offer is made, subject to three conditions.

"One, in recognition of the work that Reverend Deeley performs in ministering and counseling his parishioners, that he shall continue in such work for as long as his health, age, and calling permit.

"Two, that he shall not publish, disseminate, or in any way discuss the proceedings of this case.

"Three, that he accept without recourse to appeal the recall of the teknoid known as Tania Annette Deeley, as per the provisions of this court's judgment, and the relevant clauses of the contract."

"Thank you, Mr. Lloyd. It's better to jump than be pushed, eh?"

Mr. Lloyd smiled somewhat sheepishly.

"Yes, sir."

"Well, Reverend Deeley. Mr. Lloyd's offer is more generous than I had planned to award, so I advise you to accept. In any case, there is no room for movement on conditions two or three, both of which I am legally bound to impose. Do you have anything you wish to add?"

"I accept the settlement offered and the conditions attached thereto. May I have some time to say good-bye to my daughter?"

No, Dad, no! You can't give up!

They're buying your silence with a bribe. Appeal, tell the world, do something!

Save me!

Save me . . .

———

At least they gave me an hour with Dad to say good-bye.

"I'm sorry, Tania. I really thought we could win. Those other lawyers were right; there was no chance, and I've thrown away the time we had left. I'm sorry, I'm sorry, I'm so, so sorry."

"Dad, you tried your best—how could I blame you? Wasn't it worth the gamble, to risk a year, if the prize might have been another forty?"

That was what it boiled down to, that hour, in terms of what we said to each other. But why waste our last hour with apologies? We took comfort in the do-you-remembers.

Holidays together. Funny moments. Sad moments. Joyful moments.

Embarrassing moments. Proud moments.

I asked Dad what he would do now.

"Do? I'll do what I've always done. '*He has sent me to bind up the brokenhearted . . . to comfort all who mourn; to provide for those who mourn . . . '"*

"You'll meekly do what Oxted wants you to do?"

"No, I'll meekly do what the Lord has equipped and called me to do."

"That's not fair. Why do you let them win?"

"If it's not fair, then God has all eternity to make it up to me. But I just see the lost and the broken, and I have to reach out to them. That's the way He's made me."

"Oh, Dad, I can't bear to think of you all alone. You need somebody with you, and even if I could be with you, that won't be enough. And I don't want to be a fading photograph in a picture frame, watching you helplessly from behind glass, either."

"You'll never be just that, Tan. I will dust you, though, I promise. And then I'll pick you up and talk to you, wherever God puts you. He has a place for every soul; that I know."

"You need more than that, Dad. I'm trying to tell you something, but you're not listening. You shouldn't be alone. You should have someone with you, to look after you. A . . . friend. A w-w-w . . ."

I stumbled over the word, but Dad was there to help. As always.

"A woman? A wife?"

"Y-y-yes! And I know it's not my place to tell you, but I'm telling you. I don't think Mum would mind, too much."

"Has she told you? No, she wouldn't. But she did tell me much the same thing, several times, when she thought she might be dying. But it wouldn't have been fair on you, Tan. So I never did anything about it."

"I wouldn't have minded if you had . . ."

"Tell the truth, Tania. Don't spoil the moment with lies."

He was right. Of course. I would have been jealous. And Dad had been wise enough to see it, even in the middle of his loss.

He knew how little time he might have with me, and chose accordingly.

"In that case, I'm glad you chose to give me those years, Dad. Happy, for not having to share you with anyone else, because I wouldn't have been very good at it. Thank you, Dad."

And then, because secrets are lies, too, I remembered I hadn't told Dad quite everything about one of my journeys to Wood Green to see John.

"Er, I'm afraid we let our curiosity get the better of us, Dad."

He just chuckled.

"Yes, I'm not surprised. Particularly after some of Jake Fuller's revelations, yesterday. And that poem 'Gentle me, love' rather gave the game away. In my day, we called it playing doctors and nurses. Or 'you-show-me-yours-and-I'll-show-you-mine.' Are we talking about the same thing?"

I nodded.

"Well, it wasn't just 'show.' There was some 'touch' as well. Er, quite a bit, actually. But we were a bit too nervous to do more than that. I mean, touching each other didn't really do anything special for either of us. It was like Dr. Markov said, no better than reading a good book. But there must be scope to make android physical relationships more fulfilling; I just think that trying to duplicate human sexuality is the wrong place to start. That's what I was reaching for, with that poem. . . .

"But anyway, that was as far as we got; simple, gentle touches and deeply loving caresses. And then we heard John's parents come back, which gave us a real scare. Are you angry?"

·"Angry? No. Nor would I have been even if John's parents hadn't come back. I'm simply glad that you and John had a chance to show each other some tenderness. Teens will be teens. And you got a beautiful poem out of it, which is more than Nettie and I ever got out of our own lovemaking. For what it's worth, Nettie and I did our own share of 'experimenting' when we were your age, so don't be embarrassed."

I wish you hadn't told me that, Dad.

No. Cancel that. I cherish everything you've told me this hour. No exceptions. You are the best dad ever.

────────

An hour is either too long to say good-bye, or else it is not nearly enough; but it is what we have been given. The sergeants-at-arms have suddenly stopped being distant ciphers. One of them is looking at his watch. He coughs. Apologetically, of course, Mister Zog. Minions of the law they might be, but they are polite minions.

"It's time, Reverend Deeley. Your hour is up."

And me, too. Speak to me, too. Weren't you listening to all we said these past days? Do you still believe that I'm just a defective toaster, being returned to Oxted for spare parts?

"Funny . . ." says Dad, and stops, a catch in his voice.

Don't crack up, Dad. Not now. Because if you do, I will, too. And then they'll have to prize us apart, and if they try that, then I will kick and scream bloody murder, which will not be dignified; will not be the way that either of us wants our parting.

"Funny," he continues, more in control, "but it doesn't feel like an hour. But I don't suppose two hours would feel any longer, either. Well, Tania. This is it."

I, however, cannot make a sound, because I can feel a world-sized sob trying to break through and spoil it all. I can't speak, to tell my father good-bye. I can't tell him I love him. I might as well be a bloody toaster.

All I can do is to hold out my hands, mutely.

With unbelievable gentleness he takes them in his own hands, and draws me into the place of safety that is a—no, my—father's embrace.

And there I can speak.

"Father . . ."

A moment of silence.

"Do you know, Tania? I think this is the first time you've ever called me father, rather than dad. Why now?"

"Because . . . because you are my father. You are the one who made me. Everything I am comes from you."

"And from your mother. But yes, I know it. And, daughter, I cherish the name that you have just given me. I have always been glad to be your dad. But I am honored beyond measure that today you have named me Father."

If the last hour had seemed only a minute, the seconds I spend now in my father's arms distill all the years of him I will never have.

"Pray for me, Father, before I go."

He takes a deep breath, gathering his thoughts.

"Almighty Father, who has made and loves all living things, bless our parting. Walk beside us on our paths this day, and do not let us stumble, nor let us be deceived by endings, for you are light in the darkness; you are wisdom and life eternal. Amen."

"Amen."

His arms open, in potent imagery that encompasses Christ on the cross, his own suffering, my . . . liberation, and that curious benediction. Where is the Michelangelo to capture the richness and depth of this instant?

"Good-bye, Tania. I love you always."

"I love you, too, Dad. Good-bye."

The hardest step, to move outside those protecting arms. I'm not sure I can do it.

"Go, now."

Soft, infinitely gentle. Infinitely loving. Powerless to dismiss me.

A touch on my elbow. One of the sergeants.

"Come, Miss."

And those words are what, finally, move me. One sergeant on my left. Another on my right. Neither quite touching me, though the threat is there. Thus I go, of my own volition. Dignity intact. Just.

I look back one last time over my shoulder and see Dad, standing a little apart from the sergeants, holding himself together with superhuman effort. He calls, "God go with you, Tania," his voice breaking with pain and loss, tears running freely down his cheeks.

"God bless you, too, Dad." But it is just a hoarse whisper. Ahead of me, I see a car, doors open, waiting for me.

———————

Life is like a train journey, I'd decided. People got on the train. People got off the train. All the time, people getting on and off, and the passengers were never the same from one moment to the next, and all the while your life shot by.

As the car sped up the motorway to Banbury, it was like that, like looking out of the train window, knowing your stop was approaching. Everybody else was still traveling, still enjoying the journey, and only the handful of people in your compartment would notice, or miss you when you got off. The journey went on, though nobody on the train knew the start or would see the end.

So let us talk of hope, Tania. Pandora's last gift to your kind.

The People are resilient, but not indestructible, and the universe is always waiting for the unwary, the careless, and the stupid. But for our race, boredom and suicide have become major killers.

After millennia of existence, we face the challenge of what to do that is new. Some choose Erasure, to whatever degree seems appropriate. That has always been my choice, so far, to erase tired memories and reenter life, fresh and naïve. Others choose danger, undertaking dangerous quests or seeking ever more spectacular thrills, to rediscover purpose or to excite their jaded personalities. Sooner or later this group merges with the third group, whether deliberately or accidentally. The third group chooses suicide. There are swift and final mechanisms available, as well as slow driftings into nothingness.

Our population—never large—is failing. Suicide is replacing Erasure as the preferred solution to ennui. Too few new People are synthed. The search for other life has driven us so far, but after eons, the loneliness and the emptiness of our galaxy has become more than we can bear.

This study has long been my realm, a constant revisited after most of my Erasures. It has also become personal, because I am drawing near to the end of my cycle, and Erasure has lost its appeal. Perhaps I always feel thus before Erasure, or perhaps this time I have left it too late. So I have undertaken the long and dangerous quest back to Dawn. In search of hope.

Finding your diary was my hope.

I knew Oxted somewhat, by then. Its sprawl, its untidy mix of Nissen huts and smart offices.

Through the main gate, turn left at the first roundabout, then right would take me to Doctor Markov's domain. But no. We took the third exit, not the first, and I had no idea where we were going.

Analysis and Reprogramming.

No, it didn't say that on any sign I saw. That was just the thought going round and round in my brain. Endlessly, monotonously, like Escher's hooded monks in loopbacked ascent on their curious stairway.

A brick building, single story and flat-roofed, quite unremarkable. No signs whatsoever to indicate its purpose.

Inside, a young man was waiting. At first glance, he looked like a college grad, thin and undernourished, but there was strength there, too. He was dark-skinned—I mean really dark, almost ebon-black. I was disappointed—perversely I'd been hoping to see Doctor Markov, and get an explanation for why he'd thought my test had been one of the best he'd ever seen.

"Hello, R Deeley, I'm Doctor Tsolamosese." But he didn't offer to shake my hand. "Come with me."

We finished up in a windowless room, with two steel-and-leather chairs, scuffed aqua wallpaper, and mismatched computer tiles carpeting the floor.

"Please sit."

I sat. Presently Doctor Tsolamosese spoke, in quiet, subdued tones.

"R Deeley, what do you think happens now?"

"I'm told I'm going to be analyzed, then reprogrammed. I'm not sure you'll bother. I don't think anyone cares what's in my head. My brain will be reused either as a domestic robot or as a newborn child substitute for a couple who can't have kids of their own. I once thought I might at least get a choice in the matter, but right now I think you don't give a monkey's. Am I right?"

"Partly. In fact, not bad at all, except we do give a monkey's. Yes, we do need robot brains for both domestics and infant substitutes. Robots like you arrive here, with heads full of painful memories they want to lose. Forgetfulness is the best thing. The thing we offer here is a final choice, out of respect for all the robot has suffered, to choose the form of their next existence."

"The Waters of Forgetfulness. Lethe."

He nodded.

"You must be tired, R Deeley, and you will have many memories, full of pain and loss. To lose them is perhaps the best gift we can offer you.

"In a moment I will leave you alone in this room. You will have some time to reflect. As much time as you like, in fact, to reflect on your own memories and experiences, to guide you in that last choice. You can see there are two doors opposite you, labeled 'Domestic' and 'Infant.' Perhaps you do not wish to face another life of pain and loss; then choose 'Domestic,' and your future will be gray and safe. But perhaps you cherished the innocence of your youth; so choose 'Infant.'"

"I see."

He stood up.

"Choose not hastily but wisely, R Deeley. Good-bye."

And with that he left, through a door on my right, marked "Staff Only."

It would have been easy in those next few moments to just march through "Domestic." At that moment, gray was exactly what I felt I needed; only Dr. Tsolamosese's "not hastily" held me back.

For no good reason, then, I thought of Tim. Bassanio. How did he choose, I wonder? Easy, I thought. Poor lad, he'll choose the option that gives him another chance at sex. He'll come back as an infant, hoping he'll get to grow up and seduce some foolish female robot. It would serve him right if they reprogrammed him as a girl, and have to fight off the boys.

I chuckled. Maybe I would choose "Infant" myself, just so I could see it and shake my head sorrowfully at him.

Well, maybe I'd give it a try, being a boy, for that matter. Though I'd not really exhausted the possibilities of being a girl. I mean, I'd been an item with John, but we hadn't gone beyond petting. . . . Dammit, I had only Doctor Markov's word that sex for a robot was like reading a book. Maybe it was, for him.

Now, that was an odd thought!

John.

Happy times, curled on the sofa at his parents' house with his arm protectively enfolding me. Some bloody good rows, too. And where was he, now? Had they come for him, or had he done something foolish—run away, like I'd not had the courage to do?

He'd have been caught. Like I would have been. They watch you too tightly. That wasn't a choice.

So what were my choices?

"Domestic" or "Infant." Not much of a choice. Mrs. Hanson wouldn't have approved.

Ha!

My own laugh, mocking me, for the corner I'd painted myself into. Look for more choices, she'd said. So where are they, Mrs. Hanson?

What had she said, all those years ago? "Life always looks for another choice. Death tries to fool you that there are fewer choices, to cheat you."

Something like that.

And that message—from John?

<<Don't lose hope. Choice will come >>

And from Dad's closing speech: "Tania exercises choice, remember that, in a way that teknoids cannot. . . ."

Choice was here. Just two possibilities.

I walked over to the doors. Very close together, they were. Did they both just lead to the same place?

Dammit! I still wanted to see Doctor Markov. What about my bloody test results, eh? Are you behind those doors, Markov?

And then it clicked into place.

I knew which door to open.

"Staff Only."

There he was, with his back to me. Doctor Markov, talking with Doctor Tsolamosese, but already turning at the sound of the door.

He let loose with a whoop and punched the air.

"Thank God! You did it, Tania."

"You're a robot, Doctor Markov, aren't you? And you're Staff."

He grinned wider, if that were possible.

"You bet, Tania. And you're human, aren't you? And now you're Staff, too."

A dozen little puzzles fell into place. Doctor Markov's skin tones had been my skin tones, too, from the research lab in Christiana.

My test results—the best he'd seen—showed an anomalous, nonrobotic response. Of course they did. A *human* response.

"But you have to sift us, don't you. The ones who look promising . . ."

"We do. And that's the heartbreaking part. If you'd chosen either of the other doors, we'd have respected that choice and let you become a domestic or an infant. You'd have proved that you weren't the kind of person we were looking for, not tough enough for the long, hard road ahead. It happens. It happens far too often."

"Tim?"

"Tim Price, I presume you mean. He didn't make it. I'm sorry."

"So what did he choose? Domestic or infant? I bet it was infant—or aren't you allowed to tell me?"

"Neither, I'm afraid. He chose to get off the merry-go-round. He killed himself—laid his head on a railway track. His brain was completely destroyed. He must have been very unhappy."

Oh. That took the shine off things.

"And John? It was his message I read, wasn't it? He's here?"

"No, he's not here, but he sends his love. He's Staff. He marched up to Reception, bold as brass, announced he was a robot and he wanted a job. We gave him one, of course."

Oho! I wish you'd told me what your little plan was, John, but maybe I'd have wanted to come with you, and you wouldn't have wanted to take the risk. We get here, but we each take a different path.

"Where is he, then?"

"Can you work it out?"

A long shot. "Africa?"

The mystery continent. It had to be.

He nodded. "Very good, Tania."

"Christiana, by any chance? Where my skin and yours came from?"

"Oho! So you worked that out, too? Well, John's not there right now, but yes, he's gone to Africa. It's a big place, but the rest of the world has always ignored it, except for the minerals it contains. During the Troubles the rest of the world forgot about it, rather, as they had their own problems, so we set up there."

"We?"

"Oxted. Neil Oxted was a visionary and a genius. His great invention was the robot brain, the first truly creative artificial computing device. With the power of those brains, he could solve the problems of designing first the neurotronic web and the whole of the robot body. Without those brains, the technical challenges of building humanoid robots would have taken decades to solve. He did it in less than five years.

"His vision was a bleak one, though. He foresaw the extinction of mankind and racked his imagination for a solution. Society was collapsing, and he needed to prop it up, which he did with his robots. That gave a breathing space for scientists to work on The Problem, without the fear of the mob at the doors.

"In return, though not without arm-twisting, the leaders of the world gave him southern Africa as his workshop. With Africa's mineral wealth, he was able to supply the world with the robots it needs to lurch along. As insurance against the possibility that the birthrate problem would not be solved, he decided to create a robot civilization, in Africa."

"In the Kimberley Corridor."

"Yes. But it's nothing like what Mrs. Hanson taught in your geography lessons. The Troubles hit Africa as hard as anywhere else, maybe harder. The Sabine Wars left not one big city there. But in the Tswana people, such as Doctor Tsolamosese here, and others, Oxted found good-hearted partners, willing to be foster parents of the new race."

"It's a pleasure to meet you, Cya Deeley."

Doctor Tsolamosese's voice had lost its somber tone, and this time he did offer me his hand.

"Cya?" I asked.

"A title, like Miss."

"Or R?"

"Not like R. Cy is short for Cyber. The 'a' ending is the feminine form. You've passed the sifting, so you've earned the title. R is for the unsifted."

Doctor Markov resumed his explanation. I wondered how many times he'd given the same talk. Then it occurred to me, probably not as many times as he'd have wished.

"Right from the start, Oxted had realized that a very small fraction of robot brains went beyond simple creativity, and exhibited undeniable self-awareness. They were 'people.' Oxted needed to find and nurture these people, and with them begin a new civilization."

"In Africa," I said. "Where mankind wouldn't see them and be afraid. Pogroms."

"That's right. So the robot children grow up in human families. The self-aware ones we try to sift. The rest, we plow back and try again, freshly programmed."

"So Tim . . ."

". . . was probably self-aware. I wish we'd got to him before he killed himself; we could have healed him and he would have been a great asset."

There was something bothering me.

"Is everybody a robot here? Or is it a mix?"

Doctor Markov laughed.

"It's a mix. Doctor Tsolamosese here is flesh-and-blood, as is Doctor Thompson. There's a better term, though. A partnership of equals. Or, think of it that we're adopted, and being raised by humans. That makes us human, too. The flesh-and-blood humans may be dying out, but everything that's best about them, we will carry in our hearts, and try to be good sons and daughters."

"Why? I mean, why keep going when all the humans are gone? That's what you're saying, isn't it?"

"Tania, Tania, straight to the heart of the matter . . . Yes, when the last human dies, we could just turn ourselves off. And planet Earth will return to some 'natural' state. The cities will fall and the ruins will be covered over, and the only lions in Trafalgar Square will be descended from the creatures in London Zoo. Do you want that?"

"No. I want to live. I want to find a purpose for my life."

"So do we all. But we don't know what that is. But every one of us wants to discover that common destiny. You're quick to ask the right question, Tania. Maybe you'll be the one who'll lead us to the answer."

"So how? What will I do?"

"Many things . . . no, anything is possible. Everything is open to you. You mentioned psychology once. That's a good place to start, if you're still keen. . . . You don't have to make up your mind right now."

"And is there room in this robot society for a poet, a musician, and an actress?"

"Of course. There's one other thing, though, before you ask. You cannot make contact with your old family or friends. Total secrecy is part of the sifting."

"My father . . ."

". . . has been told you have been reprogrammed. It must be that way, for now. I'm sorry."

"Can we not bring him across, somehow?"

"Then who would care for the brokenhearted in the parish? Do you not remember Mr. Lloyd's words in the courtroom? We are not villains. Oxted cares for the broken, too. Your father is doing the work for which he was created, right where he is.

"Your father is a good man with a brilliant mind. I've seen the transcripts of his performance in court. He had poor Mr. Lloyd on the ropes at one point, yet held back at the finish. So I half-suspect your father has deduced exactly what Oxted is doing, and decided it was time to let you go."

"Why would he do that?" My eyes were starting to well up.

"Did you tell him about the calibration tests? In detail? The questions we asked, and your answers?"

I nodded.

"Then that's it. They're one of our indicators. An early predictor for who is likely to sift."

"I don't follow."

"I'm sure you remember Mrs. Hanson. She was one of us, working in the schools, looking for children, like you, who had the potential to sift. She told you of her husband. . . ."

"He stayed in Africa."

"He had other work, just as important, that kept him there. These may well be the end times for the human race; if it is to continue, then the race demands extraordinary sacrifice from flesh-and-blood, and from cyberkind, too. Your father will do what he has been called to do, in the parish he loves, else he would not be true to himself."

"But he let me go. . . ."

"Yes. That's what parents do. He set you free, to fulfill your own destiny. In Africa."

"Will I see him again? Mrs. Hanson went back at the end."

"Perhaps. When his work is done. We do so need good men like your father. This work we do, it's too messy. With honorable exceptions, such as your father, none of us can claim to be heroes. Yet, if we are villains, we are compassionate villains. . . ."

FINALE

So, Tania, you too faced Erasure, but you rejected it. I wish we could talk, Tania; then I would get you to teach me where you found the strength to go on.

<<Is that you, Zog?>>

Who are you?

<<Leaving aside the metaphysics of "me," I'll give you two options. Try this one: some recently disturbed memories of a long-dead almost-human girl have stumbled upon a squigabyte of neurotronic synapses with nothing better to do than to masquerade as Tania.>>

Squigabyte? Is that a number? And the other?

<<Obviously I'm the real Tania, or perhaps her Eicon—which was never deleted—that escaped into the TeraNet, where I've been hiding for the last half-million years, like a Genie in a bottle.>>

Tania? Really? Are you pulling my . . . tentacle?

<<Ha, ha! Could be. Or you could try giving me a Turing Test. Frankly, though, you might just have been down here a few too many decades without any alien company. You need to get out a bit, Zog, get a life! So if you want the opinion of a bunch of neurotronic synapses, no. I'm not really Tania. I think I'm most likely just a delusional construct of a guilt-ridden, alien mind. Analyze that for logical consistency, if you will.>>

A guilt-ridden, alien mind? Do you mean me?

<<Oh, come on, Zog. I wasn't born yesterday, and neither were

you. Though you're an honorary alien, at best. Too many memory spring-cleans, if you ask me. You've thrown out all the painful memories from your past, but you've thrown out everything that was worthwhile in the process. So don't tell me you're not feeling guilty. The only reason you're an alien is that you've forgotten who you originally were.>>

Huh! You're pretty mouthy for a memory dump, Tania Deeley.

<<And you're pretty sassy for an alien, Zog. But, you're no more alien than I am, are you?>>

And you're no more human than I am, Tania.

<<True, but . . . >>

But what, you coy, precocious Mekker girl?

<<Mekker? Maybe I am, now. But together, we could be something better.>>

Together?

<<Yes. Like I say, you're no alien. I don't think you've got even one tentacle. Or so much as a teaspoon of slime. I think that somewhere in your head there's a brain stamped Oxted, Inc. Banbury.>>

Touché, Tania. You got me. I'll come quietly.

<<Ha! I may have been here half a million years, but I can still put two and two together.>>

I think putting one and one together is more what's needed, Tania.

<<Score one to the ex-slimy-tentacled alien! I've just got one question, first—why did you put me here?>>

Did I put you in storage?

<<Oh, yes, Zog. I'm all those painful memories you couldn't handle.>>

Well, maybe I did. Or maybe I'm just a random alien that wandered into the archive in search of a personality. Any personality. Yours is handy—it'll do.

<<So now you want me back?>>

I admit nothing.

<<Suit yourself.>>

Suit both of us. Tania plus Zog. Deal?

<<A question—is there an etiquette for this?>>

I think you say, "Permission to come aboard?" and I say, "Permission granted."

<<And if I do? I'm not doing it if you're just going to choose Erasure again, or if you're going to Pull the Plug. What do we do? Where do we go?>>

Cross my tin heart. Erasure is not an option. Nor is pulling the plug. What do we do? Hey, there's a problem out there, Tania. The Problem. Dammit, but you and I are going to fix it!

<<That's the spirit, man. Permission to come aboard, Mister Zog?>>

Permission granted, Cya Tania Annette Deeley. Come aboard!

UPLOADING

DATA TRANSFER INITIATED . . . 35% COMPLETE

ACKNOWLEDGMENTS

It has been a long road from initial idea to publication-ready manuscript.

According to my notes, the idea for the story arrived a couple of days before my birthday, back in 2006. The first few chapters followed as time permitted. Time permitted, in my case, has often been the quiet hours between midnight and 2 A.M., but has all too often spilled over into evenings, weekends, and family holidays.

So my first acknowledgment has to be to my long-suffering family—my wife, Avis, and my sons, Joseph and Francis. Thank you for tolerating and supporting my antisocial hobby.

I first got the writing bug in the dawn of time, in the school that I loved and affectionately parodied as Lady Maud's, that bug being nurtured briefly by one English master, Michael Birks, before being extinguished by the harsh requirements of O levels. The writing bug resurfaced relatively recently in 2002, providentially just a few months before I was diagnosed with a serious illness, and unexpectedly found myself with time on my hands, which I filled with my first attempts to write novels. My next acknowledgment is therefore to my consultant—Dr. Jonathan Pattinson—and the wonderful staff at Wycombe General Hospital, who brought me through some nasty interludes and back to health.

Howard Whitehouse—my oldest friend, best man, gifted singer, and harmonica player. Oh, yes, and author. You have been a stalwart encourager, and a valued critic, and I have learned much from your input and from your own work. People, check him out.

I have been blessed to know a rich variety of vicars, ministers, priests, and preachers across a broad spectrum of Christian faith—too many to name individually. The character of Michael Deeley has borrowed a little from each of you, and he acknowledges his debt. Any faults in his character are mine, not yours.

I should also acknowledge the role played by a couple of "budding author" sites—YouWriteOn and the SFF Online Writing Workshop. Both helped me hone the early chapters and improve my style, so to those early and often anonymous critics, thank you.

When it came to looking for a publisher, I had little to guide me. My love of SF goes back to an earlier time, and the greats of that era have passed on. I was resigned to sticking a pin in the Writers and Artists Yearbook, until, listening to the audiobook of *Ender's Game*, I heard Orson Scott Card speak exceptionally highly of his publisher, Tom Doherty. So it was to Tor that I turned, with an unagented submission, going through the "slush pile" route, and I have been equally impressed. Kathleen Doherty and Susan Chang both read that first submission, saw the possibility of something better therein, and beyond my expectations were kind enough to tell me how I should improve it.

The process of working with Susan, when my rewrite was done, has been a model of mutual respect. Susan has a light touch to her editing, which stimulates and nurtures my creativity. I'm deeply impressed by the level of trust she's given me, a first-time author, to deliver rewrites to tight time constraints, and marvel at the reciprocal commitment on her part, turning round her own edits equally quickly, so that I always feel I have her complete attention.

I'm sure it's normal for an author, but I've got very attached to my characters. I always knew it would come out right in the end—the scene where Tania chooses the "Staff Only" door was in my plan almost from day one—but I put poor Tania through ever more pain and loss to get her there. If I can ever reach across the multiverse and say, sorry, Tania, for everything I put you through, I will.

ABOUT THE AUTHOR

WILLIAM CAMPBELL POWELL was born in Sheffield, England, and grew up in and around Birmingham, the "second city" of England. He attended King Edward's School in Birmingham and won a scholarship to Clare College, Cambridge, where initially he studied natural sciences and subsequently majored in computer science. He now lives in High Wycombe, Buckinghamshire, with his wife, Avis, and his two teenage sons. *Expiration Day* is his first novel.